PERCHANCE TO SCREAM

Rolen was slowing down, his body slipping into a chemically induced coma, the grip of cold sleep washing over him. He distantly sensed an endotracheal tube in his throat, and a rush of air forced his chest to expand. Blood pounded in his ears. His body was leaden.

The room lurched. Agoraphobia gripped him, along with the certainty that he was in a vast abyss, row on row of glass tanks gleaming like emeralds beneath the lights, human figures suspended in viscous liquid.

Another sickening rush of motion spun him, twisting, banks of fluorescents passing above him in alternating bands of illumination and shadow. Vertigo swept over him, and he fell in a slow, feet-first plunge into a green ocean . . .

CORPSEMAN

Joel Henry Sherman

A Del Rey Book

BALLANTINE BOOKS • NEW YORK

A Del Rey Book
Published by Ballantine Books

Library of Congress Catalog Card Number: 87-91653

ISBN 0-345-34461-8

Manufactured in the United States of America

First Edition: February 1988

Cover art by Barclay Shaw

For Carolyn and Alphonsine,
with love . . .
And
The late Richard F. Sherman, Sr.,
who knew how to tell a story.

Chapter 1

A message waited at Bacchus, Priority One, the type generally reserved for deaths or legal summonses or worse.

Rolen Iserye sensed the call as the ship dropped out of jump space and entered the Bacchus Flight Control Network; an urgent siren clear and sharp amid the conflicting signals of the first seconds of spatial orientation. He blocked acceptance instinctively. With normal space materializing around the ship, other priorities demanded his immediate attention. The interface split his mind into a dozen task centers, each one simultaneously dealing with a different aspect of shutdown. One disengaged the jump generators. Another began dumping velocity; the braking thrusters were a distant rumble in his sensors. A third adjusted docking angle. Others watched the board for failure, checked cargo, ran biological scans on himself and his passenger, conjured up an external view of the star system. He slipped in and out of the mental channels, watching for trouble, retaining as a safety measure a portion of his intellect to use should problems arise.

The siren, overriding all bands, jumped another octave.

Low-resolution optics reduced visual to hard lines and basic hues of blue, red, and yellow. Bacchus was a granular orb on his imaginary horizon, bracketed by satellite orbitals and the exit paths of two ships moving out toward the jump nexus. The stellar mass of Olympia hovered at one edge, cold Styx at the other. He preferred the three-dimensional sketch to the blinding reality of the Olympian system, an expanse of dark and light that left his stomach cold and his palms sweating. Plunging back into the internal network, he sidestepped his fear and lost himself in the tight rhythm of approach.

The Priority One added a visual signal, red block letters printed somewhere inside his skull: URGENT . . . URGENT . . . URGENT . . .

The approach program was fouled by the quirks and habits of a transient population. Rolen had his own routines aboard the *Trojan Horse,* twelve years' worth of subsystems and loops which were comfortable furnishings within the software. He cursed the unfamiliar matrix of the *Shadowbox* and the rotten luck that had forced him into a temporary command.

He was dry-docked at fiscal close. At the end of the financial year most corporations recalled their managers for annual meetings, and the demand on charter flights caused the Guild to shift all available personnel to short jaunts. Rolen normally avoided such duty—one of the advantages of a frontier run was being mid-transit and far from commerce centers when the books were tallied. But the *Trojan Horse* was due for refitting, leaving him vulnerable to interim transfer. For three weeks, Rolen had shuttled drunken executives between a dozen ports—a string of six-hour layovers and turnarounds in a cramped relic of a ship pressed into service to meet schedules. He was tired of short jaunts, blinking back and forth across normal and jump space, brain dull with fatigue; he was ready to return to his freighter and the minor demands of cargo shifts and manifests.

Switching visual from external to internal, Rolen checked the condition of his fare. The man was coming out of sleep, eyes open and staring, lights glistening on the sweat beading his pale, overweight body. Rolen found him representative of most of the executives he had dealt with in the past: soft and flaccid, with a perpetually harried look as if he were stalked by some dark creature through his sleepless nights. He jerked at the crackle of the intercom and the sound of Rolen's voice.

"Attention. Entering Olympian system. Estimated time of arrival is fifty-nine minutes. Prepare for docking." They had not met, a condition Rolen wished to maintain. He enjoyed the anonymity of the bridge and avoided even brief contact, a trait shared by most pilots. Groundlings thought in different routines. Their priorities made no sense.

By the time Rolen was ready to turn the ship over to the autopilot, his teeth were vibrating to the cry of the priority message. He merged with the flight-control computer, letting the ship be drawn toward the port on an invisible tether of beamed commands, and lowered his mental block, accepting the call. The link was direct to Bacchus Traffic Control, a bad omen. Initiating high-resolution feed, he found himself face to face with Ayn Keppler, the senior controller.

"Zenyam's *Shadowbox* acknowledging Priority One." His voice was hoarse, throat dry.

"Copy, *Shadowbox*." Keppler had a groundling's face, weathered by ultraviolet, carved by gravity, cheeks fissured and cragged. Jaundice yellowed his pale eyes. His hair was a tangle of black and gray. He bent his lips in an ascetic smile. "Took your time replying."

"Securing approach."

Keppler nodded, mouth fixed as if he were in constant pain. "Port of Origin alert issued by Yannik. Word is a local cause planted a bomb on the *Shadowbox*."

"Damn." His muscles tightened reflexively. Rolen slipped back into the system and scanned the ship for any anomaly. Trouble was, he had no idea where to look. "Scan is negative for explosive device," he said, cutting back to visual. "Any idea what I'm searching for?"

"Details are sketchy. The usual anonymous call."

"Why me?"

"Who knows? Maybe they're after Zenyam. It's their ship."

"Must be a hoax." Rolen tried to sound convincing. He thought back to loading procedures on Yannik. Everything had been perfectly normal. He had noted nothing suspicious, but he hadn't been looking for anything.

"Can't take the chance. We'll have to bring you up short to give the port a margin of safety. I'm sending a tug for evacuation."

"But—"

The controller shook his head decisively, a gesture designed to terminate arguments. "Regulations, *Shadowbox*. No exceptions. Twenty-four-hour isolation and bomb-squad inspection."

Panic washed over him, his breath racing, throat suddenly tight, adrenaline a coppery tang in his mouth. "You don't understand . . ."

"Look." Keppler consulted a screen. "Iserye, isn't it? Think of it as a twenty-four-hour vacation. Enjoy it." Keppler shrugged. "You've got no choice. Zenyam doesn't want the liability of rebuilding the port."

Rolen frowned. Nausea congealed in his guts, his mind a confusion of anger and fear. "Yeah."

"You know the drill. Initiate shutdown. ETA on the tug is forty-six minutes. No luggage. Nothing leaves the ship that isn't flesh." The man narrowed his eyes. "Sorry for any inconvenience."

Keppler broke the connection.

Rolen shut the *Shadowbox* down before jackknifing out of the system, leaving positional maintenance to the autopilot. Reaching up, he snapped the plugs from his skull. The bridge materialized around him as his vision slowly returned. Sweat beaded his forehead and made the electrodes itch.

How long he sat motionless, staring at the instrument panels, Rolen was uncertain. His body was paralyzed, his mind numb. The bomb threat caused part of his terror, but it was a vague sensation, for he lacked the personal experience to define the event. His contact with explosions had been filtered through the imaginations of others and presented in the sterile mediums of literature or holofilms, images of swelling mushrooms of flame and distant screams.

His true fear was intimate and uncontrollable, a well-studied madness that left him cold and sick. He had been born at the mining colony in Thor's Belt, a scattered ring of asteroids honeycombed with tunnels. Home was a maze of linked passages, close and comfortable, ripe with sweat and stale air, a universe of measurable distances, where the largest space was a common room that he could cross in seconds, touching the ceiling with a mighty leap. Steel, plastic, and bubble-foam sealed the shafts and held the cold void beyond the walls at bay. To venture outside, even in the protective cocoon of an environmental suit, was to tempt fate. Every door had a pressure seal. Every Friday, a decompression drill sent them scrambling for emergency shelters. His nightmares were always staged on the surface.

Rolen had passed from one womb to another, trading the tunnels of Thor's Belt for the compact reality of a ship's bridge, curving alloy and scintillating displays, narrow passages, pressure seals, and claustrophobic quarters. He had not been downworld in five standard years, and then only on a quick sprint through the corporate headquarters to print a contract and meet with the company physician.

His fear had a name—agoraphobia—a string of nonsense syllables incapable of expressing the depths of his terror. Compared with the thought of being portside, the bomb seemed a minor inconvenience.

The bridge was a cleft in the center of the ship. Telltales and gauges flickered, contacts studding the bulkhead that curved around him, each point exactly one arm-length distant. Others might have dreaded the pressure of the walls, but Rolen drew strength from the confined space. He laid his hands on the opposing surfaces, feeling the electronic hum of the components, switches, and lights pressing his palms. For a few seconds, Rolen toyed with the idea of flight, of spinning the ship on its axis and running for the jump zone. It was a fantasy. He forced his panic back into a small crevice in his brain, unbuckled the restraints, and pulled himself up into the accessway.

"Gods," he muttered, his voice strange and flat, his nakedness another reminder of the divergence between his life and the world portside. "I don't have anything to wear." His laughter seemed to come from another throat.

They gave him a jumpsuit on the tug. The white cotton fabric was soft, the sleeves an inch too short for his arms. He still felt naked; strapped into one of the auxiliary benches of the tug, his skull sockets empty, no contacts pasted to his skin, he was forced to sense the movement of the ship through the dead and distant receptors of his nervous system.

His fare sprawled in the next couch. He was short and compact, age lost in his fat, features swollen. His balding scalp gleamed. "Bombs," the man kept repeating. "As if jumps aren't dangerous enough." He gave Rolen a rubbery smile. "Be damn glad to get dirtside again."

Rolen studied the auxiliary panel, eyes mesmerized by the frantic dance of the needles and power monitors surging from green to red. Without the demands of flight to occupy his mind, he had time to curse the bastards who had selected his ship as a symbol. Despite Keppler's suspicions, Rolen was certain the attack was not aimed at Zenyam. More than likely, the terrorists had singled out his fare for retribution. The man was senior comptroller of Bolzak Manufacturing, the major employer on Yannik. They probably hoped to turn his death into a statement about their working conditions, environmental destruction, or any of a thousand complaints that flooded the media of every port Rolen had ever visited. Nothing personal, just damned inconvenient.

The clang and hiss of the docking maneuver brought him out of his reverie. Fumbling with the straps, the corporate man released himself from the couch and hurried out the lock. His voice carried down the passageway, complaining to the dock agent, snarling loudly now that he was safe in port. Iserye unstrapped and sat up on the edge of the bench. Gravity tried to draw his arms and legs from their sockets. The cabin swayed when he stood. He staggered to the airlock and leaned against the threshold, eyes closed, breathing deeply through his nostrils as if to swallow the ship's air and somehow sustain himself for twenty-four hours among the poisons of the port.

"You okay?" The pilot squinted at him from the bridge hatch. No sockets in his skull. No true contact with his ship. He might as well have been driving a truck or tractor. The man could not understand. No groundling ever would.

"Yeah." Rolen nodded.

"Watch the boards. They'll post when the *Shadowbox* is docked and cleared. Shouldn't be too long . . . twenty-four hours. If you're looking for something different, my brother runs a club . . ."

"No thanks." Rolen shook his head, took a deep breath, and climbed up into the clamor of the Bacchus Port of Entry.

The air was a thick soup tainted with grease and solvents; cold, compared with the stale warmth of the *Shadowbox*. Noise assaulted him: the heavy rumble of machinery, hissing air and fuel lines, shouting workers. His mouth tasted of chalk. His heart was pounding, his ears rang with tinnitus. Rolen strained to keep his eyes on the scuffed floor, raising them in quick jerks as he scanned for the lifts. His gaze was inexorably drawn upward, as if his head had been snagged by a line from a passing crane.

The external wall of the office structure was a flat plain stretching away toward the central spire, wrinkled and knobbed with access hatches and equipment bays. Above and behind him, the dome of the port swelled, its honeycombed surface the flat hue of a twilight sky, spanned with a spidery network of girders and catwalks. Cranes crawled along the steel like angular insects, small in scale and lost in the distance. The horizon resisted his efforts to define and focus. Vertigo wrenched at him.

Traffic raced by: loading trucks weaving through knots of passengers and crew, dock workers, security officers, shills, and maintenance personnel. He stumbled along with them, trying vainly to breathe, his vision going red, panic filling him. The gaping doors of a service lift yawned across the broad corridor. Rolen lurched toward it, electric vehicles swerving to avoid his mad dash, horns squealing, a stream of invectives following his headlong flight. He darted inside just as the doors closed; he hugged the wall, his cheek against the cool white plastic, eyes screwed shut. Sickness flooded his stomach.

"Hey, you okay, jock?" A hand touched his shoulder cautiously.

After a minute to catch his breath, he turned toward the voice. The woman was short, head just at his bicep. A mass of gold ringlets surrounded her face, blue eyes bright against the wings of dark mascara that jutted to her temples. Thin lines of rainbow colors marked the perimeter of her smile, twisting as she grinned, mesmerizing him. A short tunic clung to her figure. She smelled faintly of corba, her pupils sparkling with chemical intensity.

"No," he said, finding his voice. "Not too good. I could use a place to rest."

"Got the answer. Caliban's." Something in her voice suggested rote. She interlocked her arm with his and pulled him from the lift as it stopped, heading down the corridor toward the interior. "Best lounge in the whole damned port. I'm Miras. Miras Magana."

"Rolen Iserye," he said. Shill, he thought bitterly. Company for a price. But it was better than being alone in the nightmarish open spaces threatening to swallow him. Rolen allowed himself to be led away.

Nearer the port axis, gravity lessened, as did the strain on his muscles. The corridors reminded him of the tunnels of Thor's Belt, weaving through a network of offices and shops, communication centers, and banks. Miras remained a half step ahead of him, clutching his arm, reeling her catch with unerring precision through the crowds, exchanging greetings and slurs with familiar faces.

At the intersection of an axial tunnel and an equatorial passage, the crowd slowed, milling in confusion. Sirens blared. Blue strobes flashed. Amplified voices thundered through megaphones. Miras hesitated, searching for a path through the press of bodies.

Though styles had changed since his last port visit, Rolen had no trouble identifying the security forces—blue-and-red uniforms, gold braid, and hard, trim frames moving liquidly beneath skintight fabric. They pushed through the crowd as a precision unit, isolating a knot of figures from the snarled pedestrian traffic.

The dissenters were new to him: gray fatigues, shaved heads, skin so pale he could see the veins tracing their exposed flesh. Sitting in the center of the intersection, arms linked and swaying from side to side, they had brought travel to a standstill.

"Vasquez! Vasquez! Vasquez!" Their measured chant overrode all other noise. Hate painted the faces of many of the bystanders; some were spitting and swearing, others lashing out with fists or savage kicks. The protesters refused to strike back, raising their arms to deflect the blows, mouths set in grim lines of defiance.

"Local troubles," Miras said, answering his unspoken query. "Corpses protesting about the work again. But at least they got jobs." She spoke as if he understood her explanation, and turned before he could question further, leading him around the logjam and into a side corridor. The sounds of conflict faded with distance.

Caliban's was a tangle of stellar refuse, a split-level room filled with close shadows and cluttered spaces. His eyes adjusted slowly to a semidarkness cut by flickering neons and backlit with the soft glow of night reds, like the bridge on the *Trojan Horse*. The memory intensified his homesickness and he blinked his burning eyes. Lacquered counters and tabletops reflected the silhouettes of the patrons. Live and holographic dancers twitched in frantic spasms across the crowded floor. The place offered no cure for his fear, but the alternative was worse, so he followed the woman up a flight of Plexiglas stairs to a booth against one of the back walls. Her table. The bartender responded to her nod.

Miras smiled at him, her rainbow lips gathering highlights from the strobe. "Been here before?" She dug through her shoulder bag for a stick of corba, then flicked an arc from her lighter. The blue flame illuminated her winged·eyes and golden hair.

Rolen shook his head. "Don't usually get portside."

"Come on. Truth now." Miras laughed. "I know all about pilots. Love in every port."

He shrugged. "Haven't been offship in five years."

"Then you've got some catching up to do." Her intensity made him turn away.

The clientele and the decor represented litter from a hundred planets: drunken miners coughing up their lungs between swallows; knots of military personnel cursing their collective luck and dealing cards; solitary pilots; shills and prostitutes making the rounds, eyeing him enviously. Old antennae and communication vanes, gimbals pitted, waldoes frozen in mid-grasp, studded the walls along with a thruster flange, obsolete deck modules and audio units, ship insignias, and planetary flags. Corba smoke hung in hazy blue clouds like drifting nebulas fired with red stars. Jangling strains of music jarred his brain, a throbbing buzz he felt in his bones. The barmaid appeared with a round of drinks. The usual, he thought. Shill's was probably water. His credit paid for both.

"To company," Miras said. She raised her glass.

"Yeah." The liquor burned his throat, warming him from the inside. He gulped it down, hoping to numb the subliminal trembling in his muscles, which felt as though a tightly drawn wire were vibrating rapidly. Events were happening too fast, a progression of action beyond his experience, unreadable and intense, frightening because he lacked the computer input to decipher the conflicting data. A second drink did nothing to quell the vague unease pervading him. The third glass blurred his vision. Somewhere in the middle of the fourth, his mind shut down, body operating on automatic, reacting to primal impulses, his last memory the rainbow arc of Miras Magana's smile.

Chapter 2

The courier died moments after the exchange. Strictly business. Silence was too valuable to buy with money.

Jaleem Abbasi crushed his larynx with one fist. The man staggered against the low retaining wall, eyes wide and surprised, mouth working soundlessly. A shoulder kick tumbled him over the parapet. With one hand, the man snagged the vines clinging to the outside of the building. Desperation filled his fluid gurgle. Abbasi chopped the white knuckles. Bone snapped. The body spiraled eighteen floors to the street. Dropping the infocube into his pocket, Jaleem walked to the stairs.

Because he had paid for free passage, he was two blocks away before the authorities arrived. Every second reduced his chance of capture and eroded his tenuous link with the dead man. Jaleem matched his pace with traffic. No speed. No panic. Thirty years in the slums of the Islamic Zone had honed his skills to razor perfection. Akira never worried about mistakes. He had Jaleem Abbasi.

Jaleem crossed the city of Rohar alone. No bodyguard. A stiletto clung to his left calf beneath the loose fabric of his pants. His gray vest cloaked the bulge of his Spencer Magna. Plastic flesh concealed the fragmenter in the palm of his left hand. Sensing his readiness, street life veered from his path.

Rohar offered him the protection of mottled shadows. The city rose in layers of green, hanging gardens and sweating jungle. Vines knit the spaces between buildings, weaving trees and shrubs into nets of waxen leaves. Morning light was hot where it broke through the dense canopy. The resinous surface of the street gleamed as though liquid. Jaleem studied each arched doorway, glancing up to windows sheltered by twisting creepers, anticipating ambush from every blind corner and each cable bridge swaying overhead. He was not afraid. He was cautious. Caution enhanced survival.

Knots of flatheads and chromers watched him from darkened alleys, their sullen eyes and painted faces universal. As one band moved to intercept him, a fragment of memory twisted in his mind. Corrugated steel slums. Dirt passages. Fat flies swarming in the dry heat. The cool weight of a Kalashnikov in his hands.

The rattle of chains brought him back to the present.

"Tribute," the lead chromer whispered. Bright links wrapped his knuckles, his biceps, and his neck. A braided strand linked nostrils to earlobes. He stank of sweat and grease. "Gotta pay the toll to pass."

Jaleem recognized the anger in the hatcheted features of the boy's face, and something else, a sharpened survival instinct, raw intelligence. Street-smart. He felt a twinge of empathy as he met the chromer's gaze.

"Pay or play." The hand the boy extended was black with grime, hard-knuckled, and a chain was coiled like a snake around his thick fingers.

Jaleem decided to let him live. The boy never knew how close he had come to eternity. Jaleem saw their lives diverging in the future, forking away from this moment. Who knew? Perhaps another Akira would swoop down to pluck the boy up into one of the surrounding towers. Or maybe the next fixer would not be so charitable. He opened his vest and displayed the butt of his Spencer. The boy arched one eyebrow as though weighing his chances. Finally, he stepped around Jaleem, a signal to the others. They let him pass unmolested. Jaleem smiled. His boots clicked on the paving like a metronome.

With every stride, the infocube gouged into his thigh, a bullet with the Transport Guild's name carved on its liquid center. He had spent eleven months preparing for the present operation, going through a thousand small maneuvers to set the trap. Across four systems, a vast machine waited, trembling in readiness for the command to act. Transport was oblivious to any danger. Toshiro Akira had but to fire the first shot. Would Akira pull the trigger? Jaleem didn't know. Such decisions were not his to make, not yet. If the cube held the answer, he was unable to decipher the code it tapped against his leg.

The Akira building mimicked nature, jutting through the jungle like a stone pinnacle, a series of flat terraces encircling a central spire in staircase fashion. Vegetation wrapped the external surfaces. Flowers and vines formed small grottoes of darkness and bursts of color. Misty shafts of water plunged in graceful falls, each plume creating a distinct tone keyed by the height of the fall and the depth of the pool, a symphony of liquid.

Shrubbery concealed the hardware of the security field, an interlocking network of electronics and mechanicals designed to detect and discourage intruders. Infrareds monitored ambient temperature changes. Audios listened for stealthy approach. Hair-trigger kinetic sensors could register the impact of a leaf from a height of twenty centimeters. The foliage disguised an arsenal of defensive armament as well as the detection equipment. Tanglers waited to snarl climbers in a weighted web of plastic and adhesive, dropping them in an uncontrolled plunge to the distant street. Caustic foggers spat streams of chemical blindness. Lightning bugs held enough electricity to stop a heart. Fragmenters reduced blunderers to bloody rags. Coils of razor-wire unraveled when touched, forming brambles of knife-edged steel. And because it was not good to trust technology too implicitly, there were devices he had brought with him from the Zone—weighted deadfalls, trip wires, jangling bells strung on monofilament, sharpened sticks dipped in poison.

He was pleased with his precautions. Damn those who questioned his budget and the expense. In his five years with Akira, only one employee had been lost to subversion, and that incident smelled of collusion and revenge. Frugal people usually had more money to spend at their own funerals. It was a reward he found strangely fitting.

At the entrance, the computer read his physical scan, matched retina- and voice-prints with corporate documents, and opened the twin doors before he broke stride. Security guards stiffened in his presence. Impact glass reflected him in a dozen places, tall and thin, loose-jointed. A black turban hid his hair. Thin mustache and beard outlined his mouth. His eyes were dark pits. He inspected the lobby quickly, checking for breaches in the defense network, and, satisfied, nodded quickly to the team commander as he made his way to the lifts.

The mezzanine was a shining cavern. Four columns rose through the center of the building, height lost in the distance, level after level of chrome and plastic receding above him in tightening rectangles. Green-gray veins mottled the white marble floor. Chandeliers of brass and crystal hung like satellites in varied orbits, seeming to defy gravity, their suspension hair-thin and invisible. Delivery boys and employees scurried before him, vanishing down corridors and into lifts, dancing to a hidden beat he could not detect. The sounds of computers and chattering printers drifted down from above. Their work was a mystery to him, a side of the business in which he had little interest or understanding. It was not necessary for him to understand to perform his duty—and should the need arise later, he was a quick study.

Jaleem stepped into the lift, an iridescent hemisphere arching above him. It rose skyward.

He endured a brief moment of anxiety that passed in a heartbeat, the curse of his past. The Zone was far too primitive to have provided him with great exposure to the high-tech world beyond the demilitarized zones. Once in the employ of Akira Corporation, he had adapted, yet certain prejudices remained and he always suffered a moment of vulnerability, forced into trust and fear as he handed over his life to a technology that he once had considered magic and even now did not fully understand.

The penthouse spanned the top of the building. Partitions divided the area into semiprivate alcoves that made him think of a sterile maze. Glass walls flooded the interior with tinted daylight. Angled mirrors bounced the light from ceiling to floor. The carpet was thick and gray. Refrigerated air whispering from hidden vents chilled the sweat silvering his arms. Jaleem stood motionless for a minute, listening to the silence, cautious even in the center of the Akira corporate fortress.

As Jaleem exited the lift, the computer registered his weapons and stopped him with a stasis field, a resistance that hampered his movements. He disarmed slowly, dropping stiletto and Spencer Magna into the armory receptacle. Jaleem missed the weight of his pistol, the comfort of the knife. An electrical charge disarmed the fragmenter in his palm. Satisfied, the computer deactivated the field and allowed him to make his way to the contact room.

The door was hidden behind a holographic façade, an eternal sheet of falling water. Plunging his hand into the cascade, he touched the access panel. The illusion left his hand dry. Jaleem stepped through the holograph and entered an austere cell. A single metal chair sat before the contact terminal. Lights flickered on the modules. He took a minute to uncoil the electrodes, one pair to monitor his thoughts, a second to measure his heartbeat and trigger a detonator should his pulse cease.

The bomb was located in the level below him, its charge sufficient to blow the roof from the spire. He might be helpless while he interfaced with the communication network, but he would not die alone. Electrical discharges tingled where the electrodes met his skin. Jaleem eased into the chair.

Toshiro Akira had been in time dilation for the equivalent of ten external years. His location was a corporate secret. He was probably orbiting Rohar, lying rigid in cold sleep, his mind active but slow, body functions reduced to one-hundredth speed. Jaleem's memories were of a small man with porcelain skin, eyes slightly bulging behind heavy epicanthic folds, black hair greased to his skull. Thoughts of Akira always triggered a specific mental referent, a still frame from a nightmare: a smoke-filled tour bus littered with dead; Kalashnikov chattering in his grip; Akira watching him with the squinting gaze of a missionary priest, contemptuous and pitying; the woman's eyes as the bullets struck, surprised and angry and glazing over with the dull film of death. Jaleem avoided sleep.

He withdrew a projection cube and fitted it into the slot on the contact panel, then slid the headband over his skull. His fingers touched the switches in a ritualistic pattern, the computer accessing at his command, interfacing with the dilation equipment. His vision went dark. He sensed contact, a drawn laborious movement in his mind.

Sound blossomed in his head. "Abbasi?" The voice was slurred.

"Yes, Mr. Akira."

Another pause. "What have you brought?"

He mentally accessed the projection cube. Light filled his head, his mind interpreting the signals as vision despite his blinded eyes. A man of medium height and slender build appeared, seated at a booth in a darkened bar. His hair was clipped in pilot fashion, shaved to midskull to allow electrode contact. A trio of ceramic sockets resembled bullet holes below one ear. The bulge of jump hardware distorted the outlines of his skull, a gross swelling at the base of his neck. He was caught laughing, smile frozen on his pale features, head tilted back. His eyes were innocent, wide and naive.

Akira grunted, slow and fluid. "Is this the one?"

"Rolen Iserye. Twenty-nine years old. No familial attachments. Specializes in freighter work. Presently operating charter and courier service for Zenyam Limited. He's on Bacchus. Our people are in position."

He waited forever for Akira to respond. "And the Guild?"

"Murder is a capital crime on Bacchus, even for the Transport Guild and its pilots. Confidence rating is high."

"Never underestimate them."

"No." Abbasi inhaled deeply. "Simulations estimate ten days before Transport responds. By then, Iserye will have been executed and the corpse auctioned. They might cross-file through the Confederation courts. But to win, they'd have to prove the illegality of the Bacchus judicial system, fighting both our attorneys and the Bacchus High Council. I doubt even the Transport Guild could win such an engagement."

Akira was silent for a long time. Jaleem imagined him. Narrow face slack, skin like weathered ivory. Heavy lids, black eyes glittering. Lips pursed in a smile as if at a cutting joke leveled at some victim. The smile was the focus of his power, bending men to his will. Jaleem cringed under that slight exposure of even white teeth. He bent and broke and hated himself, but bent anyway. Even now, Jaleem found himself waiting breathlessly for an answer.

"Do it, then," Akira said. "Release the tigers."

The contact was broken as abruptly as it had been initiated. Jaleem Abbasi stripped off the contact hardware, blanked the infocube, and tossed it into the shredder. Touching his fingers to the keyboard, he tapped out a preset code and punched TRANSMIT. It was a simple action, like drawing a knife or pulling a trigger. Two lives ended at his fingertip, one in death and the other changed forever. Jaleem felt nothing. He rose slowly, gathered his weapons and went to his quarters to pack.

Chapter 3

Rolen awakened on a strange floor, curled in a fetal position beside a puddle of drying vomit. Carpeting pressed into his cheek. Breathing made his chest ache. One arm was numb and bent awkwardly under his side. His head seemed partially filled with sand, shifting with every movement, needles of pain stabbing his skull. His bloated gut was tender, stomach muscles strained from heaving. Rolen turned onto his back and stared up at the ceiling, sticky effluvia and gastric juices cold on his skin.

The room could have been anywhere: a portside apartment with rented furnishings. The carpet was green. Plastic-framed pictures and odd curios dotted the bare white walls; a holo poster of some unknown actor, a few faded lithographic prints. A traffic sign proclaimed YIELD in black letters on a yellow background. Scents of old food and pheromone perfume filled his nostrils. On his left a narrow hallway ended at a closed door. A small kitchen was on his right: two chairs and a table built into the wall, a microwave, and a square refrigerator. A vase of aged silk flowers lay on its side on the counter dividing the dining area from the living room.

He was naked, clothing gone and skull sockets empty. Without the constant feed of information into his cortex to orient and motivate him, Rolen was lost. He stared at the seamless white ceiling and tried to interpret the chemical mélange of his thoughts.

Memory was a jumble of lucid moments and blurred events. Caliban's assumed nightmarish dimensions, chasms of vacuous shadow separating the tables and booths. Phantoms of smoke swept past in ghostly shrouds. Red lights gleamed like telltales on the board of a derelict freighter. Miras's laughter echoed in his head. Her scent filled him. Her voice was heavy with the sexual tension from every fantasy his adolescent imagination had ever created. Liquor appeared at timed intervals, burning his throat and nostrils. The table melted beneath his fingertips. His hand was a flesh-tone spider crawling across the lacquered surface, touching her fingers. Nails raked his knuckles.

The camera in his head lurched forward at blinding speed, creating a collage of faces, flickering ends of cigarettes, rainbow lips arching. They danced for a time, jerking spasms timed to the electric throb of the music. Miras rubbing against him. Her mouth on his neck. Her teeth fastened on his earlobe. He reveled in the pain and the warm liquid that trickled down his neck in a sticky rivulet. Her hair smelled of cinnamon laced with the bitter tang of corba.

"Relax. Enjoy. You're my responsibility now." Her laughter filled the interstices of silence in the music. There were secrets in her eyes.

More drinks blurred time and space. He was on his back in the center of a pedestrian passage. Workers skirted him, trying to ignore his presence. Their pity enraged him. Miras pulled at his arm, misinterpreting his anger as playful reticence. He broke free, swinging awkwardly at the parting crowd and stumbling over his seemingly detached feet. The side of his face struck the wall, shoulder slamming against the floor. His vision went red and black, a two-tone chromatic image like those created by the *Trojan Horse*. He sent his thoughts out, frantically searching for the computer feed and finding only silence, a scrambled input from his own, pitiful external sensors. Hands raised him by the armpits, his legs dragging behind him; men on either side carried him at her directions.

There was a bedroom somewhere—a water-filled bed that surged under his body. The woman caressed his scalp, her tongue searching out the implanted sockets, circling the flesh and ceramic, her erratic breathing rushing over them, damp and hot. She was sweating, lurching on him. Air rasped from her throat. He pitched beneath her rhythmic motions, reacting to impulses he had thought long dead, something visceral and animal hidden deep in his being.

Another image welled up from his subconscious: a steel fang, sharp and thin and dripping with dark fluid, wavering in the air before him; the sound of a spike being driven into wet sand; a scream cut short and gurgling into silence. He tried to follow the path of memory further, but his mind was blank. It was as though his brain had been deactivated, an oddly unsettling feeling, a nagging certainty that there was something he did not want to remember.

Rolen raised himself to a sitting position with a labored grunt. His eyes were gritty, grinding beneath his closed lids. Somehow he found his legs and defied gravity, swaying to his feet. He stumbled along the wall, dragging his fingers on the smooth surface as he took a sluggish inventory of his body. His bones ached. His skin was clammy with sweat.

The mirror hanging askew at the end of the corridor reflected a skeletal figure rippled by the cheap finish of the glass, a fun-house caricature he found both familiar and frightening. He was surprised by the scratches, a network of furrows tracing his cheek and neck, crusted with dried blood. One eye was swollen and bruised. His upper lip was a purple bulge. Lacerations etched the white plain of his chest, ruddy beneath the dark curls of hair. On his right breast was a handprint, a brown stain, nails at the ends of the fingertips marked by the pink-white puckering of damaged skin and hardening scab.

Shame turned his face scarlet, his neck and chest mottled and burning. He hung his head, mind swimming with confusion. His muscles were quivering. Nausea twisted in his stomach like an eel, a rubbery convulsion that sent him staggering toward the bathroom, remembering the way by instinct, a subconscious message imprinted on his brain during the course of the night.

A gut-wrenching heave expelled a few ounces of bitter liquid. He thought of the *Shadowbox* and wondered if the bomb had detonated. His injuries might have been fatal had he remained on board, but not nearly as painful as his present condition. Rolen lay on the toilet for a long time. The cold surface against his forehead seeped into his skull and numbed his pain. Running water soothed him. He slept, draped over the fixture.

He was not an experienced drinker. Piloting promoted other habits, though he knew pilots who indulged, spending their time portside in small dives, swilling glass after glass in search of a high they could not find in their augmented universe. Rolen entertained himself with the diversions offered by direct computer link, simulations and games, fantasies created by master artisans and stored within the convoluted universe of the *Trojan Horse*'s memory. Separation from his ship had driven him to drink at Caliban's, seeking solace, not pleasure.

His last drunken stupor had occurred years ago, before contracting with Zenyam, back in the tunnels of Thor's Belt. There was a storeroom where they met, a place at the end of a shaft where the vein had been depleted and the operation abandoned. The room was furnished by subtle donations: a crate appropriated from shipping, an old chair lifted from recycling, lighting borrowed from some of the less-traveled tunnels. He remembered clipping wires and running hard, feet pounding in time to the beat of his laboring heart, electrical fixture wedged tightly under one arm, trying vainly to hide it beneath his scrawny bicep.

Burke, Halser, Kinesky—the names and faces rattled up from some dark recess in his head. And Illana Vanos, her memory always separate, elevated as if in some mental shrine that the years had fashioned out of guilt and longing. They had held their own graduation celebration, a ritual entry into adulthood complete with homemade brew and cigarettes, imbued with that perfect eighteen-year-old psyche which was strong and smart and certain their future was brighter than that of their parents.

The cups were plastic. A liniment smell rose from the brew. Burke held his drink in both hands, long fingers wrapped loosely around the transparent shell. He tipped it back, swallowed, and smacked his lips. His face was lean and long, vaguely canine. "I'm posted to Hardcore," he said, grinning tightly. "Shipping out in a week." He had signed on with the Peacemakers, a Confederation military force responsible for mediating disputes between the colonies and made up of volunteers from every member planet. Passing the mental and physical tests had earned him a ticket out of the mines. It was an occupation high up on their social hierarchy. Burke lorded his success over them, and for a moment, Rolen allowed him his small victory, an instant in which to feel superior.

"A trooper." Kinesky poured another cup. Slow, envious Kinesky. The gods had programmed him for ambition but destined him for labor. He was trapped, caught in a life that denied him success but tortured him with desire. "Beats the hell out of digging holes."

"Maybe." Rolen reached for the bottle. It was cold in his hands.

Illana leaned against him, head resting on his shoulder. Her eyes were the hue of a verdigris deposit, a brilliant bluish green. She wore her hair long, a thick fall of gold past her shoulders. Her features were strong: prominent cheekbones and nose, full lips, straight teeth. She smiled at his scrutiny, ignorant of the gulf between them.

"And how are you getting out?" Halser's voice was a strange mixture of music and nasal twang. His ears protruded under his shaggy brown hair. The mines had already claimed him; he worked after school and evenings to support his injured father and hindered family. He had a perpetual cough, wracking and deep, as if he were sucking blood from his lungs.

"Pilot." He grinned without looking up, pouring another glass and listening to the liquid splash. Illana stiffened beside him. It was the wrong time, the wrong moment, but the alcohol had loosened his tongue and the smile frozen on Burke's face goaded him into action. "I've already sent out queries. Zenyam wants an interview."

Even now, years and distance layered over his memories like belts of sediment, he still saw their shocked faces and heard the stunned silence that filled the small room. There was magic in the words and envy in their eyes. He had spoken an incantation, a whispered wish, the dream of children.

Illana lurched to her feet. Tears welled in her eyes, horror and hatred and betrayal all contained in a single glance that forced him to stare down into the cup and watch the rippling liquid. Then she was gone. He should have followed. He didn't.

They finished the bottle and he got sick in the passageway, lying on his stomach, confused and angry and yet enjoying the moment, reveling in the power he felt while destroying the future Illana had created for both of them. He regretted it later, but not while the others slurred their congratulations and loved and hated him with equal intensity.

Burke's freedom was short-lived. He died within the year, during a police action on Hardcore. Rolen was unable to attend the funeral. Pilots had other priorities.

Measured pounding echoed on a distant doorway. For a few moments, Rolen lay still to see if they would leave or if the woman would answer the knock, but he was evidently alone. He found his feet again and staggered out into the hallway.

"All right!" he roared, stabbing the lock mechanism with trembling fingers.

Three Port Authority officers stood in the hallway. Two were grunts, brute force designed to prevent arguments. They stood shoulder to shoulder behind a woman. She was precise and trim, her red-and-blue uniform starched to stiff perfection, creases like blades. She pursed her thin lips, scanning him suspiciously.

"Miras Magana?" Her voice was flat, without inflection.

"No." He shook his head and tried to clear the fog. "Rolen Iserye." The instinctive fear of authority reared in him, a convulsive tightening in his chest. Every pilot dreaded the nightmare of local justice. Stories of minor offenses that resulted in life terms were an integral part of pilot folklore, as familiar as ghost ships and artificial intelligence.

"I want to speak with Magana." She studied him closely. Her muscles were tensed. The two guards drew their weapons slowly, as if reacting to a subliminal signal, a scent or a twitch he had not noticed. "Is she here?"

Rolen shrugged cautiously. "I guess. Sleeping maybe. I'm not sure." His head was spinning. His intestines felt as if they were packed with ice.

"We've had complaints of a fight." The woman inspected the scratches on his chest and the bruised eye. "Had some trouble?"

"I don't really remember." He smiled, an embarrassed grin. "A little too much to drink last night."

She thrust a sheaf of papers toward him, their official seal gleaming hypnotically. "Stand aside. I've a warrant for search." The woman pushed him back, her hand warm on his chest. "Stay with him." The last officer in line stepped beside Rolen. The other followed the woman down the narrow hallway. They checked the bathroom, kitchen, and then the small living room. The door to the bedroom was locked. No one answered their repeated knocks.

"What's going on?" He tried to follow, but the guard held his arms in a grip like two clamps, fingers digging into his skin. Rolen struggled, his uneasiness growing. There was something familiar in the sensation, a maddening kind of déjà vu, as if he had expected trouble and left the ship searching for a confrontation.

The grunt kicked open the door to the bedroom. No ceremony, just a heavy boot splintering wood with a crash that jolted Rolen's sodden skull. He cringed. A smell washed over him, distant and sickly, like milk turning sour.

"Sweet Allah," the woman swore as she stepped into the room, the second officer trailing in her wake, his face turning ghastly white. The guard craned his neck to see, relaxing his grip. Rolen wrenched free and lurched down the passage, the officer scrambling in pursuit. The doorway yawned. He spanned it with his arms; the officers looked up in surprise, drawing their weapons.

The water bed keyed a mental chord. Twisted into pink ropes, the satin sheets glistened as if the fabric were woven of liquid fibers. The white jumpsuit he had been given on the tug was spread out on the floor, an empty husk of a man, arms wide, legs angled as though frozen in flight. A bottle leaned against the far wall, its contents a dark stain on the green carpet. An overturned chair thrust its legs into the air, casting fingers of shadow across the floor.

Miras Magana was sprawled on the bed, limbs akimbo, skin dry and pale, muscles stiffened with rigor. Her face was surprised, like the face of a child discovering a long-lost toy, her rainbow lips arched halfway between a smile and a startled gasp, frozen forever. A streamer of sticky blood and saliva clung to her inverted cheek, its progress halted just below the sweat-smeared mascara encircling her eye. The angle of her head in relation to the body was unnatural, an impossibly thin strand of flesh connecting it to her blood-spattered torso. Her eyes were dry and fixed, staring at the ceiling.

Rolen slumped. The guard caught him from behind, arm around his throat, elbow against his neck, jerking him erect. He tried to speak, gagging and sputtering, unable to breathe or swallow.

"Take him," the female officer growled, her teeth clenched and her nostrils flared. "Hold the bastard for murder."

Chapter 4

The weight machine crouched above her like a denizen escaped from some cheap holofilm, chromium limbs and cabled extensors straddling her supine form, preparing to feed on the sleek carcass stretched across the bench. Veta Pulchek struggled against the monster, flexing her arms in smooth repetitions as the clanging weights beat out a counterpoint to the tempo of her breathing, controlled gasps escaping at the apex of each lift. Sweat ran in rivulets from her hair, beading her breasts, puddling in her eyes and in the flat hollow of her stomach. Her muscles burned with exertion.

The arm was weak. Synthetic tissue was a serviceable replacement, but the amalgamation did not match the power and grace of the original. Her limb was gone, a bloody stain somewhere along the Avenue of the Stars on Farin. The memory brought fresh pain and anger.

"You're lucky to be alive," the surgeon had said. "Without the damage collar you'd have bled to death."

He was wrong about luck. Wearing a damage collar took a conscious decision; it meant that one was prepared to sacrifice a portion of the body to salvage the rest. That was skill. And one had to accept that nothing was ever as good as new. Late at night, she still sensed the phantom appendage, superimposed on the existent arrangement of artificial muscles and tendons, cultured bone, and nylon ligaments. Even as she exercised, the difference persisted, subtle but noticeable—a maddening reminder of just how close she had come to losing her life. She fought the urge to rub at the scar and strained harder at the weights.

A tone sounded—the first interruption of the morning. Veta finished the set and pulled herself upright on the bench, heart throbbing, temples pounding, and throat raw. The light from the recessed floodlamps glazed her skin. The coppery salt stench of her sweat was like a breeze around the docks at low tide. She took a towel from the dressing table and rubbed herself down with the rough fabric. Reflections moved in the mirrored walls, reaching for towels, wiping their damp faces, smoothing strings of slick gray hair back against their skulls.

"Yes," Veta said, responding to the second chime.

"Len Bollinger requests an audience, madam." The computer voice was soft and asexual, seeming to emanate from the air, disembodied and discreet.

"Get a number. Tell him I'll return his call in an hour."

"He is in your waiting room. Shall I send him away?"

She squeezed her eyes shut and sucked a deep breath through her nostrils, a smile rising unbidden to her lips. "No. Make him comfortable. I'll be there in a minute."

Standing made her thighs ache. She draped the towel around her neck and walked toward one mirrored wall, approaching her own slender form, muscles taut, ribs outlined beneath the drum-tight skin of her stomach. The scar on her right arm was a thick, dark rope, beginning to fade but in need of further sanding. Well-meaning friends called her features exotic: high, broad forehead, wide-spaced green eyes, jutting cheekbones. Others said striking. Few ever used the word beautiful. Wealth negated her severe looks, kept her from being lonely, and allowed her to acquire companions on her own terms. Intelligence tipped the balance well in her favor. She liked the arrangement. The wall slid open soundlessly, shower hissing to life as she crossed the threshold, water a myriad of stinging needles emanating from every surface. She closed her eyes and let the warmth melt away her fatigue.

Her wardrobe was designer-label—Maxwell, Arata, Feri—no nouveau fashion from any colony worlds, but the best New York and Paris had to offer, collected while her arm healed and the wound forced her into temporary retirement. Veta selected a Teche original: a silver jumpsuit belted at the waist with a wide, white sash. The color accented her hair. She left the zipper just above her navel, revealing a smooth expanse of tanned skin. Her neck chain was a triple braid of heavy gold, as thick as her little finger. A single earring dangled from her left ear, an enormous black pearl set in a gold clasp. The effect in the mirror was striking, as if she had somehow emerged from the last year unscathed and was ready to return to her life. But the longer she stared, the more certain she became that the right arm was several centimeters too long for the sleeve. Frowning, she headed for her office.

The room was designed to project tasteful elegance, a statement of success and confidence. Her desk was walnut, three hundred years old, polished to a glassy sheen. The chairs were covered in ranch leather, not cloned hide. Even her accessories were subtle: a brass lamp from a whaling ship, a fifteenth-century dagger used as a letter opener, a quill pen in a gold inkstand. One wall was glass, overlooking the water, an actual view instead of the usual holographic projection, an imperceptible distinction, yet one that made her feel more comfortable. She knew the difference and that was enough.

Len Bollinger stood at the window, staring out at the light glittering on San Francisco Bay. The Sausalito Dome appeared fragile and incomplete, like some decaying sea beast washed up in the surf, an enormous jellyfish fashioned of steel girders and monoline, thin sheets of plastic fluttering in the morning breeze. He turned at her entrance, ice rattling in the empty glass clutched in one weathered hand; the scotch decanter was open on the bar. He was tall, over two meters, past his prime in years, but still carrying himself with the muscled dignity of a man who knew how to use his body. His hair was jet, and his smile perfectly matched his craggy face, a credit to his surgeon.

"Damn it, Veta. You look terrific." He kissed her cheek and stood admiring her for a moment. "How's the arm?"

In answer, she flicked out her right hand, a knife-throwing motion blurred with speed. Though aiming for the button on his vest, her index and middle fingers stabbed his solar plexus, hard enough to make the man wince. She silently cursed her lack of control. A year ago, she could have snapped the button from the fabric without grazing flesh, holding it out in her palm before he even realized it was missing. If Len noticed, he said nothing.

"Good as new," she said bitterly.

"I hope I didn't disturb you." He moved away from the picture window and sank into one of the leather chairs opposite the couch, air hissing from the cushions. His skin seemed cut from the same hide.

"An appointment would have been nice." Veta crossed to the bar and took a goblet down from the rack, a dozen stems suspended from the overhead rack like transparent fruit, light sparkling from the facets. The glass chimed softly as she dropped in some ice cubes.

"There was no time." He narrowed his gaze, measuring her carefully. "Are you taking cases yet?"

"Personally?" She shook her head. "Not yet. But it's business as usual. I've got some of the best operatives in the field."

"I didn't come here for the second team." The man frowned. "Something's come up, a situation requiring your special attention. Do you want the work?"

"Yes." She didn't give a damn if he heard the yearning in her voice. It had been a long, slow year. She was tired of sedentary life, of shopping and social engagements, sleeping late, and waking in the cold sweat of nightmare. The time had come to step back out into traffic. Fear lurked at the fringes of her consciousness. Veta poured juice into the goblet and sipped the liquid as she turned back to the man. "Who are you representing, Len? Zenyam? Or the whole damn Guild?"

Bollinger met her gaze. His blue eyes were rheumy with fatigue and laced with red, but they still held amusement. A corporate executive, chairman of Zenyam Limited, and a member of the Guild Management Committee, he was accustomed to deference and respect. Questions were supposed to be phrased as suggestions, answers given as thoughts—a protocol of speech designed to avoid offense. Yet he treated her as an equal and dispensed with the formalities. "Transport will pay the fee. But my opinion is on the line, you understand?"

She nodded. Puzzle pieces fit and locked within her mind, large concepts created from a few small fragments. The Transport Guild was interstellar transportation—a monopoly controlled by three companies: Zenyam Limited, Alamar Industries, and Mehfil Corporation. They held the major patents for the jump interface, owned the acceleration software outright, and were responsible for recruitment and pilot augmentation. Anyone with enough credit could buy a starship and run it on thrusters through planetary lanes. But if they wanted to jump between star systems, they needed a pilot and went to the Guild with their credit slips in hand. It was a tradition with a fifty-year history, and the patent laws, coupled with the legal maneuvers of a brace of corporate attorneys, gave the Guild a solid future, a destiny worth defending. There were very few reasons why Transport would come to her. Veta pursed her lips. "One of your jockeys gone rogue?"

The man handed her his glass and watched silently as she refilled it with scotch. "We have a pilot being tried for murder on Bacchus. A backwater colony planet out in the fringe. I've got the locations and personalities, a full dossier for your examination." He slipped an infocube from his pocket and set it on the table. "We need some silent intervention."

"Guilty?"

Len laughed, a guttural sound. "Doesn't matter. Preliminary information indicates a setup. Bacchus has a specialized penal system. Prisoners are indentured, their sentence time purchased by locals. Slave labor. Murder carries a life sentence. It all seems very convenient.''

"Someone might end up owning one of your people?''

"Hardware, software, and transit codes. The whole package.''

"The end of the Guild.''

He laid one finger alongside his nose, cupping his chin with his thumb to hide his smile. "Hard to maintain control when the market is flooded with cheap copies. So we're taking defensive measures.''

Veta tossed her head, flipping a short strand of hair off her forehead. "Any legal options?''

His frown was answer enough. He spread his hands, a gesture of futility. "Acquittal chances are slim. No doubt justice has already been purchased by the opposition. We'll try to exercise our contractual and legal rights to remove his interface hardware, but those are valid only in Confederation courts, and this is going to be treated as strictly a local matter.''

"Certainly the Guild can exert some pressure on the Confederation. Why not get them to step in and move the matter into Confederation courts?''

"Never a good idea to push the Confederation. It might attract unwanted bureaucratic attention. There are certain aspects of our business we would like to keep private.'' He cleared his throat. "Anyway, by the time we got a legal judgment in our favor, it'd be too late.''

She steepled her fingertips, staring over them at the man. "A lot of trouble to plan. Why not just kidnap a pilot?''

"Using the Bacchus judicial system puts a patina of legality on it.'' Len cleared his throat and leaned forward to drive his point home. "Kidnapping him would have violated Confederation law. The Feds would be involved, whether we wanted it or not. This way is actually preferable.''

"So you come to me.''

"I never forget talent.''

Veta laughed. "Talent lost her right arm during her last run.''

"Still completed the job." There was no way to determine if the admiration in his face was real or just another aspect of his manipulative skills. "I want that kind of dedication. Name your fee."

"I will." She pushed the errant lock of hair back behind one ear. "What have you got in mind?"

"Eliminate him." He drained the scotch in a single gulp and grimaced pleasurably.

"What about his hardware?"

"The implant is tied to his brainwaves. They cease, it self-destructs."

She nodded.

"One other task." Bollinger stood and handed her his glass. "Raise the bastard responsible for this little fiasco."

"You want him hurt?"

His smile was brutal. "That part we'll handle. Just give us a name."

"Consider it done."

The man stretched and wiped his eyes as though suddenly tired. "Wish I had time to stay."

Veta matched his smile, and reached out to take his hand. "Me, too." She kissed his cheek. The skin was soft despite the weathered appearance. He smelled of cologne. Pheromones caused a primal stirring and Veta pulled away. "But I'm on a case." She escorted him to the door, flicking on the corridor scanner. Infrared showed two large heat sources on either side of the entrance.

"Mine," he said, answering her questioning stare. "It's a tough world out there. Keep me informed."

"You'll be updated through the regular channels."

"Take care, Veta." As the door slid open, his bodyguards stepped from the shadows, two burly men, their forms hazed in protective shields. Bollinger released her hand slowly. "God knows what we'll do when you really do retire." They hurried down the passageway toward the lifts, Len safely ensconced between the two like a king judiciously guarded by his knights.

Veta stepped back inside her office and closed the door. Absently, she collected the glasses and stowed them in the wash unit, wiping up the beads of water from the top of the mahogany bar. A burst of adrenaline flushed the fatigue from her system. Her mind was racing, reviewing the conversation, prioritizing actions. It was good to be working again, but her phantom arm throbbed and her mouth was dry.

In the drawer behind the bar, she found a bottle of capsules. White and red, they were chemical youth, designed to make her body forget its age and start her brain firing like a hot-running engine. She swallowed two and chased them with a mouthful of water. By the time she accessed the computer, the drug had kicked in, adding its impetus to her mental flight. She was charging, heart stoked with a linked fuel of artificial and natural stimulants, muscles tense and coiled as if waiting for the chance to strike a blow. Choices shuffled themselves in her head. Actions and reactions. Veta saw the plan laid out before her as if on an enormous game board awaiting her touch. She was the catalyst—a push here, a prod there, and lives would spin away, forever changed. She was alive.

A list of contacts in the Olympian system flashed onto the screen. Veta stared at them as if they were hieroglyphics, only one notation seemingly in English—Rocco Marin. In her drug-induced state, her hesitation must have been immeasurable, but it seemed an eternity before she touched the keyboard and placed a personal call.

Chapter 5

The holding cell was a small white square. Rolen wedged himself into the corner, drawing strength from the two cold walls against his back and the hard surface of the bench protruding beneath him. The close quarters reminded him of his ship and helped keep the spaces beyond at bay. He had time to catch his breath, time to think.

Prospects were bleak. Horror stories of colony justice were always circulating through the comm channels of deep-space freighters, cautionary tales complete with moldering dungeons and brutal forms of execution. He was lucky in one respect—the port was technically Confederation soil and as such under their jurisdiction. Whatever else might happen, Rolen could expect a uniform legal process and, if found guilty, a competent and humane punishment. A reasonable concern. Murder on Thor's Belt was punishable by spacing, perpetrators sent out to suck vacuum in an open lock—clean, quick, and an economic necessity on the small mining colony. He'd heard of others: mindwipe, lethal injection, and even a fundamentalist Islamic sect that still used beheading. No telling what the groundlings of Bacchus had dreamed up as punishment for murder.

He had other problems, too. The Guild was a jealous mistress. As long as he played the game by her rules, she would go out of her way to protect him. If he screwed up,

the backlash would be just as detailed. His Guild contract
had a directory of violation clauses, in print too small to be
completely read or totally absorbed. If he broke his Guild
contract, they could legally jerk the hardware from his skull.
Rolen had seen one such victim before, an ex-pilot staggering down a port corridor, palsied, trembling, his nervous
system raped by the removal of the interface. It was a fate
possibly worse than death. Odds were a murder conviction
was a breach of his Guild agreement.

The Port Authority offices were in the central axis of the
station, all chrome and white plastic gleaming under fluorescent banks, as sterile and functional as the workings of
a giant mechanism, with just enough gravity to keep objects
stationary. Form followed function in a familiar institution-
alized progression, reminding Rolen of the dining commons
at Zenyam's flight academy: long lines threading down a
narrow space between the wall and the steel counter, anonymous faces on the other side of the glass partition shoving
the plates back to him through the space below the divider.
Here, a stoic officer escorted him, hand on his shoulder,
pushing him through the maze of registry officers. The
drama of arrest played before him, Rolen responding
numbly to their inquiries, unable to function in an environment that had robbed him of his edge. Without the computer
feed, he was dull and senseless. Rolen floated along, a log
caught in a swift current, unfeeling and inanimate.
"Read and verify." A computer printout was held flush
against the divider, legible through the glare. He saw his
name scrawled in dot-matrix block script. The charge was
murder. Another print of his palm for authorization, and
they moved on down the line. The grunt looked bored and
tired. Beyond the glass, the clerks failed to recognize his
humanity, seeing him only as a charge, a crime, a unit of
work to be shaped and filed and slotted into some mechanical niche beyond his comprehension.
"Any valuables to declare?" An open hand waited for
watches and rings; a blank face and callous shrug were the
only expressions as a form was slid toward him beneath the

partition. "Print here." Fingers pressed his hand down firmly. He shuffled to the left, the grunt pushing hard.

"Strip and stand ready. Put this on. Hold the sign upright. Relax your damn hand."

The faces flickered by him, cold and precise, functioning on their own sensory network, reacting to impulses from which he was denied access. Anger boiled up within him, spurred by the anonymous assembly-line nature of the system. He had rights under Confederation law. Rolen cleared his throat.

"I want to speak with someone." His voice sounded strange.

The grunt glanced at him, still bored. "You want to make a statement?"

"I want counsel."

"You'll get it, for all the good it'll do." He choked off a laugh.

"I've got rights," Rolen insisted. His head was pounding.

"No problem. You'll get your chance."

"I want to contact the Guild."

The man looked down at him, his thick features shadowed, his eyes deep and hooded. A smirk traced his lips. "They'll know soon enough, if they don't already." He grabbed the other hand and shoved it down against the ident plate. "Now, why don't you slam your hatch and let's get this part of it finished."

The guard refused to answer further questions.

They dressed him in prison fatigues. Gray coarse fabric. No belts or ties to use for suicide. Soft cloth shoes. Other than that simple gesture, more perhaps for their own modesty than for his comfort, the Port Authority ignored his needs. He was left in the holding cell to sit and wait and wonder.

Had he killed the woman? The question nagged. The mental block hindering his memories was formless and featureless, with no chinks or gaps through which he could find answers. It had been a dozen years since he'd been

limited to the storage capacity of his own brain and its
chemical system of information recording and retrieval that
was so easily scrambled; even if not victimized by inten-
tional chemical abuse, it was partially erased by every passing second. He thought longingly of the *Trojan Horse*—hell,
even the creaking hulk of the *Shadowbox*—and touched the
sockets in his neck just to be certain they were still there.

Aboard a ship, connected to a computer system, the moments would have been frozen within the RAM. No need
to sweat and worry over a single word or a movement. Call
it up and replay it. Christ, relive it if you wanted, complete
with sight and smell and sound as real as the actual moment. But in this small cubicle, Rolen had only the apparatus that filled his skull, a spongy, alcohol-sodden piece of
mutated muscle that had failed to capture the murder except
in the barest of confused details.

There were flashes of clarity—her body on the bed, eyes
lazy, head angled back with a slow smile of orgasm spreading across her lips; the steel fang flashing again and again;
he was conscious now that it was not fang but blade, a
dagger flickering in the light. The hand gripping the hilt
was shrouded in darkness. Blows came from empty air, from
above and behind. Light exploded in his skull, pain accen-
tuating his pleasure. Nails raked his skin. He remembered
lashing out, flailing his arms blindly, connecting with damp
flesh and hard bone. The knife hung in the air, the blade a
ruddy gleam.

There was no way to tell if his hand thrust the weapon.
Nor could he escape the clouding eyes of Miras Magana
watching him in surprise as her life pulsed from open arteries in her slashed throat.

He hung his head and closed his eyes, trying to make the
nightmare vanish and failing miserably.

The bars slid open with a metallic clang. Rolen jerked
upright, squinting against the light. He had no idea how
long he had been out. Another glaring reminder of his hand-
icap—the inability to call up the time from some recess
within the ship computer.

Framed against the square bracket of the doorway, the PA looked huge, as square and solid as the metal bars. His hair was a short, dark bristle on his skull, like some fungus grown in dark corners and deep pits. Grinning broadly, a vicious humor in his gleaming eyes, the man stepped into the cell and let the bars slide closed behind him.

"Hear you want to make a statement, slasher," he said.

"I asked for counsel."

"What the hell for?" The man squatted before him, bringing his square face level with Rolen's. His laugh was rich and deep. "We got your ass." Square teeth gleamed behind his lips. He counted off the points on fingers as thick as sausages. "Witnesses place you with the victim at a joint called Caliban's. We got two others who'll swear they carried you to her flat. Your prints on the blade and your skin under her nails. Might as well left us films of you doing the deed."

"I'm innocent until proven guilty."

"Just my point, skyking. No real problem with the proving." He placed his hands on his thighs and leaned forward, getting close and confidential. "So why don't you just tell me all about it?"

Rolen shrugged and looked away. "I don't know . . ."

The man slid forward like a shifting load of cargo, a fluid lunge, one solid arm coming up to pin Rolen by the throat and slam his head against the wall. "You're trying my patience," the PA said carefully, his face inches away from Rolen's, his breath sour and stale and smelling of curdled milk. "I don't have time to screw around, and the way you look, skyking, nobody's gonna notice a few more bruises. So why not make it easy for both of us?"

"Am I interrupting something?" a feminine voice said, calm and cool. In the sudden silence, the clatter of the cell door as it opened sounded like alarm bells. The officer stood slowly, dragging Rolen to his feet and straightening the front of his fatigues.

"No." The PA kept his gaze locked on Rolen. "Nothing that can't wait till later." Shoving him back into the wall, the man whirled and stalked out.

She was middle-aged. There were no wrinkles on her face, yet her eyes were those of an old woman. Brown hair cut short. A painfully thin body. Her prison fatigues rustled softly as she moved. In one hand, she carried a medical kit.

"They said you need medical attention." Her voice was soft and quiet, personable, as if he were a casual acquaintance met on the street. He couldn't help returning her smile.

"Let's see what we've got." She placed her kit on the bench. Gently, she helped him peel the fatigues away from his arms and back, frowning at the scratches, cuts, and bruises, prodding and touching and careful to avoid causing further pain.

"You don't have to take that shit, you know." She nodded toward the corridor where the officer had disappeared, keeping her eyes on her work. "Not from him. Thinks he's a hard-ass, that his badge gives him some leeway. But you can file a complaint, maybe get him pulled."

"Thanks," he said quietly. "I'll keep that in mind."

Her examination continued without pause. "These look superficial. Anything feel serious?"

Rolen shook his head.

She took his pulse and temperature. "First time?"

"Yeah." There was something comforting about the woman. Maybe it was the way she went about her duties, doing her job, but still treating him as a person and not just some item to be studied and processed. He took a deep breath and tried to relax.

"A couple of pointers, then." Her expression grew serious, a maternal mask, grave and concerned. "Get your story straight. You want to be damn sure how it went down when you go before the Judicial Council. Won't be any second chances with the Jaycees."

He winced as she began abrading the wounds, cleaning out the gashes on his arms and chest. "It's all jumbled in my head. I can't make any sense out of it."

"Hey, it doesn't matter to me if you slashed the bitch or not. But you have to convince the judge. If you didn't do it, what's your alibi? If you did the deed, then why?—'cause sometimes the why makes a difference. Lots of marginal sorts on Bacchus . . . shills, thieves, slavers. Maybe it was self-defense?''

The plastic skin she applied stung and Rolen clenched his teeth. ''Wish I knew.'' He sucked air deep into his lungs to control a scream that was building. His voice quavered. ''Something happened. Went real wrong. But I can't translate. A major malfunction in my head.''

She touched a bruise on his neck, went to the kit for a syringe, and injected a clear fluid. The needle stung. She went down to a hematoma above his right nipple. The needle stabbed again. He felt the pressure of the fluid and watched as the color faded. ''She threaten you . . . try to rob you?''

Shaking his head made his skull ache.

''Maybe the bitch hurt you? They do that sometimes—get off on the violence. Did she ask for it?''

Rolen let the tears fall silently, his jaw trembling. ''I don't know.''

The doctor seemed to understand. She nodded and finished her work. After the exam and treatment were completed, she packed her kit. ''Anything else?''

''I'm hungry.'' Rolen closed his eyes and sank back down on the bench.

The woman picked up her kit. ''I'll get you something to eat.'' She walked to the bars and they slid back at her approach, closing after she had exited. In the corridor, she stopped and turned back, her ageless stare fixed on him. ''Try to remember,'' she said, her voice professional and detached. ''No one can help you but yourself.''

He nodded. Then she was gone. His loneliness was sudden and acute.

After a while, there was nothing else to do but dream. Somewhere in his mind a synapse snapped; a mental spark crossed a gap in gray matter. A segment of the past materialized, breathtaking in its detail.

The flight simulator at Zenyam was an exact duplicate of a jumpship cockpit. From outside it was a Rube Goldberg design, a cube snaked with cables and mounted on a network of hydraulic gimbals and shafts. Puddles of oil stained the concrete floor. The greasy smell filled him with a vague nausea, overpowering and rich. His bare feet whispered up the mesh-steel stairs, waffling his soles, cold serrations abrading his skin. The place was a second home, classroom and dorm for hours on end. Once inside, he was in command of a ship, the simulation so real that all thoughts of mock and make-believe were hidden deep and easy to ignore. He flew. He learned.

Standard charter runs, cargo dumps, courier flights, exploratory jaunts—all in the privacy and safety of the simulator. He reveled in the joy of command and the newfound skill of his mind meshed with a flight computer, joined at the neck to the fluid power of crystal and chemical and electric intelligence.

A specific flight segmented itself from his general memories and blossomed before him like a flower seen under time-lapse photography, swelling, bursting, passing.

He came into the Hantu system hot, ripping out of jump space and through the nexus, vectoring in on the distant beacon of the Hantu Port, his mind fractured into task centers, his consciousness flickering over the duties arrayed like dominoes before him. The priority message tugged at his consciousness, a cry from space, wailing across the normal space bands: MAYDAY . . . MAYDAY . . . MAYDAY . . .

Rolen called up external view. Enhanced, the stricken craft was a red glow against the black-and-white granular image of the Hantu system. A quick scan confirmed that he was the nearest vessel, no other ships even yet detaching themselves from the square white cube that was the Hantu Free Port. He shifted vectors to intercept and set one task center to unraveling the preset commands for deep-space rescue, feeling the suck of gravity as the ship changed course and homed in on the red flicker like a moth to a flame.

The computer identified the craft as an insystem hauler, matched spin, and increased thrust to intercept. He went to visual to follow the docking procedures, surprised by the silence from the stricken ship and worried that he was already too late for the crew. The docking port loomed. He felt the clang of steel as the ships connected, and heard the rush of exchanged air.

Immediate darkness ended the simulation, like a curtain dropped over his consciousness. A message blinked across the interior of his skull. EXERCISE TERMINATED AT 1250 HOURS. SHIP LOST. PILOT DEAD. His guts knotted. Shame burned his face. Reaching up, Rolen grabbed the plugs and pulled them from his skull, muttering under his breath as he released the straps that held him into the pilot's chair.

Collins waited in the debriefing room. Her face was sallow and pinched. She looked uncomfortable in her jumpsuit, rubbing at the arthritis that had turned her fingers into twisted sticks. "Review."

Rolen raised his hands futilely. "Standard rescue procedure. I don't understand."

The woman pursed her lips, two pale slivers over her white teeth. "That was an insystem craft."

"Beaming a mayday," he protested.

"Did you ask for the proper transit code?"

"It was insystem. They wouldn't know the proper code."

"Precisely." Her voice was a thin wheeze. "A standard trick used by pirate craft. Suck you in and strip you. You don't stop unless you get the proper code, and that means you don't stop unless it's a jump ship."

Rolen blinked and swallowed. "What if it's really in trouble?"

"Insystem ships take care of their own . . . just like us." Her eyes narrowed, shriveled lids sliding over them like snakeskin on oil. "Transit codes. I hope you've learned the lesson." He nodded. "Good. Go get some rest." Rolen left her in the room, rubbing the bulging knuckles of her red and swollen hands.

The holding cell returned, the memory fading, but not the lesson. Twelve years of imprinting and he was still listening for codes. He didn't like the silence.

The medic returned with a plastic tray. Delicious aromas steamed up from broth and stew. His stomach churned hungrily, yet Rolen hung back.

"Here. Eat." She held the tray out to him.

"Who are you?" He kept his tone low and even, trying to control his anger.

The woman set the tray beside him and slid two fingers into her pocket, exposing her PA badge glittering against the fatigues. "It's a game we play with virgins, a yin-and-yang thing. Sometimes it works." She shrugged. "Waste of time with you, though. No longer our problem."

"What's that supposed to mean?"

"Lady you cut had some strong ties to the ground. Major corporate dollars. Extradition order came through a few minutes ago." She stood to her full height. "You're going dirtside."

Rolen slumped against the wall and closed his eyes. Planetside. Sucked down into the depths of the gravity well with its poisons, masses of groundlings, and wide-open spaces. He swallowed hard. "Get the hell out."

The woman laughed softly. "Word of advice, spacer. Plead guilty and pray for clemency. Big credit wants you taken out. And credit always wins." She left him slowly, her footsteps fading with the clang of the bars.

Chapter 6

The landing craft touched down in twilight, the braking sequence pulling Jaleem Abbasi against the restraining harness. He rode it passively, letting his body jar. Around him, less experienced travelers struggled, pained expressions marking their efforts, as harnesses cut deep into tense muscles. The landscape outside the small window slowed and became distinct. The local star was a ruddy ball settling into the horizon through a fiery haze of mining dust. A flat plain stretched toward the dark shadows of a distant mountain range. Wind ruffled through dry, stiff grass bordering the tarmac, brown bristles thrusting up from the crusts of dirty snow.

"Welcome to Delphi." The pilot's voice was a mechanized whisper in the overhead speakers. "All of us at Intercon Connections hope you enjoyed your flight down and will try our hospitality again." The soft, cozening speech continued, offering discount tickets for miles flown, special prices on goods and hotel services, bait and lure.

Jaleem smiled. The shuttle firms were parasites, clinging to the leviathan of the Transport Guild, feeding on the crumbs dropped by interstellar jumpships: cargo and passengers left at local ports and waiting passage to the planetary surface. Transport created the need. Credit insured competition. Alliances shifted and flowed like molten steel, hot and quick, less dependent on the influx of material and bodies than on the benevolence of the Guild. One company basked in the glow of the Guild's patronage while others shriveled on the edge of bankruptcy. Next week, the lines might change, and other favored sons arise. Transport pulled strings and watched.

The shuttle companies would realign as the monster died. Some would. expire in the confusion. Others would shift hosts and sign other contracts, darting and fighting and gorging in the frenzy, becoming stronger and more permanent. He watched the stewardess moving down the aisle, unlocking the restraining harnesses, a plastic smile fixed on her lips. A parasite within a parasite, interlocking symbiosis. She would survive. Most employees survived corporate wars. A few even bettered their positions. But he was too close to the edge. Someday Akira's power would shift, and when it did, Jaleem would have to be ready to jump or die.

He'd spent his life learning the art of positioning, a skill perfected in a dozen different geographies. In the Zone, it was simpler—picking those to guard your left and right, choosing a sect with enough muscle to generate respect but independent of the major power brokers, or using an older, more reliable weapon rather than the high-tech machines so prone to jamming and failure in the primitive enclave of the Teheran slums. Preparedness was a trick learned as a grunt in the trenches and never forgotten by those who prospered. Success was simply a measure of the ability to create and use opportunity.

The terminal was a generic design: dark blue carpet, arrangements of native flowers and green plants, and framed posters of local attractions on the walls. Woven fabric in grays and browns covered every flat surface, softening edges and adding depth. The cool air, scented with freshener and smoke, was permeated by a dull hiss of conversation. Measured against Earth-standard, the gravity was only slightly less, but in contrast to the hard drag of Rohar he felt superhuman. He'd need a few hours in a gym to regain control of his muscles.

Security was tight. The red uniforms were bright splotches of color among the denim fashions of the colonials and the gray suits of waiting corporate types. His contacts had briefed him on the local troubles. Certain dissident factions were trying to abolish the convict labor system: liberals, unemployed workers who blamed the system for the lack of jobs, teens, students, and the slaves themselves. There were the usual demonstrations, with fiery speeches and marches consisting more of Maimers looking for fights than of those trying to enlighten the social consciousness. All this was a minor threat to the success of the Akira operation—very slight, his contacts insisted, claiming that every effort was being made to contain the problem. He had no reason to doubt their sincerity. They knew the price for failure.

Har Vogel waited in the lobby. Once he'd been the Teutonic ideal: tall and spare, with blond hair and steel-blue eyes. He still carried himself with the easy assurance of a man secure in his own strength, but his muscles lacked tone and his gut was developing a paunch. A hard blow would probably sink to the wrist in fat. The dueling ring had left its scars layered over the skin of his meaty face like Chinese ideograms. The pupil of his right eye bled into the azure blue of the iris, a gash of darkness.

Vogel smiled tightly as Abbasi approached. "Welcome." His voice was a dry rasp. "Good trip?"

Abbasi grunted. They walked in silence to the exit.

A limo waited at the curb: smoked-glass windows, polished black body—even the apron bag was fashioned of some material that gleamed in the light, a major totem in the hierarchy of corporate symbols. The door was open and a liveried corpseman waited, erect and alert. His skin was almost transparent, like a thin layer of pink gelatin, muscles outlined, veins pulsing. A chauffeur's cap rested on his hairless skull. Jaleem settled into the back of the stretch, eyes adjusting to the darkness. Taking the bench seat across from him, Vogel keyed the intercom and barked a quick command to the corpse. Turbines whined. The hovercraft rose slowly and moved off toward the distant outlines of Delphi.

* * *

"So?" Abbasi eased back against the plush seat and stretched out his legs.

"No surprises." Har Vogel opened a panel to his left, revealing a compact bar. "Drink?"

"No." He inhaled deeply. "The conviction?"

"Purchased. Used four separate credit transfers. Can't be traced. Justice doesn't know who's paying the bill, but he knows the drill. We've used him before. Very reliable. Remember," he said with a homeboy grin that was meant to reassure but only angered Jaleem, "this is our backyard— our system. We've been kinking it since long before you even thought about doing corporate repair."

Jaleem returned the smile, feral, without friendship. "My ass. Your ass. I want to know. What's the timetable?"

"We get a conviction today. Execution tomorrow, which is really straining the specs. Auction is forty-eight hours after execution."

"Too much time. Move the sale up. No more than twenty-four hours between sentence and sale. Can't give Transport a chance to react."

"Not possible. Langen Nacht will shut down all functions." Vogel's grin widened at Abbasi's confusion. "Local holiday. Longest night of the year. Big damned party."

Jaleem ground his teeth silently. A loose thread. One minor detail that his contacts had failed to mention; they probably hadn't seen it as important. He'd learned long ago that every detail was important. He forced his jaw to relax. "No way around it?"

Vogel gave him a fatalistic shrug, sipping at his drink. "Can't fight custom. But not to worry. No one else can move then, either. Nothing happens on Langen Nacht, except drinking and screwing." His laugh was a mixture of grunt and wheeze. "Transport's nothing to worry about, anyway. They're thrashing around pretty good legally. But swinging blind. They've filed for a temporary restraining order and are trying to secure hardware retrieval. It's been denied. Secondary injunctions are cropping up everywhere, but nothing's serious. Justice has postponed all proprietary-rights decisions pending the outcome of the trial."

"Good." Jaleem stared out the tinted window, watching the landscape flicker by, outbuildings and factories, sparse patches of scrub and sand. A one-man wing twisted in an updraft above the city. The skyline was a thrust of projects and corporate towers, hard-edged and gleaming in the twilight—an attempt to conform to the corporate mold by taking a segment of New York or Singapore or Rohar and thrusting it deep into alien soil. "I want holo access to the trial and auction. No one is to know I am here."

"Understood." Vogel's lips slid back to expose square teeth, with a gap where one canine was missing. "You didn't have to come. We've got it buttoned down tight."

Abbasi turned and stared at the man for a long moment. "That's not the way it works." He couldn't explain, not in any way the man would understand or accept. "Not the way I operate." He straightened the lapel on his jacket and flicked a bit of lint from the sleeve. "If I am compromised, if Akira is attached in any way, Larion House will be held accountable. We won't go down alone."

"How bad can it get?" Vogel finished his drink in a single swallow.

"War." Abbasi turned back to the window.

Once, in the Zone, years ago, he had found an uncompromised bomb shelter in the basement of some long-dead diplomat's home. English, he'd assumed from the stacks of London *Times*es he found in the cellar. Most of the buildings in the western compound had been razed; all that remained were charred beams and shattered glass, and twisted fingers of steel melted by the intense heat of raging fires. Jaleem loved exploring the ruins, clambering up staircases that led to collapsed upper floors, and darting in and out of caverns fashioned by canted walls and jagged ceilings.

The door was beneath a staircase. He found it by accident while squeezing between the wall and a row of warped shelves, recognizing the slick feel of steel against his bare shoulder. It took two hours to clear away the debris. Jaleem stood before the dark surface, smoke-scored and striped with white slashes of lath and plaster. He could sense the wealth beyond the door, feel it radiating toward him. He had visions of bullion and jewels. Crates of penicillin. Tins of meat. Credit chips.

But the hardened polychrome was beyond his ten-year-old abilities, so, after hanging a shroud of rotting drapery across the opening, he sprinted back through the narrow streets to seek the aid of Fasil the Salvager.

Fasil Mohammed huddled in the twilight of his shop. Gold light spilled from an oil lamp. An old video machine crouched against the wall, its black screen reflecting the dull glow, the words SPACE INVADERS etched mysteriously across the garish paperboard panel surrounding the display. Blankets were piled in the corner. Tin cups and plates were scattered on half-empty shelves along with yards of rope, rusted tools, dented cans of paint and nails—salvage scraped from the wounds of the Zone.

"You must come." The words rushed from Jaleem. He gasped for breath.

"What is it, boy?" Shrewd, cunning Fasil rose from his squatting position on the dusty floor and pushed his hookah back under the protection of a three-legged table.

"A bomb shelter."

Dark eyebrows rose slowly. A smile spread across his hawkish features. "Something, eh?"

The boy nodded.

"Where?"

Jaleem described the location in great detail, explaining how he had come to stumble upon such a great treasure and elaborating on his bravery and keen eyesight. Fasil listened intently. He called into the back for Hossein and Mustafa. They whispered among themselves, ignoring Jaleem. They gathered their tools: picks and shovels, a long length of iron bar, rope, a portable acetylene unit, two battered Kalashnikovs, and an old Walther PPK. Fasil rubbed the dark steel with the edge of his headdress, making the metal gleam.

"You stay here," he said to Jaleem. "Mind the shop."

"But—"

"The shop." The man stabbed a finger at him.

"I found it," he whined.

Fasil nodded. "We'll give you a share." The other men laughed, their eyes sparkling in their soiled faces at some bit of adult humor the boy could not understand but vaguely feared. "A quarter share, little lion."

They went off without him.

The shelter yielded little. There were a few watches on the desiccated corpses. The tins of food were empty. The men split the weapons. In the end there was nothing for Jaleem, except a lesson in the hierarchy of strength and the value of a man's word.

Three weeks later, a claymore mine leveled Fasil's shop and sent the Salvager to meet with Allah. It was Jaleem's first killing.

The suite was spacious, four rooms and a private comm network, certified clear. Polished wood and brass accents—the type of luxury he had grown to expect during his tenure with Akira. A tray of fruits and candies lay on the coffee table. The bar was stocked with private reserve. The air was cool and crisp and free of the omnipresent mining dust that fouled the sky.

A hotel corpse appeared with his bags, alabaster skin starkly contrasting with the silver-and-black hotel uniform. The corpse was male—heavy musculature, broad brow, and flattened nose with wide nostrils—and moved quietly, as though invisible. With his shoulders slumped and his face down, he was the perfect image of a broken man. But flashes of indignation flickered in his eyes. Not broken, Jaleem decided. Concealed.

He was not much for symbolism. Education in the Zone had not included a literary curriculum, yet Abbasi was not so blind as to fail to see what the corpse represented: a focal point for the room, a pivot upon which his actions balanced. Had it not been for a strange local law, the practice of sentencing criminals to servitude, buying and selling them like commodities, Abbasi would not be on Bacchus.

The economic realities of Bacchus had created the convict labor system, evolving it as if by natural process. Drawn by the lure of extensive mineral deposits, the first colonists were practical, conservative, driven, working hard and expecting the same from others. Tales of fabulous wealth brought the criminal element, looking for easy prey and fast credit. The first few lawbreakers had probably been executed. Bacchus had no room for convicts, no way to keep them alive. Yet any death was a waste on such a sterile world. Life was precious and demanded conservation. Some business type spotted the gap and saw an opportunity to make a profit, a method to turn an economic drain into a productive part of society by making convicts work off their sentences. A new being was born.

Time refined the system. Offenses punishable by life sentences grew more numerous. Though originally destined for hard labor in the mines, the corpsemen eventually penetrated every aspect of Bacchus industry, both white- and blue-collar. Buying instead of hiring became the corporate stance.

Sideline businesses arose, not all of them legal—buying convicts from other colonies and arranging surrogates for those with enough money to pay another to serve their time. A ritualistic execution developed: chemical injections to turn the skin pale and rid the body of hair—an inescapable signature, like the infrared heat source on a security screen, marking the beast as different and binding it to the system as securely as if with heavy chains. Those who would escape couldn't run from their own skin.

To Jaleem, the law was simply another opportunity, a weapon for his use, as innocuous as a bottle resting in a muddy gutter; shattered and clutched into a rigid fist, then thrust with proper timing, even an old wine jug could disembowel an opponent. Transport drifted with mindless abandon, its fat belly exposed. Jaleem was moving for position even as he sat in the fine room and watched the corpse empty his luggage. The bottle had already been broken, the lunge timed and initiated. The Guild would not die quietly. He sat and waited for the anticipated retaliation.

Chapter 7

Rolen dreamed of flying. Even as the dream kicked in, he recognized it as a recurring nightmare from his days in Zenyam's academy, identifying it with some split portion of his mind, automatically thinking in normal flight mode. He was jacked in, the bridge a tight cocoon around him, and input flooded his skull. Something was wrong with his head; he was sucking information in like a vacuum, but he couldn't transmit. The ship failed to respond to his frantic commands. Red lights flashed across the consoles, monitor needles pegged in burnout position. A white star glared on the screens, the ship spiraling in an ever-sharpening arc toward the glowing surface, and all Rolen could do was clench his teeth and scream . . .

He woke sweating and crying, terrified, not by the threat of flame, but by the lack of control. The sterile confines of the prison cell did nothing to dispel his helplessness.

There wasn't much difference between the Bacchus House of Justice and the Port Authority. Gray replaced white as the basic hue—the color of fog, covering everything so the surfaces were indistinct, and if he sat in the center, legs folded under him, the padded floor absorbing his weight, it seemed he was lodged in a cloud. The only fixture was a white stool thrusting up from the floor, a receptacle for his body waste, a single point on which to anchor his universe.

Gravity attacked him like a hard maneuver that wouldn't end. A slow flame burned through his muscles, and his joints ached. His skull was a lead weight threatening to snap his spine. Lying on the floor brought no relief, planetary force reaching up through the padded surface to clutch and squeeze him. He tried to imagine living the rest of his life in the grip of Bacchus and realized it would kill him, a slow agonizing death. Another reason to prove his innocence.

He hadn't killed the woman. His memory was still scrambled, but he knew he simply wasn't capable of murder. He might have been a witness, maybe didn't even try to stop it. But no amount of alcohol could have so twisted his sense of morality. Proving it was another matter. Yet, in some way, just consciously deciding he wasn't a murderer gave him hope.

A guard appeared, another face in an endless series somehow sharing a common red uniform, heavy belt studded with batons and weapons, a headset clinging to his shaved skull. "Open seven." The door whisked open with a soft hiss. "Your counselor is here." He waited in the corridor.

Rolen struggled to his feet.

Another gray room. A table and a single chair. He sat. The guard stepped out and the door closed behind him. For a moment, Rolen was alone.

Light flickered across the table, an image burn. The other half of the room became an office: wooden desk, bookshelves, potted plants. It was a very good hologram.

"I'm Layna Stanz, your counselor." The woman's face was neutral, a professional mask. Her black hair was pulled back, and her skin was taut over sculptured cheekbones and a broad forehead. "And you're—" she said, consulting a computer screen to her left, "Rolen Iserye?"

He nodded, still listening for transit codes.

"I've been assigned to your case."

"Who sent you?"

One eyebrow rose in puzzlement. "The Judicial Council. Think of me as a public defender."

Rolen had a sudden vision of a room full of attorneys, drawing straws to see who would have to take the case of the crazed pilot, their faces sour and scowling. "There must be some mistake." He shifted in the chair, trying to find a way to escape gravity. "I was expecting someone from Zenyam or the Guild."

She shook her head, a minimal gesture. "I'm it. If there were anyone else, I wouldn't be here."

Behind the woman, a breeze drifted in from a partially opened window, making the potted palm nod. It was only a hologram, so he felt nothing. Through the glass, he saw a distant landscape, jagged peaks white with snow and scrubby brush; the same view he'd had from the shuttle. She returned her attention to the screen and frowned.

"Given the circumstances, you have few options." Her voice was a quiet whisper, distant, as though she were speaking to a machine. "Guilty with intent. That's what the prosecution is trying for. Guilty with no intent. We'll think of that in terms of manslaughter, tough but not impossible. Guilty with mitigating circumstances—self-defense or accidental death. Probably impossible to prove the latter. We should concentrate on manslaughter."

"I didn't do it."

"Prisons are filled with innocent men." Both eyebrows arched for effect. The woman managed a tired smile. "Besides, that's not a viable defense, not with your confession."

A sick helplessness washed over him. His guts went tight and cold. "What are you saying?"

"Confessing narrowed the options."

"What confession?" He leaned across the table, sliding one hand into the holo as if to grab her wrist, the walnut grain of the desktop and the corner of a pad of yellow paper overlayering his skin. "There was no damned confession."

She seemed genuinely puzzled. "It's all here. Print-verified. Christ, listen for yourself." Her fingers stabbed a control.

Distantly, Rolen heard a voice. Maybe his voice, gravelly and dry. ". . . so I took the knife and cut her throat. What a frigging mess . . ."

"Some kind of mistake," he insisted, his voice edged with hysteria. "That isn't me."

"Look." Her eyes narrowed suspiciously. "You can't retract a confession. And if you're trying to prove mental instability, I must warn you, insanity is not recognized as a plea on Bacchus."

"I never made a confession." Rolen lurched to his feet, toppling the table. One wooden leg sliced through her image cleanly—there was no blood, no scar.

"Sit down," she was saying. "Just sit down."

"Listen to me."

"What you're saying—implying—is impossible. These kinds of mistakes just don't happen. Not with the Port Authority and the Judicial Council."

He balled his fists. "Maybe it isn't any accident."

"Now you're sounding paranoid. And we've already discussed that option."

"I didn't do it!" Something snapped inside him. "I didn't kill anyone!" he roared.

"Why don't I come back when you can discuss this rationally?" The woman broke contact, her image flickering to darkness.

And then the guards were swarming in from the corridor, one grabbing him from behind, another fighting to pin his arms to his sides.

"No more outbursts." Her office was darker, night having fallen in the time it had taken for him to regain control. Outside the holographic window he saw stars and the jagged silhouette of the mountains. Stanz was scowling, her thin lips drawn into a taut line. "I didn't ask for this case. I can turn it down. And then you have no counsel. Think about it. Up to you."

Time had cooled the initial flash of rage and replaced it with the cold certainty that he was at the center of some massive conspiracy. No transit codes. No computer input.

No way to separate the bogeys from the homeboys. But it wouldn't do any good to antagonize the woman. Rolen nodded slowly.

"That's better." Her face relaxed into obscure professionalism. "You're probably not very familiar with our legal system. You would have never been charged if a conviction wasn't virtually assured."

"I didn't do it."

Stanz raised one hand. A trick of the light let him see through her palm. "Look, you can use that if you want. But it won't do any good. Not with a signed confession. There are no long-drawn-out trials here. No personal court appearances. You get one statement. I suggest you make it count."

"What for? I'm already convicted. Right?"

"But not sentenced. Mitigating circumstances can make a difference. Self-defense and accidental death can mean acquittal. Guilty without intent can mean a possibility for parole. Minimize losses, Iserye. That can be very important."

"What's the penalty for murder on Bacchus?"

"Attainder." Finding no understanding in his face, she continued. "A writ of attainder is a formal declaration revoking personal rights, usually for life. The convicted felons are processed and turned to labor. Their sentences are sold, to corporations mainly."

Insight punched through him. "Slavery? You buy and sell criminals?"

Stanz looked indignant. "It is a very efficient system."

"This is crazy!"

She ignored him. "They're going to send in a team to take your statement. You'll be wired. Heart monitors, pulse, respiration. A visual picture for the judge. Just relax and tell your story. Don't leave out anything. Not a single detail. I can't stress how much his decision will rest on your testimony."

Rolen inhaled deeply. He closed his eyes tightly and fought a rising tide of dizziness. "I can't remember."

"Tell what you can. It's your only hope. Unless—" She

studied him for a moment. "—you just want to plead guilty with intent."

He pressed his face into his hands.

"All right." The woman cleared her throat. "Just a few hours left before they take your deposition. I suggest you spend the time refreshing your memory." She made a gesture as though to rub his shoulder reassuringly, her hand passing through him. "I'll be watching the procedures. Everything will be according to the letter of the law. You have my word on that." Her other hand found the contact.

He was abruptly left alone.

Sol Iserye, his father, was a mechanic, like his father before in the time-honored way of family traditions. In that respect, Rolen had been a disappointment. And in other ways. He remembered his father best in the context of his work. Certain stimuli conjured specific memories: the brine of old sweat, metallic grease, the clang of steel. Different stimuli . . . different fragments of life. He did not understand the chemical process. His mind scanned and cycled. The tunnels of Thor's Belt rose around him.

The man stood in the shadow of a borer. Grease darkened his arms, and perspiration coated his square face. He was a compact block of flesh, thick-necked and broad-shouldered. A day's growth of black stubble shaded his jawline. He worked with his mouth clenched tightly, dark eyes fixed on the rigid outlines of a stubborn nut, muscles straining along his forearm.

"Hand me that hammer, son." He kept his gaze on the interior of the borer. His voice was a soft rumble. One massive hand swung in space before Rolen, its fingers like stubby sausages. A fresh cut leaked plasma from one jutting knuckle.

Rolen hefted the forged iron and graphite, marveling at how such an inanimate object seemed to come to life in his father's hands. "Almost finished?"

"Intake's cleared." The wrench slipped. A stream of swearing accompanied the thud of his fist against the housing. He grunted and threw his weight into a final turn on the bolt.

Rolen swallowed hard, staring up at the yawning maw of the borer, its bits angling out like canted teeth. "Gives me the creeps."

"What's that?"

"Well . . . we should scrap it or something."

"Why?" His father raised the cowl and twisted the clasps, rapping sharply on the graphite panel with the hammer, a hollow thunder in the repair chamber.

"You know."

"Bullshit. Jancer won't know, son."

"But . . ." He shook his head. "It killed him."

The man stopped and looked down at him, his square face serious. He took a moment to suck on the torn knuckle, biting a loose scrap of skin from the edge of the wound. "No machine ever intentionally killed a man, Rolen. Jancer died 'cause he thought with his balls." He sucked a breath through his nostrils and grinned. "Tell your mother I said that and I'll kick your butt. But that's God's truth. Bastard liked to jump into beds where he didn't belong." He ran his hand across the smooth surface of the borer, leaving a wide streak of bright paint where the dust had been cleared away. "A machine is only as deadly as the man operating it. The secret is to always be certain of who's at the controls. You got to be aware."

Sol clambered up into the cockpit of the borer. His boots clanged on the ladder rungs. He leaned out of the hatchway, a streak of grease and dust highlighting the bones of one cheek. "Stand clear."

Rolen trotted back to the doorway. The roar of the turbines throbbed in the enclosed chamber, a pressure against his ears. He turned back to watch the borer roll forward into the access, his father waving through the grimy port.

That was how he best remembered the old man: big and thick and somehow attached to a machine as though it were a massive prosthesis; knowing as much about reality as the workings of a borer or the use of a wrench.

Truth was, the law was nothing more than a tool, a machine fashioned of precedent and inference. But Rolen couldn't see who was at the controls.

"In the chair." The lead tech pointed to the chair they'd brought, a wheeled conglomeration of steel and foam padding. Rolen did as ordered.

The testimonial team was a precision unit, mechanized and impersonal, two techs and two guards, all male. The guards stayed by the door of the cell, watching with bored disinterest.

Hardware cluttered the top of an equipment cart. He recognized a heart monitor, two holocams, and recording units. There were other cubes of electronics, mysterious and threatening.

"Open your shirt."

He obeyed numbly. The tech smeared gel on his chest and in a thick line across his forehead. Electrodes followed, familiar and reminding him of the *Trojan Horse*. Homesickness washed over him and he had to fight back tears.

"This is stupid," Rolen muttered. He tapped the implants behind his ear, nails clicking against ceramic. "Why don't you just jack in? Let them see what I really remember."

No one answered. One of the men produced a thick roll of silver tape, stripping off squares and adhering the sensor plates to his chest, his throat, and his temples. The holocams hummed softly, red lights gleaming bright against the white walls.

The lead man filched an inhaler from the medical kit—a white tube with a plastic flange on one end designed to cover the nose. He held it in front of Rolen's face. "Something to make you relax."

"No." Rolen shook his head.

The man looked back to his partner, who shrugged. "It's his funeral." After checking the leads to the recorders, the tech stepped out in front of the holocam. "Ready here."

"Go ahead." The disembodied voice was loud and mechanical.

He pointed toward Rolen with one finger. "You're on."

Rolen told his story. Even as he spoke, he knew it was not enough, would never be enough, to free him.

It didn't take long. Not nearly long enough for someone to judge his life. Maybe they hadn't even made the tape. Rolen had no way of knowing. The PA's words echoed through his head. "Big credit wants you taken out. And credit always wins." Enough credit to buy his conviction. Why? Because they thought he'd killed the woman . . . or maybe something else, strategic maneuvers occurring on some level he couldn't begin to understand.

Layna Stanz didn't have to tell him the verdict, he read it in her face. She sat behind her desk, safe in the confines of her holographic universe. It was still dark outside, snow-capped peaks ragged and gleaming. The window was closed. The woman looked at her hands, straightening the sleeves of her black coat.

"Well?" Iserye remained standing, muscles tensed.

"Guilty with intent." She met his gaze, her eyes in shadow, darkly gleaming.

"Of course," Rolen said, suddenly very tired.

"I did my best. Everything legally possible."

"But I didn't have the credit line. Right?" He shook his head slowly. "What about an appeal?"

"The decision of the Judicial Council is final."

Rolen breathed deeply. "Thanks for your time." He turned toward the door.

"It's not that bad," she said, and then looked embarrassed at her words. "I mean . . . there are worse alternatives. Many places still use capital punishment. It's got to be better than spacing."

His laughter startled the woman. "Nice sentiment. Must make it easier for you to sleep nights." He walked from the room.

The guards were waiting to take him back to his cell. For a heartbeat, he entertained the brief fantasy of charging them and letting the men gun him down in the corridor. But he lacked the strength and so fell into step between them.

Somewhere outside, the bastards who had set him up were

probably already celebrating. He had no idea who they were. He sensed the shudders of machinery moving around him, vague shapes gliding like predators at the edge of the eye. There were people in the cabs, grabbing levers, turning wheels, but he couldn't see their faces.

Chapter 8

The world beyond the glass was bitter cold, a stark tableau of white snow, gray slush, and black stone. Veta Pulchek stood at the window and stared out at the spreading twilight. From her vantage point, Delphi expanded in diminishing geometric shapes. Square, stout buildings of gray jutted on the horizon, growing smaller at the edges with both distance and construction, impacted design reflecting the mentality of Bacchus; a colony forged by heavy-metal miners, carving their fortunes from the bowels of the planet.

Night enhanced the stars above and the lights below. To the south were the occasional constellations of the corporate estates, pockets of brilliance in the unrelenting dark. Sprawling mansions of natural stone, they were set apart from the city as though the scions who inhabited them were embarrassed about and afraid of the urban sprawl they had helped to spawn.

Neon and strobes flickered along the narrow streets of the city. Decorations gleamed from store windows and shop fronts, gold spots imitating the local star, sprays of plastic flowers in reds and blues and shimmering yellows, sheaves of wheat, and wreaths of evergreen. Glowing garlands trimmed the few trees in the parks, anticipating the coming festival.

Somewhere in the night there was another like herself. A

kindred spirit. Male, she sensed, because it was a woman who had been sacrificed to gain the pilot. Worrying, she'd bet. The way she always worried when a plan had been designed and set into motion, and there was nothing to do but wait and see if the architecture would stand the stress of reality; sweating the backlash and the minutiae that might have been erroneously overlooked and tensely waiting for the other side to make a move.

A fleeting pain stitched a path down the reconstructed arm and crumpled the hand into a tight fist. It felt like alien fingers cutting into alien flesh. The thought brought a scowl to her lips. She turned from the window at the hiss of the opening door.

Rocco Marin stood in the doorway, overcoat slung over one shoulder, auburn hair swept back in a graceful fall. She was tall and slender, her narrow waist accentuated by square shoulders and the jutting thrust of her hips. Pretty. Beautiful. Breathtaking. All were justified descriptions. Her green eyes sparkled when she smiled, but she wasn't smiling as she stepped into the room.

"Hello, Veta." Her voice was a husky whisper.

"Good to see you."

"Wish I could say the same." She hung her coat across the back of the sofa.

"Thanks for the use of your place."

Rocco nodded. "Anything for a friend."

"How's business?"

"You wouldn't like it." Her hands fumbled nervously with the collar of her jacket. "The intrigues are smaller. The pay is considerably less. But so are the risks." When she looked up, her eyes were hard. "You're dragging me back into the mainstream."

"Just for the moment. You don't have to stay."

"I won't."

"I need your help."

"Just like old times." Her smile was laced with bitterness. "Always going after the big ones."

"They come to me."

"You don't have to take them all."

"Of course I do." Veta laughed softly. "I want them. I like it in the fast lane."

"Yeah." The woman shook her head. "You're talking about a pilot here. That means the Guild, 'cause no one else gives a crap about a skyking. Heavy traffic. I sure as hell don't want to get run over."

"You're setup. I'm execution. Like always. That means it's my risk." She flexed her hand; it felt distant, still alien.

"The way this one is geared, we both get to watch from a safe place." Rocco swallowed and pushed a strand of hair behind her ear. "I've secured a couple of people. They'll be meeting us here at 2200."

"Why don't I buy dinner?"

"One condition," Rocco said. "No business with meals. It's a new tradition. At least for a little while, let's pretend we're just two old friends."

"I'll do my best." She followed Rocco out the door, feeling odd to be watching her familiar shape. Like old times.

She hadn't always been involved in corporate operations, but that part of her life seemed somehow separate and distinct, as unfamiliar as her new limb. Her career wasn't the result of a conscious choice, but rather a physical response to a pleasant stimulus, like an erotic technique that once experienced becomes a compulsion. Veta had found her niche by accident, stumbling across it while in pursuit of a vague goal more consistent with the family wealth and social status. They assumed that, as with most of her endeavors, the intensity would pass, the desire fade. But thirty years later, she was still scanning the layouts of deadly targets and planning clandestine activities.

The first job was free-lance. Commission work would come later. His name was Dobrik. A thin and wasted man with a perpetually bewildered smile on his skeletal face. Skin the hue of dried paste was drawn tight over his sharp features. Veta had seen him many times in her father's office. The good right hand. The one to be trusted with every detail of the family fortune. He knew the assets and the investments, and personally handled most of the transactions. At some point, the sheer injustice of all that wealth going to someone else had twisted through his head like a bullet and ripped loose his normal sense of morality. Dobrik punched out a million liquid credits and bought night passage to Hardcore, the first link in a tangled chain of transfers and shuttles toward the frontier colonies.

Father was crushed. A minor wound financially, but the damage to his ego was substantial. He was spoken of in quiet tones at the Club. Mocking eyes followed him through restaurants and across the floor of the Exchange. The rumor surfaced that perhaps he was going slightly senile.

She had been between schools at the time, having just discovered that she was woefully bankrupt in the talent required to pursue painting as an art. There was a gap in her life and she had been drifting along for several months in a current of parties and groping affairs, rudderless, lost. Anger returned the focus. Veta bought a ticket to Hardcore.

She caught up with Dobrik in a luxury apartment above the casinos of Malacar. The man pleaded. He threatened. He cajoled. He even offered her money. In the end she took the credits, what little remained, and a portion of his anatomy. Slow surgery with a pair of industrial cutters. A present for Father. Sometimes she wondered if Dobrik had ever swung the credit for a decent repair, and if so, was it ever as good as new?

Rocco had come later, too late to save her from the work. It had already become an addiction.

The operatives were waiting when they returned.

"Jann Petski and Kol Danton," Rocco said with a nod toward each as she moved to the bar to pour drinks.

Jann Petski was street-hard. She knew the type, a pack animal now operating solo, and probably not by choice. Malnourished, short, and brooding, he looked cold and uncomfortable in an oversized jacket, its white fleece collar brown with dirt. His jaundiced face was pocked with fever scars, dark beard concealing the ravaged skin of his cheeks. He took the drink from Rocco with trembling hands, gulping a quick mouthful and nervously watching Veta over the brim of the tumbler.

She had never seen an albino before, not in the flesh; she found the pale skin fascinating and unsettling. The short stubble on Kol Danton's skull was white, and his eyes were the unnaturally perfect blue of contact lenses. A mercenary, muscle for hire, he bore the scars of his battles. The smashed lump of cartilage that had once been a nose was spread between his mouth and eyebrows like a tumor, distorted and flattened. His body was hard and muscular, maintained like a prized weapon. He returned her steady gaze, assaying her worth as though sizing an opponent in the ring, searching out weakness.

Rocco settled onto the sofa, looking at her expectantly, waiting for Veta to break the silence.

There was no need for preliminaries. Rocco would have already briefed them. "What's the program?"

"A variation on the smash-and-grab," Rocco said. "Petski's on the inside, a guard at the House of Justice. He's been keeping his eyes open. Working in the blockhouse, he sees it all."

Petski lit a corba butt, his cheeks drawn as he inhaled smoke. "A prime example of Bacchian justice. The best credit can buy." His voice was a thin whine. "Iserye went down on a slide. Clockwork arrest and conviction. Unreal. And I've seen a few of 'em before."

"Where is he now?" Veta pursed her lips.

"In the House. Saw him secured myself. Security is tight as a straight's butt." Petski grinned. His teeth were brown and stained. "Somebody's got the tempo cranked way up. Double time. Execution in twenty-four hours. Wasn't for Langen Nacht, he'd be personal property by day after tomorrow. As it is, the auction's in three days. Whoever's pulling strings wants no gaps. No errors. Beautiful, you might say, if only you weren't trying to crack it. Right?" He took another long drag on the smoke, blue haze escaping from his lips. He waved the stub. Ashes tumbled to his pants in a soft clod. His rheumy eyes were unnaturally bright. "If you want him out before execution, you'll need a frigging army."

"That's what they're expecting." Rocco continued. "Because he'd be easiest to move before the medics got to him. Once he's marked as a corpse, he's a red flag. Very tough to get offworld, but not impossible."

"What about during the execution?"

Petski laughed knowingly. "No openings there. The medico team is the top of the line. Big credit buys the best. How much you got to pay to get somebody to commit suicide? That's what it'd be. Medico pulls some stunt and the pilot vanishes while in his care and it's good-bye. Bend over and kiss your ass farewell." He laughed again. "Nobody's that stupid."

Rocco cleared her throat. "The soft spot seems to be the gap between execution and auction . . ."

"In the tanks?" Incredulous, Petski clenched his teeth onto the stub of the cigarette, speaking without really moving his mouth. "Secure, Roc. Real secure. It's a prison. Remember? Chambers are well inside the compound. Iserye will be submerged and unconscious. Gates guarded. Entrances and exits checked. Tight."

"Just where you'd want someone during Langen Nacht." She nodded and glanced toward Veta. "Any action then would be a real surprise."

"Still got to get inside," Petski muttered.

"No problem." Rocco jerked a thumb toward Danton. "You should see his impersonation of a corpse."

The albino smiled. "My best role."

"We smuggle him into the compound with a work detail. When the Langen Nacht festivities hit peak, Danton makes a move on the pilot. No one will be looking for him. My guess is they can both walk right out." She glanced at Petski for his input.

"Might be. Could be." A small smile of appreciation crossed his lips. "Won't be scanning the deaders. And there's always a righteous smoker for the shift." Petski sucked his teeth and spit a piece of corba to the floor. "Need

gate passes. Extra risk. Means extra credit. Double. Right?''
He pushed greasy black hair back from his forehead.

"Done," Veta said. His face tightened as if he had been
gambling and now realized he might have gotten triple.
There was a flicker in his eyes of anger and hatred. "Very
workable. Got one change." She was looking at Rocco now,
waiting for her reaction. "Simplify matters. My clients are
very specific in their needs. They want the hardware out of
commission. The pilot—" She shrugged. "—is not their
concern."

Rocco's jaw was clamped shut, her nostrils slightly flared.
There was another dirty laugh from Petski. "Cold-
blooded."

"How do you want it done?" The albino folded his
hands.

"Your choice. Just turn him off. The implant will blow
itself when his brain cuts out."

"Don't worry."

Setting his glass on the table, Petski rubbed his beard.
He fumbled for another corba stick. Flame winked from his
lighter. His cadaverous cheek went concave with the strength
of his draw. He met Veta's gaze. Cool. Too damn cool.
"Seems to me, we get to take the chances. What's your
gig?"

"I fix mistakes."

Petski studied the end of the butt, his hands shaking
slightly, nodded, then took another pull.

"Better shave your head," Rocco said to the albino.

He rubbed one massive hand across his scalp. "Needs it
anyway." He laughed softly.

Petski flexed his hands. "I'll get the pass."

The two men left together.

Rocco closed the door behind them, then turned and
sagged against it, staring at Veta. Her face was pale. She
looked suddenly old, drained. Uncertainty tainted her features and she shook her head in a familiar gesture.

"I don't like him."

"Petski?"

She nodded. "Real asshole. Trust him?"

"Maybe. Sometimes you've got to give a little to get what you want. We needed an inside man."

"Yeah." She paused. "You okay, Rocco?"

"Bad business. Don't like killing innocents."

Veta swallowed hard. "Sometimes it happens."

Rocco walked over to the bar and poured three fingers of amber liquid into her glass, downing it in a single motion and refilling the glass. Her sigh was a soft whisper. When she returned her attention to Veta, she seemed confused. Veta sensed her rage, a maelstrom just below the surface of her control. "Who in the hell are we tangling with?" Rocco asked.

"I don't know yet. Any leads?"

Rocco shrugged. She studied the bottom of the glass, noting the way the light bent through the fluid. "Real confused. Only Bacchus corporations can purchase convicted labor. So the major names are all local. A dozen different leads that end in blind alleys. Familiar faces. Familiar companies. But they can't be the real power—not who we're looking for. Not enough clout to be taking on the Transport Guild. That's the worst, Veta. Whoever it is . . . they think they've got enough to take on the goddamned Guild. Maybe more than we can handle."

"Never." She conjured up one of her patented confident smiles, but there was a sudden sharp ache in her right shoulder. If she flinched, Rocco did not notice. "We're the best."

"No." Rocco slammed the glass down; oily liquid splashed in gilded droplets. "Don't start thinking of us as a team again." Tears appeared, her eyes wet. "Look at what you're doing to me. I haven't slept in days. Not since you called. You brought it all back, Veta. The nightmares. The sweats. The whole frigging number." She whirled, grabbing up her coat from the sofa, slipping the garment over her shoulders. "We were never really a team. I was just a handy tool. Right, Veta?" The anger penetrated her cool facade, a momentary lapse which made her turn and stalk toward the door. "Just a weapon or a recording unit; use me. I can't believe the things I did for you!"

"Come on, Rocco."

The woman laughed, a choppy sound, strained and filled with panic. She stopped in the threshold, holding the door open. "When this is over, Veta, we're even. Don't call me again." Her eyes narrowed to slits, mouth a tight line. "I won't be there."

Outside the window, the gloom had deepened. Clouds obscured the stars. A pair of wings performed an aerial dance, glowing stripes on the fabric deltas shaped like arrowheads, pilots ignoring the slight dusting of snow whirling down from the night. Flakes brushed against the pane, a faint drumming. The lights below gleamed gold and bright, festive. Hovercars slipped along the highways.

Veta watched the traffic dance for a long time, staring blindly. No matter how hard she tried, she could not catch the thrill that usually accompanied a run. Where the hell was her edge, that pure, brilliant rush of exhilaration? A year without work, buying clothing, eating expensive dinners, travel—maybe it had blunted her senses. Maybe she'd changed.

The only sensation she had was of something wrong. The prescience of impending doom. She could lose just by imagining defeat. She knew that. The belief that one couldn't fail was a powerful charm. She tried to analyze her dread, to select the focus and remove it. Rocco? Petski? The cold black outside the window was vastly different from the brilliant nights on San Francisco Bay. She rubbed at her arm absently, her fingers searching under the fabric, finding the ridge, digging and clawing. Snap out of it. Come on, girl. Think positive. Think victory. Remember the way it was . . . the way it will be.

When she looked down at the arm, the scar was bleeding.

Chapter 9

The Blue Note was filled with revelers, early Langen Nacht celebrants come up from the mines and looking for solace. Thick corba smoke burned the eyes and shrouded the lights in blue. Mugs and tankards rattled and clanked. Laughter rumbled from wet throats. The rank stench of old sweat and sour wine assaulted the nostrils. Jann Petski sucked it in, swallowed it. Damn near as welcome as a blast. But not quite; not when the need was growing and he felt as though worms were awakening inside his guts.

He squinted against the haze and navigated the narrow spaces between the tables. He needed Comfort badly. His hands trembled, nausea churning in the pit of his stomach. The inside of his mouth was as dry as tailing dust, his gritty tongue like an alien presence against his teeth. He swallowed hard, shoved two drunken miners apart to reach the bar, and waved a hand toward the bartender.

The man behind the counter frowned and shook his head, giving him one of those patented I-can't-help-you looks, a face reserved for winos and stiffs who had tapped out financially. "Sorry, Petski."

"Hey!" His voice was hoarse, cracking. Several of the drinkers turned to stare with glazed expressions. Not interested, just startled and hoping maybe for a fight. Jann gripped the bar, knuckles turning white. "I'm in need."

"No more credit. Bern's orders."

He slammed his fist down. "Where is he?"

Glass and hand gestured toward the back booths.

Jann leaned in close. "Bring the frigging Comfort and don't stop till I say." He stalked toward the rear booths.

A single lamp on the table did little to dispel the shadows. Bern Aggutter sat with his back to the wall, watching the patrons move through his club and sipping at a glass of mineral water. His features were bloated, eyes hidden in thick folds of fat, lots of sweat on his wrinkled forehead. A mess of rotted teeth appeared as Jann approached. The grin was big and friendly, like that of a brother. Jann had seen it before, and it made him want to whirl and watch his back for a knife.

"Been expecting you, Jann." He waved one hand expansively. "Have a seat."

Petski slipped into the chair, licking his dry lips. His need was consuming. His gums burned and his vision blurred. His pulse throbbed in his skull. His ears rang with tinnitus. The spasms in his stomach made him grit his teeth against the pain. "What's the problem, Bern?"

"Business." Aggutter rolled his thick shoulders. "You owe too much."

"Have I stiffed you? Ever?" His voice rose with practiced indignation, a trait he had scoured from the holos. Act hurt. Act trustworthy. Save rage for later.

"Never given you the chance." Aggutter swallowed water, beads dribbling off his swollen lips. He looked at Petski with all the concern one would give to something foul on the street. "Jann, you got to clear up your tab. Nothing personal."

Petski was quiet for a moment. His mind raced. The slight headache he had brought into the bar was now an agony. He tasted bile. "What'd you have in mind?" His voice was a throaty whisper.

Aggutter laughed and nodded, pleased. It was the kind of expression an owner gave to a pet who had just performed the expected trick. "I hear things. You know how it is. Good news . . . bad news. Your name is mentioned."

"I'm listening." He fought to keep his composure. Fear mingled with withdrawal. Real bad. Petski knew he was about to do something very stupid, very foolish. But he was really hurting.

"You know how business works?" the man asked languidly. "One man has something another guy wants. They get together. Do a little trading." He was playing, using the moment, carefully gauging the hysteria and the evident need. "Your skin itch, eh?"

Jann set his jaw and stopped rubbing his arms. He reviewed his assets and came up short. A few credits, but not nearly enough. Payday was only a distant dream, not even tangible yet, just a promise. The only item of value he owned was a corpse he'd won in a recent card game. But Aggutter had more corpses than he needed; to him they were just another commodity. Still, it was a chance. "You want my corpse?"

"The woman?" Bern shook his head. "No. Something else. Think, man. It should come." His cheeks bulged with a broad smile. "Even to you."

He had the feeling that something big was being offered and he was blowing the deal without even knowing the score. Something clicked in his brain. He sucked a breath through his teeth. "The pilot?"

Bern gave another low, rumbling laugh. "Now we're talking business. You got to have something I want."

Real bad news. The face of the woman appeared in his head. What was her name? Veta Pulchek. Cold bitch, killer type. The definite wrong type of bitch to cross. "You're crazy."

"And you're hurting." The man drummed the table with fat, stubby fingers, amusement lighting his eyes. "Who else is going to sell to you? Nobody. Not once the word gets out that you stiffed Bern Aggutter. But it doesn't have to play that way. You know what I want. You wouldn't deny me, would you? We're family. You don't stiff family for some offworld heat. Not good. Not smart. Offworlders go home. But I'm forever, Petski."

"This is too big." He managed a pained smile. "Come on, Bern. Something else. Anything else."

"Supply and demand. Yesterday, you were just another Comfort King. Got a thousand of 'em on the books if I got one. One more or less doesn't matter. Today, though . . . different story. You suddenly have become a VIP."

Jann lowered his face and looked at his hands. The tremors were strong, making his fingers appear blurred. He buried his face in his hands. Sweat was cold on his skin. It trickled between his fingers. The worms were writhing in his intestines. Any minute he'd start to puke. Then things would get really bad. Time was wasting. He had to move. He looked up at Bern. "Who's in?"

"Me and you. I'll take half of what's left after you've paid the tab."

Jann started to roar, stopped, and swallowed his rage. His dimming vision transformed Aggutter into a hazy cherub, face gleaming with angelic light. "I'm taking the risks," he whined.

The man probed his teeth with one fat finger and re-chewed the liberated morsel. "I've got the Comfort. Supply and demand." He waved to the bartender and the man drew a blast from the cooler. Jann heard the hiss of the injector. His mouth started salivating, and Aggutter just sat there looking smug and content. "Business, kid."

Petski watched the waitress pick up the container and carry it over her head on a tray, dodging drunks. The crowd was lethargic, herd beasts watching with disinterest. He turned back to Aggutter, wanting to grab his fat throat and squeeze until his eyes bulged and his pasty face went red with strain. A tremor racked him. He nodded.

"Good." The man took the tube and passed it over to Jann. "Prime stuff. Take what you need and go celebrate. Happy Langen Nacht." His hands lingered, holding Jann's wrists. "But remember. New game now. New league. You just crossed from minor inconvenience to major debtor. Blow this and you're dead."

Petski shook his head vigorously. "Truth. All the way. You'll see."

"I'd better." Aggutter stood and struggled out from the booth. "Enjoy." He drifted away into the crowd.

The cylinder was ten centimeters of polished aluminum, cool to the touch and rimed with frost. Jann held it in his trembling fingers. His skin stuck to the metal and pulled free, leaving small pink scraps of raw flesh on the fingertips. Tilting his head back, Jann slid the nozzle into one nostril and squeezed. The fluid burned his sinuses. Tears welled in his eyes. Thrusting the tube up the other nostril, cutting the nasal passages with his clumsy touch, he sucked blood and the dregs of the narcotic into the back of his throat.

The rush hit him hard, a wave of heat surging through his veins, a tangible line spreading down from his head and into his limbs. Voices in the bar grew suddenly loud. Individual words became overwhelming. Every tone was isolated and distinct: the ring of glass against steel, droplets of liquor splashing from a loose spigot, the click of a fingernail on a wooden banister, boots crashing against the floor. Rainbows encircled the dim lights with prismatic crystals. And he was hot, a burning cinder, heat cooking the sickness out of him.

His muscle cramps faded. The twitches in his eye gradually subsided. Or did they? Could have just been overwhelmed by the force of the drug. Point was, he didn't care. Felt so good, so fine. Humming through life now. The bar became kinetic, a scene from some damn holofilm and all the patrons were like actors, playing roles in the script of his life. When he moved, they would react. He was the center. He was a damned god.

Crumpling the cylinder in his fist, Petski rose from the chair and headed back to the bar. Aggutter watched him quietly, nodding acceptance to the man behind the counter. Jann took a fistful of Comfort, five or six cylinders frozen into his palm, clinging to his flesh. They looked enormous in his hand, like metal digits. He sucked another at the bar and headed out into the street. Beneath the streetlamp on the corner, he snorted his third, leaning against the wall for

support and swearing at the tongues of fire that licked his
nasal linings.

Comfort made the slums beautiful, even in the depths of
a winter night. Snow skirled down from the darkened skies,
twisting, spiraling, as if the stars were raining down around
him. Jann heard each flake hit with a soft crunch.

He did not want to go home. There was something ulti-
mately depressing about his flat. It was even worse now that
the corpse was there, hovering in the background as his
mother had once haunted him, always watching with wide,
sad eyes, a kind of pained expression as though his very
presence was a big damned disappointment. Not the place
to blow a clutch of tubes.

The Blue Note was in the center of his territory. He had
no property rights like Aggutter or the Leatherboys. To
claim landscape one needed an army. Force had to meet
force. But he had the slums mapped. Jann knew the tangled
maze. There were places where a man could go and blow
four tubes of Comfort in relative safety, little alcoves where
the rats were afraid and the street soldiers didn't bother to
prowl—neutral zones in the gaps between Leatherland and
Aggutter's stake. He moved quickly, gliding through the
narrow streets and alleys like the wind and the snow.

Temporary Housing . . . a local joke. A hundred years
earlier the first colonists had laid out a grid of prefabricated
structures with labels like Temporary Housing and Temporary Offices. The original shells were still standing, but-
tressed with brick and wood, pilfered aluminum, and scrap
steel. The once-painted surfaces were pitted and peeled by
the constant wind. Shattered windows had been repaired
with fragments of cloth and sheets of tin.

The result was a diseased geometry. Lower levels were
set back from the alleyways. Stilts supported overhanging
porches and second levels. The buildings jutted, hard angles, obscure bisected surfaces, triangles merging with rectangles and octagons. Geodesic domes swelled from
trapezoidal lower floors.

Even in the depths of the filth and squalor, signs of Langen Nacht appeared. Candles burned behind dirty glass. Snatches of song drifted with the wind. The smell of spiced wine and evergreens touched his nostrils, intensified by the chemical rush.

He hurried through the narrow streets, jumping greasy puddles and scattered trash. On one corner, crackling flame filled a barrel. Three figures huddled near it—Leatherboys, their jackets gleaming like dark oil, covered with melting flakes and beaded with moisture. They sipped from steaming cans, keeping watch on territory. They stared at him. But the night was cold, and he stayed to his side of the street, just beyond the borders. Maybe on another night, or if they'd known he was carrying Comfort. But not in the late hours of a Bacchus winter evening.

This was hard country. His whole life had been spent trying to climb up and out, like trying to crawl out of an elevator as it plunged down a shaft. Every time he made some headway, the whole structure seemed to settle further down into the depths. Sometimes it got real hard to face. Sometimes reality was a definite bitch. He shoved his hands deeper into the pockets of the jacket and felt the tubes burning his fingers.

He walked down two more mean streets, left and right, his feet dancing, breath forming clouds. The ladder was just in reach, bottom rung cold against his fingers. Jann swung up. His boots scraped on the catwalk as he skirted darkened windows.

The crevice was a dark space between two buildings, a slot in the total structure, both addresses merging above and below, leaving the alcove between. He slid inside and dropped the rubberized canvas drape over the entrance. Against the back wall was a battery lamp. He fumbled in the dark, then flicked on the faint light to reveal an old blanket and a crate for a chair. He went down on one knee and dug the cylinders from his coat pocket.

Jann lay back against the wall. The aluminum was cold. Jamming the inhaler into his nostril, he left the planet, if only for a few brief hours.

* * *

It was almost dawn by the time Petski reached home, and the rush was fading fast. His throat was tight, his tongue thick. He fumbled with the lock, cursed loudly, and shouldered the door open, stumbling between the racks of sleep boxes to the lifts. Somebody muttered a garbled curse as he jarred their cube. The doors parted and he stepped inside, clutching at the wall for support as the cage lurched.

The face haunted him: silver hair and tanned features, and the coldest eyes he'd ever seen. Veta Pulchek was one dangerous lady. He couldn't believe he'd agreed to Aggutter's plan. Only a fool crossed a fixer . . . especially a freelancer. Sure, he had thought about lifting the pilot. But those were just fantasies. This was real bad. His fists clenched reflexively. His hands were trembling. Sweat ran down his face. Suppose someone knew? Suppose she'd had him followed to the bar? Maybe they were waiting for him outside the lift . . . maybe in his room? He crouched against the wall of the cubicle and drew his knife.

The hallway was empty except for a transient crumpled at the far end. The man regarded him warily. Petski hurried to his door, punched the entry code, and clawed at the panel as it slid open, straining against the growling retraction mechanism. He keyed the closing sequence as he stepped inside, and held his breath until it was securely locked. He listened for footsteps in the corridor, but all was silent.

The corpse was standing in the doorway to the kitchen when he turned, her sudden appearance causing him to jump and feint with the knife. "Damn you," he roared, pointing the knife toward the pale figure. "Don't ever come behind me again, never. Next time I'll split you open."

The pale face displayed confused emotions—hate, anger, despair. She was small, with a figure that belied gymnastic training: slender waist, muscular legs, small breasts. Her eyes were brown, her skin translucent due to the execution process. Her bow-shaped mouth was tautly set, shadows cutting her face below high cheekbones. Petski shoved her aside and went to the liquor cabinet, grabbing the one remaining bottle, half-empty and cheap enough to qualify as fuel. The liquid burned down his throat.

Her eyes followed his every move. She never made a sound, had not spoken since he'd owned her. Her hairless skull reminded him of Aggutter, as the man might have looked fifteen years earlier. Petski emptied the bottle, watching her as he swallowed. He could not help but see the disgust flickering in her face.

The rage hit him like an embolism in his brain, a desperate need to hurt something as badly as he was hurt. He lunged for the corpse, hands catching her throat, slamming the woman back against the wall, pounding her skull against the plaster. She did not struggle, just watched him with those liquid eyes, her face rigid. Petski slapped her hard, again and again, his hand stinging, blood flushing her cheeks. The flesh around her eyes discolored, swelling quickly. Then they were on the floor, Petski on top of her, fumbling with his trousers, spreading her legs with his knees.

She was unconscious before he finished. Petski lay on her for a long time, feeling the slow rhythm of her breathing. He was suddenly sorry, guilt stabbing him. Tears flooded his eyes, and he rolled free of her, curling into a fetal position on the hallway floor, sobs racking his trembling body.

No doubt about it now, he was in deep trouble.

Chapter 10

Two guards came for the pilot. They might have been clones; both were tall, trim, and black. They made him stand and turn around, sealing his hands behind his back with warm plastic. Their callous indifference was more frightening than his uncertain future. The two grunts shoved him out into the corridor, falling in step behind him, giving directions with the blunt end of a swagger stick, and making future plans as if he were already dead.

"You free next off day? A few of us are going hunting."

"Chasing Vasquez again?"

"Somebody's gonna get that reward."

"Easy as catching a fart in your hand." The guard's laughter was out of place, another blatant reminder that for them it was just a job.

The corridor unfolded before him. Rolen thought of computer-generated designs and geometric shapes. Perspective turned the gray wall panels into long trapezoids. Bars of light bisected the ceiling. The black floor was scuffed, white scars exposing the lighter hue of the backing beneath the dark surface. He was led down another corridor and through a double doorway, swagger stick prodding him first left, then right, along with thrusts in the spine to keep him moving forward.

His senses were razor-sharp with that peculiar intensity

he'd always come to associate with stress. He could smell the moist, fungal stench of his sweat and the sweet-gum aroma of the wax the guards used to paste their hair to the sides of their skulls. Their shirts rustled with each step, arms pumping in unison. He heard the soft whispering crunch of his own bad knee joint, the scraping of their soles on the floor, and the distant creak of the swagger stick's leather strap each time the guard extended it. The tip felt like a piece of bone, the finger of God pressing down on him.

When they entered the hallway leading to the execution chamber, he recognized it instinctively. The guards grew subdued; their banter faded. Reflections wavered in the glass partition dividing the corridor from the storage area below them. Beyond the glass stretched a wide expanse of open warehouse. Row on row of clear tanks extended to the far wall, a stationary formation of crystal cubes filled with green fluid. Floodlights cast the angular shadows of catwalks and hoists across the rippled surfaces of the tanks. A pale body hung in each cube, floating in the viscous fluid; some were twitching slowly, others were frozen in rigid postures, backs arched, mouths taped around endotracheal tubes, eyes open and staring blankly. As he watched, a brace of white-smocked technicians lowered a net-wrapped form into an empty unit. He was uncertain whether agoraphobia or something else caused his fear.

The subconscious does not create nightmares from whole cloth, but scavenges materials from the memory. Brain loops bleed across in ways that would be unacceptable in a machine. His mind had been very busy constructing scenarios, recycling parts of old dreams, bits of once-viewed holos and snatches from books and vid tapes. His mental image was of a dark chamber, edges lost in shadow, a single spotlight illuminating the wooden frame that rose above him. In his dreams, he had never been able to examine the structure too closely. When he tried, the design shifted and changed. Beams jutted without support. Chains and ropes hung in abstract patterns. Occasionally there was a hooded torturer;

other times he was alone, hanging from his arms, swaying as if buffeted by the wind. He remembered splintered wood, hemp rope with the bristles cutting into his wrists, the red glow of a hot iron, and the smell of burning flesh.

Real time was a vivid disappointment.

Somewhere, there must have been a factory spewing out prefabricated medical facilities. Dump in the right mix of plastic, aluminum, chrome, and glass, and a hospital was squeezed out of the far end, supplied and fitted with standard equipment, waiting for doctors from another assembly line. The place was a collage of white and silver, blindingly clean counters and tables, and glittering instruments. A battery of machines—cardiac monitors, respirators, transfusion hardware—and shelves littered with canisters and bottles formed a stark backdrop for a single bed and steel tray standing beside it.

It could have been the Zenyam clinic. If he closed his eyes, he might have relived hardware implantation. The memories were there, waiting for him, infinitely preferable to his present reality. It had been so good . . . all of it, so damned good. Now it was gone. Unbelievable. He suddenly realized that he didn't know how to believe it. Without computer input, there was no reality.

Two medics waited for him in the execution chamber. One was tall and gangling, draped in a white smock. His hair was clipped short in the old style, his forehead broad, temples twin concave depressions in his skull. He had pale, sure hands with long fingers. "See the fight last night?" he asked his colleague.

The other executioner grunted, a meaningless gesture. Short and tending toward weight, the man approached Rolen. His eyes were bloodshot, stark against his black skin. Gray peppered his wiry hair.

"Judas Priest, Venom's got a wicked uppercut. But that's why I had twenty riding on her." The man turned his attention briefly to Rolen.

"You can strip or be stripped. Your choice." He glanced back to the other medic. "I've got front-row seats for the next one. Need a raincoat because of flying sweat. It's like being in there with 'em.''

Rolen didn't move.

The black medic nodded toward the guards. "Do it, then. And carefully, unless you want the warden on our tails." He moved to his machines. A subliminal hum filled the room.

The guards took him gingerly, removing the sealed plastic from his wrists. He didn't struggle. It would have served no purpose. He'd never been one for displays of bravery. Besides, they were no more his enemies than the techs at Zenyam had been his friends. They were only performing duties at the orders of others, others who'd never needed to soil their own hands, people he'd probably never see face to face. Standing motionless, Rolen let them peel the jumpsuit from his back. His naked reflection glared back from a dozen polished surfaces; pale skin, dark thick hair covering his chest and genitals, his expression bewildered and scared.

"Put him in the depilation chamber," the white one said.

The unit was an upright coffin with an interior of silver foil. Overhead lights flicked on at his entrance. The door sealed with an audible hiss, a slight pressure on his ears. The close quarters were almost welcome, not familiar, but he felt safe out of habit. The light increased and the heat grew intense. He closed his eyes.

Illana was waiting for him at Malibu.

The heat exchanger at the steam generation plant was the hottest place on Thor's Belt. In a controlled environment where the temperatures tended toward the frigid, the novelty of heat was always welcome. Illana had made some sketches of a beach scene gleaned from a library tape. Old Earth: California. Down in the space between the holding tanks and the furnaces, they'd constructed a cheap facsimile. The sand came from discarded hydroponics filters, fine and white with black grains of iron and charcoal. Someone appropriated a few stunted trees. The overflow tank served as their ocean, flat metallic water the temperature of urine. They called the place Malibu.

She was sitting on the white sand. Grains clung to the backs of her thighs, forming a continent of grit. There was no reaction to his approach. She stared down at the silica, blond hair pulled back behind her ears, high cheekbones flushed with color, back stiff, and her neck forming a rigid arc. He could see the muscles working along her jaw as if she were chewing meat.

"So?" she whispered, her voice soft and cold. Her hand made patterns in the sand, scooping and letting it sift through her fingers.

"I signed with Zenyam." He presented his best disarming smile, one of his social weapons designed to melt instructors and ease parental anger.

"You bastard." Illana scissored up from her cross-legged position. "You selfish bastard."

"Don't . . ."

She was on the edge. Rolen sensed her controlled rage fighting to surface. Her voice quivered. She swallowed hard and wiped at her eyes. There were no tears. "Why did you even come back? Did you want to see my face? Did you want to know it hurt?" Illana pushed past him. "So sorry to disappoint you."

He shook his head. "I can't stay here."

Twisting back, the woman threw her arms out in a gesture of helplessness. "They'll cut you up. You know that? When Zenyam has finished, you're damaged goods, man. Brain damage. They'll have you forever. You've sold your soul."

"I've been thinking this out for a long time. It's what I want."

"What you want?" Her teeth were white and even behind her pained grimace, half shock and half hatred as though she couldn't believe he had finally said it. "What about me?"

Rolen had no answer.

"I feel . . . Christ! I don't know how I feel." She chewed her lips fiercely. "We had plans. We had a future. The two of us. What about that? All this time, you let me dream. Sat right here, listening to me, smiling and laughing, and somewhere back in your head it was all some stupid joke 'cause you weren't planning on being around. How could you do this to me? Answer me!''

He dug one toe into the sand, etching a pale groove.

"Go let them cut on you. Go die in space. But don't think I'm home dying without you."

"It's not you, Illana. It's this place. Can't you understand that?" He put his hands on her shoulders. "I love you."

She had a wicked uppercut. Her right arm blurred, swinging in a savage arc, fist hitting him in the eye and filling his vision with stars. Rolen went down hard, toppling over a stubby tree, his head crunching against the thin layer of sand. She loomed over him, punching again and again and swearing loudly. "You frigging bastard. Someday, it'll even out. Everything always does. And when the wheel turns, I'm gonna know. Some way, I'll know."

He curled up in the sand and let her swing until the rage subsided and she staggered away blindly. He never saw her again.

He hadn't thought of Malibu in years, not with the thick armor provided by the computer, layers of ROM-generated simulations encrusted over his real memories. The vague and unsettling data from his past could find no channel to haunt him, and if it did, he had only to call up another game, request another fantasy, to occupy his mental circuits. Only now there was no input and no way to stop the vicious onslaught of memory.

Worst part was, he suddenly understood just what it was he'd lost and what he was about to lose again.

A sudden silence expanded in the depilation chamber, penetrated by the rhythmic click of cooling steel. Soft ash covered his skin. The acrid stench of burning hair was thick in his nostrils. The hatch swung open soundlessly.

A stinging shower of astringent fluid scoured the scaly crust from his flesh. The jets of liquid burned his skin. Gray silt swirled down the drain in ropy syrup. When he stepped from the mists, he was more than naked. Without the dark halo of body hair, his arms were sticks of flesh. His chest was a pale slab, nipples dark circles on alabaster. He felt oddly defenseless, as if alopecia conjured up some primal memory in his fetal brain, an animal fear of predator claws.

"Here." The lead medic slapped his palm onto a padded table. White cloth draped the stainless-steel rectangle, its legs reflecting the lights and the color of his smock.

Rolen rolled onto the table. The cloth was coarse against his back, starched and stiff. A corona of light and shadow stretched across the tile ceiling, pebbled acoustics for soundproofing. Gleaming mirrors encircled the spotlights above him. The light was hot and bright. Image burn danced across the inside of his eyelids.

Fingers cloaked in thin surgical rubber gripped his right arm. A cold alcohol scrub abraded the inside of his elbow, an icy rasp on new skin. The sharp stab of a needle made him wince; he felt the sliver of steel twisting and finally seating, pressure, and dull pain radiating up his arm. Tape whispered from a roll. The quick hands pressed and moved in rapid succession, adhesive strips anchoring the needle and the long umbilical of intravenous tube to his forearm.

Both executioners leaned over him, heads together. "Be glad to finish this one. Bad business," the thin one said sotto voce to keep the guards from overhearing. The other arched his eyebrows and nodded. His hand trembled as he lanced the needle of a syringe into the umbilical yoke.

Tingling flushed Rolen's limb. The drug was a hot rod twisting down to his fingertips and up through his shoulder. The artery in his neck was a line of fire. He thought of inquisitors armed with branding irons and imagined the stink of crackling fat and muscle. As he watched, the skin around the IV faded from white to clear, like a deep, subcutaneous blister expanding in the crook of his elbow. The fuzzy edges spread rapidly, exposing the stringy fibers of bunched muscle and the nylon-white strands of tendon. The vein was a purple cord stretched tightly across the bicep. When he flexed his hand, he saw the slick bone pressing up through the skin.

The two executioners performed an intricate dance, moving from task to task without pause, their conversation reduced to nods and grunts. Medications coursed into his arm. Cold accompanied the second and he shivered violently. The third made the lights intense, brilliant halos whirling above him. Numbness followed the final injection, oozing out along his arm, as if the segments were somehow being detached from his brain, like useless waldoes, dead and frozen.

"Heart rate?" the lean man asked. His voice was strange, abrupt and distorted.

"Slowing steadily." The reply was wrong, an odd pitch, an octave higher than a moment before. Rolen thought of a recording being played back at the wrong speed. "Respiration strong." The words were compressed, recognizable, but occurring within a fraction of the normal interval. Even the bleat of the heart monitor was off, its tone a staccato note, sharp and quick.

Rolen tried to concentrate on their faces. Movements writhed across their features, eyelids fluttering, brows twitching. Expressions materialized and vanished instantly, smiles and scowls like spastic convulsions of the muscles. The drug was hitting hard. He was suddenly unable to follow their movements. He tried to focus his attention on one man's hand: one moment on his chest, then on his arm, then hovering before his face, tension stretching the surgical glove to yellow translucency. The executioners lurched from point to point, too quick for him to see, as if teleporting around the lab, visible only while stationary. Within minutes, their movements were mere flickers against a lighted background.

Time dilation: it suddenly made sense. They weren't accelerating, he was slowing down, his body slipping into a chemically induced coma, the grip of cold sleep washing over him. He was about to begin life as a commodity, and dilation would extend his shelf life indefinitely. The prospect of an eternity of labor, broken by intervals of time dilation, periods when he would be returned to the shelf for some other product, stretched before him in a terrifying panorama.

He distantly sensed an endotracheal tube in his throat and

a rush of metallic air that forced his chest to expand. Blood pounded in his ears. It took him forever to raise his arm. The limb was alien; there was a glassy sheen to his skin. Veins and arteries crossed his palm and snaked down his wrist, weaving through white strands of tendon and pink threads of muscle. He tried to stand, but his legs wouldn't respond. His body was leaden.

The room lurched. He dimly recognized the blur of motion. Agoraphobia gripped him as he was overwhelmed by the certainty that he was in the center of a vast abyss, a huge room filled with row on row of glass tanks gleaming like emeralds beneath the lights, human figures suspended in viscous liquid.

Mesh overlaid his vision with a distorted lattice as though he were enveloped in a fine netting. Another sickening rush of motion spun him, twisting, banks of fluorescents passing above him in alternating bands of illumination and shadow. Gestaltic images assaulted him: rows of coffin-shaped tanks brimming with liquid, a spidery network of whitewashed catwalks and beams, twisting growths of plastic tubing, and contorted bodies floating motionlessly.

Vertigo swept over him. He fell in a slow, feet-first plunge into a square of green ocean. Amniotic fluid lapped against his skin. Warmth closed around his legs and swirled up to his waist, splashing his chest and neck. The solution closed over his head and took the sound. He was alone in a liquid universe, his body swaying gently to the currents of the disturbed medium.

He thought of Malibu and cried.

Chapter 11

The Spencer Magna molded to Jaleem's hand like added flesh. Squat and dark and balanced at the end of his arm, its weight was negligible. His body heat caused the grips to melt and shift, mirroring the contours of his palm. He kept the pistol flat and his movements fluid as he swung across the crowd, picking assassins out from the sea of faces. His shoulder absorbed the recoil, brief magnesium strobes marking the impact of each explosive shell, victims twisting; they were stick figures, arms and legs drawn with sharp angles.

It seemed he had spent his life with a weapon in his hands, a necessity in the hell of the Zone. He'd had a knife as soon as he could make a fist; a homemade pistol at the age of twelve, wooden block for grips, a length of pipe for the barrel, and strips of surgical tubing and a nail for the firing pin. His first rifle was a Kalashnikov, the wooden stock etched with ceremonial scars reminding him of the palm of his mother's withered hand when it pressed against his cheek. An eon of human development existed between the hard, oiled surface of the Kalashnikov and the Magna he balanced in his palm. The Magna was the present pinnacle of ergonomic design, soft and curved and clinging to his hand like a living thing. Point and kill, the ultimate power. Death at his command, as silent and soft as a caress when compared to the growling kick of the old rifle. Yet sometimes he still wished for the simplicity of the Kalashnikov.

Echoes roared through the shooting range: the hiss of the projectiles as the Magna launched them on a rope of magnetic force, the deep, guttural *kachung* of the shells exploding. He left the protective muffs hanging from a peg on the black wall, wanting feedback from all senses, ears tuned beyond the normal sounds of the range, listening for the creak of the door, the click of a hand on the lock, or the rasp of footsteps. A portion of his mind was set aside, ready with contingencies and reactions. The gun jerked. Red blossoms appeared on the dead. The computer recorded the impact of each shell, calculated its position relative to the holoprojection, and adjusted his score. An extravagant video game. Some arcades already stocked them, training youth for future employment.

Crowds made him think of the Islamic Zone. Childhood was a mental montage of screaming faces and echoing chants, a monolithic cube of bodies. Images flickered through his head like those odd dream sequences that were so popular with the latest music-holo fad. He remembered: Allah's storm troopers in tattered rags and fluttering headdresses marching with defiantly raised fists through the littered, choked streets; the instant hell of firefights, Kalashnikovs and rust-scabbed M-16s against Walther buzzguns which scattered fragmentation shells like flaming chaff; feral packs of children stripping the dead of weapons and meat. He remembered the taste of human flesh.

It was hot even in the dark band of shade created by the single remaining wall of the bombed-out building. A fine grit of dust coated his face and his mouth. His Kalashnikov was ambient temperature, warmer than his hands and reeking of the rancid fat that Jaleem used to grease the breech. Mazen leaned against the wall where the plaster had fallen away from the mud brick below, a dirty brown ulcer on the white facade. His dark eyes watched the rooftop where the directional antenna of the sending unit was a line of silver light in the glare from the midday sun.

The hoverbus hove into view, a whirling snarl of dust and debris spraying from beneath the fan shrouds. The darkened windows and lacquered surfaces of green and gray looked like the head of an enormous insect pushing through the cloud, black glass reflecting back the rubble, computer mind scrambled by the rogue signal, following remote commands into the center of their ambush. Mazen gave Jaleem a toothless grin and snapped the safety on his ancient M-16. The fringe of tassels hanging from the muzzle shook obscenely.

Across the street, Omar and Persis crawled along the slight cover created by a scorched foundation. He saw the humped shapes of their backs, spines detailed against the thin fabric of their fatigues, the pack of extra claymores an angular bulge on Omar's shoulder. Persis popped up for a quick glance. Her bladed features were grim, mouth a dark line beneath her prominent nose. She raised her fist in victory.

Jaleem's heart was pounding. He watched the bus roar between them, the front apron hooking the trip wire. Panicked faces pressed against the windows, watching in horror. The tourists had wanted to see the war, but from a safe distance where they could snap pictures and nod their heads with superior wisdom. Now they would live it for a brief moment.

The crump of detonation throbbed through him, lifting the ground and dropping it suddenly. Blades splintered, flashing through the net apron and spraying out across the street. The hoverbus lurched and twisted as if in pain, front turning toward the shredded hindquarters like a dog nipping at a bullet wound in its back. Swinging toward him, the front caromed into the remaining fragment of wall and brought it down in a dusty cascade around him. The rear collided with the foundation and pitched to one side, springing the accordion pleats of the central union and spewing two security guards out from the rupture. Mazen dropped them with a burst from the M-16, laughing at their surprised expressions.

The driver was furious. He staggered from the bus with his clearance papers fluttering in the wind and his pale face red with rage. He was European—blond hair and blue eyes. Spittle flecked his lips. He tried French and German, finally settling on halting English.

"We paid. We paid." He waved the papers. "Clearance. *Vershtehen Sie?* Yes. Clearance, you rag-headed bastards."

Omar actually looked at the documents and the driver relaxed, smug assurance settling over his face. It was a Western attitude, the foolish belief that money could buy safety. They brought their credit slips and funneled in to see the barbarians at play. Travel agents made deals with terrorist factions, buying safe passage through turf and war zones, a loose chain of treaties and agreements with Free Palestine and the Arabic Liberation Army. But the borders changed from block to block. The rules blurred. New factions rose. And these particular tourists had left the safe territory three kilometers back when the computerized navigation unit on the bus veered left at the signal from their sending device. Omar nodded and smiled and put a bullet through the man's broad forehead.

The shot galvanized them into action, and they broke into their preassigned tasks. Mazen took four others to the entrance of the alley to set up an ambush for incoming security squads. Others scrambled across the roof of the bus, seeking out the homing transponders and fragging them with rifle bullets. Omar ordered the sending unit to start broadcasting false signals, jamming frequencies to confuse and blind the security choppers that were probably already in pursuit, airborne at the first sign of trouble from the hoverbus. Jaleem followed Persis into the front of the wreck.

Somewhere at the threshold they left the Zone. Cold crisp air filled the bus, the cooling unit working on auxiliary, still pumping a frigid draft in whispering currents from the vents. The floor was thick carpet; a stairwell curved up and past the empty chair where the driver had been sitting; the console formed a parenthetical arch across the darkened glass windshield. Red lights gleamed against the black and chrome. Static buzzed over the Muzak system.

Persis took the point, stationing herself in the aisle with her Uzi leveled. Her weapon was an older design, but he could not look at it without a pang of envy. The chatter of Japanese faded abruptly and left soft weeping, a few moans of agony from injured passengers trying to stifle the sound and stay anonymous, to force the attention of the terrorists onto another and away from themselves. Sacrifice friends and acquaintances, but stay alive—a motivation Jaleem understood.

"Down!" Persis barked in her best English. "Down, bastards!" Heads burrowed at her words, trying to slip under the seats and through the carpet, praying for invisibility.

The man was seated in the back on a long wide bench. His sharkskin coat reflected the overhead light, fine silver thread in the weave like steel mesh. Black hair was trimmed into a glossy skullcap, a stark contrast to his porcelain skin. His dark eyes were almost hidden by the wrinkled flesh of his epicanthic folds. Instead of dropping with the others, he leaned his head back slightly, a faint smile on his thick lips.

Persis swung the Uzi toward him. "You! Down!" The threatening muzzle of the gun got no reaction, and she nodded to Jaleem.

Heading down the aisle at a run, Kalashnikov raised butt first, Jaleem anticipated the crunch of wood on skull. The man waited, a secure smile on his lips as if he were laughing at a private joke. He waited until Jaleem was within two meters before raising one hand slightly, palm up—a brief gesture, minimal effort, designed for effect. Jaleem stopped.

"I'm Toshiro Akira." His voice carried to Persis.

"Down, bastard," she screamed in her limited vocabulary, rage twisting her sharp features.

"You don't want to kill me." His Arabic was flawless, with no trace of accent. The dark eyes glittered. "I could be your future employer."

Jaleem was frozen, unable to move. He knew his mouth was gaping; the Kalashnikov was suddenly heavy in his arms.

"Your choice." The other hand came up, palm raised in supplication. "Even if you don't know me, you know what

I'm offering. Or would you rather stay here and die in the service of a God neither one of us believes in?''

The bus seemed suddenly to contract around Jaleem. A rivulet of sweat oozed into his eye, burning. He sensed the wealth of the man, credit drenching him in the stench of Eurodollars and colonial banks. A decision point. Jaleem saw the future diverging before him: stay and die for Allah, or go and become a soldier for this man who waited before him. He swallowed hard. The strap clasp on the rifle rattled as his arms trembled with strain.

''Jaleem!'' Persis took a step toward him, Uzi swinging toward the back of the bus.

''What will you have?'' The man's voice was level, even, so calm as to be unbelievable.

Jaleem gritted his teeth. He whirled fluidly, Kalashnikov coming down, stock against his shoulder, hand molded around the trigger. The concussion bruised his ribs. Smoke rose from the breech as the fat burned. Persis gaped, her wide slash of a mouth falling open. Blood appeared as if thrown from the cowering tourists, gleaming and red on her soiled fatigues. She tumbled against the back of the seats, pitched forward, and collapsed into the aisle. Jaleem stumbled to her corpse, jerking the machine gun from her clenched hands. Akira refused the weapon, pushing it away with the back of his hand.

''Your job,'' he said, still smiling. The man withdrew a pair of dark glasses from his coat pocket and slipped them on, twin black ovals perched on the wide bridge of his nose, sucking in the light. ''Let's go.''

Omar had shifted all personnel to the rear to meet the security forces. The back streets were wide open. They went out the front, Akira stopping to blow the emergency exits as he passed the cockpit. The other passengers rushed the doors, dropping down to the hard-packed dirt. Mazen's beloved M-16 started barking, bullets spinning around them, scattering them like panicked animals. Akira went first, running hard, sharkskin jacket a steely gleam. Jaleem followed, firing over his head, roaring in guttural Arabic, a sham of pursuer and pursued.

No one followed.

"We need an open area," Akira said as they pulled up against the wall of a vacant hotel, its broken windows gaping, the torn shroud of the entrance pavilion a flap of bloody skin hanging across the splintered wood of the front door.

Jaleem nodded and took the lead down through the twisting streets, passing rusting hulks of automobiles and trucks. Within two klicks, they reached a plaza. The man produced a cube of electronics from his pocket, finger keying the contact. If anything happened, it was far too distant for Jaleem to hear.

The chopper came in low over the buildings. Rotors popped with a tangible concussion, sending a wave of hot air over them. Jaleem stared up, squinting into the dust as the insectile shape dropped down to meet them. Akira smiled. The doors hissed open and a huge grunt swung out. He wore a dark suit and dark glasses; the flat, black plastic Spencer was dwarfed by his hands. Not security, but part of a private force. Akira shouldered past him and into the craft. He turned back to Jaleem, smiling at his awkward stance.

"Get in," Akira said, laughing slightly.

The grunt took his weapon as he passed. "Junk," he said. "Get you something better." Tossing the rifle to the dirt, he climbed in behind Jaleem. The door hissed shut. The chopper rose skyward with gut-wrenching acceleration. Akira pursed his lips as if at some private joke.

In retrospect, Jaleem recognized the planning, and the tactical risk the man had taken to find him, or someone else like him: a person with special talents forged by hardship until survival was instinctive. The incident was an exercise in spiritual bonding, the memory of the tour bus chaining Jaleem to the man forever. He never made the mistake to think that Akira had wanted him specifically. The man had wanted the animal he was. But for the hand of fate, it might have been Mazen, or Omar himself. But these thoughts occurred only in memory. As the chopper gained altitude, Jaleem could only remember the twisting cavern of Persis's mouth and the red blossoms on her shirt.

* * *

When he came back to the present, the pistol was empty, breech clicking as he mindlessly squeezed the trigger. At the end of the darkened shooting alley, a street in Delphi stretched into holographic infinity. Snow crusted the pavement. Wind whistled down the space between the tall buildings. A group of youths crossed behind a hovercraft, leather jackets gleaming and wet, hair shaved in flat wedges and dyed white. Jaleem kicked the pause bar with the toe of his boot and the gang halted in midstride, vicious grins and narrowed eyes frozen in place.

He slid a new clip into the Magna and called up his misses on the screen. Four wide shots and three dead bystanders. They all were Oriental. Freudian slip, he thought wryly. Jaleem reached across to hit the reset.

The door swung open behind him. Jaleem peripherally detected the shift of light and spun to bring the Spencer up, then saw Har Vogel framed in the opening. The man froze, eyes wide, hands open. A swallow traced his throat.

"Sorry." His voice was steady.

"Announce yourself next time." Abbasi did not lower the weapon. Vogel's surprise turned to a scowl. The light carved his face with shadows. His damaged eye gleamed, torn iris resembling a cat's, slit vertically. "The execution has been completed."

"Any trouble?" He lowered the Spencer slowly.

"None." Vogel forced a laugh.

Jaleem keyed the reset. The machinery whined. "Anything on the Guild?"

"Not directly. Except for legal channels. And those are jammed." He rolled his shoulders as if working out a kink. "Something suspicious, though."

Jaleem glanced back over one shoulder. "What?"

"Local security by the name of Rocco Marin," Vogel said. "Asking questions. Making waves. Passing some heavy credit."

"Ever had trouble with this one before?" Jaleem turned his attention back to the range. A man was running at him, brandishing a knife, close and deadly. He stitched a pattern of shots across the assailant's chest, red dotting the holo.

"No. She's strictly small-time and low-profile. Embezzlers and divorce cases. But you said to watch for any angle." He cleared his throat. "Thought you should know."

"Commend your people on their work."

"Shall we take steps to eliminate any interference?"

"Get me a dossier and keep your eyes open."

Vogel nodded. "As you wish."

He watched the man leave, following him with his eyes until the door closed behind him. Three assassins burst from a waste bin to one side of the hologram.

Jaleem blew their heads off with three successive shots.

Chapter 12

Petski had to kill Danton. No way to avoid it. The albino was too loyal to bribe and too stupid to see the pilot's potential . . . or maybe he was too damn smart.

Strangulation was his method of choice. A shot would rouse the guards from the warmth and wine of the Langen Nacht smoker. So would a scream, and Petski wasn't sure he could knife the albino without noise. The wire was Aggutter's idea. Silent and deadly—if he was quick and strong enough. If.

A garland of plastic flowers bordered the doorframe of the observation room, red and yellow clusters faded with age and dusty from a year's storage in a lower-floor closet. The faint odor of polystyrene evoked flashes from previous Langen Nachts, memories of running with the Leathers through the crowded streets, pumping up, being free. Eons ago.

The garrote was a stiff coil in his pocket.

Images shifted across the bank of display screens before him: Front Gate, Lower Community Level, Corridor A, Dining Area 2, and a dozen others all labeled with block-script captions, white on black. The House was quiet. Few moved through the empty corridors, most grunts already in the common room where the senior staff was setting up the smoker for all but essential personnel, for every post except

Front Gate and Observation; his duty, a gift from his supervisor in retaliation for one-too-many late arrivals.

On the display, steam spiraled up from a bowl of spiced wine. Trays of fresh fruits littered the tables, imported from some distant hot world where winter never came. It was the longest night of winter, and they were laying out a summer barbecue in the common, flipping off Mother Nature. Above the door, the garland swayed in the draft from the heating vent, plastic flowers bright against the gray wall.

Jann rubbed his hands nervously over the bulge the wire made in his pants.

At eleven-thirty, a work crew approached the front gate, six deaders shuffling in a ragged formation. They skirted the guard, passes raised, sullen features set, eyes staring into space. The video unit was at eye level. A facial shot showed glassy skin, bright veins, and expressionless faces.

Kol Danton hesitated before the camera. He'd oiled his skin to make the natural transparency more acute; his face and skull gleamed. It seemed as if he were staring right at Jann, meeting his eyes through a maze of electrical gear. His lips curled in a faint smile. As if he knew. Jann swallowed hard and looked away.

"You okay, Petski?" the other guard asked. He was a new kid—young, with no trace of beard on his face. Jann couldn't remember his name.

"Yeah." His legs were vibrating, feet bouncing, heels drumming the floor. He willed them to stop, pushing against his thighs with numb hands. "Just fine."

The kid shrugged and pointed up to the screen displaying the common. Someone was carrying in a huge bouquet of live flowers, exotics, all mingled purples and crimsons and gold. Moisture beaded the leaves. "Those set somebody back a stack. Probably the warden; she can afford a line or two," he said. "Gonna be some bash."

Jann searched his memory and placed a name to the face. Baxter. He cleared his throat. "Say, Baxter." The kid grinned broadly at the sound of his name. It meant acceptance—someone other than his supervisor knew him. "Wanna go tonight?"

"To the commons?" It was as if the thought had never even occurred to him.

"Yeah." Petski managed a grin and tried radiating warmth. "No reason for both of us to miss it."

Baxter looked thoughtful, his brow furrowed. "I don't know . . . I'm still technically on probation. Don't want to lose this gig."

Jann made a needless adjustment on one screen, sucking the focus in and out, trying like hell to seem nonchalant and experienced. "Go or stay. It's nothing to me. But if you wanna go . . . I'll cover." He leaned close, whispering. "Hell, the supervisors got their own celebration. Won't even see 'em for the rest of the shift." He gave a wink and a broad smile. "Go on. You can bring me back something if it makes you feel better."

"You think?" Baxter glanced back up at the screen. Someone was taking an early dip into the punch bowl. Liquor splashed. The kid licked his lips.

"Get out of here."

He scrambled to his feet. "Thanks."

Then he was gone and Petski was alone in the observation room. His throat was dry. The garrote squirmed in his pocket like a living thing.

Eleven-forty. The first few strains of drunken song echoed across the speakers. The tinny voices were shrill and off tempo. Petski mouthed the words absently. His heart was slamming hard against his chest in time to the chanting.

Danton slipped away from the work party without incident, turning right when they turned left. The other deaders never looked back; it was not their job to be watching him. Jann followed him with camera selections across the prison. He had an easy, rolling stride, as silent as a shadow, radiating confidence. Danton was trouble, not the best choice for a murder victim.

He'd never killed a man. The albino had terminated a few, but Jann had never found it necessary. The street demanded a posture; one had to act cold-blooded, but knowing when to melt into the crowd was a basic survival technique. He was living proof that a smart individual could usually keep his hands clean. The secret was picking enemies who wanted to stay alive as much as you did. There were three options for an intelligent man: run in a pack, choose down, or don't choose at all. The philosophy had kept him bloodless—until tonight, and in a way he was still abiding by it. Better to take on Danton alone than face the muscle Aggutter could purchase. Choosing down.

Danton glided slowly through the prison. Every so often he'd stop and glance up at a camera. Just as if the bastard knew what was playing in Petski's head.

Eleven-forty-five. His corpse made her appearance at the front gate. Her breath was a white plume, her shapeless jumpsuit the same color as the chain-link fence. The guard insisted on checking her papers—examination by the numbers. The House was operating at a tenth of normal security, most swilling it down in the common room, and Front Gate was running book checks on corpses. Petski swore under his breath, leaned forward, and keyed the intercom to the guard station.

"Front Gate."

The guard looked up, still holding the pass. "Yo, Station One. Go ahead."

"Let her pass. She's mine."

"Precautions . . ." He pawed through her backpack, a grin spreading over his face as he rifled the contents: two shriveled apples, a banana the color of shoe leather, some Garnsworld oranges, and a plastic jug of wine. Fifty standard credits' worth of camouflage—a minor investment. Pocketing the oranges, the guard waved her through. The man smiled toward the camera. "You have a good time now, Station One." He was still laughing as he swung back inside the booth.

Once she was past the front gate, he put the deader out

of his mind. She was small and quick, she had a pass, and no one on the inside ever looked twice at a corpse.

Crossing to the junction box for the screens, Jann slid the panel back to reveal a maze of chips and wiring. From his coat pocket, he pulled out an integrated circuit, a small dark square, metal jacks extending from the sides like silver legs. Running his finger along the existing ICs, he pried one loose and plugged in the replacement, his eyes on the screens. The unit displaying the Mausoleum went blank, then flickered back to life. The scene was constant: sarcophagi gleaming under the lights, white-cocooned corpses twitching slowly in the green vats. The repeater took the incoming pattern of impulses and continuously duplicated them, re-creating the picture for an infinite interval. After a while someone would notice that nothing on the screen changed, everything frozen, lighting and shadows identical. But by then, he'd be gone or dead. Definitely persona non grata. Either way, it wouldn't matter. All he was buying was time.

In the other pocket, Jann had a half-dozen ampules of reddish-amber fluid. He fished one out, and held it up under his nostrils. The shell was cool in his fingers. Pure Overdrive. High-power and medical-grade from Aggutter's labs, just the thing for someone who needed an hour of boosted muscle. He'd seen addicts before who'd pumped up on amps and operated for days, rutted into a mindless task, running, singing, or writing a single word over and over, until their feet were bloody, voices shot, hands too cramped to grip the pen. Not the effect he usually sought in his drugs. He tended toward the gentle euphoria of Comfort and Pax. But he needed momentum tonight, courage he didn't possess naturally, and Aggutter had assured him it waited within the plastic shell. He crushed the tube and sucked it deep.

Eleven-fifty-two. His corpse appeared in the doorway, watching him timidly. He was charged, the Overdrive burning through him. Hyperactivated, his senses were as keen as a blade, detecting stimuli far beyond human norm. Her scent was a pungent musk. The soft rasp of her breathing roared in his head. A clamor of discordant voices wailed from the speakers, holiday songs rising and laughter rumbling like thunder.

He took one more scan across the screens. Everything was normal. He jammed his hand into his pocket and clutched the coiled garrote. His stomach knotted and he had to breathe deep to keep from being sick.

"Let's go." He pushed past the corpse, reaching back and jerking the door shut. "Move."

His muscles were hot and fluid. He was liquid, quicksilver in a microswitch, running it down through his head like an icy program. On his way to kill a man. His hands twitched, fingers tightening, fists balling into hard knobs. He was so ready it was terrifying.

The corpse stayed a step behind him as they hurried through the halls, taking a back route far from the clamor of the common. The passages were empty. Every post was vacant. As they went deeper into the prison, the silence grew stifling. Like a frigging tomb, he thought, and grinned at the joke.

A moment of panic hit him at the threshold of the Mausoleum, uncertain whether to try surprising Danton or to walk inside as if he'd confused the plans and take Danton once the man relaxed. The searing emotion was amplified by the Overdrive, doubling him up like a physical blow. Gasping for air, Jann sank to one knee and peered cautiously around the corner.

Twelve. Kol Danton was standing before a bank of coffins. He was twenty centimeters taller than Jann, and his arms were long and roped with muscle. His greased skin shone like wet plastic, sweat forming globules on his forehead and cheeks.

With thirty meters of open space to cross, there was no way to rush the albino, so Jann stepped out into the open. Danton jerked around to face him, dropping into the groveling crouch of a corpseman, then scowling as he recognized Petski.

"What's this?" The man watched Petski warily, his blue eyes cold. "This is supposed to be solo."

"No problem. Supervisor sent me out for some holiday cheer. Feeling benevolent on account of the season. Couldn't turn him down. Not without being suspicious." Jann affected nonchalance. "Nothing to worry about. Whole damn staff is in the common. Observation Post is unmanned. I was the last one out. We got all night." He smiled. "Better this way. Now you got some help."

"Who's the deader?" The albino nodded toward the corpse.

"A present. The boss said dipping my wick might calm me down some. I told you it was a party." He laughed softly. "Anyone shows, I'll say the three of us were looking for some privacy."

Danton watched him, running his own program. Finally, he grunted and turned to the tank. His neck was the diameter of a tree trunk. "Don't like it," he muttered.

Jann had a sudden insight, reducing the event to its most basic elements, life and death. He was going to kill this man, wrap a coil of wire around his throat and leave him floating in the pilot's tank. No reprieves. He felt a potent rush of energy, knowing he held a life in his hands. Balanced on the edge, his vision clarified by the Overdrive, he visualized the act: stepping up behind the man, the garrote cinching around his neck, the steady pressure of the wooden grips against his fingers, Danton's dead weight as he fell, Jann standing over him like a gladiator in some frigging holo. He was invincible. Superhuman.

"Move it, Petski. Don't got all night." Danton activated the overhead hoist, swinging it into position above the sarcophagus where the pilot floated in mindless oblivion.

This was it. Now.

Reaching into his pocket, Jann palmed the garrote. His mind was racing; turn away and open the wire, swing back and loop it over his head, pull tight. The pattern of the act beat a furious rhythm in his head, overlaid by the jangling notes of a popular tune, throbbing music timing his actions as he stepped up behind the man—a kinetic dance. Spring tight and as sharp as glass. Death.

Swinging around, a wooden handle in each fist, Jann

whipped the bright arc of steel through the air. Danton reacted a second too late, turning as the noose skinned across
his nose and hooked on his chin. His face, reflected in front
of the tanks, didn't even look surprised as he drove his
elbow into Jann's eye. Impact staggered both of them, Jann
falling and the garrote jerking tight against the man's throat.
Off balance, Jann yanked down on the handles.

Danton squealed, a wet sound as if his lungs were full of
fluid. Squatting, he lunged back, pinning Jann against the
sarcophagus, battering away with elbows to the body, ham-
mering his greased skull into Jann's face. Jann heard the
plastic snap of his nose breaking, a wedge of pain driving
into his forehead. One massive hand clubbed at his head.
Nails dug into his flesh, grabbing his ear. Danton's fingers
were slipping and gouging for a hold. Warm fluid coursed
down Jann's cheek. Darkness clouded his vision.

He reined hard left, slamming Danton's head into the
tank, rolling opposite in the same moment, and kicking his
legs free. On his knees, Jann hauled him out onto the floor
then gained his feet, raising Danton's skull off the tile by
the garrote, and straining on the grips. Blood welled on the
albino's throat. Jann sawed the wire, jerking and twisting,
energized by a fuel of terror and Overdrive. Danton was
strong, groping blindly behind his head, seeking the handles, fingers slick and red. How long before he'd die? Seconds? Minutes? Jann's arms burned and still Danton kept
flailing at him, struggling for life, gasping and squealing
and laboring for one last breath.

A moment later the man went limp. The albino slumped
forward, his weight hanging from the wire, neck kinked and
a froth of crimson bubbling out of the wound. Jann kept the
garrote snug, watching the man's fingers and hands for
movement. The body spasmed as if some final fragment of
consciousness finally released its tenuous hold.

Jann let the garrote slip free. His fingers were cramped
into claws, agony when he tried to flex them. Danton remained upright for a second as though he were a particularly realistic statue, a violent wax diorama. Then he toppled
to one side, head bouncing against the floor. Blood seeped

from the wound, forced by gravity now that the heart had stopped. Jann was shaking violently, wracked by dry sobs. He sagged against the tank, sliding to the floor, his arms locked in a death grip.

Guilt punched through him, amplified by the Overdrive, crushing him. He couldn't drag his gaze away from Danton, from the hatred etched on the man's distorted features. He turned his face to the sarcophagus and pressed his cheek on the glass. His reflection stared back at him, blood dribbling from both nostrils, purple bruises encircling his eyes. Over his shoulder, Danton still stared at him, one blue contact missing and the red iris like a bullet hole in his head.

Around him, in their quiet universes of green fluid, the corpses twitched, huge maggots writhing to the pulse of some internal nightmare.

Twelve-ten. He was suddenly aware of the terrified woman watching him. He managed to generate enough reserve strength to stagger unsteadily to his feet, wiping at his bloody face with one wobbly arm. She took a half step back, a small gesture that fired him with a quick burst of anger.

"Move your ass," he snapped.

Jann grabbed at the hoist controls. His hands were awkward. On the third attempt, he snagged the ring at the top of the net and swung the pilot out over the floor. Amniotic fluid splattered across the slick tile, green puddles on the eggshell white. The netting clung to Iserye, snagging in his curled fingers and toes and gripping his slick skin. Struggling and swearing, Jann finally pulled it free, spreading the pilot out on the floor.

"Get the kit," he said.

The woman nodded, stripping off her pack and producing the reanimation drugs from a pouch secreted between the interior of the bag and the cloth backing. The stuff was refinery-grade, not the industrial-strength type used by the House, but another quality product pulled from Aggutter's private supplies. There was an addict for everything, and Aggutter knew his markets.

"Shoot 'em in order. One. Two. Three. And no frigging air. Understand?"

She hurried to the pilot's side, fumbling with the first syringe.

Muscle spasms crawled along his arms, signaling Overdrive crash. He dug another ampule from his pocket, snapped it beneath his nose, and jumped onto the roller coaster for a second ride, leaving his pain behind. But the guilt hung on, a little demon flying with him, just over his shoulder. It had Danton's face.

The albino was as awkward to move as a bag of wet sand, heavy and yielding. He left a ruddy trail of fluid as Jann pulled him toward the net. His open eyes were dull and glazed, his mouth locked in a grimace, tongue protruding. With the Overdrive pounding through Jann, it was easier to strip off Danton's jumpsuit and wrap him in the plastic filament. He used the garrote to tie the man's neck to the top of the net and keep him from slumping, trying to make him look as much like a corpseman as possible. The hoist chattered, raising the man slowly, a segment at a time—head, neck, back arching, knees breaking contact with the floor and letting the body swing freely, feet dragging.

The woman was injecting the third dosage, stabbing the needle into the intravenous tube; she triggered the injector.

The pilot's eyelids fluttered.

Danton sagged into the tank. His blood made brown streamers in the green fluid.

Chapter 13

Why wouldn't they leave him alone?

He was jacked into the *Trojan Horse*, entering the jump nexus at Saratoga and firing up the generators for a hard flex into null space. He felt good, the best he'd felt in days. His mind was fractured, functioning on high, augment force-feeding him a hot stream of data. Rolen read it all at once—hull temperatures, thrust vectors, fuel pressures, flux percentages—visualizing the interior of the ship down to the exact placement of cargo crates, feeling them through a myriad of sensors feeding back through his skull in layered precision. It was a sensual power bordering on orgasm.

But he got no peace. Collins, Zenyam's flight instructor, entered his mind through an open channel. Hunched and bent with age, silver-and-gray uniform loose on her twisted frame, knobbed hands clutching the head of her cane, she speared him with her usual disgusted scowl. Her thin lips rode up across the white slivers of her teeth, an expression reserved for his worst training errors. He anticipated her tirade, a litany of lost ships and penalties spiced with frequent references to the location of his brain and its apparent lack of function.

"Come on, pilot," she barked.

The voice was male.

* * *

He felt movement—up toward the light, body being compressed by gravity, warm fluid receding past the top of his skull, across his face, down his neck and torso, his genitals, his feet. He was suddenly cold, rolling with uncontrollable spasms, a hard surface beneath his back and shoulders. Shapes fluttered around him. A burning tide rose along one arm.

Coming up was like the first time he'd ever gone on-line with a flight computer, the techs feeding him a diet of controlled impulses so that he saw the ship gradually—a flux generator, impulse engines, sensor vanes, holds, a scattering of unrelated fragments that suddenly congealed into a cohesive unit. Except this time there was no ship. Voices evolved from the stillness. Light and shadow became real objects; the dark expanse of the floor stretching away from him: a hard vertical plane resolving into the face of a glass tank filled with green fluid; sharp bright patterns of light working across his eyes, the reflections of the overhead fluorescents bouncing off the rippling surfaces of the vats. The endotracheal tube snaked from his throat and he gagged, spewing out a mouthful of bitter liquid in aquamarine puddles on the tile. The air was cool and sharp.

"Damn it, pilot. Move!" The male voice returned; this was definitely not Collins. A man with an accident victim's face loomed over him, dark mad eyes set deep in a pair of livid bruises, cheeks pitted and pocked with scars, black beard and brows, sharp teeth. His nostrils were crusted with blood. "Get up!"

"What?" He was more than disoriented—totally dislocated. He stared at the apparition, trying to make sense of the data and thinking mainly that this couldn't be standard procedure for bringing a slave out of dilation. Rolen coughed hard, as if still trying to dislodge the breathing tube.

"Time to be going." The man rose to his knees, pulling Rolen upright, a frantic urgency in his motions. A metal name badge glinted on his shirt: J. Petski. "Heat could be all over us any minute now."

"Not yet," Rolen slurred, trying to roll to his side and curl into a fetal position. "Need some sleep."

"Later." Petski snagged him under the arms and lifted him from the floor, fingers digging into flesh as he held Rolen up like a rag doll. "Right now you just move your friggin' ass."

Rolen's legs seemed soft and yielding beneath him as if the bones were still forming. A female corpse stood to one side, watching him anxiously, fear painting her features. Her skin matched his own.

Petski shoved him into the arms of the corpse. "Get him dressed." He took up a position at the doorway, watching the corridor.

The woman produced a jumpsuit from her backpack, the standard gray uniform of a slave. She leaned him against the wall and struggled silently to get his legs into the fabric, moisture making the cloth cling to his skin. No way this was standard procedure, but he couldn't seem to frame any questions; not all of the parts of his body were responding yet. Somehow, she managed to get him inside the suit and snug it up tight. The metal zipper was an icy line up his belly. Draping his arm over her shoulder, she helped him stagger to the doorway.

"Who are you?" Rolen asked, managing to produce a sentence and being oddly pleased by its coherence.

Petski clamped a hand on his face and forced his head against the wall, neck arching over the bulge of the implants. It was hard to breathe around the man's fingers; air whistled through his nose, and Rolen fought the urge to vomit.

"Listen." Petski's voice was a tense rasp. His eyes were dark flickers in the bruised sockets. "Too damn bad we got no time to do this right. Give you a couple hours to start running smooth, but we got a slight problem. This isn't a scheduled release. Catch my message?"

Rolen nodded slowly.

"You got two chances to get out of here, slim and none, and I'm both of 'em." His breath was bitter, some type of drug fire burning inside him with nova intensity. The man didn't come across as Guild material. Rolen realized that he was still waiting for transit codes, for some small sign that the man was on his side. Petski's rat-like face twisted into a deadly mask. "Follow me. Do what I tell you, when I tell you. No screwups or we're all terminal. Understand?"

Rolen nodded again, and the man released his grip. Rolen swallowed hard. "You from Zenyam? The Guild?"

"I'm your friggin' guardian angel." He stabbed a finger at the pilot, nail red with dried blood. "Shut up and stay close. We'll discuss details later." Petski slid away from the wall. Another glance out into the corridor and then he was motioning for them to follow. The woman supported Rolen with an arm around his waist, half-carrying him out into the hallway.

She was trembling.

They moved through a back route, a maze of identical corridors and blind intersections. The walls were sprayed fiber, wrinkle-textured, painted gunmetal gray with a thick layer of industrial-strength latex. Conduit and piping snaked along the panels, around electrical boxes and the occasional red gleam of an alarm unit. The floor was uniform black, as though a frozen tide of some indefinable substance had been sheared and buffed to a semigloss, abstract patterns of scars and grooves exposing the raw white backing. Doors were spaced at regular intervals, black access mechanisms with block-letter stencils announcing MAINTENANCE, COMMUNICATIONS, or any of a dozen other designations. The place was hospital quiet; even their footsteps respected the silence, whispering across the tile.

Petski stayed ten meters ahead of them. He wasn't like any corporation man Rolen had ever known, either the suave, stylized version portrayed in the holos, or the bloodless types Rolen had met in his dealings with Zenyam. They were professional, as cold as a darkside. Petski's movements were a little like those of a circus clown performing a tightrope act, wobbling, pretending to almost fall, and looking terrified. Only Petski wasn't faking. He radiated fear, holding his arms out at his sides as if expecting attack from every side. He moved in jerking, spastic bursts, a me-

chanical motion induced by the drug, peering around each
corner and spinning back at every sound.

The man led them through the prison with the kind of
certainty that implied a familiarity bred by many hours
roaming the place. His uniform was standard prison issue.
Not a businessman, Rolen decided, but a free-lancer, an
inside man probably operating for the reward no doubt being offered by the Guild. Rescue might explain their absence
from his trial, lulling the locals into a false sense of security
and then spiriting him out in the dead of night. Once outside
of Bacchus jurisdiction, he'd have a chance at an unbiased
trial and an attempt to clear his name. The thought gave
him strength, and though his body was still slow, his nervous system scrambled by the effects of dilation, Rolen
managed to pull free of the woman and navigate under his
own power.

Laughter echoed down the passage. Petski froze and
waved at them with one hand, palm open, stopping them in
midstride. He flattened against the wall. The laughter dissolved into slurred cursing. Petski crab-walked to the nearest door, a black plane with PURCHASING etched in white
across the dark surface, and slapped the lock. The door slid
open with a soft sigh. He motioned to them.

"Inside," he hissed. "Gotta check it out. Keep your
mouths shut." He shoved them both inside and closed the
door.

They were in a government office. A counter bisected the
room, formica countertop, a glass partition above divided
into teller windows. Desks and terminals dotted the space
beyond the counter. On the near side were a few chairs, a
table, and a water cooler. A memo board ran the length of
the inside wall, hung with clipboards and computer tear-
sheets. In the twilight gloom of the few active fluorescents,
he could read the headings above each sheaf of paper. NEW
ARRIVALS. RETURNS. TERMINATIONS. ANNOUNCEMENTS.

Rolen approached the wall slowly, his eyes locked on the
sheets, reading lists of names and identification numbers, a
brief description of each item, the crime committed, talents

and skills—advertisements of labor for sale. His attention was drawn to the announcement column. It was a laser-printed handbill detailing an upcoming auction:

    BY SEALED BID ONLY
    DEADLINE: 4/38/21
    ISERYE, R.
    24311K
    Crime: Murder.
    Skills: Certified Jumpship Pilot.
    Class: Prime (Special)

Prime special. He thought he was going to be sick.

The door whispered open. Petski slipped inside. The sweat on his face was washing paths through the dried blood.

"Dice game ahead. Have to go around." He jerked a thumb toward an exit at the other end of the room and hurried off.

Rolen stood staring at his name. The woman had to pull him away.

They walked through another empty corridor, this one narrower, with an unused feel. They passed a bank of elevators, doors closed, and took the stairs instead. Bare concrete with dust piled in the corners, the staircase twisted around itself like a geometrically designed serpent trying to swallow its own tail.

The doorway to the lower level was propped open with an ashtray stand. The stench of corba and tobacco nauseated Rolen. Singing drifted from far away. Someone was retching loudly in the hall just beyond the door. Petski halted in the crack of light cast from the opening, rigid and tense, his eye pressed up to the space. He waved them through behind him, waiting until they were almost to the next landing before following. On the succeeding level, all was silent. Petski darted past him and opened the door into the empty corridor.

Through the lower floor and up another set of stairs, they encountered no resistance. The place was empty, and except for the dice game and the drunken party, they were the only ones moving. Every checkpoint was abandoned, internal gates standing open.

Subtle changes told him they were nearing the outside of the building. The corridors were wider. New paint and brighter colors suggested areas open to the general public. Glass panels replaced the solid doors of the deeper prison. Windows gave glimpses of the night, curious flickers of torchlight in the distance.

Petski tensed, clenching and unclenching his fists, looking pale beneath his beard as though the drug was wearing thin or something ahead was real trouble.

"Okay," Petski said, stopping at a corner. "This is it. Down this corridor and we're outside. Nothing between us and the gates. Get past the gate and Langen Nacht will give us plenty of cover. Melt into the crowd. But Front Gate is trouble. Running book checks. No way you'll pass." He licked his lips. "So I gotta take him out. Problem is, he's wired, damage relays. Something frags his vitals and the gates shut automatically. Means you got to be moving through before that." He winced as if aware of a sudden pain. "We need to be real close. Watch me. When I jump him, you better be running for the nearest traffic. Get beyond the fence. Until then—" The man glared at Rolen. "—be a corpse. Do what Carta does. Nothing suspicious. Don't look up. Don't speak. Nothing. You got it? We're gonna walk right up to him and he won't know what happened.

"One more thing." His firestone eyes gleamed, spit shining on his ferret teeth. "If it goes bad, follow the deader." He jerked a thumb at Carta. "Be real crazy in the streets, but she'll get you out to a safe place. Stay with her. No one else. Understand?"

"Yes."

Petski fished through his pockets and produced an ampule, crushing it in his fingers and inhaling the fluid. The drug brought him up fast, returning the spastic jerkiness to his movements. He swung around the corner without looking back.

A short passage extended before them. Cold wind blasted in through the open doorway, filled with distant smells, ice crystals and woodsmoke, organic effluvia assaulting him. An instantaneous agoraphobic reaction swamped him, iron bands tightening across the chest and fear welling up inside him. Tremors racked his body. The woman shoved him from behind, forcing him to walk.

Don't look, he thought furiously, a desperate plea in his skull. Rolen forced his gaze down to the floor, watching the alien reflection of something pale and vaguely human moving along the dark gloss like a creature trapped beneath a layer of black ice. Somewhere in his mind, that part of him which abhorred the open sensed the wide, gaping space before him and twisted violently. He staggered, caught himself against the wall, and stood there, arms spread, trying to inhale enough air to keep from passing out.

Carta grabbed his hand and pulled him futilely. Footsteps thundered behind him, then Petski jammed his mad face close.

"You're blowing it, pilot," he snarled. Clutching his jumpsuit, the man swung him out into the corridor, dragging him forward. "Move!"

The wind whipped past him. Twin iron gates gaped ahead; beyond them the courtyard was dark. The lights of flickering torches moved in the distance. It was like looking down an open shaft. Carta held him around the waist and kept him from falling, carrying them both. Then they were across the threshold and out into the night, black flooring giving way to a broad expanse of concrete plaza.

Ice whirled in the breeze, pungent with damp soil and the stench of wood fires and burning grease. Erratic music caught his ears—jangling tunes, horns, bells. Explosions rumbled above as a sudden brilliance flared. Rolen staggered and stared up into the sky. Fireworks painted the night, blossoms of color flaring: streamers of burning yellow, crimson novas, whorls of magnesium brilliance.

Beyond the fence surrounding the prison, a mob seethed

and roiled in confusion, spilling out from the streets, jamming alleys and avenues. Torches sputtered in the darkness. Knots of carolers sang competing tunes, trying to outscream the others, collapsing in laughter, other songs sprouting from new alliances and new voices. Rolen stared numbly, agoraphobia forgotten for a moment.

The guard came out of the shack as they neared. Petski angled toward him, laughing and singing, staggering as if drunk. The woman kept Rolen moving toward the open gate.

"Hey, bro'," Petski was yelling. "You're missing the greatest smoker."

The guard stopped between them, a puzzled expression on his meaty face, his uniform binding across his swollen gut. He squinted suspiciously. "Petski?"

"None other." He lurched forward, wrapping one arm around the guard's shoulder.

"What happened to you?" The man glanced back and forth between them. "And who's in Observation?"

"Who gives a shit? It's Langen Nacht."

"Just a minute," the guard ordered as Rolen and Carta continued toward the gate. He shrugged off Petski's brotherly embrace. "Let me get this, will you, Petski? Duty calls." Then he was almost on top of them, not smiling, but instead bored by his position and his call of duty on this blessed night. "Let's see some passes."

Petski slid up behind him, darting across the concrete. His face was grim. His eyes gleamed. He raised his joined fists in a solid unit, bringing them down with a grunt on the back of the guard's skull.

The guard collapsed to his knees.

"Go," Petski screamed.

As Carta jerked him through the gate, Rolen stared back over his shoulder to watch Petski bring his fists down again. The man sprawled onto his face, turning slowly, his expression stunned, mouth gaping. His mouth worked soundlessly. He reached for his pistol, hand crawling along his leg. Petski kicked him hard in the side. Ribs cracked. He kicked again, and the man groaned in pain. A third kick rolled him across the paving, blood oozing from his mouth.

Petski stooped down and scooped the pistol from its holster. He started toward the gate.

The guard snaked out one hand and clutched his boot. Petski spun, waving the pistol awkwardly, then pointing it at the man. Flame roared from the muzzle. Still the man hung on grimly, Petski dragging him across the concrete and firing a second time; Petski wrapped his fingers around the gate to pull himself through as it began sliding closed, and finally kicked free of the man's death grip. The guard sprawled flat on the paving. Alarms wailed. The gate rattled shut. Shouts echoed from the corridor. There was the sound of running feet. Long shadows stretched out of the doorway.

Then Petski was behind them, shoving Rolen into the street and into a narrow gap in the waiting crowd.

Chapter 14

Because Veta was cautious, she and Rocco were both on-site. Expecting trouble, she'd worn her emergency kit—some mag blinders, gas grenades, and a pair of Shintu crickets. The kit added extra weight, especially the crickets, but they gave her tracking capability. Rocco refused her offer of a weapon, accepting an ear bead and transmitter. As a final precaution, Veta struggled into her damage collar.

But Veta still wasn't prepared when Petski terminated the guard.

She hadn't been able to shake her instinctive dread as she climbed on top of the hovercar for a better view of the House of Justice. But a certain dosage of anxiety helped keep the senses sharp. The crowd jostled the hover, the field of vision inside the infrared nighteyes bouncing, bodies painting red blobs of heat on the cold, blue stone of the prison walls. Following her lead, two drunken celebrants levered themselves onto the hood and segued into a frantic dance, twitching arhythmically to an unheard song, out of sync with the carols being shouted by the mob. A nude woman riding the shoulders of a painted gent loomed across Veta's view. A red breast with a purple nipple left an image burn in the goggles.

The House of Justice was unlike any prison she'd ever

encountered. Veta knew the high-security prisons of New-
ark and Solitary. She had expected a sprawling complex
with exercise grounds, turrets and searchlights, and barking
dogs patrolling the perimeter.

But Bacchus justice had a different evolution and the design of its security facility reflected the altered nature of its
prisoners. The place resembled a factory: five levels above-
ground, each story low and flat, a fifty-meter span of open
territory to the barbed-wire fence, and one guard station at
the single entrance. There wasn't much visible security but,
she reasoned, they didn't need much force to control prisoners held in time dilation. Rather ironic. The House of
Justice really was a factory, a processing plant using hu-
mans as raw material and producing slaves. An odd vision
flashed through her brain of a line of pale bodies laid end
to end on a conveyor belt, being stamped and processed
and dropping out the far end with a price tag tied to one
leg.

More blossoms of flame appeared overhead, fireworks exploding with dull concussions. Clots of ash and the smell
of gunpowder drifted on the wind, acrid and burning. Midnight had brought madness, crowds spilling onto the street
into a growing festival—the legendary Langen Nacht.

The two dancers finished their set and stumbled, arms
linked, to the front of the hover, falling forward into the
milling press of bodies. Veta watched them disappear,
handed arm over arm into the depths. A barrage of flying
wine bottles glimmered in the greasy yellow light of the
torches, glass crashing as they hit the wall of some distant
building. The riot continued undaunted. She'd been to fes-
tivals before, even the famed Mardi Gras of New Orleans.
But the others were mild compared to Langen Nacht. Maybe
it was the juxtaposition of hard labor on a bleak world and
the frenzied abandon of this night that made it appear so
intense. But whatever it was, the celebrants reveled with a
savage force that bordered on the purely primal, a mind-set
that interpreted violence as passion. It was an attitude she
herself occasionally craved.

Glancing up the front of the next building, Veta spotted fireworks reflected in the lenses of Rocco's nighteyes, which showed up as mirrored orbs in the darkness. The other balconies were thronged with bacchanalians. Streamers of confetti spiraled down in slow clouds, fluttering and twisting in the ragged breeze. Continued explosions dotted the sky: chrysanthemums of magnesium brilliance, green flame, and scintillations of crimson and gold.

She checked her watch. Danton was due any moment.

A trio of figures appeared in the doorway of the prison, silhouetted in the open doors. Veta thumbed her goggles to night vision and scanned the group. The one on the end had dark hair and beard, and pocked skin like the cratered surface of an asteroid, light and shadow. Jann Petski. She swore under her breath, clenching her jaw. What the hell was he doing?

"We got a problem," Veta whispered into the bead microphone thrusting from behind her ear, a lance of dark wire with a black marble dangling before her lips. Her headset crackled.

"I see him." Rocco's voice was tinny and charged with static.

Veta examined the other two and found that both were corpses. One was small and definitely feminine. There was something odd about the other deader, a quirky way of moving as if stumbling blind—and two bulges on the base of his neck, reflecting the light. Implanted hardware.

"Veta, you copy." Rocco was frantic. "That's the goddamn pilot!"

"Don't know what's happening, but I'm taking him out." Veta drew her Spencer from its shoulder holster and raised the pistol with both hands, aiming with the electronic sights, an emerald circle gleaming in her nighteyes. She centered it on his head.

Somewhere on the other side of the city, a fireworks crew released another volley of festival artillery. The flash of detonation overrode the goggles and left her momentarily blind, blinking back tears. She jerked the goggles away from her eyes, her vision reduced to stars and whorls of phantom brilliance.

"Christ!" Rocco was screaming. "He's got the guard down. The guard is down."

The crowd rocked the hover and Veta was falling, gripping the Magna tightly, her sight tuning in from blinding white to gray and then to the fuzzy images of the chaos. A band forced through the packed bodies, horns blaring and pointing like the eyes of an alien creature thrusting out in brass stalks. There was no way she could get a clear shot, but she looked in time to see Petski take the guard's gun and nail a pair of rounds into his back.

"Damn. Damn . . . goddamn." Rocco swore a monotone litany across the headset as she watched the crazy bastard make them all accessories to the murder of a Bacchus Security officer.

"Got to move. Can't hit them from here." Veta squirmed toward the prison gates, tucking the weapon under her arm to keep it concealed. "Keep your position. Spot for me, Rocco. Get me close."

"Are you crazy? Drop it. Time to evacuate."

"Rocco . . ."

"You wanted my help. A quick project. Small risk." Her voice choked with panic. "This is murder one. A guard, Veta. Bacchus Security. They don't ever quit. In a matter of days we'll be inside the House looking out if we don't get our butts offworld. Leave it, Veta."

"Come on, Roc. A minute more and it'll be done. Give me some direction. I'll cover your butt. Nothing to worry about. Just help me finish. Tell me where they're headed." A man in a bathing suit and straw hat loomed before Veta. His skin was blue with the cold, teeth chattering as he stumbled along with the mad flow of the compacted bodies, grinning insanely.

"Find him yourself. I never wanted in, Veta. Now . . . I'm definitely out." A crackle of static punctuated her words and then there was only silence.

"Rocco?" There was no reply. "Rocco!" She craned her neck to stare up toward the balcony. It was empty. In fury, she ripped the headset away and threw it into the mob. The gesture cleared her mind. No time for anger now. She'd deal with Rocco later. Petski was a much more immediate problem. Sucking air through clenched teeth, she erased her rage and turned her attention back to the hunt.

A wailing siren echoed from the prison, the ululating cry somehow part of the ambiance of the midwinter insanity that had overcome the population. She figured there were better than ten thousand citizens jammed into the streets. Ahead of her was a living collage of arms and legs, bodies nude and dressed, drunk, sober, and drugged into a dead stupor, held upright by the flowing river of humanity. Veta clawed her way through them, moving diagonally across the avenue, trying to pick a line that would intersect the fleeing Petski.

Rotors thundered over the tops of the nearest buildings, security choppers rising above the jagged skyline. Fireworks illuminated the aircraft, multicolored glare splashing across ebony panels and flanges. Searchlights carved the rabble.

Finding a light standard, she reached up to dislodge a drunk from the perch. The concrete stanchion allowed her a view over the horde. Approximating their speed and position relative to her own progress, she sectored the mass and searched for familiar faces. She found them fifty meters away, moving north, flowing along with the human current. Petski was driving a wedge through the celebrants, pulling bodies from his path and chopping with the pistol. There was no clear shot for her Spencer or a cricket. Cursing, Veta slipped back into the chaos.

There were ways to move through a crowd. The secret was to stay low, to move with the grain rather than against it, and to try to fit through existing openings instead of creating new ones. Bowing her head, she kept her weapon sheathed and lunged forward, twisting and clawing madly as she used the lines painted on the street for direction.

Her next observation point was the bumper of a cargo trailer, which a group of leather-draped teens had turned into a stage. Music blared from their amplifiers, a throbbing jungle rhythm of clashing harmonies and screeching voices.

They were battle-dancing in stylistic combat, arms and legs flying. Contact wasn't faked. One had gone down under a blow to the face, and the others were stomping his chest in chorus-line fashion, bloodlust in their bright eyes. Veta darted up to the bumper, spotted Petski only thirty meters ahead, then melted back into the surrounding mob before she had time to become a target of the whirling punks.

A chopper circled overhead, its fore and aft lights panning independently, red strobes flickering on the underbelly. Megaphones crackled, but the speech was lost in the roar of the street. Most of the herd, assuming it was a new event in the party, gawked and shouted back, adding to the din. The chopper headed north, searchlights stabbing the ground-floor entrances on both sides of the avenue.

Veta surfaced. She didn't see Petski, but the pilot was standing on the edge of the crowd, the smaller corpse at his side, a drunken bystander rubbing at the bulge of the jump hardware. Then Jann appeared against the wall of the building, checking for pursuit and looking back toward the prison where an army of security guards was trying vainly to advance into the press. Somehow, in the confusion, the rotten bastard locked eyes with Veta, seeking her out as if with an internal radar, a self-defense mechanism that all good survivors possessed. His mouth formed a small circle of surprise and fear. He grabbed the pilot's arm and bolted, shoving his way toward the entrance of an alley.

The mob was a solid entity, congealing around the nucleus of the brass band and throbbing to the jiving rhythms of the screaming horns and pounding drums. A seam opened before Veta, a fissure slicing to the curb. She squeezed through the gap. The building towered above her, steel and concrete sparkling with hoarfrost. Staying along the wall, she probed the fringe and slipped into the narrow lane.

Little more than a crack between the two structures, the alley ran straight for thirty meters and then made a hard right. The overhanging balconies and emergency exits blocked the light from above, leaving the cleft in darkness. Stagnant water had frozen into slick patches of black ice in the central gutter. Harsh voices echoed ahead. Drawing her Magna, she followed.

Around the corner at a crouch, weapon raised, all systems up, she was ready to fight, and more importantly, primed to kill. The three were frozen in the center of the alley. Iserye was bent over, body rigid. The corpsewoman was trying to hold him upright. Petski had one hand on the pilot's collar as though to drag him farther into the shadows. Seeing Veta swing into view, he raised his pistol, but even as he moved, his whitening features showed he knew he was too damned late.

Her mind was functioning at machine speed, prioritizing her actions in nanoseconds. Petski had a weapon raised, so he'd go first, the pilot second. The little female corpse got to live. Just an impulse.

A heating vent from inside the building pumped a cloud of steam across the narrow street, melting the ice. The stench of raw sewage boiled up and a memory slotted, hitting her like an avalanche, the incident on Farin loading and running through her skull even as she squeezed the trigger, muzzle leveled, green sight centered on Petski's heart. She relived it: the explosive shell striking her right arm just below the shoulder; slug penetration followed by the warm wetness of vaporized blood; gobbets of flesh splattering her face and chest as she went down into a slime-choked gutter.

Veta flinched. Her right arm jerked, the Magna elevating a tenth of a centimeter as she fired. Petski slammed into the building, but the wound was high in his shoulder—not fatal. He squeezed off a round that chipped fragments of brick from the wall above her head and sent Veta rolling for cover around the corner.

A stupid mistake. The type of idiotic lapse made by dead amateurs or old operatives who'd lost their edge. The rope of scar on her right arm itched madly. Footsteps and curses faded. When she screwed up enough courage to glance around the bricks, the alley was empty. There was blood on the street, a steady pattern of gleaming droplets. She loped after them, crossing from side to side, watching the darkened doorways and shadowy mounds of litter for ambush.

The lane opened onto a small courtyard, a patch of sky visible above, the building terracing up and out at an angle. Suddenly, it was as bright as noon, the street bathed in a white glare. Popping rotors deafened Veta; a downdraft whipped ice and grit into the air. A chopper hung in the gap, only thirty meters up, floods stabbing down into the darkness.

"Freeze!" The loudspeaker crackled as the mechanically amplified voice echoed down the alley. "Drop the weapon. Raise them high."

Whirling, she lunged into the closest doorway. The door was locked, but she shattered the mechanism with a single bullet and tumbled into a tight hallway. Behind her, the searchlight slashed the alley with impotent fury, and sirens shrieked.

The hall was narrow; half the lights were burned out, and the air was thick with the aromas of old dinners and damp clothing. The first two apartments were occupied. The third was unlocked and empty, the owner probably out in the street with half the other population of the building. The closet yielded a heavy winter cloak, drab and nondescript. She wrapped it across her shoulders, then found a window with a view of the front street and slid it open. Two drunken men climbed inside before she could slip past them and into the crush beyond the glass.

A troop of muscle types in G-strings carrying a litter neared her position. On the mobile dais there was a woman made up to be some type of ice maiden, nude except for a trio of strategically-placed snowflakes, her skin painted white, thick hair frosted and lacquered to jagged peaks. Veta squeezed between two of the bearers and rolled onto the litter. The ice queen grinned numbly and thrust a jug of wine into Veta's hands. As Veta tipped the bottle, she turned her head and looked back toward the entrance to the alley.

Security officers were forcing their way into the lane.

Amid whistles and shouts, the officers were using electric batons to beat a path through the throng. The chopper was buzzing above the building like an angry hornet, floods swinging around. A second bird rumbled in from the north.

No use trying to track the pilot now. What she needed was a place to think for a few hours and time to talk to Rocco, to convince her to stay. Rocco would know where Petski might crawl to hide. Pushing after the man right at the moment would only compound mistakes, and she'd made enough of those for one evening.

Veta handed the jug back to the woman, but the snow queen had passed out, sprawled on her back, head dangling off the edge of the litter. The bearers either didn't notice or didn't care. She placed the bottle at the woman's side and slipped off the platform, turning her back on the alley and letting the crowd carry her off toward the center of the city.

Chapter 15

"Freeze!"

The magnified voice, firm and assured, reminded Rolen of the persona of the *Trojan Horse*. He tried to stop, but Petski thrust him into a dark crevice that angled away from the alley and shoved him up against the mortar, keeping him still and silent until the rotors subsided and the searchlights panned over to the other side of the courtyard. A sharp report, the bark of a single shot, echoed around them. Petski winced, probably with memory. His shirt was sticky and warm where it touched Rolen's arm.

It was strange how he'd managed to keep a portion of his intellect aloof from the action. It might have been an inherent trait or perhaps a talent acquired through his years of piloting. In the *Trojan Horse,* the interface split his mind into separate workstations. In the dank stench of the alley, his mind divided itself, one segment calmly recording the incident, the other fragment fighting agoraphobic paralysis.

Rolen had never witnessed a shooting. Compared to holofilms and computer-generated fantasies, reality appeared contrived: Petski turning back to goad him into running; the woman darting into the open, her weapon raised; Petski reacting in slow motion, his body jerking as the slug ripped through his shoulder, his right arm recoiling as he returned fire; the woman vanishing behind the safety of the pitted mortar wall.

In the holos, the two would have stood their ground, exchanging shots until one went down and the victor smiled grimly. In real time, Petski staggered backward, weapon raised, mouth working soundlessly as if screaming in a pitch beyond human hearing.

"Come on!" The man found his voice and snarled. "Come on, you bastard." Rolen had been uncertain if Petski was taunting him or the woman. The pistol wavered, the man's left arm hanging limply. His shirt was slick and gleaming, a stain spreading down across his breast.

Then Carta was shoving Rolen from behind, and the trio was running down the alley, staying just ahead of the arc of light from a hovering chopper.

They waited a few minutes in the silence. Finally, Petski sagged away from him, prodding Rolen with the barrel of the pistol and directing him forward along the fissure in the tectonic formations of the apartments. The passage was dark and comfortable and very much like the tunnels of Thor's Belt, except for the band of stars far above him.

A huge mound of rubbish partially blocked the opening. It was a teetering structure composed of crates and splintered wood, discarded wall panels, electrical wiring, and household items that had collected over the years in sedimentary fashion, trickling down from the windows of the upper floors. The only way through was a short tunnel created by a slab of wood that had lodged between the buildings at an angle, supporting the accumulation above it. He had to suck in his chest to squeeze past the blockage. Carta was close behind him, the plume of her breath a mist above his shoulder.

"Gotta slow 'em down," Petski wheezed. Rolen looked back in time to see him struggle beyond the pile and then, with his good arm, snag a lower crate and yank it free.

Even if he hadn't been wounded, Petski couldn't have reacted fast enough to escape. With a shriek of steel on steel, the entire formation shifted, collapsing toward him—

splinters of wood, boxes filled with packing materials, scraps of meat, and kitchen offal. Petski had time to raise one arm and shield his head before the mass engulfed him. The ripe stench of fetid decay billowed out as the lower putrefied levels were churned up to the surface. In seconds, the space leading back to the plaza was sealed, as if a doorway had swung shut, the avalanche swirling around their legs in a confetti-colored landslide of orange peels and plastic cups, aluminum rivets, and bubble-foam. Rolen lurched ahead, using the walls for balance, legs pumping slowly, churning through the mire.

Thirty meters away, he stopped and surveyed the damage. A few minor slides shifted and then everything was still. The gap was almost level, a uniform drift of garbage.

"Keep moving." Carta went around him. Her eyes were wide, mouth grim. Her breath swirled around him. She kept her voice in a low hiss as though afraid Petski might somehow overhear. "Hurry!"

"But . . ." He nodded back toward where the man had fallen.

"Forget him."

Petski surfaced, his dark head penetrating the rubble. Blood streaked his face in war-paint stripes. The whites of his eyes seemed to glow in the dark. He tried to rise and fell back. One arm wormed free, fingers seeking purchase on the bricks, trying vainly to pull him out of the tangle. Damp plastered his black hair in wet curls against his forehead.

"Carta!" His voice was raw, as if the words were ripping the length of his throat. "Carta!"

Rolen grabbed her jumpsuit. "Help him."

"Him?" Carta chopped at his hand. There was something in her face—hatred, not for him, but for the man face down in the garbage. "Wouldn't help him do suicide. Bad news, him. Gonna get us all killed. You wanna play savior, fine. But I got four Incorrigibles on my record already. Only stayed with him 'cause I couldn't risk number five. That's terminal." She turned to stare back down the gap. "But now, hell . . . he's hot. And if I'm caught with him, then it's five anyway." The woman returned her gaze to Rolen, measuring him. It was an expression she'd kept hidden while Petski was in charge. "So I'll take my chances alone, thank you."

"What about him? You can't just leave him."

Petski was moving again, rocking back and forth from the waist like a jack-in-the box. His shirt gleamed like red plastic. Above, the chopper made a circular pass, its search-lights trying to penetrate the depths and failing, illuminating overhead catwalks as black-and-silver bars.

"No time to argue. Simple choice, pilot. Stay here with him. You're a first-timer. Prime special. Same rules don't apply to you as do the rest of us." The woman frowned. "But I think I'd take my chances with Vasquez rather than Security or that asshole."

"Who's Vasquez?"

"Damn, you're really green." The woman swallowed hard, blinking her eyes. "I wouldn't advise you to stay here. Recommend putting some distance between you and him. Otherwise, you'll probably get yourself killed just trying to surrender."

Sobs were rising behind them—choking noises and muttered swear words.

"But Petski's from the Guild."

"That what you think?" She laughed. "Must have left your brain at home, skyking. Petski's a merc. An opportunist, understand?"

His head spun with confusion. He tried to find the computer input, the interpretation of the data. Instinct told him to listen to the woman; she seemed less dangerous than Petski. But his training reminded him they were both groundlings, operating in a gravity well with a program that he couldn't read.

"You're just potential credit to him." She moved away through the gap between the buildings. "If you don't believe me, then stay and help him. None of my concern. Maybe it'd be best for you," the woman called, her voice seeming to emanate from the fabric of the night. "Probably don't have the programming to cut it on your own."

"Carta, damn you!" Petski jerked upright, flailing at the rubble, his arms rubbery with fatigue. He gained a little, but then his strength ebbed and he sank back, chest heaving for air. Bits of white packaging clung like feathers to the blood on his shirt.

The woman reappeared at his shoulder. Reaching out, she took Rolen's hand. "I'm probably gonna live to regret this, but it'd be murder to leave you alone. Come on." She headed off again, hauling Rolen in tow.

Rolen switched to automatic, his fear activating him like a command burst from the flight computer. He followed the woman down through the thick shadows, stumbling over boxes and cans. Carta moved like a cat, weaving around the obstacles. Behind them, fading with distance, he heard Petski swearing, a sound that grew thin and watery and eventually faded to a whispery scream of blind fury.

The alley meandered without apparent direction, left and right and right again, following the random contours of jagged buildings. Ice made the cobbles as slick as glass, cold and sharp under his sandals. As they neared the street, the light grew brighter and he was able to discern specific elements of his surroundings: the carcass of a CRT screen like an open mouth studded with green glass fangs; a wad of vinyl fabric resembling the pebbled skin of a dinosaur; the skeletal remains of an old mattress. The roar of the crowds increased from a dull murmur to a chaotic din, music and singing, shouts and screams. She halted at the entrance to the street. Darkness concealed her face, but Rolen was certain that the corpsewoman was smiling.

"A few rules to live by," Carta said. "You're a corpse, and the secret of survival is not attracting undue attention from the norms. Out there—" She gestured toward the street. "—you keep your eyes down. Avoid contact with civilians. Don't speak until spoken to and then mumble. Humility, pilot, that's the key." She held one hand before her face, peering at him between her fingers. "Be invisible."

He wiped the sweat from his eyes. A memory kept nee-

dling him: the flight simulator, and Collins screaming at
him about transit codes. He had his own rules to live by.
Transit codes were the keystone of any pilot's philosophy.
Groundlings didn't know the codes. Carta was a groundling, so how far could he trust the woman? How far could
he trust any groundling? "Who are you?"

Her features softened in pity and understanding. If she
was trying to manipulate him, the woman was a master.
"Just a deader. Pretty standard version. Trying to make the
best of a bad situation."

"And you weren't sent to get me out?" He leaned against
the wall, facing her, his body suddenly tired. Staring at the
gritty surface of the alley, Rolen convinced himself they
were safe in a tunnel, and held his panic at bay.

She shook her head. Her breath fogged. Droplets of moisture beaded her naked scalp, running in crystal rivulets
down her translucent skin. "Till two days ago, I didn't even
know you existed. See . . . Petski holds my papers. Means
I do his bidding. He got contracted to take you out. Part of
a team effort. Don't know who was calling the shots. Only
he decides to cut his own deal and brings me in as labor.
Crossed someone. Someone big and bad. His troubles are
just getting started." Her eyes gleamed like two chips of
obsidian. Air whistled between clenched teeth. "Anyway,
he was just looking for some middle-man action. Gonna
sell you to the highest bidder."

"And you?"

A shrug, shoulders jerking quickly, eyes averted. "I'm
going to ground. Safety. Course, that's a relative term. But
better than your chances on the surface."

Glass crashed distantly, and they heard the sound of steps
scraping along the alley somewhere behind them. She levered herself away from the wall with her elbows, peering
back down the constricted gap. "That can't be anything
good. Let's go."

She pulled him out into the crowd choking the avenue.

Thor's Belt had a population of five hundred and twenty,
stable and growing slowly. He knew most by name. Every

quarter the entire colony met in the common chamber for the financial report. It was an event requiring new jeans and shirts, and scrubbed faces. He remembered sonorous voices, rustling papers, the rasping sound of a miner clearing his throat, and the scents of soap and aftershave. The room always seemed jammed to capacity and made him vaguely uncomfortable.

Langen Nacht: Thousands of drunken groundlings spewed up from the depths of the mines to drink and sing and raise a collective fist of defiance in the face of winter.

Sensory overload kept him moving, too much data influx for him to concentrate on any single aspect, even the pervading terror of open spaces. One hand gripped tightly on her shoulder, he trailed in the woman's wake through a forest of human flesh. The strain of attempting to assimilate all of the chaotic images taxed him as much as did the tug of gravity and the biting cold. His exposed hands were numb; his feet throbbed in the thin fabric sandals. He watched in wonder as nude and partially clothed figures passed around him, skin the color of slate, appearing almost bruised by the frigid temperatures.

They had the look of miners. He was not so long away from the colony to miss the signs. All had muscular arms and legs, but most of the men had developed fat around the gut. They suffered from the pervading belief that hard work made up for hard living, the same attitude that allowed every individual to look down at his own sagging belly and never see the same one that protruded over the others' belts. Perspective—all in the angle from which one looked.

Raw knuckles provided additional evidence. Back on Thor's Belt, every person who spent more than a day in the mines wore a permanent cut or scab like a badge of honor, each old one replaced before it fully healed. If a person was really clumsy, it was a cherry welt on the cheek or forehead topped by a dab of nu-skin and invariably described as a minor wound from a recent brawl. And there was always dirt, as if the dust from the frac-bits had tattooed the pores.

There were corpses in the crowd. Rolen counted a dozen in the first few minutes, all sharing the same gray jumpsuits the color of old ash, shaven skulls, and skin like nacreous glass. Most were with their masters, bearing sacks of fruit, jugs of wine, or other supplies for the mobile festival. A few had been dressed for the party by callous owners, gray replaced by bright frocks adorned with flowers. One male was wearing a hat festooned with plastic fruit. Rouge daubed his cheeks, and a greasepaint mouth of crimson was perpetually leering. His real lips were pursed. Rolen watched him drift away, surrounded by jeering revelers hounding him deeper into the mob.

A deader drew one of three responses from the civilians: indifference, fear, or hate. Most ignored them. Corpses were part of the landscape, like the buildings or the lines of hovercraft parked before the apartment complexes, and worthy of no more attention than a curb. Others reacted to contact with a corpse in disgust. Brushing against them conjured a horrified expression, as if touch risked contracting a dread disease that would somehow cause the victim to snap, exploding into a nova of violent crime ending with his own skin the hue of waxed paper.

And then there was hate.

The contact was accidental. Carta was moving fast, her head down, picking a route between the tangled press of bodies and sliding through the cracks. Spotting an opening, she squeezed through, but it closed before Rolen could follow. Instinctively, he forced a shoulder between the two men and pushed them apart.

A dull face turned toward him. The hair was a ragged snarl. There were no front teeth behind the lips. Stale wine and cheese soured the man's breath. His vacant expression went from surprise to dark anger.

"What the hell you doin', deader?" His voice was a liquid slur. A hand the size of a shovel grabbed Rolen's jumpsuit. "No friggin' manners?"

"Bust 'im," his companion hissed.

"Goddamn deader shoving me." He jerked Rolen close, his voice a ragged yell. His eyes were small and deadly. "Bastards. Takin' all the goddamn jobs. Leavin' respectable people to starve. You mistake me for one of your own? Maybe I should point out the difference between you and me.''

Hatred twisted his face, but the underlying joy was more terrifying. Here was a chance he'd been waiting for all night, the opportunity to seize on something less than him, something under his complete power. The man brought his meaty fist back slowly, relishing the act, already feeling his knuckles connecting with Rolen's jaw.

Carta slipped in behind the man. Her leg caught the miner behind the knees. He collapsed, his knuckles grazing Rolen in a glancing blow that spun the pilot away. Another corpse had somehow gotten close and accidentally leaned into the man's partner, sending him toppling over the other, both down and swearing and trying vainly to get to their feet. A space opened to Rolen's left as the new corpse subtly made room, his face stupid and blank. Carta and Rolen darted through and found another gap, other deaders giving them access without apparent plan, creating a linked chain of accidents and misdirections.

As they passed each, Carta made a quick gesture: the little finger of her hand extended, wrist twisting in a short arc. The sign was returned in kind, the only acknowledgment as they raced by. Near the edge of the crowd, the going was easier. They continued along the fringe until Carta reached another alley and dove for cover in the thick shadows.

He sank against the wall beside her, panting for breath. ''Real slick,'' he said. ''Thanks.''

''Sure. But I hope you're a fast learner. Otherwise, you're gonna get us both killed.''

It suddenly occurred to him that his old codes were no longer valid. He needed to learn a whole new set. ''So where are we headed?''

''Vasquez.''

''Another friend?''

''Oh, yeah.'' Carta grinned tightly, laughing at a private joke. ''And I think you're gonna need all of them you can get.''

Rolen nodded. Out in the avenue, motion in the crowd far behind them caught his attention. For an instant, he glimpsed a man staggering along the wall, with wild eyes, pocked cheeks, and dark beard. But before he could call Carta, a group of youths swarmed across the front of the alley. They had their backs to Rolen and Carta, paying them no attention as they handed an aerosol blaster back and forth, each taking hits of some type of aspirated narcotic.

Carta leaned close. "Best be vacating before the natives decide they want to play games," she whispered. "From now on, we stick to the back routes."

Silently, they drifted away into the night.

Chapter 16

Jaleem Abbasi hated waiting.

There were two phases to any operation: planning and execution. In the planning stage, he expected long periods of idle thought, time spent gathering and arranging, calling in old debts, studying physical and economic structures for weakness, and probing for corruption. The beauty of sound strategy was an acquired taste, something he'd developed at Akira along with an appreciation of fine wine and satin sheets. In the Zone, random factors dominated tactics, uncontrollable events often causing an entire operation to collapse, success dependent directly upon the ability to react quickly to a situation in flux. And though he'd never lost that skill, Jaleem enjoyed the machinelike precision of a finely tuned scenario.

During a Zone operation, he'd never had time to worry because he'd always been on the firing line, Kalashnikov chattering, busy just trying to stay alive. Now, though, he was generally on the fringe, watching the developments pass like points on a line, ticking by him at a safe distance.

Waiting.

For something to go wrong.

"Have you ever seen anything like it?" The woman shifted position slightly, her arms forming parenthetical curves on the balcony railing. She had red hair and eyes dark with mascara, blackened triangular wings extending to her temples. He could not remember her name. A present from Larion House, she was their response to his refusal of attendance at the traditional Langen Nacht celebration. She had appeared at the door with a basket of fresh fruit, wine to be heated in the microwave, and half a kilo of Salonas corba. The smoke was a fading taste in his mouth, stale and rank in his nostrils. The wine upset his stomach. Even the sex act was distant and forgettable.

Jaleem turned his eyes out toward the city. Madness reigned thirty floors below. Torchlight flickered. Snatches of song were carried on the biting wind. A wing navigated the fissure between the buildings, trailing a stream of scintillating particles. No, he'd never seen anything like it. The chaos seemed more war than celebration, the city grinding to a halt, impervious to his actions. Making him wait. He suppressed a shiver.

"Do you want to go down into it?" Her lashes fluttered, curls of ash across the orbs of her eyes, emerald contact lenses shining. An orchid adorned her hair, crimson and pink and overtly sexual. "It's like nothing you've ever done." When he didn't respond, she continued. "Our two claims to fame. Hard ores and Langen Nacht. We can dig and we can party. It's not such a bad place to live."

From somewhere up and left, a voice screamed. "Good Langen Nacht to all!" The echoes died slowly.

Jaleem scowled. The streets were jammed. He had a vision of the city as a living organism, the pulsing streets like veins about to hemorrhage. Traffic surged and flowed. Groups formed and dispersed randomly, marked only by the flicker of torches. Fireworks roared in the sky. Off on the horizon, a single chopper hovered, searchlights wavering, rotors grumbling faintly. A single sign of control—not enough to ease his anxiety, it actually made the feeling more acute, reminding him of the pilot in the House of Justice, guarded by fools who were probably stumbling drunk by now.

Jaleem had seriously underestimated the effect of Langen

Nacht. A local festival, it had conjured up thoughts of prayer and fasting. Solitude. A quiet time that lent itself to highlighting disturbances. Not this caroling madness. He swore softly under his breath.

"I know a place," the prostitute was saying, her red hair swirling with the wind, the blanket curled up around her neck, concealing her body. He remembered pendulous breasts, a waist almost narrow enough to be encircled by his sweating hands, and the soft hemispheres of her bottom. "The best spiced wine. Open till dawn. A band which knows every song you've ever heard." Her smile was fixed, professional. "Then maybe we come back here again." She opened the blanket; he saw a brief flash of white skin, rosy nipples, and freckles.

Anger washed over him. She *was* Langen Nacht—her darkened eyes and ready smile, breath sweet with wine and corba, she was an entangling web of sensual pleasures. It would be so easy to succumb. No one would be working on such a night. There was no reason not to relax and enjoy, and, had he not been working to spring the pilot, no better opportunity. Jaleem pushed back from the balcony rail, his robe opening slightly and letting the wind cut across his chest.

"Get out," he said softly.

The woman never changed expression. Her smile fixed, her eyes shining, she nodded slightly and walked from the terrace. A few minutes later, the door to the apartment hissed shut, leaving him alone with his nerves.

An hour later, the sound of a chopper penetrated his reverie. A Manzano Elite, all hard angles and sharp planes, its rotors were silver halos against the darkness. There was an insignia in white and green upon the black plastic canopy, an L and an H forming the walls of a small house, a canted roof over the alphabet building. Larion House. The bird hovered outside the window for a moment. He felt their eyes on him and sensed fear and confusion. He knew there was trouble long before the craft rose toward the roof port and footsteps echoed outside in the corridor.

* * *

Har Vogel looked ill, his puffy features white, his lips blue from the cold. The damaged pupil of his eye seemed to be running, a clear fluid seeping across the cornea. His clothing accentuated the serious nature of his visit. He had come straight from the party, and his frown was out of place against the backdrop of his silk shirt, bow tie, and black dinner jacket.

"There's a problem." His voice quavered.

Jaleem did not speak as he donned his shirt. A pair of baggy black trousers hung from the bedpost. He concentrated his efforts on pulling them up and tying the waist, letting Vogel stammer through a poorly rehearsed explanation he must have been planning enroute.

"The pilot is gone."

Jaleem gave a sharp nod, just enough motion to acknowledge hearing.

"An inside job." Vogel averted his gaze. "One of the prison guards. We weren't expecting disloyalty in the local security force."

"Obviously."

Vogel grimaced. He was strictly local talent, a fighter retired from the dueling ring with no aspirations. The position of fixer at Larion was supposed to be quiet, a place to spend his days, and though he knew it involved risk, he had never really expected anything to happen. Jaleem almost understood his position. Almost.

"What happened?"

"Still trying to piece it together. Inside man appears to have been a guard named Petski. He was on station in Observation."

"One man breached the security at the House?"

The man cleared his throat. "It's Langen Nacht. Things were lax."

Jaleem found a pair of black gum-soled shoes in the bottom of his closet.

They fit like skin, his bony feet outlined against the soft leather, and made no sound when he moved. He glanced up at Vogel. "You let me down."

Vogel's face reddened. "We've got a dead man in the storage area. He'd been impersonating a corpse."

"How'd he die?"

"Strangled." Vogel licked his lips nervously.

"Odd. Only fatality?"

"Guard at the front gate was killed in the break. The pilot, Petski, and an unidentified corpse were last seen heading north, away from the prison. They escaped into the crowds."

Jaleem armed himself silently. The Spencer Magna slid into his shoulder holster with the oiled precision of regular use and familiarity. He liked the weight of the chromium dagger against his calf, its knobbed hilt pressing into his muscle. "Any other prisoners missing?"

"No."

He picked up his emergency kit, a fanny pouch stocked with electronic gear, scanners, code breakers—essentials he needed to deal with problems. Slinging the nylon around his waist, he cinched it tight and adjusted the bulge beneath his jacket.

"The chopper is waiting to take you to the House of Justice."

"What for? The pilot isn't there."

A hard swallow traced Vogel's throat. "I thought—" he stammered. "It's a place to start."

Flexing his left hand, Jaleem cocked the fragmenter, feeling the trigger cock with a sharp snap, arming the single-shot tube that had replaced his left ulna. "Take me to Rocco Marin's."

Surprise registered in Vogel's face. "As you wish."

The Manzano was as fresh as a newly minted coin, and ripe with the signature of new plastic and factory cleaners. As it climbed into the night sky, Jaleem sank into a lambskin seat. Nearly soundless, the rotors were a slight throb more felt than heard. The bird bounced through pockets of turbulence. He kept his stomach tight against a sudden elevator-shaft drop of open air.

Bacchus spread out below them, an electronic grid: streets rivers of torchlight, buildings highlighted by tower strobes,

and skylights casting up shafts of yellow illumination. The
shadows and structures resembled a massive circuit board,
offices silicon chips of dark glass, roads like copper and
gold strips laid out inside the guts of an old computer—not
like the clean chemical units of the present, but the type of
computer he'd have seen in the Zone, old and dusty with
use, and burned by electricity.

Beyond the edge of the city, he saw the mines dotting the
hills, stark sculptures of conveyor belts and skeletal towers.
The white fire of klieg lights reduced the apparatus to bare
essentials, lines and etchings on the horizon. There were
no dust clouds, so he assumed that the mines, too, were
inactive due to the holiday. Was there no business on this
planet not frozen by the paralysis of festival? Only himself
. . . and those working against him. An anomaly clicked
into place in his skull, a wrongness like an Oriental face in
the dust of the Zone. A thing demanding study.

Jaleem turned to Vogel. The man was facing him, a band
of darkness cutting across his forehead, slit eye watching
him, oddly feline.

"You're certain the pilot lives?"

Vogel nodded, stripping away the bow tie with one hand.
The butt of his pistol projected from the waist of his pants.

"Doesn't make sense."

The man looked at him as though trying to understand
an equation for which he lacked key variables.

"Should have killed the pilot," Jaleem said. "Can't be
used if he's dead. Alive, he's a liability until they get him
offplanet." He raised one hand to the back of his neck,
forming a gun with thumb and index. "One bullet through
the implants and it's over. Nothing left for Akira to salvage.
That's how it should have been done—the way I would have
done it."

"Maybe he's too valuable alive."

"No." Jaleem stared at his hand, a pistol forged of flesh
and imagination. In his head, fragments were coalescing
into an understanding. He pointed the finger at Vogel. "Few
are that important. Certainly not him. I checked before se-
lecting him. He's a cog, just an employee. Like you or me.

And if we were in the same position?'' The flesh gun bucked, and he blew imaginary smoke from the barrel of his finger. "Heart or head. Quick and clean.'' Jaleem had a sudden memory, standing in the center of the bus, Persis falling in slow motion, blood forming red roses on her fatigues. He shrugged it away.

"So?''

"It didn't go as planned.''

It was a good address, uptown, fashionable. The snow was increasing as they touched down on the roof pad. There were no witnesses on the rooftop, the bitter weather having driven them all indoors, but the streets were still jammed. Guttering torches wavered along the avenues.

The apartment was on the top floor. Outside the door, he drew a Kiran scanner from the butt pack and scoped her security rig, finding it primitive and easily jammed—another indication that Marin was operating above her normal range. An infrared scan showed no one home; only the pilot element of the wall furnace registered. The door lock was a Hollingsead digital, obsolete and quickly sprung. Affixing a magnetic seeker to the unit, he set the program and watched the numerical sequence flicker in red LED, fingering each key as the code appeared. The door slid open.

The decor was strictly new wealth. Low furniture of designer caliber was covered in brown and beige weaves. Imported tapestries hung on the walls—a moonscape in stark hues of midnight and gray. There were statues in white marble for accent pieces. He clipped the Kiran to his belt, set it on infrared to alert him of any approaching heat source, and fit the listening bead into his ear.

Vogel stood awkwardly. His existence had been severely warped and he was still off balance. A week before, he'd been enforcement for a local powerhouse whose reputation had served him well enough as a shield. The dueling ring had seemed a long way away. Now suddenly he was in the middle of a war. Fear showed in his white face. He swallowed hard. "Should I do a search?''

"No need.'' Jaleem squatted beside the door, the man

taking a position beside him. "Remember, this is my score. You're backup. We'll have a brief discussion with Marin when she returns. Until then, we wait."

Akira.

The man would have to be told. A difficult task, formulating a progress report to the man. The wording had to be perfect, suggesting difficulties under control, impending success—as delicate a task as disarming a bomb. Otherwise the mantle would be passed from him.

A skilled businessman, the consummate corporate ideal, controlled, calm, bloodlessly rational—Akira defined the form. But he was not rational concerning the Guild. Perhaps the time in dilation, hours stretching with nothing to occupy his mind except the myriad offenses of the Transport organization, had skewed his perceptions. The credit wagered was enormous, as was the potential return. But Jaleem wondered if the risk was not beyond the value. The man was offering his empire against a single card.

In the Zone, a man had only his life to lose. But it was a poor existence and the threat was nullified by the rewards: If one survived, then there was food and drink, the glory of retelling the battle, and the chance to fight again; if one died, it was a short walk across Al Sirat to paradise. Even now, seen from the dizzying heights of the corporate structure, Jaleem realized that he still wagered only his life. But while before it had been forfeit for God, now it was payable to Toshiro Akira.

The Kiran whined. One tone—a single heat source approaching from down the corridor. Jaleem knew it was Marin. Intuition told him—he didn't even need the Kiran. He sensed the woman, detecting her hurried steps as she neared the door. Her fingers stabbed violently at the keyboard.

Scenarios flashed in his head, an array of response sequences arranged like computer commands. If she came in fast—let her pass, spring hard and take her from behind, letting momentum collapse them both, one arm snaked around her throat and a hand at her mouth to stop the screams. If her entrance was slow—grab her arm and throw her forward, allowing her weight to take her down while bringing the arm up against her back and slamming her face to the floor. A dozen other reactions awaited her move.

The door hissed open and her shadow spilled in from the hall, framed in a white rectangle of fluorescent blue light. The woman entered slowly.

As Jaleem moved, reaching up for her arm, she was already countering the attack, swinging her coat in a short arc, blinding him with heavy fabric. He snagged her hair, a fist full of red, fingers snarled in the thick curls. Marin kneed him in the groin, sending Jaleem staggering, still clutching the locks, trying to keep her off balance. The gun came up, wicked and small in her hand—lethal. Not the way he had expected to die.

Vogel found his legs. One arm looped over her neck and under her armpit, and a hip roll flipped the woman into the corner. She spun, arms and legs extended, gun pointing at the ceiling. Bone crunched as she hit the wall, her neck canted at an impossible angle. A breath spasmed across her chest, reflex muscles, a last attempt to cling to life. Then she was still.

He checked anyway, knowing it was useless, feeling for a pulse on her neck as he squinted his eyes against the pain and tried to breathe.

"Damn," Jaleem muttered.

"Sorry." The duelist shrugged. "She'd have killed you."

Jaleem nodded, massaging his groin, nausea spreading up through his guts. He could not argue; the local had proven his worth.

"I'll take care of this." Vogel must have remembered how to act like a fixer. He rummaged through cabinets until he found a felt-tipped pen, a thick black sausage of plastic. When he was done, the letters gleamed black and stark on the pale blue wall:

END ATTAINDER
VIVA ANTONIO VASQUEZ

"Local cause," he said. "Let them take the blame. You ready to move?" He stared at Jaleem. "Don't want to be around when the authorities arrive."

Abbasi got to his feet as Vogel levered the woman's body from the floor. He raised her overhead. Her skull bobbed like a rag doll, boneless and slack, a stream of drool oozing from between her lips. For a moment, they were both reflected in the glass of the picture window, her body balanced on his thick hands. Vogel strained with the effort, then he grunted and heaved the woman forward through the thick glass. Shards expanded out in a glittering halo.

The wind rushed in through the gaping hole, clearing Jaleem's head. They left the apartment, walking normally and chatting softly.

"He can't have gotten offplanet. No corpse would ever get clearance without a pass." Vogel opened the door to the roof.

"Still on Bacchus," Jaleem mused. "If you had something to sell, something of questionable value and carrying definite heat, where would you go?"

"There are a few places."

Jaleem smiled tightly. "Get me some names."

Chapter 17

The security squads were in foul moods; no doubt they'd been roused from their own private parties and sent out into the cold madness to hunt down reports of gunfire. They were precision triads, not beat forces responsible for crowd control. As she walked along the street, a strange cloak over her shoulders with the hood pulled down to cover her face, Veta Pulchek wondered about the identity of the bastards financing the operation. They had to have heavy credit to secure the services of Bacchus Security.

Transport had a multitude of enemies. While most of her clients didn't qualify as benevolent organizations, monopolies had a particular ability to alienate corporations, and the Guild was no exception. Even their allies were suspect, bought with a percentage of the excess credit siphoned from industries forced to pay Transport's high shipping fees. Alternatives to the Transport Guild existed, but they were slow and unreliable. Transport was the only entity with the hardware to manage jump space. That was its trump card. As long as Transport held it, the corporations queued up to pay the ransom.

Should she include the Bacchus planetary government on her list of possible suspects? A good question. Walking slowly with the crowd toward the center of Delphi and Rocco's office, she toyed with the idea. Bacchus would certainly benefit from the collapse of the Guild. It would be hard to find a colony that wouldn't. Everybody hated the Guild. Critics agreed it wasn't because Transport failed to provide a good service, but simply because there was something inherently evil about monopolies. If free enterprise were allowed, competition would enhance trade. Truth was, most hated the Guild because they didn't have financial interest in the monopoly. Envy was a motivation she could recognize and identify. Yet the magnitude of the present operation implied something beyond greed, something sinister and pervasive that smacked not of business but of vendetta.

Bacchus Authority was probably innocent, not of complicity—complicity could be bought—but they wouldn't have planned the score. There was a massive amount of credit changing hands, possibly more than the planetary council could raise, and definitely more than they'd want to wager on a risky operation. Besides, Bacchus couldn't risk the Guild's embargo. A corporation always had the option of dissolution if the Guild decided to refuse service. Ownership of new entities could be disguised and hidden under mountains of paper or red tape. A planet didn't have that luxury. Guild embargo meant political upheaval. Heads would roll. And finally, a vendetta wasn't colonial style. Governments rarely acted out of personal vengeance, because there were too many people involved. Vendetta meant individual behavior, cutting her suspect list drastically.

She came up behind the triad, drifting, but angling toward them as she worked her way through the mass of people. Two women and a man. The man was tall and slender. The women seemed squeezed from a single mold, hard-muscled and wiry, like gymnasts. All three wore their hair clipped short, stiff bristles forming narrow wedges on their skulls. They wore skintights the color of midnight, and flak-armor plated their chests and backs. A single gold epaulet on the right shoulder identified each as Bacchus Authority. Storm troopers.

"Check that control," the man said, speaking into the bead of his headset. "We're ten blocks south, and there's no sign of suspect or any riot."

His eyes were shielded behind enhancers, goggles set close to his skull, lenses rotating to focus as he panned his gaze down the street. The glass gleamed purple. His lips were tight and thin. The triad was heavily armed: buzzguns in belt holsters, batons shining black, and chemical grenades clipped to shoulder webbing. Veta noted that they were carrying stunners in hand. A blast from a stunner would drop an elephant, but wouldn't kill it. That was an important distinction. Whatever they were hunting, someone wanted it taken alive.

"Negative for trouble here. You want crowd control at the homicide?" His voice was flat and emotionless. He clipped his words tightly. One of the women looked at him with interest. He shook his head. "Right. We'll circle back to House. Keep our eyes open. Team four out." With one hand, he pushed the bead away from his lips and raised his nighteyes.

Veta wandered closer, appearing to concentrate on something in a shop window, studying the guards in the reflection and picking up bits of errant conversation. They didn't notice her interest.

"Trouble?" one of the women asked as she filched a cigarette from her belt pouch and struck a match. The glow lit her cold features. Her smile was chilling.

"Got a termination in the Heights."

"So?" The other woman ran her fingers along the barrel of the stunner, a strangely sexual gesture.

"Sloganed. 'End Attainder.' Sound like anyone you know?"

"Vasquez."

"Shit." The smoker sucked a drag. "Holy shit."

"War time."

"Could be," the man said. "Nothin' we ain't been expecting. Sit-ins, protests, strikes. A short walk to burning pedestrians." He flipped his goggles back into position. The lenses focused with a soft whine. "Screw the stunner." It fitted into a metal bracket on his belt. The man loosened the strap on his buzzgun. "If we hit rogue deaders, we do the terminating." At a jerk of his head, the triad moved off into the mob, a space of isolation opening around them. Even in the midst of the party, storm troopers generated fear.

Rogue deaders.

The officer's words seemed to reverberate in her skull as she watched them prowl away into a landscape of torches and staggering revelers. Rogues were a natural by-product of any slave system, a waste material like wood pulp or tailings—useless matter dredged up during normal operation and discarded.

Veta had encountered slavery before on other planets. Salome maintained pleasure slaves. Hardcore used an indenturing program that allowed immigrants to work off debts incurred during transit. These examples were minor compared with the industrial labor force the corpsemen represented on Bacchus.

A successful slave operation hinged on three major factors: supply, identification, and containment. On Bacchus, the supply was a seemingly endless chain of prisoners and convicts processed by a ruthless judicial system. Rumor had it some criminals were actually imported from other planets, shipped to Bacchus as the raw ore from which to forge more corpsemen. Whatever the truth, supply was no problem. And as long as the system ran smoothly, the Confederation didn't see any reason to meddle.

Every slave-owning society had to devise a method for differentiating the slaves from the citizens. Salome pleasure slaves were kept isolated and identified by a bracelet. On Hardcore, indentured workers wore a standard uniform and carried term monitors, an electrical tracking system that marked off the remaining time in service and was removed once the debt was paid. Bacchus used a permanent method. Antimelanin injections destroyed the skin's color and left the epidermis the hue of Depression glass. The result was irreversible and very difficult to conceal. She scanned the crowd and easily picked out two slaves; they stood out like glass statues against the backdrop of drunken miners, whores, and packs of predatory teens.

Containment was a double-edged sword. Every system had rogues, people determined to escape. On Hardcore or Salome, it was difficult to duck the authorities, but not impossible. One could lose the bracelet or term monitor and escape from the camps. Hotheads always had the opportunity to escape, and those who did were the very individuals with enough strength to lead a successful rebellion. A natural equilibrium existed.

Bacchus authorities were proud of their supposedly perfect record. No corpse had ever gotten away from the system. Rogues dropped out of circulation and managed to survive on the fringe, living in abandoned mines or old warehouses, surviving on scraps gleaned from refuse bins. But escape to free colonies was said to be impossible because they couldn't diguise their altered skin well enough to pass through the gauntlet of security inspections.

She thought of a science experiment from her school days: heating water in a sealed bubble without an escape vent. Sooner or later the bubble had to shatter, giving way to the pressure building inside it. So it was on Bacchus. If the rogues were banding together in an attempt to overthrow the government, it was because they had no alternative.

Veta took a deep breath and cleared her head. She was being paranoid again. In her old age, she was seeing life through warped lenses that interpreted every action as threatening. Her private filters brought everyone into focus as an assailant. Bacchus couldn't possibly be behind the attempt on the Guild. The triads were prowling tonight trying to prevent an uprising by the corpsemen. The pilot had somehow been mistaken for part of the unrest.

She looked down the narrow street. A group of Leathers were surrounding the triad in mock combat postures, three of them moving into a dance routine. The triad ignored them and continued north. She turned slowly and followed the flow of traffic southward.

By now, Rocco would be frantically rummaging through her apartment, suitcases scattered in a wide arc around the room, clothing and equipment lumped in random piles. The thought made Veta smile. This was not the first time Rocco had bolted under fire, nor would it be the last. She was the best positioning operative Veta had ever used; she could scam together a strike in her sleep, but was totally worthless in a fight. Too emotional and too impulsive.

Veta had learned that during their first run.

She was working for the Burgoyne Cooperative on a smuggling operation, inside/outside work. Someone on the interior was pirating software, feeding it to an external contact who, in turn, passed it on to a Taiwanese concern that replicated it and flooded the market. Burgoyne was slowly bleeding to death, drowning in a sea of red ink created by its own ideas. In three weeks of solo work, she'd spotted the outsider and ferreted out where the information was received and funneled into a waiting freighter bound for the Taiwanese Colony at Lido. As for the insider, Veta had identified the mole, but she needed proof to take to the Co-op.

Proof was difficult to obtain. There was no smoking gun in such a case. What she needed was evidence of the credit transfers between the three parties, something demonstrating that a particular systems programmer had access to more credit than he should ever hope to possess. She needed a look inside the local banking system. That would be her own inside/outside job, making the whole operation resemble a Chinese puzzle box, bribes within bribes. She loved the irony.

There were three probable contacts within the local financial institutions. One was a loan officer with access to the central computer system, a prime location for checking balances. The second was a credit analyst with new suits and small paychecks, easily swayed by the promise of extra income. But Veta chose the third: a bank examiner, Confederation employee, the archetypal struggling civil servant, one with a weakness for zero-gravity racquetball and hard gambling.

Rocco Marin.

The Courthouse was a minimum-gravity exercise club at the interior hub of Burgoyne Station. Typical gymnasium, as Veta remembered them: all white and chrome, heavily padded, smelling faintly of antiseptic and sweat. Marin played Tuesdays and Thursdays, against a tight rotation of regular opponents whom she'd been fleecing for months with a wicked short game and an overhand smash that was legendary. Veta assumed the role of a visiting executive, spread some credit around to learn the particulars of the gambling circuit, then bought herself a chance with the local champ.

The first match was after hours. Marin drifted into the court, her racquet, black graphite with red strings, slung in her right hand. Her flaming hair was knotted into a braid and coiled tightly against the back of her skull, the severe style pulling her facial skin taut. Her green eyes sparkled, a half-smile playing about her lips. The black-and-yellow neoprene jersey molded the hard planes of her body; she had wide shoulders, narrow hips, and a wasp waist, the physique of a person who spent countless hours with racquet in hand, slashing at the blue sphere as it arced back from the wall. She flipped the ball to Veta, appraising her with a long stare.

"Visitor's honor. You serve." Her voice was softly intense.

Veta smiled back and sent the ball screaming toward the front wall.

Those were hard matches, grinding physical play more war than game. Credit changed hands between the players and the small core of onlookers. Veta won the first two sets, a ploy to boost her confidence and raise her wagers, then her opponent settled in and took the next four in straight games. Marin, grinning broadly as she rested, cleared her throat and sent a globule of spit into the vent.

"How much you down now?"

"Five thousand." Veta frowned and wiped her brow.

"Had enough?" The smile grew broader—a shark's grin, predatory and satisfied. She was already counting her money.

"One more chance to recoup." Panting, Veta squinted her eyes and looked away. In the spectator's gallery, a small core of four individuals sat and drank in the front row. "Ten thousand on the next set."

Marin's face grew suddenly solemn, mind working hard, calculating. Veta knew the bet was beyond the woman's means. Just beyond. She could almost hear Marin's thoughts as the woman reviewed the previous games, weighing the chances. "A lot of credit," Rocco said.

"Just how good are you?"

"Good enough." She bent to stretch her thighs, then smiled up at the gallery.

Veta took her in four straight games.

Tears replaced Marin's smile, silent sobs of frustration and panic. Veta hadn't expected so much emotion. Wiping the sweat from her face, she sent the towel spiraling toward Marin.

"Thanks for the games."

"Yeah." Marin stifled a sob and looked at Veta suspiciously. "You got better." The woman knew she'd been had. That showed real intelligence, and Veta found herself pleased with her selection. "About the credit. I'm a little short."

Veta raised one eyebrow in a calculated gesture. "Shouldn't bet what you can't cover," she said after a moment.

The woman shrugged. "I'm good for it . . . if you give me some time."

"Tell you what." Veta took a deep breath. "I'll take your note. I'm going to be in port for a few more days. We'll work something out." She ran a hand through the wet strands of her short gray hair. "I'll be in touch." As Veta kicked out of the court, Marin chopped at the wall with her racquet. Graphite splintered.

Within the week, Marin agreed to scan the transactions, and printed up a sheet of incontrovertible evidence. Burgoyne gave her a bonus. Veta sent ten percent to Rocco along with an invitation for another game. The partnership evolved, like a natural progression.

And even after it had dissolved, Marin still ranked as the best point operative Veta had ever known.

Sirens wailed, dragging her out of the depths of memory and back to the madness of Langen Nacht. The sound nagged at her, her stomach tightening with nervousness. The red flash of the ambulance lights melted across the fronts of the buildings, reflecting back from black glass and droplets of moisture mixed with ice. The crowd unconsciously swayed to the throb of the sirens, eyes fixed on the open circle cordoned off in front of the apartment complex. A pair of kids scrambled to the top of a light standard for a better view. Overdose, Veta thought, watching the faces of those around her and trying to pick a pathway through to the entrance of the building.

A dozen security officers moved beyond the line, taking measurements, working around a sheet-draped body. Several stared up into the night. She followed their gaze, up the side of the building glittering with reflections from across the street. The broken window was eighteen floors up, a ragged hole of illumination in the flat plane of mirrored darkness. She felt her stomach twist and had to remember to breathe. Her eyes traveled slowly back to the shrouded form.

A big miner stood next to her, huge arms thrusting from the torn sleeves of his shirt. He wore black jeans, with braided cable for a belt and a buckle fashioned from an old gear. His bare feet were blue. He breathed into his hands, his nails light crescents against his darkened skin. The man stared at her numbly.

"What's happened?" She had to ask him twice.

A grin spread over his sluggish features. His eyes were glazed and unfocused. "Bitch tried to fly." Laughing slowly, he rubbed one massive hand across his jaw. "Didn't make it."

"Suicide?" Her mind was racing. She wanted to lurch forward and rip the sheet away. Part of her was crazy with fear. The rope of scar on her arm was a burning flame, electrical discharges of pain flickering along the muscles.

"Goons say murder." Another rippling laugh. "Say some deaders pitched her through the glass." His face grew troubled, fleeting anger followed by confusion. "What's happenin' to us, hey? What the hell's happenin' when corpses start snuffin' citizens?"

Others took up the cry. The miner moved off after the sound, which swelled like a wave. Someone thought they saw a corpse across the street. The crowd followed, chanting; the madness was growing, the festival mood turning sour.

Veta pressed against the orange tape cordoning off the area. The security officers watched the crowd, boredom in their faces, trying to look professional and detached. A white-smocked woman hovered over the victim. She was a coroner; Veta knew the type. Two aides stooped and lifted the body onto a litter.

Thick auburn hair tumbled out from under the white sheet.

Her vision went suddenly telescopic, as if Rocco's body were viewed at a distance while her surroundings were blurred and indistinct. Only the red hair was in focus, the ruddy glare of the ambulance strobe washing over it with metronomic precision. Veta turned away, her legs leaden, and stumbled blindly into the mob.

For a time she wandered aimlessly, allowing the initial shock to drain away, but not the anger. The rage she sharpened to a keen edge. No way the deaders were responsible for Rocco. Instinct and experience told her that Rocco's dive was linked to the pilot. She'd have to follow the chain back to get even. It was not business anymore. Now it was vendetta, and she had only one place to start. Veta saw his face as though on a holographic wanted poster: dark hair and beard, pitted cheeks, yellow teeth.

Jann Petski.

He was a dead man.

Chapter 18

Rolen was lagging.

It was easier to let the woman lead him, easier not to think but to follow as if jacked into her skull and reacting to commands from her software. Not piloting, but riding—a passenger. No hands on the comm, no input required, no control. It was like free-falling, similar to the moment when the ship shuddered and dropped into the nexus, and the generators twisted the universe. For a few seconds everything was out of the pilot's hands. If the ship went nova, it didn't matter. There wasn't anything he could do to save himself at that particular point in time. Pilots called it lagging. A mildly derogative term, implying submission. And yet he lagged, content to coast in her wake and allow the woman to be responsible for his survival.

He had, he realized, spent most of his life either coasting or trying to achieve that desired state. Pursuing the path of least resistance. Going to ground. As a child, he'd been accepted as part of the group, but never as the leader. In school, he'd kept his grades blessedly average and was thus insulated in the center of the student body, safe from the attention and demands placed upon the very bright or exceedingly dull. Piloting had seemed a strange vocation for him, surprising to most of his acquaintances, an ambition beyond his normal range. Yet, in truth, it meshed perfectly with his goals. Despite the romanticized versions popular in the holos, the job was routine and dull, safe because he traveled along well-explored routes. There was no need to plan his future, as his schedule was programmed months in advance. After twelve years, there was no need even to think, because repetition had embedded his duties into his mind like autonomic reactions.

He'd forgotten how to make decisions, so he clung to the fleeing corpse and tried desperately to keep pace.

"Be easier going now," the woman said, stopping to peer out from the alley toward the deserted avenue. "Industrial sector just ahead. Be quiet tonight. Everyone's up on the hill."

The city had changed. While they had traversed Delphi through a network of linked passages and alleys, the urban landscape had shifted. To the south rose the monolithic range of apartments and corporate towers. North, the city flattened out into low warehouses and a collection of gritty factories, smokestacks, and tin roofs. Beyond them, Delphi abruptly ended, the mining district spreading across a confusion of stark ridges and gullies, open shafts marked by jagged heaps of useless rock, and steel forests of draw works and conveyors. In the darkness, the twin rails of the train tracks were two knife blades cutting across the devastated landscape. A few lights gleamed in the night, blue-white halogens blazing like misplaced stars. Humped angular shapes jutted on the serrated horizon: spidery networks of cranes and crushers; pyramids of dross; the prehistoric silhouettes of earthmoving equipment and boring units.

They were in a narrow band of suburbia between the two sectors of Delphi. The darkness was lit by the occasional flicker of a dying neon sign. Iron bars latticed the storefronts. Litter fluttered along the sidewalks. Black patches of ice dotted the street.

A group of young girls thundered down the fire escape of one of the remaining apartment complexes, a mean and decaying structure that sagged and seemed about to implode. Their footsteps drummed along the steel; their white robes flowed and swirled in the breeze. Each wore a head-dress, wreaths of flowers studded with four white plastic candles. The candles were electric. The arcs buzzed softly. The girls passed, laughing and chattering as they hurried off to join the procession wending toward the center of Delphi, a river of torches flowing slowly into the central plaza. They paid no attention to the corpses.

Gripping the banister, Rolen swung around from beneath the stairs and sank onto the bottom step. For a time, the narrow confines of the alley had helped keep his agoraphobia controlled. But now, with the broad deserted avenue stretching before him, he felt it return. He tried to inhale deeply, but it was as if there were a shunt in his throat that allowed the air to bypass his lungs. Dizziness made him close his eyes. He vaguely heard the woman sit beside him and distantly sensed the cold steel stair beneath his legs.

"Okay?"

"In a minute." Hanging his head, he watched Carta obliquely, studying her with his peripheral vision and attempting vainly to keep his attention away from the open space beyond the edge of Delphi. Dim light carved her profile: delicate skull, curving and fragile; wide forehead; upturned nose; lips pouting; chin trembling slightly with each breath. Her eyes were large and luminous, her pupils wide and fathomless. An enigma, she was more child than hero, with a terrible fatalism clinging to her that made him very afraid. She was a corpse, so she had a criminal record. She was no saint, but instinct told him to trust the woman. "Which way?"

Carta pointed toward the horizon, a jagged darkness against the starry sky.

"Vasquez?"

She nodded.

"Look," he said, raising his head slightly to face her. "I don't handle open spaces well." He choked back a panicked laugh. "Actually, I don't handle them at all. You may end up carrying me."

The woman grinned and shook her head. "You're some

piece of work, pilot. You can push a lump of steel through jump space, but you can't walk across a road.''

Rolen shivered, teeth chattering.

She inspected him thoughtfully. "You're serious?"

He fought nausea and nodded.

"Man, 'cept for heading out into the beyond, there's no other way to get to Vasquez."

"Who is this Vasquez? Before I go out there"—he kept his eyes on the woman—"I want some input. Right now I'm operating without data. I don't like it."

"Depends on who you ask. Put it to a citizen and he'll say Vasquez is a radical, revolutionary. Some might even say . . . terrorist." She sniffed loudly, coughed, and spit. "Mention him to a corpse and you'll get a different story. Most deaders think he's a saint. Me, I'd say he's smart and he's got potential. And right now, he's got cover, food, and shelter. More than I can expect to find waiting for me with the authorities." Carta rubbed her hands together for warmth. "But if you were from Bacchus, you wouldn't have to ask. For him or against him, you'd know Antonio Vasquez. Got a price on his head. A list of charges half a klick long: treason, inciting to riot, terrorist activities. Pure trouble for the straights. But for a corpse, he's the last resort." Carta gave him a tight smile. "And you're a corpse."

A warning klaxon went off in his skull. Terrorists. He looked down at one hand, bit a ragged nail, and inspected his work. "I still got options."

"Sure."

He massaged his neck. "Really. The Guild. Zenyam." Rolen tapped a finger on the implants at the base of his skull. "I've got value."

"More than you know." Carta laughed. "Enough to get you terminated." Her eyes narrowed, not in hate but in pity. "Look, when I said Petski was part of a team sent into the House to take you out, that's what I meant. They were supposed to pull your plug, pilot. Only reason you're still breathing is Petski needed credit real bad, figured to sell you off to the highest bidder. Word's out that big credit is changing hands for your option. Taking you out alive was his scam. Original intent was to snuff you.''

It was too crazy to be believed, and yet . . . The night flashed into focus, a microburst of highlighted replay. Was anything too insane right now? ''Who'd want me dead?''

She rubbed a hand across her scalp, a gesture retained from when she'd once had hair. ''Don't know. But they got big credit, the kind of clout carried by someone about the size of the Guild or Zenyam. Definitely Fortune Five Hundred. You want to go back there and take your chances finding out, you do it solo.''

He closed his eyes and bit his lips. It was too much to absorb all at once. His mind was hitting overload. A bubble of panic welled up inside him. He glanced back down the street and then quickly out to the mines. The darkness tried to hold his eyes, but he managed with a superhuman effort to turn back to the woman. ''How do I know you're telling the truth?''

''You don't. And I don't friggin' care.''

He stared up at her. The gleam from a distant streetlamp caught her features and softened her jaw and brows, giving her a child's face. ''Then why help me?''

''Wouldn't be, if you weren't so damn helpless.'' She shrugged. ''Maybe I've got a soft spot for idiots. Anyway, like I said before, if I'd gone down with Petski, it would have been a fifth offense, which means termination—and as much as I hate being a corpse, I don't really want to die.''

It was a good answer, one he could possibly trust. God, he wanted desperately to trust someone. He nodded slowly. ''Vasquez will help me?''

''Much as he can,'' she said softly. ''But no guarantees. And he might have his own price.''

Carta turned quickly, as if tracking something down the street. Rolen jerked his head to follow her gaze and might have seen a movement as he turned, or maybe it was just a stray reflection. The street was silent. Torchlights wavered far in the distance.

''Time to go. Can't stay here any longer.'' She pushed

away from the wall and turned toward him. "Do what you want. I've done my good deed for the night."

He licked his lips. "I wasn't kidding about open spaces."

"Nothing out there." Carta gestured toward the skeletal frames of the distant mining apparatus.

"That's the problem." Reluctantly, he reached out and took her hand, keeping his head down as she pulled him away from the protection of the stairway.

The ground was hard and rough, sharp stones cutting like teeth through the thin soles of his sandals. Rolen kept his face down, his eyes half-closed, trusting the woman to lead him to safety. Deep ruts carved the surface, the rugged hieroglyphics of berms and blade scars imprinted by heavy equipment. The edges of the road fell away into rills of silt and mud, steaming pits of violet and orange that glowed with soft phosphorescence from the intermingling chemicals of drilling mud and milling fluids.

The wind was thick with hard pellets of gritty snow. From somewhere to the south, a loose tin panel on a tool shack pounded out a cadenced tempo to their march. A raw sewage stench welled up from the open sumps, their glowing surfaces hammered by the gusts. Gravel crunched like bones underfoot. The emptiness enfolded him. The mining crews had gone to the city for the festival, and Delphi seemed light-years away. The two corpses might have been the last surviving life-form on the planet.

They passed close to an equipment yard, where the hulking shapes of the earthmovers and borers stood silently brooding. White layers of snow coated the horizontal surfaces. The acrid pungency of fuel washed over him, a thick heady brew of hydrocarbons, burnt rubber, and grease. Scabs of hardened oils crusted the soil beneath his feet, darkness hiding the mounds and ridges that staggered him. He longed for the smooth regularity of a ship's deck, the protection of a hardened alloy hull, and the sanctity of the bridge.

Rolen was vulnerable, and fatigue attacked him. He had been running for hours now, gravity tugging at him with every step. His muscles were as tight as spring steel, trembling and burning. Every breath scored a raw swath in his throat. He imagined himself a child's toy on a string, bouncing and jarring across the ground.

Lagging once again.

"Shit!" Carta stopped and turned as if at a sudden sound.

Rolen sank to his knees, head down, trying to keep from passing out. He heard it now—the deep, throaty rumbling of a chopper in the distance.

Delphi was a glittering mass in the valley. At one edge he saw the slashing blades of diamond light that were the search beams of an aircraft. It was dancing along the fringe, a mad firefly pausing at each structure to peer and probe as if seeking food. Running parallel to their path, it seemed only a distant threat.

"If those bastards make an infrared scan," she hissed, "we might just draw some unwanted company."

The woman scanned for cover and her gaze locked on the conical towers of a thermoelectric plant rising a hundred meters to the left where steam venting from a crack in the planet's surface was transformed into cheap power for the mines. Silver pipes snaked across the ground. Rags of vapor twisted on the breeze, hurrying phantoms that dissipated instantly.

"Just what we need. Something hotter than us." Carta glanced back and forth between the plant and the circling chopper. "If we can get between them and it, the generator's heat signature should screw up their seeker." She helped him stand. "Besides, heat and rest might do you some good."

They were not on a slope, but he struggled as if climbing a hill. A loop of expansion pipes rose above him, hoops of aluminum designed to suck the contractions from the tubing as fluids of various temperatures were pumped through the interior. Rolen needed expansion joints in his head, a mechanism to keep his brain from shattering under the pressure of the conflicting images warring within it: Miras Magana laying spread-eagle on the blood-spattered bed; a prison guard taking a bullet in his spine and going down hard; a corpse twitching in a vat of green fluid; Petski writhing on his throne of trash.

Carta squatted against one of the tanks. Heat radiated from its metal flank. He crumpled beside the woman, sprawling on the dirt, ignoring the jagged rocks beneath his back and wishing that he could somehow melt into the soil. Overhead piping framed a segment of the night sky, wisps of steam dancing across the stars gleaming in the gap. He felt vacuous inside, empty, and the weight of the open space above seemed to be pressing down and crushing him. The fragment of control he had been clinging to slipped slowly from his grasp, ebbing away into the darkness.

"They're turning away," Carta whispered. "Must have blinded the bastards." Her laugh was a dry chuckle. Pipes clanged in the background, pressure surging.

Rolen heard her distantly. The night was killing him, compressing him and changing the basic elements of his being. His arms and legs were leaden sculptures. He stared up at the sky, the square of dark and stars calling him, vacuum seeking him, pushing down through the insubstantial veil of atmosphere to suck him dry, leaving a husk to crumble and drift on the wind, to end up as grit in some miner's mouth.

The woman leaned over him, her face jutting into his framed segment of the sky. "Pilot?"

He could make no more answer than a sibilant hiss between tight lips.

She lifted his head gently but awkwardly, as though it had been a very long time since she'd given anyone comfort. Her hand stroked his face tentatively, making patterns on his cheek, her skin warm and dry.

"It's all right," she said softly. "It's okay. Relax, pilot. Just relax. Nothin's gonna get you now."

After a while she grew tired of rocking him, or maybe she was afraid he really was going to die, and she made a pillow out of her pack and placed it under his head. "I gotta get us some help," she explained very patiently, though she had no idea whether or not he could hear. "Be right back."

The woman shifted beyond his narrowed field of vision.

Dark sky and burning stars beckoned him. He heard the gravel crunching as she moved away into the night, and then there was only his heart pounding; he half expected every beat to be the last and the silence to become complete.

Later—maybe minutes, maybe hours had passed—footsteps approached, slow and soft. Voices carried on the wind.

"Here. Help me."

"I don't like it." Shapes moved at the edge of his vision. "Bad timing. Too convenient. He could be a plant."

"Look at his goddamn neck. You think those are friggin' real or what?"

"So what." He felt hands against his implants, touching the skin. "Could be cover. We had some Security trying to get in a while back, all made up to look like a standard deader. Would have made it, too, 'cept I'm careful. Got an awesome responsibility, lady. He depends on me. Maybe those bumps are show. Maybe not. But Vasquez don't need no friggin' pilot anyway."

"Maybe you better let him decide that."

There was a long pause while the stranger considered. "Just so's you know it's your ass." He called to others in the distance. "Hossing! Murtch! Got a load for the tunnels. Gimme a hand here."

Chapter 19

"Damn!" Jann Petski muttered a curse and pounded the soil with his good arm. Jagged pebbles gnawed his flesh.

The situation was downgrading fast, taking another step lower on the scale between success and failure as he watched the deaders collect the pilot, lifting him like some random casualty of a Leather clash and carrying him toward the nearest cavern.

Time to panic, boy. Time to be afraid.

There were four of them: three men and the woman. The pilot didn't count, not hanging between them like a sack of grain. Four shots and he could take them out. But the pistol was lost beneath the rubble back in the alley. What then? His left shoulder was useless, no longer bleeding, covered by a wad of cloth forming a makeshift bandage, but it burned as if a flare were lodged in his flesh, a core of liquid phosphorus eating away at him. He couldn't run an assault on the four of them. No way to move the pilot with one arm, and a struggle would likely bring others. The situation was more than he could handle.

"Damn."

They staggered across the boulder-strewn landscape toward the dark pit of the nearest mine. He heard the equipment lift groan and the cage door clang shut. And then he was alone in the night.

The pilot was gone.

He fought tears, squinting his eyes tightly and pressing his face into the hard-crusted ridge on which he lay, trying to stifle a scream that had been building since he'd gone on shift in the House. A fortune—a damned fortune for which he had already killed—had been within inches of his grasp, and yet it had slipped away like a night at the games. It was his typical betting luck, the same rotten fate that always kept him at the dice machines long after his credit line was tapped, running on borrowed funds and the thin intensity of adrenaline, knowing it was sour but punching the keys again and again because if he stopped he'd never have the chance to win, and somebody always won, and someday it had to be him, maybe on the next damned roll.

Time to regroup, he thought bitterly. Got to minimize losses.

Dealing with crossed partners or betrayed allies required a skill bordering on an art. If a boy wasn't big enough to power his way through the packs of Leathers who'd staked out Delphi's slums, then he had to use his brain to fabricate a diversion, a magician's trick to turn their attention to other problems. Some lessons were so hard-imprinted, etched on his memory with an acid so hot, that he never forgot them. He had learned this one particularly well. Jann remembered, unwillingly.

He had been a disposable child, in the strictest sense implied by the dark-suited social worker who came by once a month to make sure his father hadn't killed him in a drunken rage. The old man didn't care if he came home or not, just as long as he stayed out of the way. His mother always watched him prowl the rooms, as if uncertain of his origin, as if he were some fixture of the dingy apartment that had somehow come to life. He never spent much time at home.

A few blocks east of the squalid arcology where his mother passed her days in a drug coma and his father went to piss and sleep, there was a row of burned-out offices. Labor troubles had led to a few well-placed bottles of kerosene, and the resulting fire had gutted both the structure and the corporate assets. So the buildings moldered, the rain pouring through great gaps in the roof, and the Leathers going into the vacant rooms to punch the latest drugs and practice their budding sexual techniques. He liked to wander the darkened corridors, staying quiet and keeping out of the way.

The cat lived in the remains of the third-story washroom. Cats were nothing new. Ships brought them into the port. They smuggled their way onto the surface of Bacchus. Most considered them a nuisance and a plague. This particular one was a questionable specimen: gray fur lusterless and matted; one ear missing; one eye white with scar tissue. Wild and mean, it never let him get close enough to touch. Yet there was something familiar about the way it moved, some vague affinity that kept him bringing scraps of food and spending long hours watching the animal stalk its territory.

His cat. The association gradually became automatic.

He avoided the Leatherboys—at least they would grow into the title. At thirteen they were already brutal. Cassick, with his darkened brow and first whiskers, sporadic stubble like a fungus on his cheeks. Pollard, who claimed to have already killed once and carried a fingerbone in his pocket as proof. And Hawkins. She was the worst, sour and bitter and strung out on Overdrive, living on hatred and what she found in the streets.

They cornered him in the third floor, in the restroom. They must have heard his footsteps above the room where they were shooting liquid Comfort.

"Looky, looky," Cassick rumbled, trying to keep his voice deep. His biceps were huge, jutting from his leather vest. A cobra earring sank gold fangs deep into one lobe. "And just when we was wantin' some fun."

Pollard rubbed one hand against his thigh, polishing the fingerbone between his palm and his jeans. His grin was tight and deadly. He just laughed.

"Wanna play?" Hawkins blurted, her words almost intelligible. She was on an Overdrive high, speeding. Her arms jerked spastically. "What'd ya say, Pets? Wanna play a game? Wanna have some funnnn?" She stretched the word. Her fingernails were black lacquer. Her pupils were as small as birdshot. The three moved in behind him to plug the exit.

A shadow cowered behind the porcelain fixture, a dark stain against the dust and soot. He saw their eyes move, following, watching dumbly. Maybe he thought the cat would flee at the first missile. Maybe he figured it could escape. But truth was, he was so sick with fear he didn't care. Jann stooped, found a wedge of fibrous plaster, and threw low purposely. It clattered against the wall.

"Betcha can't hit it." The words spilled from him in a rush of breath as he bent for more ammunition.

He'd found a diversion, something else to maim—something they could actually kill. The cat arched its back and hissed, fueling their interest. The scarred eye gleamed white. Hawkins palmed a clod and pitched it hard, howling as the animal clawed at its damaged ribs. The hail of plaster grew heavier and they closed in, moving toward the corner and leaving the doorway open. Petski broke for the street. They didn't follow, too engrossed in the death at hand to worry about him.

Later, he went back and buried the carcass—just the body, because, for a long time, Pollard wore the head on a thong around his neck.

Jann raised his head slowly, shaking off the memory. It was time for more magic. He examined the area, isolating landmarks. The thermoelectric generator rose on the horizon, an abstract of silver cylinders and piping. Fifty meters north was a rusting hulk of a draw works that had been stripped for parts. The third leg of the triangle ended at a bladed mound of rock and sand. He memorized the location.

Serious trouble—that was the best definition he could assign to his present status. His apartment was now hostile territory. The cold, hard face of Veta Pulchek flickered through his mind—lethal eyes, dark and flecked with gold, with as little heart in them as in the wall of a mine shaft.

Once she knew where to look, she'd come gunning. For a minute, he actually considered running to the woman and offering the corpse's location in exchange for his life. The thought died quickly. Cross me once, shame on you. Cross me twice . . . He didn't need to finish the couplet. A meet with Veta Pulchek was a terminal suggestion.

Who, then? Not the authorities. His own freedom was forfeit. A dead guard was a one-way ticket into the House of Justice. Stupid, he thought angrily. Stupid greed. If he'd taken the credit from the woman, he would right now be doing a snort of Comfort and smoothing out the rough edges of his life. She'd be bearing the weight of the law, not him. Another perfect plan in shambles.

Only one alternative: Bern Aggutter. It was real risky, but Aggutter had the most to gain from his success. Dead, Jann was a debt to Aggutter. Alive, he had a potential for a profit. The exchange rate was different—his life for the pilot. He thought in terms of misdirection and timing.

Diversions.

Jann rose to his feet slowly. He needed a blast, an amp of Overdrive to rev his engines and kill the dull pain in his shoulder. But he'd used it all pursuing the corpses across Delphi, and his pockets were empty. Comfort was south. There was nothing left for him to do out in the sprawling darkness of the mines. Grimacing, Jann picked his way down the hillside and followed the road back toward the center of town.

It was early morning when he reached The Blue Note. The party mood was waning. Dim lights revealed catatonic celebrants, some scattered over tables, others moving in slow motion as if under liquid. Prostitutes rifled the pockets of the unconscious. He saw slack faces and blue smoke—home. He felt relief as he staggered into the doorway, relief tempered with fear, but still it was good to be in familiar territory. Jann could smell the bitter tang of Comfort, a Pavlovian response conjuring images of frosted aluminum and burning nostrils.

Aggutter squatted at his table. Something slender and

young rested in his lap, a boy with the soft feminine shape of a twelve-year-old girl—a castrato, an acquired taste. At Jann's appearance, Bern stopped stroking the child's shoulder, his fat hand pausing on the smooth white skin. The boy pouted, but slid down with a shove from Aggutter, padding away into the back to wait, perhaps, in a darkened bedroom for the fat man's continued attention.

Bern sucked a deep slow breath, his huge chest expanding. There was no welcome, no greeting, just his cold humorless eyes staring.

"Bad news," Jann said quietly.

"So I heard. Very bad."

"I need help."

"You killed a guard." He looked at his hands, examining his nails. "Need more than help. You need a friggin' miracle, Petski. Maybe a priest."

"We had a deal." He made the words a flat statement of fact. Jann crossed to the table and sank into a chair.

"Business is an exchange. You give me something of value and I reciprocate." Bern's face wrinkled with a smile. "But markets are always changing. Some prices go up. Some . . . down. The value of your skin to certain people just went through the roof. Maybe I sell you to the Council. Or perhaps I sell you to a woman named Veta Pulchek. Either way, I make a profit."

"I've still got the pilot." He sucked a breath through his teeth. The first panicky twinges of hard withdrawal added an edge to his pain. Cotton mouth accompanied his headache. Sound gained a tinny quality.

The man paused, studying him closely. "Not what I hear."

"Maybe you don't hear everything."

There was another long pause. Aggutter raised his glass of mineral water and took a long sip. Wheels turned somewhere behind the wrinkled fat on his white forehead. By the time he placed the glass back on the table, Jann knew that the man had decided there was no harm in listening further. "Explain, Jann. Make me believe you still have worth."

Diversion time. No more games. One of the bodies at the bar was very alert, watching them as if looking for a signal—Aggutter muscle waiting for orders. Jann thought of Kol Danton and the wire garrote, of the pressure on his fingers. He swallowed hard. "I don't have him. But I know where he is." He leaned across the table. "I could lead somebody to him. You or anyone else. Anyone with credit. Anyone willing to make a deal."

"Ever see a man drown?" Fat fingers drummed the tabletop. Somewhere from the back booths came the sounds of retching and laughter. "He grabs on to anything for one final breath. Sometimes takes his rescuers down in his panic." His mouth turned down into a frown. "That kind of risk makes me think only a fool tries to save a man who's going under."

Jann caught the metaphor, nodding grimly. "Business. Supply and demand. Somebody wants the skyking. Somebody must want him more than they want me. An outside chance, but still worth trying. We could be even. I don't even want a profit. Just a chance to square accounts."

"I think I hear someone drowning." He laughed. "What do you hear, Petski. Are you listening?"

"You want to be part of it? Cut a deal." Jann leaned back in his chair, wincing at the agony in his arm and shoulder. "If not, then I got people to see. I'll do it alone."

"Either way—you do it alone." He gave Jann his killer grin, a brief flash of what Aggutter must have been on the way up, cold and brutal. "No matter what arrangements we make, I'm not part of it. Understand?"

Jann imagined Leatherboys throwing stones at a cat and closed his eyes. "You don't want a cut?"

"Never said that. Look at it this way. I'm a major fan of the duels. Like nothing better than seeing a good bash. And it's business for me. When I go to the duels, I earn heavy credit. But you don't see me climbing into the pits. I'm a noncombatant. Still, my take is always more than the stiffs taking the punches. That's the way of it, son. Getting someone else to run the risks."

"Like me."

His laugh was more like the hiss of escaping gas. "You, now, you're damn straight in the center of the hole. You're no dueling man. You're just some bystander who was standing too close and fell over the rail. Got combatants to your left and right. They're making the war—life and death for them. They aren't even looking at you, but you're just liable to buy it in the skirmish. Not a good place to stand, son." The man picked at something lodged in one brown stump of a tooth, licked it off his finger, and swallowed it. "I'm still on the outside looking in. I damn sure intend to stay there."

Jann nodded.

Bern continued, his voice softly droning, hypnotic and flat. "A difficult sale, without having the pilot. Always a chance that they might find him through other channels. Need to move fast."

"Who's looking?"

"Two parties want him bad. Pulchek and Larion House."

"Not Pulchek." Petski coughed, the muscle spasm tearing at him, stabbing pains in his shoulder. He jerked a thumb toward the bloody hole in his flesh. "Her currency I can skip. The bitch gets no second chances. Won't likely miss twice." Petski straightened in his chair. "Larion is local. What do they want with the pilot?"

"Both of them are fronting. Running cover for offworld firms. Pulchek is an independent with Guild connections. Larion runs the program for a corporation by the name of Akira."

"The deal goes to Larion."

"No problem, so long as they don't know it's a closed market. It'd lower the price."

"How do I contact them?"

"You don't." Aggutter shrugged. "Consider it my investment. We'll use the proper channels, son. Grapevine. Don't worry. Send out a whisper, it'll reach the right ears." He raised one invisible eyebrow. "Won't keep Pulchek out, though. She'll still be sniffing around. And Akira's got its own heat on Bacchus, a fixer by the name of Jaleem Abbasi. Rumor says he's pure machine. You've already snagged his operation. He's not going to be in the mood to deal. He'll be looking for a pound of flesh, someone to carry the weight of responsibility. Answers, son. You might be one of them.''

"I got what he needs."

"Better hope so."

"So now what?"

"You wait. There's room in the back." He stood, his legs like columns, fat rolling beneath the fabric of his jumpsuit. "Someone will be along to treat your wound."

Jann chewed his lips slowly. "Thanks."

The man grinned. "Never confuse business with friendship." He waddled away into the darkness of the rear alcoves.

Petski sat quietly for a few minutes, staring into space, his eyes unfocused, his mind a blank. After a while, one of the bartenders moved to close up, wiping down the bar, rousting the last few patrons, and shutting the doors. Jann walked to the bar and grabbed two blasters. They were cold in his hands.

One room in back was unoccupied. He did the Comfort and then he slept soundly. He was home and safe.

He still had value.

Chapter 20

Rolen smelled rock and dust, the lingering familiar scents of a mine shaft, metallic and copper with faint hints of alkaline salts, fuel, sulfur, and cordite. Somehow, he was back on Thor's Belt. He was safe. He opened his eyes slowly.

A rugged arc of stone curved overhead, its dimpled surface marbled with shadows and peaks of light like old pictures of the lunar surface at sunrise. Mica glittered in wide bands, speckles of quartz and feldspar. The shaft was old, the rock oxidized and the cuts dull with age. No microscopic grit swirled in the yellow glow from a lamp driven deep into a crevice. Electric cable hung in black loops, snaking out into the passageway. His eyes adjusted to the soft illumination. Ceiling became wall with a gentle curve, merging into a rough-cut floor, none of the hard, straight edges of ships or stations, but the womb-like oval he had loved as a child. He was not on Thor's Belt. He wasn't so confused as to persist in such a fantasy for longer than a few heartbeats. But somehow he had escaped the yawning darkness above and had found safety in the womb of the rock.

The woman was a warm mass beside him, her head propped against the wall, the silver-foil emergency blanket pulled up around her neck. She smiled as he rose up from the floor, a flickering of maternal instinct across her pale features.

"Feeling better?" Her question was polite and stilted, as though she'd planned something more pertinent and then in the last instant fallen back to the inane and familiar.

Rolen nodded and stretched, rubbing the crusts from his eyes. He felt slow, his mind drugged with fatigue. "Where are we?"

"Safe."

"Vasquez?"

Carta nodded and leaned back against the stone.

"How long have I been out?"

"Two, maybe three hours." She scratched beneath the blanket, never taking her eyes from his face. "I expected a week."

"Sorry about what happened up there," he said, grinning awkwardly. Damn, it felt good to be enclosed. "Open spaces. Warned you."

Carta shrugged.

"And thanks again."

Embarrassed, she looked away. "Yeah. Well, don't start expectin' me to always come to the rescue. You'll need to start fendin' for yourself—and soon."

Despite her words, Rolen couldn't help feeling he had an ally. Something had slotted on the surface, some programming loop that linked them. "Yeah. I guess, since I'm safe, you'll be moving on."

"Why don't you just let me decide when I'm leavin'? Green as you are, probably hurt yourself goin' to the bathroom alone." She drew her knees up to her chest, tenting the blanket. "Might've worked this mine. All look the same to me. Did a stint in the holes with my third owner. Local corp by the name of Larion. We parted company on my first Incorrigible." The woman sighed softly. "Anyway, the district's riddled. Vein runs out and they abandon the hole. Others move in. Home to all kinds of castaways. Rogues. Druggies. Dangerous out here. Open shafts and unsavory types. No place for decent citizens or stupid pilots."

"How'd you know where to find Vasquez?"

"Vasquez owns everything out here." The woman laughed, a bitter sound. "Least as long as possession is nine-tenths, skyking. He's taken what the straights have cast away."

"How'd you know where to look?"

"I keep my ears open. A corpse has to be good at listenin'. You hear things, bits of information that citizens don't understand. You're a pilot. If something goes down on a flight, you've got contingencies, right? Steps to take. Actions and reactions. Same here. I know where to go when things heat up. Didn't have exact locations, but I got us close. And when we did, Vasquez found us. That's an important difference. He wanted to find us. Otherwise . . ." She did not finish her statement.

"You working for him?"

She gave another quiet laugh. "That's like asking if you worked for the Guild. Every corpse works for Antonio Vasquez, whether they want to or not. Even the most docile pleasure slave is helping Vasquez. Even you."

"So when do I see him?"

Her face was serious. She adjusted her knees beneath the blanket and shivered with the cold. "He'll come for you when he's ready. When he can. Till then, stay here. Not safe for you to be roamin' the passageways." Carta closed her eyes.

While she slept, he prowled the chamber. His muscles were stiff from fatigue. His chest hurt. Hunger rumbled through him like an earthquake.

The far wall was stacked with fiberboard cartons containing an odd mixture of parts and equipment. Blankets filled some crates. He found bandages and medical supplies in others. Some held blank infocubes and spare chips, Burgoyne flow processors. A public commlink booth lay on its side, wires protruding from the base like a thick tuft of copper hair. There was useless garbage, as well: one crate was full of stuffed animals, monkeys with plastic faces gaping at him, eyes holoformed so they seemed to follow him from any position in the room.

In a weird twist of logic, the assortment suddenly made sense to him. The runaway corpses had to have accumulated supplies by stealth and theft, lifting entire containers, some by design and some by accident—a stream of pilfered materials finding its way to Vasquez in hopes some might prove useful. He remembered similar missions he'd run on Thor's Belt, stealing a UV unit for Malibu or appropriating furniture for their alcove. Kid's play. Only the corpses weren't playing, and Vasquez had somehow been anointed mad king of the mines, ruling an empire whose wealth was comprised of items reported to their owners as lost or damaged during transit.

One box in the corner held a treasure, a personal computer. An old model, disk technology instead of the newer infocube format, but the basic design was uniform enough for him to assemble. Miraculously intact, the CRT was a small square, white plastic and dark screen. He linked cables and snapped together couplings. In minutes he had the unit complete. Power was a problem, but he finally rigged an umbilical off the light cable. Still, Rolen was amazed to see the console light, the red telltales gleaming as the drives scanned for program.

Hardware. He longed to jack in, set a pin into his sockets and feel the power feed into his brain. A stupid fantasy. There was nothing there for him anyway, nothing but ancient firmware. No ship commands. No pipeline offworld.

His fingers touched the keyboard and remembered old rhythms, commands from his childhood. He typed the program, tentatively at first, then with growing speed as each line served to draw out the next.

When finished, he hit RUN apprehensively. The drive cycled. A wand of color appeared from a point in the center of the screen, moving silently, transforming its path with a stark pattern of green and black, and weaving the hues into checkerboards and gingham prints. The image was everchanging, infinite, the processor reacting to the looped command chain.

Rolen found a position near the woman, where he could share her meager warmth and still watch the screen, the soothing patterns hypnotizing him.

''They call me Sister Gemini,'' she said, by way of introduction. ''And I'm sent to bring you to him.''

How long she had been standing in the entrance was a mystery. She might have grown there, conjured from the stones. A tall black woman, dressed in black; the dark jumpsuit was not the usual uniform of a corpse, but was designed for invisibility in the night. Execution had faded her skin to gray, the color of stone. He could not guess her age.

''Both of you.'' She spoke musically, as if accustomed to some rolling dialect, English not quite suited to her mouth. Suspicion marked her movements, wary and careful. She was unarmed, yet Rolen had no doubt that she could use her fists. ''Now. He's a busy man, got no real time for such as you.''

At the entrance to the passage, she pressed her sandaled foot onto the floor and made a show of pointing out the print it etched in the dust. ''See here, now. You see those?'' A faint smile curved the ends of her mouth. ''You place your own feet in them, very carefully, and you be breathing much longer, my children.'' Her laugh was rich and full as she slipped out into the tunnel.

Certain phases of mining were universal, and Rolen was able to adjust his knowledge of Thor's Belt to his immediate surroundings. They crossed from exploratory adit to major artery, a broad passage where heavy cars had once rolled through with ore bound for the surface mills and dross to backfill abandoned stopes. When the corporation left, they'd ripped out the tracks and winches, and scavenged most of the old steel and the computer links that had tied the automated transportation system into a greater surface network. Only a bed of rough gravel remained, stretching before and behind. The arched ceiling was ten meters above his head. Boxes of supplies lined the walls. An erratic network of overhead lights cast sporadic illumination. Everything was temporary, easily stripped or abandoned on short notice. Nothing was permanent.

Guards squatted in small alcoves. They carried no weapons, but each was stationed leeward of a deadfall: precariously balanced loads of rock in overhead shafts; beams and scrap iron waiting to crash down on the unwary. Cables linked to the traps ended within close reach of the sentinels.

They squeezed through several tight openings that could be quickly blocked, shutting out potential aggressors. At one point, Sister Gemini took great care to reveal a camouflage net of woven fiber, lifting the edge as a brief demonstration. An open pit fell away into darkness, a damp draft wafting up through the gap. He remembered to walk slowly, concentrating on placing his feet in the woman's tracks.

The chamber was a small hollow just outside a massive underground gallery. The half-finished adit served as mute testimony to the death of the vein, one wall a crumbled mass of tailings blasted free and never removed. A metal folding table and a quartet of steel chairs furnished the cavity. The single overhead light cast a yellow cone of brilliance.

Sheets of monoline stretched across the mouth of the gallery. Through the clear plastic, Rolen could see the blurred shapes of makeshift shelving and trays stacked with electronics, display screens, comm units, a battery of cube drives and keyboards, and other constructs cryptic and familiar. It was the first real hardware Rolen had seen since his trial.

A slender figure, standing under the collar beams, turned as they approached. A man, yes, marginally. He was hairless, as were all corpsemen—but that was where the similarity ended. His face was piebald, a horrifying construct of translucent pink flesh and leathery plastic. The seam joining the two continents of his face meandered through one eyebrow, down across his nose, and out the corner of his mouth, traversing the side of his throat to disappear into the neck of his shirt. Steel teeth gleamed behind pale lips.

"Come in." His voice was hoarse and dry, metallic. One leg was a chromium prosthesis, a circular pressure plate for a foot, pins and hinges articulating with a slender rod that vanished into his pant leg. He walked with a jolting limp. Servomotors whined.

"Please sit . . . sit." There was no arm on the left side of his ravaged frame. Two waldoes protruded from slits in the shoulder of the jacket, gimbaled heads swiveling, hooked digits like claws. "Make yourselves comfortable."

"I must apologize for your wait." His skull pivoted, skeletal face angling toward them. "A bad host, I'm afraid. The press of business makes it difficult to find time for amenities. But then, which of us has all the hours we need?" The right side of his mouth pulled into a grin. "Sister Gemini will escort you to the commissary as soon as we've finished here. Ask her for anything you need. We are well supplied. Amazing where one can find the necessities of life if one knows where to look."

Vasquez clicked and hummed to the table, whining down to perch on the edge of the chair. He studied them with one human eye and one orb of crystalline sensor, probably infrared. Mirrored facets glittered. "So," he said, his gaze fixed on Rolen. "You are the pilot?"

"A pilot." Rolen swallowed and smiled uncomfortably.

The soft grunt was maybe a laugh and maybe a lung dysfunction. "No, my friend. You mustn't sell yourself short. You are *the* pilot. That is certain. There can't be two like you on Bacchus." His aspect grew suddenly serious. "Now, we must decide what to do with you."

"I'm trying to get back aboard ship."

"Home, of course. Back to your ship where you can forget about Bacchus. You would like to be safe again. A common dream for all of us." A flicker of longing crossed the human half of his face. "You are not the first corpse who has come to me for aid. You will not be the last. 'Go to Vasquez,' they say. 'He can do anything.' " He gave another phlegmy laugh.

"I was told you'd help me." Rolen stabbed a glance at Carta. She stared at the floor.

"We help ourselves, pilot. No other agencies available to a corpse. Bettering our position must be done with our own strength. Of course, such actions are treason and I'm considered responsible for the unrest among the slaves. A bit like holding a bullet responsible for murder instead of the one who pulls the trigger. I'm just a catalyst, an old man with some crazy ideas. No magician or savior.''

"Then, you can't do anything for me?"

"Get you to the Port, yes. That much is easy. But getting a corpse past customs and onto a ship is a tall order. Could be impossible. I'll have to study the situation.'' His good eye shifted in its socket. "What would you do to help yourself?"

"Anything.''

This time there was no mistaking the laughter. "So we'll see.'' In jerking, birdlike motions, he levered up from the chair with a hiss of hydraulics, groaning pressure. He inspected a glittering outcropping of pyrite, his waldoes scraping the wall. He was crazed—a broken caricature, not really man, not really machine. Something else. Something frightening.

"You're safe with us, but not for long. There is a great deal of interest in recapturing you. Comm channels are jammed with messages concerning your possible whereabouts. They'll be coming for you as soon as they know you are here.''

"Who?''

"Bacchus Security, Port Authority, no doubt there are many others.'' He massaged his face very carefully with his hand, avoiding contact with the pseudoflesh. "The problem is that we don't need company right now.''

The man turned slowly. Rolen expected to hear his spine ratchet. "Our position here is very precarious. Every few months, Security makes a show for the citizens by trying to round up escaped corpses, an inconvenience which in the past required rapid deployment to new locations. Fortunately, a hundred years of mineral harvesting has provided us with ample concealment.''

Vasquez nodded toward the gallery where silhouetted

corpses moved against the glare of the displays. "But right now, we can't move from this place. We've sacrificed our mobility to mount an offensive. A great deal of work has gone into this installation, special venting to eliminate suspicious heat signatures on the surface, air diversion to combat the occasional fumigation attempts by Security."

He studied them pensively. "We have some actions of our own in progress. Plans, pilot. You appear to be a major hindrance to their success. Several of my advisers are suggesting we deliver you to the authorities rather than risk an untimely interruption." Vasquez grinned at the concern in his face. "I haven't made a decision yet. Perhaps there is a way to turn you into an advantage. I'd hate to discover it after you're gone. So you can stay . . . for a while."

Rolen let a breath slowly escape between his teeth. "I'm just trying to get back aboard ship. I don't want to cause any more trouble."

"I'm afraid it's too late for that. You have already become trouble," Vasquez continued, eyes fixed on Rolen. "The natural reaction of a man caught in a mine collapse is to kick and struggle. But that uses up valuable air. To survive, one must stay calm, study the slide, and determine which rock to move to attain freedom. The secret is to understand the forces that brought the roof down. Takes a great deal of strength. How strong are you, pilot?"

Rolen started to answer.

The man held up his good hand in a gesture for silence. "Just listen. The first thing you need to learn as a corpse is to stay quiet and listen. In silence is strength." His tone was not angry, but paternal, as if he were talking to an errant son. "I have perfected the art of listening. Every corpse on Bacchus listens for me. Surprising, the news I gather."

Raising one curved prosthesis, Vasquez sighted along the hook at a point in the wall. "The prime question is, what to do with you? Where do you fit? Everything is coming together, plans we've been laying for years. I can't stop it for you, can't even put it off for a few days. The revolution is coming. Like it or not, Rolen Iserye, you're involved."

An aide appeared in the doorway. Vasquez regarded her with his mechanical eye. "What is it?"

"The specs are in from Mining Central. Programming would like your opinion of the workup."

The old man closed his eye for a long moment. Rolen saw the fatigue etched in his human features. "Business," he said, looking back to Rolen and Carta. "Go and eat. I must discuss matters with a few wiser heads. We'll speak again shortly. In the meantime, get some rest." He limped toward the gallery. "Iserye," he said, his rasping voice echoing in the chamber. "You said you'd do anything to escape. Don't forget that. I may hold you to that promise."

Chapter 21

Because her credit was exceptional, the link was prime. She stood in a salon complete with Victorian furnishings, Tiffany glass lamps, and a wooden bookshelf stocked with leather volumes—the familiar comforts of her personal comm-holo. Veta stood at the window and stared out at a street scene of Victorian London. A carriage rolled by, rattling on the cobbles. It was hard to imagine that the place existed only in an arrangement of electrical impulses, the product of a top communications designer, a holographic image being beamed through the nexus across a network of relay stations back to Earth.

"Veta?" Bollinger's voice was calm, but she couldn't miss the restrained anger. "I thought we'd agreed on the usual channels for contact."

She turned slowly. The man was seated on the divan, his weathered aspect serious. "This couldn't wait."

"Trouble?"

Veta nodded. "It's gone sour. Very poor chances of success. Wanted you to know. Give you time to prepare yourself for the fallout if it goes bad."

Len pursed his lips, waiting.

"I don't expect you to understand." She shrugged. "I lost an operative. Christ, Len . . . it was Rocco." She let

a few seconds of silence pass, fighting a momentary lapse
of control. "I have to . . . make amends."

"We had an agreement, Veta."

"This takes precedence. Besides, if I pull it off, the contract will be completed."

"And if you don't?"

"You lose." She met his passive gaze. "I thought you'd
want to be informed. Give the Guild a chance to prepare."

"There are other fixers available."

"If you send somebody in, tell them to keep out of my
line of fire." Veta approached the man, bent quickly and
kissed his cheek, feeling nothing as the holos merged.
"Good-bye, Len."

She broke the contact. The salon dissolved.

It was a typical hotel room, with twin beds, neorevision-
ist art posters, and a matching cherrywood dresser and mirror. She peeled the contact hardware from her head and
dropped it onto the laminated desk. Crossing to the bed,
Veta poured a cup of coffee from the tray that room service
had left on the nightstand. Bitter and black, it burned her
mouth and soured her stomach.

The first step complete, Bollinger was forgotten. She sat
down on the bed and planned her next move.

Jann Petski. Finding him was the key. He wouldn't go to
his apartment. His kind always had safe houses, places
where they could sleep and eat and wait out trouble. Petski
was a pack animal, so he'd never select a place where he
was a stranger, where he could be secure in his anonymity.
He'd want allies, a home away from home. There were always clues to such a place, if you knew where to look.

The keypads of the comm were warm to the touch. She
entered Rocco's office number from memory, and while the
machines linked, a segment of the past downloaded across
her brain . . .

The operation was a run for Rache Laboratories. A low-
level tech was stealing raw materials and supplying them to
a neighborhood Overdrive plant. Rache wasn't being be-

nevolent by trying to stop kids from doing the drug and blowing their brains. They were purely profit motivated, wanting to plug a hole in the finances. Orders and credit came down the line; close the gap. She did her job.

Rocco had never run the program. Already a legal partner, she'd always worked the outside, taking care of information and arrangements, watching the action from a safe distance. Deciding to do the search was a whim, an uncharacteristic urge to see what it was really like in the field.

She was like a kid on a first date, her nervous mood infectious. Rocco was giggling hysterically as Veta snapped a codebreaker onto the digital lock and cycled the door.

"We can't really do this," Rocco whispered, her voice high and tight. "Breaking and entering is illegal."

Veta laughed, turning for a second to stare at the woman; Rocco was not a day over twenty-five, her red hair coiled in ringlets, her cheeks flushed with excitement. "Hell, no." She stifled a laugh and hissed, "We're frigging going to ask him to let us in for a little search." Then the laughter came, the door slid open, and they stumbled inside.

Nobody was home. The tech kept his chemicals in vials, hidden in the ice machine in his freezer amid a scattering of frozen Swansons and a pair of protein steaks. They switched it with distilled water, hurrying out to the street to find a bar where they could drink and revel in the unique sensation of pure power that came only with a successful run.

Rocco never realized that the boys at the Overdrive lab would kill the tech until his body was dragged from a cycled airlock.

CODE PLEASE. The message flashed on the screen.

SAM SPADE, she entered. That was Rocco's sense of humor. Veta's smile turned to grief as she thought of the body sprawled in the street.

The menu flickered up onto the display. She selected the operative volumes and punched in Petski's name. The file appeared—a listing of cryptic notes. There was an address.

Veta committed it to memory before she backed out of the system.

Information provided a city directory, Delphi spread out in grids of blue and white lines. Mapping out a direct route to the apartment, she picked out street names and landmarks, tracing her path with the nail of her index finger. Residential district, the map said. Interpret as slum. Inhabited by unemployed workers displaced by the corpsmen. Hard times. No chance he'd be there, but it could be a clue to his present location. Something small.

She checked out of the hotel. From a booth in the lobby, Veta rented a hover, a small, nondescript two-seater. She drove north toward the residential district.

The sector was similar to others she'd visited on a half-dozen worlds. With narrow streets designed for foot traffic and small hovers, it was a place set aside by the colonists for housing. The space was adequate for a few, but had gone bad with growth and was swollen with population. The inhabitants clung tenaciously to their small segment of Delphi, pushing the roofs of the buildings higher, adding levels with available materials, a patchwork of plastics and alloys, wood paneling, and scabrous patches of stonemasonry. Someday, a corporation would swing through, buy it up in blocks, and convert, displacing the dwellers to another corner of the town where they would fester and rot. Recycling.

A half-formed arcology, the building spiraled up into the night. Eight levels were completed; the lower decks were already breaking down. Those floors above the eighth were unfinished, twenty meters of scaffolding and girders. They were dark, like the lair of some giant beast, a tangled nest of steel and cable. Construction had ceased years ago, from lack of funds or simple apathy. Her reflection rippled across the bank of glass doors in front, half with broken panes repaired by thick scabs of resinous plastic, yellow with age. Veta slid inside, into a darkened lobby that smelled of moldy carpet and steamed vegetables.

Her eyes adjusted to the interior light, not bright but different from the darkness outside, a twilight created by a half bank of flickering bars. Once it had been a grand lobby, but the insane construction had penetrated the lower floor and the mezzanine was partitioned into small cubes. She thought of Japanese sleep coffins. The cubicles were stacked three high, draped with cloth for doorways. Gas lamps gleamed through tattered fabric.

The lifts could not be trusted. They had no exits and, if Bacchus Security had managed to find the place first, the clatter would warn any guards stationed at his rooms. In several minutes, she located the stairwell, down two narrow alcoves between the sleep units and against the wall of the central core. It was darker inside, most lamps burned out, the few remaining so coated with dust and grease that their illumination was transformed into candle glow. Her boots clicked softly on the concrete stairs as she climbed, watching above for movement, ears straining for warning sounds, Magna drawn and ready.

The landings were occupied. Brat packs in leather huddled against the cold and watched her with sullen eyes. A New Universal Catholic zealot offered her potential salvation. Something in a box growled in a low, throaty whisper as she passed.

The hallway was empty. She pushed the door open and left the stairwell silently.

The lock on the door was thirty years outdated. Veta marveled that it still functioned, technology so far beyond its limits as to make the lock a formality. Three attempts and she'd broken the code. The door slid open with a squeal of tortured rollers on bare metal.

The apartment was a three-room prison with salvaged furniture: a sofa with broken springs and torn upholstery the color of old feces, two mismatched lamps of black plastic, and a folding cafeteria table. The place smelled like an old trunk opened for the first time in years. The glitter of the city bled through grime-streaked windows.

As she had expected, Petski wasn't home.

The bedroom was small, the bed a foam pad on the floor. The sheets were dirty and mottled, like the skin of some reptile. Holographic porn posters lined the walls, a seated woman spreading her legs as Veta passed. She missed Rocco's laughter, and the searing, caustic remarks Rocco would have made on the condition of the matted carpeting or the semen stains on the mattress. Anger burned.

Somewhere in the back of her brain, instinct kicked in and she went to the closet. It was nearly empty, except for two uniforms, a brace of wrinkled shirts, a fading Levi's jacket, and some leathers. Rifling the pockets produced a handful of litter. A crumpled Comfort blaster. Several credit slips. And what she was looking for—half a dozen markers from a place called The Blue Note.

She found the address through the compline, under the polite listing of *Taverns*.

Mean streets. The center of the war zone. Just the place where a ferret like Petski would crawl to lick his wounds.

The bar was on the corner. A flickering sign, blue letters stenciled on an opaque background, glowed dimly in the gathering twilight. Stairs descended, metal banisters like the tracks of a subterranean railroad. The windows at street level were so caked with filth as to appear cut from waxed paper, reducing light and movement to shadowed silhouettes.

Surveying the territory, Veta looked for a place to crash with a clear view of The Blue Note. Most of the buildings were moldering apartments and tenement houses, rotting arcologies. Soot stained the façades, black streaks on dull paint. Tattered pieces of paper and fabric fluttered from a few of the broken windows. These were not the type of streets holoed by the chamber of commerce for recruiting advertisements.

Movement attracted her attention. In the sky directly overhead, the delta shape of a wing coiled down like a spinning maple seed. Air strained against the carbon-reinforced nylon, the color of night and as silent as a shadow. There were no light strips on the lift surface to allow for dark flights. The power plant was inaudible, though the blades were spinning. The pilot pulled out of the dive a dozen meters off the deck of a neighboring building and set it down as gracefully as a falling leaf. Private courier or smuggler, Veta thought. Transportation outside of legal channels. He was no threat to her, just another symbol of urban decay.

A rundown hotel squatted on the opposite corner. Once the place might have catered to wealthy colonists and prospective corporate types awaiting arrangements for proper housing. It had been stately once, perhaps even stunning, but the years had not been kind. Bare metal showed in the window frames. Half the outside light fixtures were broken shards. A handwritten sign hung from the punctured remains of the marquee. *Daily rates available.* One tired male prostitute leaned against the doorway trying to stay out of the cold.

Inside, the hotel smelled like a urinal. The prostitute fluttered his lashes and turned on his smile. Veta brushed past him without a word.

The counter was long, made of dark wood scarred and etched with names and comm numbers. A clerk moved out from a back room. Stick thin and jaundiced, he wore a ragged jester's outfit left over from Langen Nacht. Bells jingled as he approached.

"Help ya?" His bored voice was like a mechanical rote.

"One room." She displayed her credit card, a square of platinum always met with quick smiles and raised eyebrows, and followed by open doors and premium service. "Second floor. Facing the street. Directly over the entrance."

He glanced over his shoulder at the occupancy board. "Sorry. Occupied."

"Make some arrangements."

While bells rang, the man took the card and slid it into an ancient credit monitor. The approval bleat was almost instantaneous. "Cost you extra," he said through a mercenary smile.

"Whatever it takes."

He motioned to a bank of chairs against the lobby wall, a wilting palm between them, red leather cracked and seamed. "You can wait over there."

Veta sat and ignored the gigolo hovering around her like a fly on a bloated carcass.

* * *

She took the room in at a glance: a bed, a dresser, and a square shape of brighter blue on the faded wall where a picture had once been hung. Through the open door to the bathroom she saw rust-stained fixtures.

A corner window opened on a wide segment of the street. Dawn was rising fast, a pale salmon sky above the jagged plateau of the city. The flickering cobalt musical note on the bar's sign lost its luster in the growing light.

On the top of the nightstand, Veta took a brief inventory of her war chest. One Spencer Magna in a breakaway shoulder holster. Three clips—twenty-seven rounds plus five already in the pistol. She had done battle with less. In her belt emergency kit were three magnesium blinders, one small gas grenade, and the pair of Shintu crickets. A meager bag of tricks, but enough in the right situation. The secret was choosing the proper moment.

Veta idly picked up one of the Shintus, three centimeters of brown plastic with gossamer wings that flicked out when she touched a contact. The single-chip brain had enough capacity to lock on a line-of-sight target, and the power pack gave it a flight range of a hundred meters. Lock it in and let it go. Then programming would take over, instructing the device to seek, conceal, and attach to the target. The tracking signal had a fifty-klick radius. In the name of aesthetics, some Japanese designer had shaped it like a cricket, complete with plastic legs and fine antennae. A lucky cricket. She needed all the luck she could get.

Petski had to sell the pilot. If he was in The Blue Note, anyone wanting to deal for the jockey would have to make an appearance at the bar. The sharks were no doubt already circling. If she could wait, there was a chance to take them all out at once, the pilot, the buyer, and the traitor.

Rage killed; that was a rule of the trade. Anger caused otherwise rational operatives to make stupid mistakes. She never tolerated it in her hirelings. Crouching by the window, her eyes drawn to the front of The Blue Note, Veta felt the rage pumping through her like a drug, cranking up her systems, screwing with her rational processes. Reason said she should go back to safe territory and regroup. But in her mind she kept hearing the soft music of Rocco's laughter and seeing the bloody rags of her hair on the paving.

"You're crazy," she heard Rocco saying, her voice carrying across a gulf of years.

The office on Mars was on the plain, Mons Olympus rising like a wedge in the distance, a ruddy pyramid still catching the evening fire of the sun, gleaming through the darkened lenses of the picture windows. Two leather bags lay like stones in her path as she entered the doorway. Rocco was standing on the threshold of the bedroom holding a third. Her face was very pale.

"You're walking away from more credit than you'll see in your lifetime. Which of us is really insane?"

"Damn it!" Rocco twisted a strand of her red hair back into the thick braid and tossed it over her shoulder. "I was hoping to be gone by the time you returned. You'll find a message on the comm. I'd rather let it explain."

"What's this all about?"

"My God, Veta." Her lips trembled. "You really don't know? You broke his neck." She shuddered.

"He wasn't supposed to be in the office. That was your screwup."

"Don't lay this on me."

"Terminations are part of the job." Veta shrugged.

"I was there. I saw your face, Veta. Pure orgasm. That scares the hell out of me."

"Roc—"

"Don't." The woman swallowed hard, her hand rubbing nervously across the nap on the back of the velour sofa, leaving darker prints on the cobalt blue. "You're going to tell me to forget it. Don't think I haven't run this scenario through my head a few hundred times. I'm an operations specialist, remember?" She managed a weak smile. "I don't want to be without you. It hurts bad, Veta. Worse than anything. But I can't stay. I just can't." She rearranged the bag on her shoulder, moving over to collect the two others. "I hope you understand."

"So what are your plans?"

"Low-level work, divorce proceedings and insurance recovery."

"You'll do okay."

"Yeah. I had a great teacher. I'll call when I'm situated. Let you know where I am."

"Sure. What about your percentage of the profits?"

Tears filled her eyes. "You don't owe me anything."

She was wrong.

One last job, one last call to Rocco for her help. An easy smash-and-grab, slip in and terminate a pilot convicted of murder. Veta still heard the hesitation in the woman's voice as she agreed. Guilt twisted deep inside her, a living thing trembling and spasming.

She stood and walked toward the dirty glass. Outside, the brief day was flickering to brilliance, a moment of light before the long shadows of winter stretched back across the streets of Delphi. She turned her gaze down toward the bar. The row of windows below the street were draped and dark. A flicker of lampglow caught her attention, gold illumination behind a drawn curtain pulled back by a pale hand.

A face pressed against the smeared pane: black beard, pitted cheeks, and coal-black eyes.

No mistake.

Petski.

Chapter 22

Still scowling, Sister Gemini led them down to dinner.

The commissary was an old vault, a pocket where the vein must have spread and the miners hollowed out a cavern from the rock. Arches of ribbed stone curved above them, scored by the teeth of boring machines, loose areas coated with lighter patches of a carbon-laced sealant. Five tunnels entered at various angles. The lighting was lashed to the central supports. Plastic, layering the floor to control the dust, crackled under their feet.

Rolen thought of Thor's Belt, its central chambers superimposed on this place, an odd juxtaposition of memory and reality. He half expected familiar shouts and Illana holding a place for him at one of the tables.

There were no familiar faces. A scattering of corpses occupied the makeshift tables fashioned from slabs of aluminum paneling sawhorsed across packing crates.

The food was pungent, a rich brown gravy that coated his mouth with grease, and lumps of unknown vegetables. He chewed slowly and longed for the bland predictability of ship food. His stomach rumbled and churned.

Insanity: being in this hole in the ground, buried alive with convicts and criminals under the direction of a half-human lunatic intent on revolution. Madness, he concluded. He picked at his food and muttered softly under his breath.

"What's that?" Carta paused, her fork raised.

He shook his head and stared at his plate. "Nothing." He pushed around a lump of something yellow. "Just wondering how it all tracks. What programs somebody like him?"

"Vasquez?" Carta asked.

He nodded and chewed.

Sister Gemini presented a carnivorous smile, teeth pointed and gleaming. "Hate," she hissed. "Hate and . . . love." Her voice was sibilant and soft, a musical whisper, and after a while, his meal forgotten, Rolen laid down his fork and listened . . .

He might have been a priest in the reconstructed Universal Catholic faith, Father Antonio Vasquez, or he might have been a drifter who assumed the collar for other purposes and somewhere along the line found a conscience worthy of a cleric. Either way, the order provided him with a platform from which to fan a spark of moral outrage into a roaring conflagration threatening the existence of the corpseman system. His tongue was golden, and when he mounted the pulpit he gained immediate attention, not all of it benign.

The High Council knew how to handle discontent. Long years of rule had exposed them to most of the manifestations of social reform. They knew when to listen and when to act. Father Vasquez was identified as a potential source of trouble and steps were taken, subtle actions that had yielded desired results in the past. A few well-placed bits of evidence, a financed list of acceptable witnesses, and the patron saint of corpsemen went down on a smuggling charge. The deaders' new mouthpiece joined them in their iniquity.

Down in the depths of the mines, he was assigned to a blasting crew and the dangerous, gritty work of loading charges into the stope face.

Though they had drained the color from his skin and taken his hair, they had not destroyed his voice. He still spoke. The corpses listened. Word reached the High Council. They asked that he be silenced, surreptitiously, in an accident, where he might die a miner instead of a martyr.

One of the survivors recounted later how the mining collar had come down on Vasquez as he left the lift cage, a sturdy beam that had held for two dozen years suddenly collapsing without warning. His crushed leg was replaced by a steel construct. There was no need to waste cloned tissue on a corpse. He limped, but retained his resonant voice.

A rock blast caught him sixteen months later, a week after he had organized a work stoppage on his crew to demand more machinery and better rations. Two days passed before a search party was dispatched to locate survivors, and that only as an effort to appease the striking corpses who had refused to eat or work until the corporation acted. More steel replaced his left arm.

Still he had not learned the value of silence.

Nine months of recuperation and he was back in the mines. It had become a duel of honor. Vasquez was now a symbol, and the High Council knew they had to avoid killing him. Death would make him more powerful than ever. But impugning his reputation might consequently disarm his tongue. There was a great deal of speculation about the explosion that took a portion of his chest and neck and blinded him in the left eye. Rumors circulated of a failed suicide attempt, his sense of honor and outrage so skewed by his life that he saw his only opportunity for change in the ashes of his funeral pyre. The Council put him back together, half man and half constructed being—an example for the rest of the slave population.

Shortly after he returned to the holes, Antonio Vasquez walked away from a stope face at shift end and vanished into the old mines. His disappearance seemed a blessing to the High Council, a silent ending to a difficult problem. The news was low-key and small-print. But six months later, strikes began to cripple the mines with startling regularity . . .

"He found some friends," Sister Gemini said, spooning up another mouthful of the stew and shoveling it in between words. "We got the dream. We're gonna take their hate and use it against them. Nobody can stop us. Not with fire or force. Nobody, my children."

At the entrance to their chamber their guide stopped, bowed, and made a dramatic wave of her arm. "Here you are, children. Facilities and blankets. What else could you require?" She gave him a mocking grin and rolled her shoulders in a disarming shrug. "If there is anything, you have but to call. I'm down to the other side there." She pointed toward a distant opening, a dark shape beyond the clear gleam of the nearest light. "I shall be listening."

"Or guarding?"

Her laughter was a deep resonance in her chest. She snaked out one foot and prodded a patch of dust, her sandal hooking against a concealed wire. A mechanism twanged and clattered, and they felt a rush of air as the overhead beam swung down in a chopping arc, just clearing the floor of the tunnel and slamming against the far wall. "No need for guards. There is complete freedom here. Only place a corpse can really be free." Her biceps bulged as she grasped the wood and hinged it back into place, resetting the hidden mechanism jammed into a crevice in the stone. Her eyes gleamed as she looked back at him. "Only thing is," she said softly, "you got to watch your step."

For a time he sat and watched the changing images on the screen, while Carta tried to repair the torn sole on one of her sandals. His sigh broke the long silence that had stretched between them.

"Something?" she asked, looking up from the task.

He shrugged. "Just thinking I'd rather be anywhere but here. Shipboard. Home. Wherever."

"That's two of us."

"Back to Delphi?"

Her smile was sad. "Isaac's World."

"How'd you end up here?"

The smile vanished. "Bad form," Carta said after a moment. "Etiquette. Some questions aren't asked. The past is a deader's private domain."

He felt his face flush brightly, blood warm in his cheeks. "Sorry."

Carta met his eyes, her lips tight. "No problem. Partly my fault. Forgot you're not local. Me, I guess I don't know much about pilots either." She looked back at the sandal. "Prostitution. That's what the court records say . . . I was a prostitute."

He had a sudden vision of a room with green carpet and a rumpled bed, and blood oozing from the rainbow lips of Miras Magana. He closed his eyes tightly but could not escape the images. Sitting near her, Rolen unfolded the blanket and draped it over his shoulders to cloak the sharp edges of the rock.

The woman stabbed a stitch through the fabric of the shoe and pulled it tight. "Only real crime was poverty." She held her voice at a whisper, part breath and the very slightest part sound. "Economics. My father was dead. Mother had her habits. Any idea what a twelve-year-old girl is worth to a slaver?"

He didn't answer, just stared down at the floor where his fingers were making circles in the dust.

"Of course you don't. Skyboys don't think about groundlings. Don't think about corpses, just make their runs and dump cargo. Maybe send a picture of one of us back to the folks at home. 'This is a Bacchian corpse. What a quaint custom.' The disgust was thick in her words, as if she had just found worms on her dinner plate. "Don't imagine the slave system was a bad idea in the beginning. Nothing's ever shitty to start. A couple of centuries back when the colonials were organizing, they must have seen it as the most friggin' humane solution to a big problem. But then the corporations got ahold of it and things soured."

"Entropy."

She glanced at him sideways, cocking her head. Her hard-bitten expression faded. The light gave color to her skin and for a moment he was struck by the beauty of her carved profile and bow-shaped mouth.

"A law of nature," he continued. "Any system, no matter how well designed, will eventually break down. Minor items. Say in a computer, corrosion builds up in contact points, heat degrades materials. No external damage but the system eventually crashes."

"And twelve-year-old kids become commodities. I wonder how much you're worth. Bet a pilot would bring a helluva price." She closed her eyes. When Rolen stared closely, he thought he could see the outlines of her pupils beneath her lids. "Anyway, price doesn't matter. One day I'm on Isaac's World, doing what kids will do, going to school, dodging trouble. The next day, I'm on a Guild freighter bound for Bacchus." Her laugh was dry, bordering on hysteria. "You know what the last thing she said to me was?" Shoulders shaking, Carta inhaled deeply. " 'Be a good girl. Do what you're told.' "

Somewhere in midlaugh, tears appeared, forming slick paths on her cheeks, glossy against the transparency of her skin. She bit her lip and stared at him through the moisture in her eyes. "Pretty funny, huh?"

"Sorry," Rolen answered, as if it were necessary to vindicate himself. Or maybe apologize for some other pilot. Had he hauled similar cargo? There was no telling. He had never paid much attention to groundling transport. No codes. No reason to be involved.

"What the hell for, jock? Wasn't your problem then. But that's changed, hasn't it?"

"Yeah." Rolen held up his hand to the light, studying alien fingers, bones wrapped in the cellophane of his new skin, gleaming and plastic, fluid moving in the muscle tissue. He still felt the weight of something in his hand, a phantom presence—a knife. It made him cringe. "I didn't kill her."

"Doesn't matter."

"It's important." He swallowed a lump, turned, and glared at her fiercely. "To me. Don't you see? I couldn't do that . . . killing. No excuse for physical violence. No reason to kill."

"What if it's the only way to get back to your ship?" She

wiped angrily at her eyes as if they had betrayed her. "You'd do it then. I would. Betcha money you'd snuff somebody. Just got to get mad enough."

He was silent, clenching his jaw. The muscles were sore from chewing groundling food, and from the tug of gravity.

"Economics, pilot. What're you willing to pay?"

"Leave it."

"Truth, isn't it? Do *anything* to clear atmosphere from this rock. That's what you told Vasquez."

He shook his head, confused and bewildered. "What do you want me to say? That I'd kill to get home? You want me to admit I'm as much an animal as Petski? As whoever it was who offed that woman?" There was so much pain in him he couldn't think. "Why are you badgering me?"

"Because," she replied, her voice breaking, all the emotions she'd been keeping pent up for years suddenly coming to the surface, "if you make it back to your ship, you can leave. You've got an exit. That's the difference between you and me, you and any corpse on Bacchus. You can walk away. Make it to your ship and you're clear." A tremor wracked her. "Don't you understand, you dumb bastard? It's what we've all dreamed about, the one thing we've stayed alive for—the possibility of somehow escaping from this shit hole. Me. Sister Gemini. Vasquez. Every damn one of us." Carta buried her face in her hands.

Awkwardly, Rolen touched her shoulders and felt the muscles trembling beneath her shirt, knotted and tight. Her emotions seemed to surge up his arms, like shocks from a charged cable. He slid his hand down to the small of her back, pulled her close, her body shaking against him. He was reacting to long-dormant instincts, some fiber of humanity he had not completely subjugated to his desire to become a pilot, something not killed by time and ambition.

"Christ," she sobbed. "Don't you see? That's why I helped you. That's why I stuck my neck out for somebody for the first time in ten years. You got something magical. And I thought maybe, just maybe, I'd get caught up in it and be sucked along in your draft when you blew clear. Find some way free. Because you've got a chance!"

"Slim," he said, mocking Petski's rasping voice. "Slim and none."

"It's not funny, damn you!"

"All right." He held the woman tightly, rocking back and forth. "I promise you, if I get off this rock, you're coming with me."

She pressed her face against his shoulder. Her tears were hot and wet through his shirt. And somewhere in the middle of comforting her, rage was transformed, became understanding, became need, and then passion. Her lips brushed his cheek with fire. His hands moved of their own accord, seeking and finding, pushing away the hurt and replacing it with a more basic sensation. No thinking now. No need for input or control. His mind was reduced to a single task center, a basic unit, functioning automatically. Thrust and clutch and hold, shuddering with bestial intensity.

There was a certain peace in being animals.

Later, her sleeping warmth and the soft susurration of her breathing consoled him. He lay for a long time, listening to the distant hum of activity in the warrens, the sounds of the corpses gearing up for battle. Vague and unreal.

Lagging, he realized. That's all he had done up to this point. He'd been cut free and was drifting without power or motivation. His eyes were drawn to the computer screen, the green-and-black display an odd anomaly against the concave stone of the far wall. The wand of logic swept across the face, transforming its path into a pattern of ebony and emerald, rewoven with each pass, dull and hypnotic. The tangled length of cable, snarled against the wall, cast the shadow of an abstract sculpture.

Anger fed him now, flooding him with impulses, filling up his mind with the pure bliss of rage. He had been living behind a barrier, a wall erected by the last twelve years of his life, created by the plastic and insulation of the ships' bridges he occupied. Don't like the temp—simply think up a new one. Different chow—no problem. Any small irritation vanished with a single thought. Complacency was as deadly as a gun. Rolen saw that now, recognizing it for the first time in years.

He felt cold, cool anger—the emotion that could make things happen. He raised his hand and stared at the flesh. It was different, alien. But it was still his hand. The transformation was permanent. He'd get used to the new color. But he'd never get used to life in a gravity well. It was simply not in him to adjust to the life she lived. Impossible.

That narrowed his choices: death or escape. Either way, no more lagging. Computer feed or not, time had come for action. Carta was right, he thought with bitter understanding. The *Trojan Horse* waited. Whatever it took to get back to her was justified.

He had hope, and that made him all the more dangerous.

Chapter 23

Day came and went in minutes, a wave of light, an arc of sun on the distant horizon, and then the long fingers of rose twilight again grasped at the purple sky, tinting the clouds.

Jaleem sat at the table, drinking thick, rich coffee. Oils shimmered on the surface of the murky liquid. He stared out at the panorama beyond the window without really seeing.

A knock came at the door. He muttered a response. Har Vogel appeared, his party attire gone, replaced by somber tones, dark jeans and a heavy jacket against the cold. The man was calmer now, settled into the routine and ready for the next step. The light caught his damaged eye and made the slit cornea seem to flow and ooze.

"What is it?" Jaleem raised the cup slowly to his lips, studying the man over the brim.

"Contact." Vogel adjusted his jacket. The butt of a buzz-gun peeped from the shoulder holster under his thick arm. "A reliable source. We've found the guard, Petski. He wants a meet. To discuss some business."

"When?"

"Thirty minutes. A bar called The Blue Note. I've already got it staked."

Jaleem drained the cup and stood, smoothing the wrin-

kles in his suit, touching the bulge of his Spencer, feeling
the hilt of his knife, and flexing his hand to arm the fragmenter. The moves were automatic, the closest he came to
a nervous tic. "Let's go."

Downtown was where the used and discarded went to
die. The narrow streets were choked with punks in leathers,
chain gangs swaggering, their silver links making threatening music, and derelicts sagging against the walls like infectious eruptions on the skin of the buildings, waiting to
be reabsorbed into the gray surfaces. This sector had a different feel than the slums of the Zone. Here, the despair
was more acute because the poor remembered what they
had lost.

The stretch flattened out most of the holes in the pocked
paving, whirling up a fog of litter and snow. Jaleem saw the
city reflected in the glossy black paint on the front panels,
a thin skin of dust settling on the net mesh of the apron,
the bag bulging and rippling as they slid along.

Akira had not been pleased.

The man did not like delays and was angered by the intricate maneuvers now required to regain what he had already considered to be his property. His obsession was a
thing beyond reason.

Jaleem's reassurances had stalled reaction for a time, but
he was walking the edge. Jaleem was certain that another
failure would bring the blade biting deep, cutting him away
from the corporation. It was enough to make a man tense,
if he were weak, if he could not think clearly. He had to
take one step at a time—action and reaction. He glanced at
Vogel, wondering if perhaps similar thoughts circled through
the man's head, and then turned back to the street.

The Blue Note sign gleamed cool azure in the dark.

As the hover door hissed open Jaleem stepped out, un-
folding from the interior while scanning the street for ambush. One of Vogel's operatives raised a hand from across

the roadway. Another gave him a brief nod from a doorway two addresses down. Jaleem turned his attention to Vogel.

"Wait," he ordered.

Vogel raised one eyebrow. "What if there's trouble?"

"Won't be." Stepping back, Jaleem allowed the door to seal, black sheen reflecting back his slender form and the metallic shimmer of the threads in his suit, a lightweight body armor woven into the fabric, capable of stopping a standard load or slowing down a blade. He straightened the lapel as he stepped down the stairs to the door.

The atmosphere was close inside, smoky and dim. The lights had the soft yellow glow of gas lanterns. A bar stretched the length of the right side, countertop the dull gloss of cheap plastic and printed with a wood-grain veneer. The place was a split-level, the first holding a scattering of small tables and the second elevation reserved for booths. The decor was done in dark tones: earth and wood, blacks, greens, and browns. Corba smoke hung in a thin layer, twisting as barmaids moved through an equally thin crowd. Eyes followed him silently.

Glancing at the mirror behind the bar, he saw only the legs of the single bartender reflected in the glass and the handle of a shattergun exposed on one of the shelves. A few grunts sat at a gaming table to the left; hired muscle, they were drinking and slapping the contact panels languidly, but he could see the nerves in their eyes, waiting for him to make a wrong move. The rear of the place was too close, not as deep as the building appeared outside, hiding rooms and who knew what else. He scanned for firing blinds and found two possible locations.

The bartender caught his eye. The man was short, stocky, his hair a grizzled mass of gray and black. Without speaking, the man nodded toward a back booth. Jaleem returned his tight smile.

He went up the stairs slowly, his movements fluid. Jaleem kept his hand close to the bulge of his Spencer, left arm angled up where the fragmenter could be brought to play with a flick of one wrist. Despite the setbacks, he was aware and alive, prepared. The meeting was within his realm of experience, and he knew he could handle any contingency during the next fifteen or twenty minutes.

There was no light directly over the booth, but rather off to each side so that the table was almost in shadow. This was the booth he would have chosen if it were his meeting— a place where a person could sit and watch the rest of the tavern, with no glare to distract or blind. In the shadows one could hide a weapon, appear relaxed and quiet, yet raise and fire before someone in the light could react. A killer's place. He grinned appreciatively.

"You the buyer?" The voice was dry, nervous, the words slightly rushed.

He stood over the table, looking down at the man silhouetted before him. He saw a slight figure and a thin face with blunted features as if the sculptor had been called away in midswing and never returned. "Depends. What's for sale?"

"One-of-a-kind items." The rasp from the shadows might have been a laugh, or perhaps a gasp of pain. "Name's Petski." With one foot, he shoved the chair out before Jaleem. "And you're—"

"The buyer." Jaleem sat down slowly. The changing angle brought the man's face into view. A dark beard hid most of his pitted, cadaverous cheeks. His eyes were small, set in a pair of yellowing bruises. One shoulder bulged unnaturally as if hiding a wad of cloth, or a bandage. He favored it visibly when he moved. Jaleem filed these mental notes quickly, planning out his movements if the meet should go bad: lunge forward and jam a fist into the wound; blow the man away with the fragmenter against his face; head for the doorway into the back. Breaking for their turf would be unexpected, give him a few extra seconds, all he would need. He settled into the chair.

"You alone?" Petski asked.

"Think I'm that stupid?"

Petski rubbed the side of his nose reflexively. His nostrils were unnaturally dilated, a telltale sign of blaster use. His breath was sweet. "Something to drink?"

Abbasi shook his head slowly, keeping his eyes on the man's face. "You have something of mine."

"I've got something. For friggin' sure about that. But whose it is hasn't been decided yet."

"Mine," Jaleem repeated. "Any idea the trouble you've caused me? You don't want to create more problems."

"Business. Supply and demand." The man leaned forward, straining to smile and appear nonchalant. "I took a big risk. Deserve something for my trouble. If I didn't step in, then the pilot would be history and where would you be?"

There was a moment's pause as Jaleem reflected. "Granted." He scanned the room. No one had moved. The few drinkers had returned to their cups. The muscle had gotten involved in the electronic diversion that the game table offered. "Just how much was that risk worth? How much do I owe you for being a concerned citizen?"

"Half a million standard credits."

Jaleem chuckled softly. "I should kill you right now."

"And transport offplanet."

"More?"

The man licked his lips, a red slash in the dark curls of his beard. "That's all."

"Far too much. There are other pilots."

"Look." Petski sucked air through his nostrils, making a liquid sound, blood somewhere back in his throat. "I know who I'm dealing with. I know the operation. I was part of it—from the other side. Now, you got a mess of capital involved here. An investment. You can't walk away from it. No profit in that, is there?"

"Sometimes cutting losses has its merit."

"Cut the crap. You buying or not? Otherwise, I got other people to call. Lots of interest in this item."

"Not if you're dead." He stroked the thin fringe of his beard.

Petski's hand trembled slightly as he lifted his glass. He struggled to control it and managed to swallow a mouthful. "Then my partners sell him. And he doesn't go your way. Leaves you explaining things to your superiors. How you screwed up. Not the way I want the deal cut, but not the way you want it either. Right?"

"I'll have to see the merchandise first."

The man glanced down at the table, studying his hands. Something was wrong; Jaleem sensed it. He moved his arm, bringing his fingers closer to the butt of his Spencer, a subtle gesture, covering its intent by straightening his sleeve with the hand.

"You do have the pilot, don't you?"

"Got to take my word on that."

"Don't screw with me, Petski. I want to see him."

Petski regarded him hesitantly. Fear was painted on his features. The jaundiced whites of his eyes seemed suddenly large. He flexed his hands, working his mouth soundlessly for a moment as if trying several openings. Nerves. Bad nerves. Jaleem grew uneasy, drawing his fingertips within centimeters of his gun.

"It's like this," Petski said slowly, "I don't exactly have him—"

Jaleem lunged, driving the wedge of his fingers into Petski's injured shoulder. The table tipped back and pinned the man to the wall of the booth. Jaleem snapped him into the vinyl cushions, slamming his fragmenter-armed hand into the man's forehead while drawing his Spencer with the other. Petski was a heartbeat away from dying; all it would take would be a simple flex of his wrist. The muscle was caught by surprise, three of them sitting dull and stupid at the gaming table, frozen for an instant. One instant too long.

"No!" Petski screamed. "Lemme explain! Lemme friggin' explain."

"Answers. Now!"

Petski's face was ashen white; he squirmed to shift his head but Jaleem only pressed harder. "Okay—okay," he blurted. "Listen. I don't have the man. But I can tell you where to find him. You got no idea now. No location. Might never find him without me."

Jaleem twisted his palm, letting the metal tube hidden under the plastic flesh grind into the man's skull. Petski's pupils were pinholes. Sweat beaded his forehead. Somewhere a clock was ticking. Ice shifted in a glass. They heard a slight cough, stifled for safety.

"Dead, I can't tell you anything."

Jaleem released Petski's head. Slowly, he eased back into his chair, still holding the Magna.

Petski swallowed and pushed the table back into position. His hands were shaking badly. He looked as if he might be sick at any moment. He lifted the empty glass before him and tried to find a few remaining drops of liquor. Finally, he placed it on the table between them like a shield, a glass wall.

"Figured you'd be reasonable." He sounded a lot more cool than he looked. "I'm gonna reach into my pocket now. Don't get nervous. No weapons. Something I want to show you."

The man stared at the Magna as he slid his hand into his coat and pulled out a small black cylinder, a holograph projector. He placed it on the table between them, thumbed a stud, and activated the picture. A schematic drawing, three-dimensional, sketched in red and yellow lines, rose before him, thirty centimeters of abstract slashes. It took Jaleem a moment to identify the odd configuration of a mine shaft, central column in yellow, ancillary passages branching off in red vectors. Petski lit a corba stick and blew smoke through the image, blurring the lines slightly.

"Skyking has gone to ground," he said. "This is what you get for the price." A nod toward the holo. "Interior diagram of the mine, so you can plan the run. The exact location after I'm safely away."

Jaleem raised the Magna a millimeter, just to remind the man of its presence. "I could kill you. Take the projector."

"Well." He swallowed hard. "You could. But there's no ident code on this recording. So you'd have to sort through about ten thousand registry sheets to match it up and get the location." The man managed a sly smile. "Figure that takes about a week. Meantime, the pilot might move on. Be easier to pay me. Consider it a business expense."

"You'll give me the right location?"

Petski laughed. "Hey, if I don't, I'll be looking over my shoulder for the rest of my days."

"Better do that anyway."

He shrugged and sucked another drag from the butt. "The risk you take."

"No deal."

"I sell to someone else."

It was Jaleem's turn to smile. "My terms right now—or you're dead."

The man whitened still further. "Wouldn't ever get out of here. This is my turf."

"Your friends at the game? I'll take my chances. But you go first."

"Hey," Petski said, stubbing out the butt. His hands shook as he dug for another stick. "Negotiation's part of business. Name your terms."

"You lead me to him. Payment on recovery."

Petski looked down at the table, then up to the ceiling as if invoking a higher deity. "Then what guarantee have I got? What assurances?" He took a deep breath and met Jaleem's gaze.

"The risk you take." Standing, Jaleem shrugged and laughed. "Take me to him. We might do business. Otherwise, you're wasting my time." He still had the pistol leveled, and glanced peripherally at the muscle. Their game was forgotten, but they weren't handling their weapons either, just waiting and watching. They were not supposed to keep Petski alive, he suddenly realized. They were somebody else's grunts, probably the bar owner's, standing down to keep the peace.

"Look at it this way," Jaleem continued. "If I kill you, I've gained nothing. But I'm still alive. An enviably better position than yours. Who knows, your partners might make an offer."

It took Petski a few seconds to decide, as if death might have been a viable option, but in the end he conceded. "All right. Your way, jock. You name it." He lowered his eyes.

"Excellent." Jaleem nodded. "There are arrangements to be made, supplies to gather. I'll return in two hours. Be ready.'' He turned and moved away from the booth, keeping his eyes on the grunts.

"One other thing,'' he called back over his shoulder as he was heading down the steps and across the floor, weaving between the tables. "You're safe in here. But don't go out on the streets. Never know who might be waiting for you.'' He pulled open the door, and a blast of cold air swirled in with the darkness.

Halfway up the outside stairs, Jaleem paused. The banister was cold in his hand. He heard the hover idling, felt the warm blast from beneath the airbag. Overhead, a few stars were visible in the crevice of sky between the roofs. Through the greasy windows of the bar, he saw Petski seated at the booth. The man had his head buried in his hands.

"Well?'' Vogel pursed his lips.

"He's in an abandoned mine.''

"Then the rogues have him. Not good.''

Jaleem raised one eyebrow.

"Be futile to go after him. They know the mines too well. Better to stay on the surface. Wait him out. Security will find him eventually.''

"Can't wait.''

The man shrugged. "It's your funeral.''

"No. It's ours.''

Chapter 24

"Ah, pilot." Vasquez looked up from a printout, a tired smile on the flesh side of his face.

He waved Rolen into his private chamber, where there was less chance of being disturbed. The cavern was simply furnished with an olive-drab cot, a desk fashioned from an old door supported by twin stacks of plastic crates, and a portable mechanic's lamp providing light. A display screen rested on one corner, its keyboard the color of old bones. Heavy blue plastic covered the floor, wrinkled, creased, and marred with streaks of soil.

"Again, I find myself apologizing for delays." He straightened the papers, his movement with the waldoes surprisingly deft. His human eye met Rolen's gaze. The sensor in the opposite socket sparkled. "However, I'm sure you'll forgive me any inconvenience. You were, after all, the subject of discussion. Your disposition caused a lengthy debate among my advisers. The motion to turn you over to Security almost passed, but in the end, cooler heads prevailed."

"Yours?" Rolen asked, settling onto a folding chair.

A self-deprecating grin was his only answer. "It may be possible to return you to your ship. But there's a price."

"Can't pay anything now," Rolen replied. "But the Guild and Zenyam are probably offering a reward."

"Oh, yes. A most generous sum." The man rested his chin on his good hand. The shadow from the lamp made his scar appear to be a centimeter-wide fissure in his face. "For your head on a platter."

"Wanna run that by me slowly?"

"Well, we don't have the full story either, just bits and pieces. There's an advantage in having one's spies employed in most of the offices on Bacchus, but slaves can't ask too many questions." He cocked his head, the plastic flesh on his neck folding under and layering. "From the rumors we've gathered, it seems there was an attempt to break the Guild monopoly by a corporate raider named Akira. He needed a weakness, some pressure point the Guild couldn't protect. That's where you came in."

"Akira? Name means nothing."

"Akira didn't want you specifically. He wanted the hardware in your skull. You, my friend, were in the proverbial wrong place at the wrong time. Though why they didn't just kill you and take it is beyond me."

"Can't." Rolen managed a grimace. "The Guild has taken steps to protect its investment. They got the right to jerk the implant from any pilot who tries to quit the Guild. Removal leaves the pilot partially brain-dead, so nobody voluntarily walks. Anybody trying to grab it by force would get junk. The unit has a self-destruct mechanism tied to the brainwaves. They cease and it blows. And the few pilots who've tried to go rogue have all ended up terminal."

Vasquez nodded. "That fills in a few missing pieces. Akira apparently chose Bacchus for the operation to take advantage of the legal system. If it had worked as planned, he'd own a pilot by now, and any attempts by the Guild to exercise their hardware-retrieval rights would be snarled in the Bacchus judiciary."

Rolen's mind was racing, trying to assimilate the sudden flood of data. "Then I was set up," he said fiercely.

"It appears so. If you did kill the woman, it was very convenient." The sterling smile returned. "Either way, you presented the opportunity and Akira took it. The Guild couldn't get you off Bacchus because Akira had already purchased a number of Judicial Council members. So they took the next logical option—sent someone in to kill you. It should have gone smoothly but, luckily for you, something went very wrong."

He ran his finger down the edge of the computer printout, aligning a microscopic deviation. "It's bad for everyone else—Akira, the Guild, Zenyam, even Bacchus. The High Council is suddenly facing an embargo from the Guild if they don't turn you over. Akira is exerting some major economic pressure of his own. If he pulls out, a large number of local corporations would be left swinging. Consequently, Bacchus is leaving no stone unturned searching for you. And the problems are all due to the intervention of one small operator."

"Petski."

"Exactly." Vasquez paused to dab a bead of saliva from the corner of his plastic lip. "He slipped into a system that didn't even know he existed. Petski can't possibly survive; he's probably dead already. But in an odd twist, you owe the man your life."

"He'd have sold me to the highest bidder."

"God, my friend, works in mysterious ways." Vasquez raised his good arm in a gentle shrug.

Rolen was silent. It was as if a scene he had been watching with his peripheral vision had suddenly snapped into focus. He thought of an old optical illusion he had once viewed as a child, an odd-shaped blot of ink that was an old crone or a beautiful woman depending on how one's mind initially interpreted it. He was suddenly cold. Everything had fallen into place; random factors were no longer random. Motivations were clear: Petski, the Guild's apparent silence, Zenyam's failure to appear, and even his own mysterious confession. He understood everyone now—except Antonio Vasquez.

"What do you want?"

Vasquez expelled a long breath. "Wish I could say I was going to help you out of the kindness of my heart. That's something both of us could stand to hear. But the truth is, there's a catch." He slowly stroked his upper lip with one finger, as if he were feeling for a missing mustache. "I'm going to ask you to do something for me, something for every corpse on the planet, and I want you to know what's at stake."

Rolen kept his expression neutral.

"Freedom, my friend, yours and mine. Freedom for every corpse on or under the surface of this world." Vasquez regarded him very seriously, his brow arched, his forehead wrinkling. "What do you know about Bacchus?"

"Vectors, fees, and dock approaches. Port codes." Rolen shook his head. "Things a pilot needs to know."

"Needs change." He chose his words carefully, concentration and a little madness evident in his face. "Ask a pilot about Bacchus and he'll give you flight information. Speak with a metallurgist and you'll get a litany filled with technical data on ore purity and dispersion ratios. Financial analysts know returns on investments and projected heavymetal prices based on present availability. But not one of them is probably aware that the entire planet's industry rests on the backs of half a million slaves. You see my point?"

Rolen stared at him blankly.

The man reached up to flick a bit of lint from his faceted eye, fingernail scraping across the sensor. The effect was unsettling. "The point is, as long as the system is running smoothly, no one cares. We've got to make them care."

"Won't be much sympathy for convicted felons," Rolen said, rubbing his hands together, still startled by the jewellike translucency of his flesh.

"God, you are naive. People love causes, especially emotional issues. Entire populations have supported genocide when it was properly presented." A dry laugh escaped from his throat. "We both know the crime and conviction rates on Bacchus. I'm not saying that every corpse is innocent, but a blind man could see the abuses in this system. An unbiased group needs to examine it and make some rational changes. All we have to do is to get the attention of the right people on the outside."

"And I'm the messenger?"

"In a manner of speaking." The digits of his waldoes

opened and closed slowly, creating two steel fists, as if he were pumping a bulb on some invisible device. Light glittered across the silver surfaces. "Bacchus has reached a crisis point. The civilians have no idea, but the High Council has a vague suspicion. They've been getting ready for the revolution for years. We've been conducting a battle of sorts—strikes, slowdowns, machine damage, anything we can do to express our rage without using violence. Face it, they could handle violence. They're prepared for it. But the strikes, now that's something different. It keeps them off balance and stirs up resentment in a large segment of the unemployed population."

Rolen thought of the crowd of loudly chanting corpses he had encountered in the Port, angry crowds pressing around them. "I've seen one."

"Then you know how the Council reacts. Brute force. Sometimes we lose a few people. A drastic price, worth it if changes occur, but the lack of progress is turning some of my people desperate. There's only so long a person can continue to turn the other cheek. Sooner or later they'll strike back. And when they do, it'll degenerate into a bloodbath."

For the first time, Rolen was aware of the strain in the man's face. His voice was heavy with tension. Fatigue had scored his flesh with wrinkles and lines, and a dark circle under his good eye—signs of a man who did not sleep well at night, if he slept at all.

"Think of it as a computer program, a series of conditional loops. The computer attempts each loop, but the conditions aren't correct, so it aborts that option and moves to the next command. Each abort eliminates an alternative. We're down to two, maybe three options left. The last alternative is war. Thousands of innocent people will die. I'm trying to avoid that. I need a major ally."

"The Confederation."

"You'd have made a good revolutionary." Vasquez nodded. "To get their support, we have to gain the Confederation's attention. Takes a real loud noise. Economic matters always carry major decibels. Jam the flow of product from

Bacchus, and the Confederation will come looking to see what's wrong. Same basic tactics we've been using against the Council, only on a much larger scale.''

"Why would the Confederation react any differently than the Council?''

''Because the High Council's trying to save a social institution. The Confederation won't give a damn about salvaging a system with traditional roots. One of the beauties of an organization like the Confederation is that too many planets are represented to allow any one particular aspect of an individual colony to interfere with the interests of the whole. If we can demonstrate that the High Council can't control their own soil, the Confederation will step in and do it for them.''

"Still haven't said how you get to the Confederation.''

"With something dramatic, like a complete shutdown of planetary functions.''

"That's—''

"Crazy.'' He nodded, a slow and fluid movement. "But not any crazier than enslaving a fifth of a world's population.'' The intensity of his speech gave Rolen a vision of him as he must have been in the pulpit, his eyes flashing, waving his arms for emphasis. "We're going to turn their strength against them. A tremendous portion of the Bacchus industrial complex is automated. Most of the automated equipment is controlled by a handful of central processors which organize the various demands of the transportation network, the mines, and the smelters, and choreograph the distribution of manpower and resources to meet those needs. The planet runs like a mechanical timepiece, each cog and gear dependent on the others, each movement affecting the whole machine. Beautiful and sensitive. We're going to throw some grit into the works.'' The man shifted position, hydraulics whining faintly with the gentle pop and hiss of pressure surges. "I'm asking you to provide some of the sand.''

"How?'' Rolen asked warily.

"If you wanted to dump a ship, stall it permanently, how would you do it?''

"Crash the system."

"Well—" The flesh around his good eye wrinkled in response to a feral smile. "Bacchus is nothing more than a big freighter in a fixed flight path. That's exactly what we plan to do."

"There must be backup systems, security, defenses. Can't take it all out. Can't pull the plug on an entire network."

"We've got complete access to the systems. But we don't want to turn it off. Remember, we're attempting a bloodless revolution. If we deactivated the system, thousands would die just through the loss of emergency functions. We want to leave everything intact, using the existing emergency network to springboard the entire operation."

He picked up an infocube, square crystal, blue and innocuous, from his desktop. "Every message passing through the system has a priority code. Say there's a tunnel collapse, every instruction regarding the collapse takes priority over shift changes or other mundane jobs. By inserting a new command into the master programs, we can alter the order in which messages are received and acted upon. It's a parlor trick." The cube glittered between his stained fingers. "This contains a self-replicating command sequence. Released into the network, it scrambles the existing code system. No requests except coded emergencies get action. Shipping, mining, manufacturing—all grind to a stop. It'll take hours to debug. We have corpses in position to insert it into every network on the surface, even most of the Port computers." He tapped the cube softly with a fingernail. "A fragment of grit, pilot. And—" his voice grew soft—"in return for getting you onto your ship, I'm asking you to feed it into the docking network."

Rolen choked back a nervous laugh. "That's a felony. Port computers are Confederation property."

"Exactly." Vasquez turned his head so that only the pseudoskin and the jeweled sensor showed. He didn't look even vaguely human. "As I said before, if you want to get the Confederation's attention, you've got to use the proper incentive."

"I'd be trading one prison for another." He stood, his hands trembling.

"If it goes as planned, mitigating circumstances should gain you immunity. If it doesn't, the Confederation will extradite you to their own courts and you still wind up free of Bacchus."

"Rotting in a Confederation establishment."

"We're all risking something."

"You're a corpse," Rolen hissed, his voice quavering. "You don't have anything left to risk."

Vasquez grinned broadly, his metal teeth flashing. "Have you looked in the mirror lately?"

"So," Carta said, after she'd listened to his retelling of the conversation. "What've you decided to do?" She handed him the water bottle.

For a moment, he busied himself with taking a drink. The tepid fluid was warm, tasting of plastic, reminding him of the water on the *Trojan Horse*. "I don't know. I didn't give him an answer." He tightened the lid with a vicious twist and tossed the canteen to the blanket.

The woman tossed her head and laughed. "Wouldn't have had to ask me twice."

"Not your butt, either." Rolen stared over at the computer screen where the wand still circled, green on black. She'd never understand. Neither would Vasquez. Codes again. They were asking him to go against twelve years of conditioning.

"Look," he said, turning to face the woman. "Every ship coming in from the nexus is on automatic, following instructions beamed to them from the Port. If I punch that cube, every incoming ship gets cut loose. Leaves a lot of steel flying blind."

"No contingencies?" She regarded him carefully.

"Sure." He nodded. "But maybe some pilot is slow to react. Maybe something doesn't track. Unexpected difficulties. I mean, I always jacked out of the system and let it come in on auto. Let's say a ship punches a hole through the Port. Suddenly the revolution isn't bloodless anymore. I don't want blood on my hands.''

"Then you gotta take me along. I'll do the switch." The woman shrugged and looked away. "Means nothing to me."

"They're my people, Carta."

"Were," she said. "We've been through this before. Economics, pilot. Everything's got a price."

"Yeah," he said, and added very quietly, "So I'm learning."

Chapter 25

The stretch was back.

Night had returned to Bacchus. Dark transformed the harshness of the district, softening the edges and hiding the litter and graffiti under thick shadows. Streetlights assumed a mystic glow passing through soot and dust, wide swathes of yellow spilling down onto the paving.

Veta Pulchek watched the dark shape of the hover glide along the street, its enameled body reflecting the night shapes of Delphi like mirror shades. Hard-shelled and bulletproof meant important cargo. That it was back for a second visit in a three-hour period indicated a special interest in The Blue Note, something beyond drinks and prostitutes. Her instincts bristled as the stretch slowed before the bar, engines winding down to a soft purr as the vehicle settled onto the pavement.

The door flicked open like a beetle's wing. A man climbed out; a tall man, slender, his hair covered by a modified turban. His jacket shimmered—light armor. A weapon bulged beneath his arm. He was a man who had killed before, the type who might have killed Rocco. There was reserved strength in his fluid stride as he navigated the steps and vanished into the bar.

A buyer.

In the darkness of the room, Veta reached out and placed

her hand on the emergency kit, her fingers closing on the small bulk of a Shintu. If the transaction was taking place inside, she wanted to be able to find the buyer after she'd finished here—after Petski was dead.

She brought the sighting unit up to the windowsill and jacked the cricket into the imprinter with a length of coaxial cable. The stretch was dark green in the display. Veta sighted on the rear fan shroud and punched the stud, locking the location into the bug's memory. The window was open, permanently jammed, a ten-centimeter crack gaping. Someone had tried to plug the gap with a rag, but she had stripped it away earlier. She pushed the cricket out onto the ledge with her fingertips and depressed the activating stud.

The Shintu took a second to orient itself, antennae waving, small faceted skull pivoting until it matched the target with the image in its memory. Darting forward on plastic legs, the bug dropped off the ledge. A few seconds later, she spotted a flicker of gossamer wings against the stretch, visible only because she knew where to look.

The tracking signal was clear and strong.

She settled back into her crouch, forcing her body to stillness despite the adrenaline now flooding her system, washing out the poisons of fatigue. A sense of urgency, keen and sharp, cut through her. The waiting was almost over. She was ready, dancing on the edge.

Somewhere in the back of her skull, Len Bollinger's voice was whispering the opening lines of her eulogy.

Five minutes passed before she spotted movement in the stairwell and saw the turbaned man retracing his steps. His face was placid. Behind him, another figure appeared in the doorway.

Not the pilot, but Petski.

The door on the stretch yawned. The interior light allowed her a brief glimpse inside the vehicle. Two grunts occupied the front seat, two more sat on the center bench, and another reclined in the rear. Assault armor distorted their shapes. Three sacks of gear lay on the floor between the center bench and the back seat. A rack of buzzguns clung to the window dividing the driver and the passenger compartments.

Petski came slowly up the stairs. His head bobbed nervously, scanning the street from behind the cover of the railing. Though he was expecting major trouble, there was no chance of him spotting her position. Her room was dark and she was back far enough to be out of any reflected glare. Even so, his eyes slowly ticked off each window in the hotel. Satisfied, but still cautious, he mounted the last steps and walked out to the hover.

He was momentarily in the open, but Veta resisted the urge to shoot. Something didn't track. There was an excess of firepower in the stretch, no sign of the pilot, and as Petski climbed into the hover, his face was as white as that of a man about to be executed. Patience, she thought, easing her finger away from the trigger. Opportunity didn't always mean success. The secret was finding the right opportunity.

The door on the hover levered shut. Turbines whined. The stretch glided away from the curb.

Veta checked the signal from the Shintu. It was reading perfectly. Her first impulse was to follow in her rented hover, but she had learned long ago that initial impulses were not always the best choices. What she needed was a way to cover territory quickly and silently, a way they would not be expecting, if the stretch was anticipating pursuit at all.

She remembered a delta shape, a maple seed spinning in the wind.

Methodically, Veta strapped on her emergency kit, collected her weapons, and left the room.

The rooftop was wide and flat. Glyphs of fluorescent tape marked out the landing zone in stencils of cool green luminescence. A Day-Glo orange windsock, vaguely phallic, dangled limply from an antenna. The hangar was half of a corrugated steel pipe, cut lengthwise and anchored to the building. One wing was chained down to a strap of cable snaking along the roof. A second was a shape inside the hangar, overhead light making dull circles on the dark fabric of the lift surface. Parts were scattered in random clusters: twisted bits of frame, a cannibalized power plant, a tattered rag of nylon, struts, and cables.

She approached the hangar openly, hands at her sides. The man bending over the wing didn't seem to notice, muttering to himself as he worked with the power plant, humming a few bars of a song over and over.

"That's close enough," he said, still not looking up from his work. "Don't like people in the shop. Insurance rates and all that kinda shit."

Veta stopped just beyond the threshold, staying out of the shaft of illumination that spilled from the hangar.

The man tightened a final bolt and turned toward her, wiping at the grease on his hands with a rag. He was tall and lanky. His coveralls were too short, his calves and knobby ankles protruding from the cuffs. He was sharp-featured, and gapped teeth showed as he gave her a cagey grin. "Somethin' I can do for you?"

"Want to rent a wing."

"Place down by the shuttlefield does a fine job of that. Reasonable rates, too." He concentrated on cleaning the grime from his black-rimmed nails.

"Looking for a special type of wing."

"And what kinda bird is that?"

"Fast. Quiet. Something with no running lights. Something maybe that doesn't show up on a scanner."

He nodded sagely. "Don't expect you'd find that down to the field. Course, a bird like that might just be a man's way of makin' a livin'. Don't know that he'd be willin' to part with somethin' like that cheap. Maybe not for any price."

Veta held up her credit chip and let it flash in the light.

His gapped teeth showed again. "Could be we got somethin' to talk about after all. Gimme here." The man moved close and plucked the card from her grasp. Gliding over the tools and parts, he cleared away a spot on the bench and produced a portable credit unit. The plastic was smeared with oil and grease. He dropped the card into the slot and nodded when it beeped.

"Course you know how to handle a wing?" He glanced over his shoulder and studied her. "Yeah. Betcha can."

"How much?"

"Don't worry. I won't take it all. Not even close. Besides, you don't really give a shit about the price anyway, do you?" He took the card and flipped it toward her. Veta caught it on the fly. "And before you go drawin' your weapon and tryin' some strong-arm crap, I'd like to point out my able assistant. He's the one with the shattergun pointed at your spine."

Veta turned her head slowly, just far enough to see the outline of another man, ten meters away, shattergun a squat bulk in his arms.

"Make a real friggin' mess from that range. Know what I mean?" The wingman grinned. "Betcha do." He grabbed an ambient suit from a pile on the counter. "Put this on and I'll give you the five-minute checkout."

The wing was as dark as night. The fabric had been dyed to match the cloud cover that seemed a permanent fixture of the Bacchus sky. A bladed power plant was mounted on a tripod above the lift surface. The pilot harness draped below the delta like the coiled legs of a butterfly. The man stooped and unclipped the landing chain.

"These are the controls," he said, running his finger across a row of contacts clustered at each end of the control bar, where her hands would rest. "Power on right. Leg cable release and retraction on the left. Don't forget those, less you want to land on your gut." He laughed dryly. "This is the jammer." The man patted an electrical box affixed to the upper crossbar. "Don't leave any signature at all. Never see you comin'."

"Any weapons?"

"Courier wing, lady. Ain't no friggin' gunship." His gapped teeth were green in the dim light. "In my line of work, can't afford the weight of arms. Weight is for cargo. But she'll run like the wind. Brand-new fuel cells. She tops out at seventy klicks and is stressed for dives no sane man'd even attempt. You wanna fight a war, best be doin' it on the ground."

She nodded.

He unclipped a pair of nighteyes from his belt. "Throw these in for free—'cept if you lose 'em or bust 'em. Ready?"

"Yeah," Veta said, pulling the goggles over her face. They had a dry, musty smell.

The man helped her strap in, tightening the cinches and fitting the collars to her legs. The weight was negligible, the bulk of the wing a construct of graphite, carbon, and nylon. Even the power plant was mostly ceramic and polystressed carbon. A gust of wind caught the delta and lifted her a meter off the ground. She dipped the nose and touched down softly. He smiled at her skill.

"No stranger to birds, are you?" Helping her keep the nose level, the man led her over to the parapet. "From the sky, the glow strips form a pentagram. Look for it on your way back. That's north, south, east, and west." He pointed in the different directions. "You have a good flight now. Hear?" Chuckling softly, he released his hold on the nose and let Veta slide off the edge.

The wing caught the breeze, then flattened out into a shallow curve from the initial gut-twisting dive. She thumbed the power contact and felt the blades bite, vibrating through her hands. The sound of the power plant was a dull whisper. Banking hard, she climbed, with the same motion pressing the cable retracts to pull her legs up flat with the rest of her body hanging in the harness.

On the rooftop, the wingman wandered back into his hangar, his figure cutting across the lines of the pentagram. The glow strips were brilliant white through the nighteyes. The city receded into a grid of light and dark.

Veta checked the signal from the Shintu. It was still strong, the directional indicating that they were north of her position. Turning again, she brought the wing in line.

The edges of the wing fabric fluttered, a dull accompaniment to the dirge playing quietly in her head.

Chapter 26

In the surreal landscape of nightmare, Rolen murdered his family and friends.

The dream initialized on the bridge of the *Trojan Horse*, with its close comfortable walls and flickering displays, and the subliminal hum of power. The soft tickle of data feeding into the base of his skull was like water running over stones. The implant mulched the information into digestible bytes and shunted them to activity centers. He flew, and for the first few moments, it was beautiful.

An unfamiliar system blossomed in his head: scattered stars, a belt of debris, asteroids. The tableau snapped into focus on Olympia and Styx, and Bacchus swinging through her constant orbit. A vague flicker of unease nagged him, an oddly erotic recognition of trouble.

Vectors appeared, painted across the digital representation of the system in the hard angles of computer graphics. Arrows of red light on black space rushed toward him, incoming craft being reeled in on a tether of beamed commands. He was not the Port, but they were angling his direction anyway.

Sounds punched through his skull, an eerie mélange of bleats and pulses—the constant buzz of insystem chatter. Familiar voices evolved within the matrix of noise. He knew them: Burke, Halser, and Kinesky, speech patterns he hadn't heard in a dozen years washing over him with the warmth of past friendship. Illana Vanos, his father, and his mother all called out to him.

The vectors closed, points of light spearing at him like a barrage of enemy missiles. They were all going to impact. Panic clawed at his heart. Sweat oozed from his pores. He begged them to turn, to stop, but their cries of joy at seeing him overrode his voice.

A keyboard appeared in his lap, the old style, a flat square box with a coil of wire twisting into the bulkhead. The keys were stylized, adorned not with letters but with faces, gleaming etchings of razor-steel. The blades caught the light, so bright as to make the cutting edges invisible in the glare.

He watched distantly, his hands moving of their own volition. His index finger hovered above the portrait of Burke, a three-dimensional hologram carved in silver. Burke's mouth was moving, his lips shaping Rolen's name. Jamming down hard onto the contact, the blades sliced through to the bone with a clean, sweet explosion of agony. Burke's voice rose above all the others, a scream of terror silenced as the corresponding vector blinked out of existence.

After a few minutes, his fingers were ragged stubs. Blood coated the keyboard and the sleek gleaming walls of the bridge.

He came out of the dream sucking air and gasping, staring down at his hands for signs of bleeding. Gradually, he became aware of the woman leaning over him—Sister Gemini, a smile on her bloodless lips, mocking him.

"Sweet dreams, flyboy?" Her laughter grated.

Rolen shuddered and sat up slowly, flashes of the dream still erupting in his head in technicolor bursts.

"He wants you. Now." She swept one hand toward the exit. Carta was already standing in the tunnel, staring at some activity farther down.

He managed to reach his feet and noticed for the first time the curious lack of pain in his muscles that signified the beginnings of acclimatization to gravity.

"You got any prized possessions, best get them now," Sister Gemini drawled. "Won't be coming back."

Rolen stared at the woman. Her eyes were dark and unfathomable.

The passages were a frenzy of activity. They wove through a tangle of corpses pushing dollies or hefting cartons of equipment across the loose gravel. Swearwords echoed, along with grunts of strain and the harsh bark of urgent commands. Tension permeated the dust-choked air, panic overlaying the taint of grease and pulverized rock.

The corpses were consolidating, making an attempt to gather the important supplies. Crates of food and electronic gear were being moved deeper into the mine, while useless material was abandoned or used to form barricades and siege walls. Behind them, under the spectral glare of some portable kliegs, crews rigged an avalanche of rock and loose steel. The depths vibrated with the clang of steel and the hum of machines.

"Company coming," Gemini said, in answer to Rolen's questioning glance. "Soon."

He snapped his gaze back down the tunnel, but could see nothing beyond the frantic labors of the slaves.

Vasquez was in the computer center.

They entered through a trio of baffles in three consecutive walls of monoline membrane. Sister Gemini had to force each flap open against the internal pressure, holding it so they could squeeze by, air roaring out around them.

"A bloody pain," she said. "But it keeps the dust from the machines."

The vault was huge, larger than the commissary. The interior walls were lined with monoline, sealed at the seams and vented and kept inflated by a steady inflow of cold pure air piped down from the surface. Thick sheets of mylar reinforced the flooring, wrinkled to the appearance of battered tin, but the reflection helped disperse the light and made the place as bright as day. Rolen counted a dozen rows of low tables stacked with an amalgam of peripherals;

kilometers of cable supplied power and linked the units to a massive block of major hardware, a chemical design. Dozens of techs were hunched over terminals, their faces painted with the spectral glow from the displays. Others moved between the stations whispering orders and collecting printouts.

Vasquez approached. Despite the cold temperature, sweat beaded his flesh; the plastic parts remained dry and shining.

"No doubt, you now have some idea why moving our operation would be so difficult. It's gone too far now, too much is at stake. We will make our stand here."

"This links you with the rest of the planet?" Rolen glanced around, trying to absorb the scene.

"We're actually linked to the mining net." He pointed toward the central hardware unit. "That's tied into one of the abandoned communication trunks. The mining district is riddled with them. Every active mine is under the control of Central, and we're riding on their coattails. Gives us access to many other units, too. Those we aren't connected to, we've got people in position who can access through other links. Lot of corpses are trained as comptechs. Corporate philosophy—why hire when you can buy?" His teeth flashed.

Rolen nodded.

Vasquez grew serious. "But I didn't call you here to discuss computer links. Your presence has drawn the attention we feared. Our surface pickets have spotted an approaching force."

"Security?"

"Mercenaries. Probably Akira's or the Guild's."

"Changed your mind?"

"About turning you over to them?" Vasquez's laugh was liquid and phlegmy. "Hardly. Nothing for you to worry about. We'll take care of them."

Rolen frowned. "Thought this was a bloodless revolution."

"It has been, until now. Told you, pilot. Fewer and fewer options." He looked away. "If these people found you, the others won't be far behind. So we've advanced the timeta-

ble, both yours and ours. We're sending you out tonight. If
it goes as planned, you'll be aboard ship by 1800 hours.
That's approximately twenty-four hours from now.''

Rolen tried to mask his relief.

''The timing is imperative,'' Vasquez continued. ''At
1800 tomorrow, it all goes down. A master stroke. We close
the planet for an unscheduled holiday.'' He drew an infocube from his pocket, reached out, and dropped it into Rolen's palm. ''You wouldn't take this last time we spoke. I'm
hoping you've changed your mind.''

Rolen stared at it as if expecting the crystal to burn
through his hand.

Vasquez shrugged, rolling his good shoulder. His waldoes grasped fitfully at empty air. ''I could tell you it's
payment for our help. Make you give me your word that
you'll plug it in. At least then I'd have guilt on my side.
Guilt is a powerful weapon. We priests have been using it
for centuries.'' He smiled. ''Could even send someone
along to force you to do it. But if I did it that way, then I'd
be no better than the High Council, making slaves of innocent people.''

The man limped to the edge of the table and leaned back,
hydraulics surging. ''As soon as you walk out of here, you're
functioning on free will. Not my slave. Not Bacchus's, not
even the Guild's anymore. Free.'' His good eye narrowed.
''Can you understand that? You've got a slave mentality, my
friend. Had it even before you made planetfall. Bacchus just
gave you a skin to match your mind.''

''You're crazy.'' Rolen said, but he closed his fist on the
cube. It was as heavy as lead in his hand.

''Maybe. But at least I know what I am.'' His steel teeth
gleamed. He turned to Sister Gemini. ''Better get him out
of here. The surface crew is already in position.'' The man
looked back at Rolen. ''1800 hours, Iserye. We'll see if
you've a conscience then, won't we?''

Rolen didn't answer.

Sister Gemini stopped where the auxiliary passage inter-
sected the main tunnel. ''Best make your farewells here,

since this is where we part company." She moved off a few steps to give them privacy.

"Well," Carta said. "I'm probably gonna regret letting you go alone, but I guess it's good-bye, pilot. And good luck. You'll need it."

"You've been kind of responsible for my luck," Rolen answered. The sudden realization of how much he had come to depend on the woman surprised him. His chest felt tight and there was a lump in his throat. "Thought you were coming along." He stared down at the floor, avoiding her gaze.

"Just be in the way. Anyway, surface isn't a good place for an Incorrigible. Be better off staying down here with the rest of them. Work to do, and all that crap."

"Look." He swallowed hard. "I don't want to go up there alone."

"That's the way it's gotta be," Carta said softly, trying hard to sound convincing. "This is where we part company. You see, I'm an Incorrigible. Security nabs me, and I'm terminal. They catch you with me, it might go worse for you as well. So I'm not going."

Rolen met her gaze, startled by the tears he saw fighting to appear in her eyes. She wiped them quickly and kissed him lightly on the lips. Her tough smile returned. "Maybe I'll see you after this is all over. Take care, pilot."

"You too."

She squeezed his hand. "And, pilot? Give my best to your people—one way or the other."

Rolen watched her swagger away, hands jammed into her pockets. She never looked back.

"I don't understand. I promised her . . ."

"Couldn't come, pilot. Be hard enough to smuggle one person up, a second would likely be impossible. She knows that. So would you if you'd thought about it."

He turned but the passage was already empty.

"Come on, lover," Sister Gemini drawled. "We got a schedule to keep."

Chapter 27

The draw works jutted like a gallows on the ridge, a dark shape against the sky. The night gave no indication of there ever having been a brief moment of day. Langen Nacht marked the longest night of the year, the days would continue to lengthen toward the solstice, and Jann Petski had an uneasy sense that his last sunrise had already passed.

He shivered in the cold wind and turned back to where the grunts were suiting up. The four hired guns, broad-shouldered and silent, were pulling on dark thinskins over the bulges of their flak armor. The one called Vogel was already dressed, fitting the clips into the buzzguns and dividing up the rest of the arms from a pair of canvas satchels. Abbasi was sitting motionless on the front of the stretch, his dark eyes watching the road and the night.

Jann had never been so frigging scared. His palms were slick and his mouth was dry. He wished he had a blast of Comfort.

Vogel didn't look up as Jann approached. He busied himself separating a box of gas grenades into five sets of two. The grenades were dark metallic cylinders, and he placed them upright in the sand, like the stools of some strange beast dropped in passing.

"You got something for me?" Petski asked, squatting beside the man.

Vogel looked at him blankly, his cut eye gleaming.

"I mean, Jesus, you look like you're going off to war. Maybe I should be carrying, too." He tried to smile.

"Nothing for you." The man went back to the box of grenades.

"Problems?" Abbasi queried. He was still watching the darkened horizon. It gave Jann an eerie feeling, how the man could see when he wasn't really looking, and how much he seemed to encompass with his cold eyes.

"I was just asking if there were some . . . accommodations made for me. Something for defense?"

"Think you need a weapon?"

Jann swallowed hard, but the clot of bile in his throat remained. "You tell me. You're packing for trouble. Maybe I should have something just in case."

"Not to worry, Mr. Petski. You're reconnaissance. They're support. We'll take good care of you." Abbasi's smile was chilling.

"What about some armor?" He rubbed his shoulder gingerly. "Already taken one hit. Don't want to catch another."

Abbasi slid down from the hover. His sharkskin jacket shimmered in the darkness. The Spencer was a solid bulge under his arm. The man stooped over one of the canvas bags and retrieved a pair of nighteyes. He threw the goggles to Petski. "All you'll need. Let you see what's coming." Still smiling, the man walked up toward the draw works.

Jann had never liked the mines. As a kid, he'd listened to his old man's descriptions of hellholes choked with dust and fire. They were mostly lies, he knew, like the other stories the man told when drunk on his butt, between curses and laments about how the frigging deaders were slowly taking all the jobs. But they were real enough to etch his young mind with fear and hate. And when the old man went terminal in a rock blast, it was a final indicator that life existed only on the surface of the world. Underground was for the dead.

As he stood along the edge of the shaft and inhaled the

dank coffin fragrance billowing up from the depths, Jann imagined his father waiting somewhere down in the dark, skin hanging off him like white rags, waiting for his boy to come home.

"Something else, Mr. Petski?" Abbasi scanned the upper frame of the draw works.

"Look," he said, following the man's gaze. "I brought you here. I've done my part."

"Not our deal. After recovery."

"You don't need me down there."

"Sure I do. You're point man." Abbasi walked to the edge of the shaft and looked down into the dark. "A very important role."

Jann crossed his arms and tried to keep from shaking. "He's yours, Abbasi. I don't want any part of it. Just let me walk away. No credit. No deal. Understand?"

"What about your partners?"

Bern Aggutter seemed nothing more than a distant threat compared to the cold efficiency of the man. "Screw him."

Abbasi laughed quietly. "Too late for that now."

The grunts and Vogel marched slowly up the hill.

The equipment lift was operational, its motor whispering to life when Vogel hit the breaker. Blue sparks danced across the contacts, writhing inside the housing.

"Check it out," Abbasi said to no one in particular, his eyes back to scanning the horizon for signs of trouble.

At Vogel's nod, one of the grunts slung his buzzgun across his broad back. He levered himself into the framework, using the beams as a ladder, his boots scraping on the iron. The thinskin made him invisible against the dark sky, a blot moving slowly along the girders. A moment later, his voice rang down to them, echoing past and into the depths of the shaft.

"Stand clear."

Metal snapped. The lift cage dropped, caroming from the framework. The clatter of its fall faded into a distant rumble, sparks along the edges of the rock marking its plunge.

"Cable was cut above the brake," the man said, swinging down from the scaffolding.

Jann sucked a deep breath and tried to keep from puking.

Abbasi grinned and flicked off the safety on his Spencer. "Now we know the game."

"Use that?" The grunt pointed toward an inspection-ladder clinging to the side of the shaft frame.

"No doubt sabotaged as well. We'll use the climbing gear."

The grunts set to work rigging up the ropes. One of them shoved a pair of slides into Petski's hands.

He stared at the aluminum pulleys and hooks for a long moment, at first not understanding what they were for, then feeling his panic evaporate as he realized they'd have to leave him behind. "With my shoulder? You're crazy." Jann laughed, giddy with relief. "No way I can make that climb."

"He's right." Abbasi nodded sagely. "Better lower him. First."

It was a death sentence.

Jann stood motionless while the grunts rigged a sling around one thigh and drew the rope up over his good shoulder. He wished he had the strength to try and run, even though he knew they'd cut him down before he'd gone ten meters. At least it would have been quick. But his body was numb and his muscles leaden, as if he were already terminal.

"Better put your goggles on," Vogel said.

"Keep your eyes open." Abbasi bared his teeth.

The grunts swung him out over the pit, lowering him in a smooth, steady descent.

Chapter 28

Veta Pulchek climbed to fifteen hundred meters as she passed over the industrial sector. The Shintu was calling from deep inside the mining district, and once she left the fringe of Delphi, there would be no more structures to block her craft from line of sight. She needed altitude for cover.

The wing was a smuggler's dream, as quiet as a whisper and responsive to her every move, but she took no pleasure in the flight. She was running on hate now, and as a drug, hate overrode everything, even the strong desire for self-preservation.

The air was bitter cold and her hands were numb. Her face felt like a layer of frozen rubber stretched over the bones, but the ambient suit kept her body warm and reduced her heat signature to a minimum, venting the surplus warmth along a row of flaps set into the spine. Anyone trying to spot her would need phenomenal equipment or terrific luck. It gave her one advantage, surprise, and there had been plenty of times when that had been enough.

Beyond the city was a darkness broken sporadically by white floods around the active mines. Valleys and dry washes gave the land the appearance of a rumpled cloak. Spines of stone jutted from the humped ridges like armored plates on the backs of long-buried dinosaurs. Pale stripes of gravel road twisted along in serpentine loops on which heavy trucks and ore trams rumbled below, headlights forming bright cones in the dust. Farther north, the territory grew more desolate, the active sites dwindling to a few oases of brilliance in the night.

As she neared the Shintu, Veta climbed again, rising another five hundred meters, thumbing the power and shifting her weight back to make the nose spear upward. Grabbing quickly with one hand, she found the contact on the night-eyes and faded into infrared. A mottled landscape appeared, mostly blacks and dark violets, but scattered here and there were random clots of red and yellow, pools of blue, and bands of aquamarine. The signature of a thermo generation plant blossomed far to her left, a crimson glow intensifying to white. Steam pipes painted ruddy lines across the ridges.

She spotted the limousine abandoned in a small valley, the arch of a hillock concealing it from the entrance of a nearby mine. The area had long since been tapped of its wealth and deserted. Heat eddied up from the engines of the hover, maroon blots slowly losing definition. She circled for a long time, searching for other signatures; finding none, she dipped the nose and put the wing into a sharp dive, pulling up a scant fifty meters off the deck and skimming over the top of the craft.

The surface was clear, which meant they'd gone underground. Banking into a hard power turn, she made another circuit, dropping close to the mine shaft. The top of the draw works loomed almost at eye level as she went past.

Petski had chosen an excellent hiding place for the pilot—zero permanent population, and little cover for anyone to make an unseen approach. If he had support, and there had to be someone staying with the pilot, they'd spot Security or trouble long before it reached them.

Veta circled above, looking for a place to stage an ambush. The vague glimmerings of a plan started to gel in her head. The buyer and his party consisted of six people. Petski needed at least four in reserve. Two to watch the surface in four-hour alternating shifts, and two splitting the duty on the pilot. Operating with any less was sheer suicide. That meant she'd be facing at least eleven armed grunts. Not good odds.

Still, there were ways of cutting the odds in a hurry. A magnesium blinder detonated against the hover's fuel tank would turn it into a raging inferno. Properly timed, that would take out the pilot, the buyer, and his party, reducing the equation quickly to five on one. She only wanted one of them—Petski. No reason to hunt the others; she could hit and run and leave them wondering what the hell had happened.

Of course, if the blinder failed or Petski had more than four in the hole, she'd end up as food for whatever lived in the bottom of the shaft. Veta pushed that thought from her mind and concentrated on picking out a viable sniping position.

Something moved on the edge of her vision, a boxy blot of light and heat. Veta twisted the wing into a sliding turn and dipped below into the cover of a narrow valley, running as close to the ground as possible, trying to get beyond their line of sight before she climbed. She came up hard, G forces wrenching at her, feeling the thrum of the blades through the frame as the power plant labored in silence.

By the time she'd gained altitude and swung back around, the intruder was identifiable as a service truck rolling slowly up the gravel road in the next valley beyond the mine. The truck idled to a stop. The lights flashed twice, then a two-man crew climbed out and started work on a stalled road cutter.

Puzzled, Veta angled toward them, staying high and running straight. There was a ventilation shaft on the back side of the ridge, hidden between two fingers of granite. She'd have missed it except for the blot of heat in the mouth of the tunnel. The signature calved into two figures moving slowly down the side of the hill toward the truck, staying low, using the boulders and gullies for cover, two red specks wriggling across the ground.

Veta tabbed the magnification setting on the nighteyes. The first signature was normal, but there were two curious blue blotches marring the second, high around the neck.

She bumped the magnification again, and the swellings took on shape and definition.

Implants.

Recognition gripped her. The pilot.

There was no way to take him out from the air, but she wasn't certain she wanted to kill him now. Maybe Petski's people were crossing him, or maybe Petski was stupid enough to try and cross the buyer. But possession of the pilot would change everything. The pilot was the key. If she took him alive, she'd have the bargaining chip.

They'd come to her . . . and she could pick them off at her leisure.

She circled above and waited.

Chapter 29

The first level was a short adit, a dry bore five meters deep floored by a thick mantle of undisturbed dust. The miners had once used it as a garbage dump, and it was still ankle deep in moldering litter. Across the shaft, the opposite end of the tunnel was blocked by a collapse. One of the grunts inspected it and pronounced the cave-in old and solid.

Thirty meters down, they reached a second passage. It was as quiet as a grave. They ran it in a modified phalanx, taking cover behind blade-sharp outcroppings and abandoned ore cars, Petski leading, two of Vogel's grunts following him, then Jaleem and Vogel, with two more covering the rear. Both sides proved clear and empty.

A smashed crate rested on the lip of level three, a red plastic cube with white lettering stenciled on the outside. PROTEIN PASTE. White tubes were scattered on the ledge. Several had been smashed underfoot recently. Vogel stooped and probed the glue with one finger.

"Fresh," he droned. "An hour or so."

Jaleem gestured with the Spencer. Petski grimaced and moved slowly forward, hugging the wall for protection, while two operatives took up positions on either side and slightly behind him.

The operatives were loose and ready. They moved fluidly,

without hesitation, buzzguns held ready, barrels pointed
forward, waiting for the squeeze of a hand to spray a lethal
arc of explosive pellets. Their mouths were serious lines.
The only sounds were the whisper of the thinskins against
the rock when they passed too close, the creak of body
armor, and the soft crunch of their boots on the gravel.

An intersection loomed, two side tunnels breaking off
into the darkness. Jaleem's nighteyes cast a pale glow on
the boxes of additional supplies spread along the walls, pyramids of blue and green plastic, marked with white letters,
the scrawled grease pencil of a customs officer. The stacks
were in disarray, evidence of recent use and hasty retreat.

"Knew we were coming," Vogel said dryly.

Jaleem kicked at a box. "Maybe us or maybe Security."

"Be that much harder."

"Keep moving."

They encountered more intersections. Drafts of stale, cold
air blew in from occasional ducts, square ports carved into
the stone and faced with rusted steel gratings. As he walked,
Jaleem swung his head from side to side, expecting ambush
from every opening.

Vogel was right. A colossal and possibly dangerous waste
of time, this chasing after shadows in the deep caverns. But
anything was better than sitting in the quiet madness of his
rooms and thinking of Toshiro Akira, seeing his pathetic,
disappointed smile. A scrub run, but it helped keep his
mind occupied.

They heard a distant echo of steel on steel. The grunts
froze. There was another clang, far down the tunnel.

"Go," Jaleem barked.

The mercenaries knew the drill—hustling now, run and
cover in rotation. Falling into the rhythm, Jaleem took his
position on the right side, his Spencer held flat before him
as he ran.

"I got heat," the point called back. "Forty meters. Moving away."

"How many?" Jaleem couldn't catch the signature.

"Lone," Vogel hissed. "Running hard."

"Take him."

They were sprinting now, using the wall as a place to bounce back out toward the center of the passage and leaping the fragments of scarp and trash on the floor. Minor details stuck in his head: a discarded glove wadded like a dead animal against the cold stone, the shattered handle of a tool, a drill bit jammed deep into the wall and bent flat toward the floor.

The hostile stayed just out of reach, always ahead of them, as if purposely leading them. Jaleem remembered tactics from the Zone—ambush and massacre.

"Eyes open," he ordered, panting for breath and feeling the dust coating his teeth and tongue. "Be ready."

The passage opened into a small gallery, with a downshaft in the center and two other tunnels intersecting. The painted steel gleamed white in the dimly lit world of his nighteyes. Sweat beaded his face, making the plastic slick where it pressed against his face. He blinked back the saline burning his eyes.

"What the hell is this?" he demanded, rounding on Petski. "This wasn't part of your map."

Petski swallowed hard and shrugged. His face was very pale, skin gleaming like a corpse's against his beard.

"Looks like the rogues have done some work on their own," Vogel said. "Joined with another mine. Could have linked dozens of them by now. Klicks of tunnels. He could be anywhere."

The soldiers fanned out, two moving toward the right passage, two breaking for the left, following the curve of the wall around the downshaft. Their boots rang on the steel grating over the lower dross chutes. The overhead grates bulged, metal hammered by years of waste rock passing through to fill the bottom of the shaft. Jaleem snapped his gaze back and forth between both tunnels; both were cold and dark. There was no sign of the hostile.

Vogel turned back to him. "Which way?"

Jaleem shrugged, squinting down each bore and finding only darkness. The operatives stayed close to the edge of the downshaft, using the lift frame for cover, crouching and trying to catch their breath. One hacked and spit into the depths. Another raised his nighteyes and wiped his face.

Pointing his Spencer, Jaleem nodded toward Petski. "Your show," he said. "Time to earn your fee."

Petski shook his head. "I don't know. I only saw them bring him down."

"Pick it." His voice was cold.

"Crazy." Vogel cleared his nostrils, looking up into a trickle of dust from one of the overhead chutes. "Sweet Jesus—" He didn't get a chance to finish.

The grates exploded downward with the force of a directional charge. Jaleem rolled toward the wall. Thunder drowned out the screaming and swearing of the operatives. The impact of the avalanche jarred the stone floor. Jagged rocks whirled around him, cutting his face and arms. A thick blanket of dust billowed. He coughed, trying to suck air through the thick effluvia of grit and soil. A buzzgun discharged, and exploding rounds flashed in the darkness as bullets whined around him. Jaleem curled against the wall, wedging himself into the base of the cut and trying to bury his head in his hands.

Echoes faded gradually, rumbling back and forth through the tunnel like a trapped freight train seeking escape. The flood of stones slowed to a trickle of sand and grit, gravel, and small bits of litter. Jaleem raised his head slowly.

A rock had smashed one lens of his nighteyes and gouged his cheek; blood seeped down his neck. The silence seemed permanent, as if the noise had deafened him. He rose slowly to his feet, breathing through his clenched teeth to try to filter some of the airborne grit.

Movement brought him to a shooting stance, Spencer clutched in both hands, finger on the trigger. Vogel waved him off.

"It's me, Vogel." The man stumbled close, one arm hanging limply. "Frigging setup. They were waiting."

Jaleem nodded and spat dirt and saliva.

Only one operative joined them, bleeding from a gash in his skull and walking blindly, his nighteyes swept away in

the confusion. There was no sign of the other soldiers. Jaleem leaned out over the downshaft, but saw nothing in the
darkness.

They found Petski beneath one of the grates, a length of
angle iron through his breastbone and out his back pinning
him to the floor. His eyes were open, orbs coated with dust,
and his face was contorted in a rictus of terror.

"What now?" Vogel grimaced in pain.

"Don't know." He thought of Akira's disappointed smile
and cursed.

They headed back to the surface in silence.

Chapter 30

Half a klick from the ventilator shaft, a pair of corpses were repairing the operating system of an automated road cutter. Rolen held his breath and ran, keeping his head down. Their work light was a gleaming beacon, partially illuminating the massive angular shape of the cutter, revealing yellow flanks streaked with dust and grease. Someone had scrawled VASQUEZ WAS HERE with a fingertip in the grime.

One of the repair crew jumped down from the top of the blade and met them at the service truck. He smiled briefly and swung the back bay open. A draft of solvents and oil drifted from the interior. Racks of tools and spare parts hung on the side walls: a pair of hydraulic jacks, jumper cables coiled like mating snakes.

"Right on time," he said, reaching in for a circuit board. "Be through here in a minute. Make yourselves comfortable." The man walked slowly back to the cutter.

Sister Gemini reached into the van and pulled out a wrinkled jumpsuit, kelly green. A red emblem on the sleeve showed a stylized wolf and the words LUPINE PRODUCTS. "Put it on," she commanded.

He shrugged out of the gray jumpsuit, the icy wind shriveling his flesh. The green uniform was stiff with dirt. Finished, Rolen levered himself into the van, Gemini shoving him from behind. He had a momentary vision of himself as a plastic crate, bulky and inanimate, passing from hand to hand. He found a place against the front. The steel of the wall was cold and hard.

"You forgot this," she said dryly, handing him the infocube and waiting while he secured it in his pocket. "You're in competent hands. Do what they say."

Rolen nodded.

"He's counting on you."

"Goes both ways."

Sister Gemini smiled. "Good luck, pilot." She moved away into the darkness.

A minute later, the cutter roared to life, billows of smoke boiling from the exhausts as the vehicle turned and growled up the grade toward the new section. The repair crew tossed their tool bags onto the floorboards.

"Next stop, Delphi," one said softly.

The doors slammed shut and left him in darkness. He heard the crew laughing up front, and heard the engine rumble, vibrations drumming through the bed. The truck lurched forward, jarring over the rutted road, gravel clattering in the wheel wells.

After a time, the battered mining cuts ended and the truck rolled onto the smoother surface of a maintained highway. The rubber tires droned as the vehicle picked up speed. City sounds penetrated the van: horns, squealing brakes, and the whirring roar of passing hovers. The truck made a series of slow turns, accelerating and coasting, winding through heavy traffic. After the chaos of Langen Nacht, it was hard for Rolen to imagine the streets filled with vehicles. Instead, he conjured up a nightmare of the service truck rolling along a road paved with bodies.

The truck finally idled to a stop. He rose to a crouch. The back door cracked and swung on oiled hinges, protesting softly. A corpse appeared, female, squinting at him in the dark.

"Hustle now." She gestured with one arm as though

threatening to jerk him from the interior. "Get yo' ass movin'."

He steeled himself for a rush of agoraphobia and crawled out of the van.

Vertigo assaulted him, a strong wrench that twisted his horizon before he managed to focus his eyes on the paved lot. Rolen got a quick view of a low, flat building, lighted windows, and the diamond pattern of a chain-link fence. The woman caught his arm to keep him from falling and escorted him into the factory. Behind them, the repair truck throttled up and rumbled away into the night.

"Listen now." She gave orders as they walked, scanning him swiftly as if to determine what made him so damned important. Her eyes fastened on his implants. She turned his collar up to cover them. "Got no time for mistakes. Stay with me. We're goin' down thermal line one to the box sealer. The automated loadin' unit's fouled." She grinned. "Screwin' with the command modules does that to 'em. Anyways, they got a manual crew doing the work. We gonna step into the loadin' line, take a box from the end, and up into the truck. Only you don't come out. Loadin' crew will take you from there. Got it?"

Rolen nodded.

"The civilian super is in the john with one of the ladies. Being attended to." The woman made a gesture, index finger inserted into a circle formed by the fingers and thumb of her other hand. She laughed grimly.

Corruption and bribery, he realized, were timeless. The process never changed, only the currency. And there was always someone who was willing to make such a sacrifice, not for him surely, but for a cause.

"Stay close."

Then they were moving out into the center of the shop.

The building resonated from foundation to roof with the pounding of rolling conveyors and surging hydraulics. Ninety percent of the work was mechanized. Thermal presses roared, hissing out clouds of steam in vaporous rags. Servos whined. Hoists chattered, sparks arcing from electrical contacts. Corpses moved in and out among the mists, effecting repairs and doing maintenance in a scene from a mechanical hell.

They followed a long conveyor line studded with presses and cutters. The product was some type of foam-backed fiberboard; he couldn't divine its use or purpose. The smell of formaldehyde and alcohol washed over him in ripe waves.

Rolen felt the stares of other workers stealing glances as he passed. At the end of the line, roller bearings chattered in a jarring tattoo. A human chain of corpses fed cartons into a waiting truck, a pair lifting each, one on either side, and disappearing into the interior. The truck was poorly mated with the loading dock; there were gaps of darkness around the edges where the night and the frigid air from outside whistled in to tear at the rags of hot moisture coming off the presses. He shivered as he got in line.

The carton was heavy. Rolen almost lost his grip and stumbled. Someone behind him, ready for the possibility, stepped in smoothly to right the load and get him headed across the ramp. The hollow cavity of the truck enclosed him.

"Here." Fingers clutched his shoulder. The loading man was big, barrel-chested, and older than Rolen. Except for his translucent skin and hairless visage, he was like many stevedores Rolen had encountered. He gave Rolen a sharp shove toward the corner where an alcove had been left in the stacks. "Stay down. You'll find another uniform. Leave the old one in the corner." The man ignored him then, as if the pilot did not exist or was simply another crate in the bed of the truck.

Somehow he managed to change in the confined area. By the time he finished, the loading was complete. He wadded the old jumpsuit into the corner, then felt a hard lump in the fabric and remembered the infocube.

Rolen dug the object from the clothing and cupped it in his hand. It was just an infocube, the most common method of upgrading software or altering the operating system. He had used them thousands of times and knew the drill by heart: open the packet, attach the unread instructions to the front of the change-record manual, load the cube. The repair squirt in the cube did the task, altering some routine or loop in a change so subtle that it usually went unnoticed on the next run.

That was what was so frightening about this cube—it looked so frigging normal.

Footsteps approached his hiding place. Startled, Rolen jammed the cube into his pocket and looked up to find himself face to face with the loading man.

"All done here," the man said. "You sit tight. Be somebody waiting for you at the other end."

Rolen nodded. The man moved away. The door slid down on protesting bearings.

For a long time after the truck reached its destination, Rolen waited in the darkness. Outside, he heard the distant roar of a landing craft climbing up from gravity, punching a hole through atmosphere on its way to the Port. The sound made his heart pump madly.

Light accompanied the chatter of the door rolling up on its tracks, a brace of automated loading units waiting on the ramp. A corpse stepped up the ramp, weaved between them, and made his way back through the narrow aisle between the crates.

"Yo, little brother," the man said as he got close, appearing to inspect the stacks. "Same drill as last stop." He didn't turn around. "Just step up and follow me. And put this around your neck to hide the bumps." He dropped a packing blanket onto Rolen's head.

Rolen stood, his legs stiff and cramped from the ride. He draped the blanket over his neck, pulling it forward with his hands like a scarf, and followed the man out of the truck. As they exited, the loading units lurched to life, rumbling up the ramp to lift a forkload of cargo.

"Going up," a corpse whispered as Rolen passed. There was an almost festival air about them, the certainty that something big was about to break. The mood was infectious and Rolen grinned back.

The box was two meters tall and a meter wide. It looked

uncomfortably like a coffin. There were ten others beside it, all identical, each with a warning notice stenciled in black on the white plastic surface:

ATTENTION
TEMPERATURE SENSITIVE
MEDICAL SUPPLIES
TEMP RANGE
15 – 25 CEL

"This is bound for the pressurized hold. Gonna be close inside, but it's not airtight, and they got to keep 'em warm." The man raised the hinged lid. "Better get inside 'fore we draw attention."

Rolen climbed into the crate. The man threw the packing blanket in beside him.

"To help cushion liftoff," he said. "Be someone waiting for you Portside." He reached in quickly and grabbed Rolen's hand. "Good luck."

The lid hinged shut. He was in darkness except for a thin sliver of illumination where the edges of the lid met. Through the gap, he could see a wedge of the warehouse outside. Corpses moved back and forth across his line of sight. Once in a while, a civilian hurried by.

Time stretched. He couldn't judge whether it was minutes or hours before he heard the whine of an approaching loading unit. Servos clattered against the side of the crate. The lift mechanism took the box straight up with surprising force. His head spun as the loading unit reversed direction, pivoted, and lurched forward. For a few moments, the machine rolled on a level surface. The motor howled as it hit the inclined ramp into the lander. Once inside the hold, it lowered him fast, crate bumping against the bulkhead. He heard the machine reverse direction and trundle away. Another load followed. A few minutes later, the pressure door swung shut and latched. The sliver of light vanished as the outside floods winked out. Then all was silent.

It was warm and close in the crate, more comfortable

than he'd been at any time since leaving the *Shadowbox*. He must have drifted off to sleep. The groan of an inspection hatch opening roused him quickly. He lay very still, listening intently. Nothing to worry about, he thought, just a preflight check.

The hatch swung shut. He brought his eye up to the crack and found it was still as black as midnight in the hold. Someone was moving around in the darkness, quietly and slowly. It was time to start worrying—no one ran inspections without light. His heartbeat accelerated. He was afraid to breathe.

The approach circled to his left, angling closer. He heard cautious footsteps. Fingertips scraped along the cartons. Clothing rustling against restraint netting. Rolen gritted his teeth and tried to keep from moaning in terror.

It's another corpse, he prayed. Some wrinkle in the plan they forgot to mention. Any moment a voice would call his name and reassure him. But no assurances came and the intruder moved unerringly toward his hiding place, as if drawn by his warmth or by some sound he was emitting on a frequency too high for him to hear.

Three meters to his left now.

No more than two.

Then whoever it was was outside the crate, close enough to sense his terror through the thin plastic box. Hands brushed the lid. Fingers slid down to find and grip the edge. Rolen tensed himself to strike, muscles coiled, ready to slam the cover up as soon as it started to rise.

He sprang, homing in on the sound, arms blindly extended and windmilling. Rolen grabbed a handful of hair and encountered the angular bulge of some type of night goggles. A flattened palm caught his chin and drove stars into his skull as a fist slammed into his groin, a warm agony spreading into his guts that made it impossible to move or breathe. Rolen slumped helplessly to the floor, his fingers twisting in the restraint netting, fighting the overpowering nausea that swept through him.

Something cold pressed against the back of his skull. He dimly registered the muzzle of a weapon.

"Get up." The low, quiet voice was female.

He rose to his knees. The gun barrel followed his head unerringly.

"Back in the box. And make some room. You're going to have some company."

Rolen tumbled into the carton. She climbed in beside him. He had a sense of a thin, hard body, with small breasts pressing against his back. The gun was a cold weight on the side of his head. He heard the woman lever the lid into place.

"I imagine somebody's going to get a real surprise," she said quietly. "Two for the price of one." Her laughter was like the wind through dry grass.

Chapter 31

Despite the heat in the box, the pilot shivered.

"You from the Guild?" he asked, after a long silence. "Or Akira?"

Veta smiled in the darkness. "You know a lot, pilot."

"It's the Guild, isn't it?" There was a slight edge of belligerence to his voice.

"Yes." She kept the weapon against his skull. The band of scar on her arm was hot and itched madly. She ignored the discomfort. "Whoever set up the run to get you aboard the lander was very good. Almost lost you at the factory. Had to hope you were on the first truck to leave after your arrival. When it made for the landing field, I knew you were on it. The rest was academic. Couldn't hide you with the passengers, so I checked the pressurized hold. Your heat signature was easy to spot. Maybe I'll suggest sweeping the hold with infrared to Bacchus Security. Might be a reward in it."

"So when do you kill me?" His voice was perfectly flat.

"Figured most of it out, haven't you?"

"Enough."

"Not everything. Been a change in plans. There's some personal matters that need attention. Your help could make it much easier. So I'm going to make you an offer. We help each other. You might just make it back to your ship and offplanet.''

''What about the Guild?''

''Live or dead doesn't matter to them. Keeping you away from . . . Akira, was it? That's the target. Interested?''

She heard him swallow. ''What do you want?''

''Cooperation.'' She stretched out her legs and massaged a cramp. ''We've got some mutual enemies. I intend to take them out. Your help would make it much easier. Otherwise, I blow you away and do it solo.''

''If those are my choices,'' the pilot answered, sarcasm thick in his words, ''then I guess I'm your man.''

Veta breathed deep, noticed she was rubbing at the scar, and stopped the rhythmic motion suddenly. ''All right then. We need a neutral zone at the Port. Someplace we can use as a meet point. Any ideas?''

He shrugged.

''Come on, pilot. Surely you've had free time on Bacchus. Give me a name. I don't want to be operating blind.''

''Caliban's,'' he said softly. ''It's the only place I know.''

''Caliban's.'' Veta rolled the name off her tongue.

A throaty growl vibrated through the ship, the first thunder of liftoff. She lowered the weapon as the roar increased.

G forces neutralized both of them.

The box passed through customs without an inspection. Veta wasn't surprised. Most Ports tended to concentrate on keeping contraband from flowing between the Port and the nexus. Getting articles from the planet to the Port was usually no problem. Moving them off-Port was an entirely different prospect.

The Port contact was a short corpse, thin and wasted, wearing a hooded jacket against the cold. He was smiling when he raised the lid; his smile froze as Veta chopped him across the skull with the Magna. The man went down hard and didn't move. The pilot bent to check him.

''Still breathing,'' he said.

''If I'd have meant to kill him, I would have. Get his jacket. The hood will cover your implants.''

In the light, the pilot seemed carved of plastic. His features were the same as the holos in his dossier: deep-set eyes, broad nose and brow. Without his beard, he seemed smaller, wan and sickly. He stripped the coat from the man and slipped it on, standing up carefully. It was too small, but the hood did the job.

They were alone in a small warehouse. From the doorway, she could see the curve of the docks. The way was clear, the nearest unloading activity concentrated on the far side of a shuttle four bays down.

The pilot was tense, staring off down the docks with longing in his eyes.

"You make a dash now and I'll cut you down." She shrugged. "You stick with me, and I'll personally get you aboard. Your choice."

Iserye didn't answer. Walking slowly, careful not to attract undue attention, they headed toward the interior of the port.

Traffic in the corridors was light. Iserye stayed close, keeping his head down and his eyes on the floor. There was a commline by the lift on level three. Veta punched in her card and called up the location map for Caliban's, making a hard copy of the direct route. A slip of paper fed out of the printer. She tore it off and, dragging the pilot by the shoulder, stepped into the lift as the doors opened.

They rode to level four in silence.

Her credit card was magic. One flash of platinum and the doors to Caliban's opened wide. They were given a room in the rear, a portable comm unit, food, and drink—no questions asked. She used a piece of tape to cover the holocam and deaden any outgoing visual signal. Then, using the credit card again, she placed a call to The Blue Note.

It took several minutes to make the connection. Finally, the display screen blinked to life, static crackling, sparkling electrical fireworks highlighting the face of the bartender. Hazy background details framed his head: a rack of bottles of various colors, glasses stacked in crystal columns, the handle of a beer tap wrapped with black tape. Music throbbed. The slack-jawed barkeep squinted into the holo-cam.

"Blue Note." He yelled to be heard over the buzz of conversation and music.

"I have a message for one of your patrons." Veta said.

The man fiddled with the comm unit. "Something's screwed with your visual. Who'd you want?"

"Name's unnecessary. I got an item for sale, something rare. You know what I'm saying?"

A feral look entered his eyes. "Maybe."

"You get the word to whoever's looking for air power. I'll return this call at 0600. If the interested party is there, then we do some business. If not, they go home empty-handed. Got it?"

"Maybe."

"Good." She broke the connection.

The pilot sat across the table, picking at his meal and watching her sullenly. There was no telling what was going through his mind. He seemed bone-tired and disoriented, baffled. Perhaps it was a façade to catch her off guard, but Veta doubted his ability to act. More than likely, his discomfort was real. Unarmed, his thin frame offered little threat. She pulled her plate close and made short work of the meal.

In her head, common sense was screaming at her to kill the man. It would be safe and easy, the right action. She could raise the Magna and blow him away. But common sense had lost its power on the street in front of Roc's apartment.

Only waiting until the trap is set, she thought, then he's terminal. But there shouldn't have been any trap. One bullet in him and she'd have fulfilled the terms of her contract. Letting emotions enter into business was a cardinal sin. Probably get them both killed.

She thought of her father, imperial and graying, sitting in his office and meting out his orders with the dispatch of a Roman emperor. She was only given audience on special occasions, those times when her transgressions had exceeded the abilities of the nannies and governesses who provided her with guidance in her youth. Her apologies and entreaties always fell on deaf ears.

"But why?" she once had asked, fighting back the tears and trying not to break before him, as crying was worse than any sin she might have already committed. "I said I was sorry. I didn't mean to offend."

That had been so long ago that the sin was now forgotten, as well as the punishment. But not his reply.

"Because," he said, his gravelly voice dry and monotonous, "absolution is not so easily purchased as that."

So it was even now. A life for a life. That it might be her own was not really a concern.

Chapter 32

The attacker came at Jaleem from the left, approaching in a swift crouch with knife held out in his right hand and a dark knit stocking mask over his face. Jaleem whirled and kicked, driving his foot up into the holographic face and blocking the knife with one elevated arm. The floor bounced under his feet; his muscles burned. He pushed himself harder, driving the hologram across the padding as he concentrated on the rhythm of his body. But the mindless, meaningless exercise was failing miserably to calm his shattered nerves.

His control was slipping away. The operation had gone wrong, was damn near unsalvageable at this point. Vogel had feelers out, trying to find a way to pry the pilot loose from the mines, even making offers, but evidently nothing had materialized. And every tick of the clock made the chances of success slimmer. Jaleem likened it to the work of a blacksmith—every moment away from the flame made the iron harder to shape, and made each strike less effective. The steel was growing cold.

Sooner or later, he had to report to Akira. Jaleem swallowed hard and fought the twisting in his guts.

The door hissed open and Har Vogel entered, walking awkwardly, favoring the arm and its pink inflated cast. Jaleem stopped his attack and left the hologram slashing at empty air. Wiping the sweat from his eyes, he turned to Vogel.

"Turn up something?"

"Nothing from my people." Vogel watched him closely, as if the events of the last few days had opened his eyes and he somehow found Jaleem lacking. Abbasi resisted the impulse to break his jaw with a sudden kick. Instead, he turned back to watch the hologram circling at the edge of its programmed world, seeking an attacker, knife blade held warily.

"Another call from Aggutter at The Blue Note." Vogel pursed his lips.

"And?"

"Someone claiming to have him. Wanting to deal."

"How do we contact them?"

"They'll call you, at The Blue Note. 0600 hours."

Jaleem nodded.

"You could be grasping at straws." Vogel adjusted his injured arm and grimaced with a sudden flash of pain.

"Sometimes a straw is all it takes." He padded softly toward the showers.

The call came on schedule.

After a flicker of static, the image on the screen resolved into something coherent: a slight man, features pronounced, mouth and nose seemingly carved from a block of translucent stone. Twin bulges swelled at the base of his neck—white and silver implants. Rolen Iserye.

"I've got a list of instructions," Iserye said flatly. His eyes tracked something beyond camera range—his captors, perhaps. He fumbled with a scrap of paper. "The Commerce Bank is waiting for a blind transfer of five hundred thousand credits. There is a flight leaving for the Port at 1400, a single seat reserved in the name of John Marcus. Be on it—alone and unarmed. A messenger will meet you at the dock with further instructions." The pilot looked back up at the camera. "Any deviation from the instructions will be considered bad faith and the deal is off."

The screen went blank.

Abbasi whirled on Vogel. "Who's got him?"

The man shrugged. "No leads."

"Dammit, this is your turf. You're supposed to know."

"It's your plan." The reply bordered on a taunt. Maybe, like most animals, Vogel smelled panic. A smile crept across his lips. "Will you go?"

"Yes."

"Could be a trap."

"Or a solution." He stood abruptly, not looking at Vogel while stripping off his weapons. Abbasi clenched his left fist, feeling the barrel of the fragmenter pushing against his palm. "Either way, I'm not without certain skills."

"John Marcus to the courtesy comm. John Marcus to the white courtesy comm." The pronunciation was precise, the voice nonthreatening and universal.

Jaleem made his way across the dock to where a bank of courtesy comms stood gleaming and spotted the name MAR-CUS blinking in dark capitals on the marquee. He stepped into the booth and keyed the receiver. A message flickered across the display.

YOU HAVE TWENTY SECONDS. HARD COPY OF INSTRUC-TIONS IN PRINTER. TAKE THEM AND LEAVE BOOTH. NO DE-VIATIONS.

Reaching down, he tore the scrap of paper from the printer and stepped back out into the lobby. Scanning the crowd, he picked out several possible tails, but no one who expressed any undue interest in him. Whoever he was dealing with was a professional. He'd been given no time in the booth to contact support. There were no calls to trace.

He turned his attention to the paper. "Caliban's. Fourth Level. Section 2A. Identify yourself at the door as John Marcus. You have fifteen minutes to reach your destination."

The lifts were on his left. He checked his watch. 1715. Hurrying, he made his way toward the elevators.

All plastic and steel, Caliban's was a niche carved into the wall between a bank and a medical supply outlet. Where

The Blue Note had been a warm construct of simulated wood and brass, decaying but somehow all the more comfortable for its flaws, Caliban's was a split-level nightmare of flickering lights and polished tables the hue of ebony. Neon strobes and night reds cast a molten glow over a crowd of soldiers and pilots, prostitutes, shills, and dockworkers. Holograms and drunken civilians staggered across the tri-level dance floor.

The bouncer was a massive chunk of a man, with arms as thick as tree limbs, a columnar neck, and a blunt face. He looked up, a question mark in his narrow eyes.

"I'm John Marcus."

"Private party," the man grunted. He dug for something behind the counter and produced a wafer thin electronic key for a card lock. "Room in the back. Go on through. This'll let you in." The man grabbed his shoulder with a thick hand and squeezed hard, fingers digging in through the fabric of his jacket. "No trouble. Understand?"

Jaleem Abbasi laughed and took the card.

He walked up two flights of stairs and across one dance platform, through several dancers that proved to be projections and one that was not. An ancient EVA suit stood near the rear doors, like a decorative suit of armor. He saw his own pale face reflected back in the mirrored visor.

Through the doors into the kitchen, he could see corpsemen squatting down on the floor. Swearing floated toward him, barely penetrating the thunder of the music.

"Back to work, you lazy bastards . . ." the voice trailed off and was lost.

"Vasquez! Vasquez! Vasquez . . ." their chant droned monotonously.

He flicked the card into the lock and snapped his wrist to activate the fragmenter, feeling it snap as the firing mechanism cocked. The door swung open, black glass casting back the twitching images of the patrons behind him.

The room was small, with a table in the center, four chairs, a sideboard with glasses and bottles; a gambling alcove. Jaleem stepped inside, his eyes adjusting slowly to the bright lighting. In the chair next to the table, the pilot sat rigidly, watching him, eyes wide. Against the wall, a woman with silver hair and a dark tan kept a Spencer leveled at him.

"I'm Marcus."

He got no reaction from the woman; her face was like stone. "Inside," she said tightly. "And close the door."

He kicked the door closed behind him, keeping his hands away from his body, palms up, left hand with the fragmenter implant pointed idly at the woman. Jaleem nodded toward the pilot. "My merchandise."

"That's debatable."

"Paid for; check with the bank. I'm alone, unarmed. Followed your instructions to the letter."

A grim smile. "Plans change."

He felt adrenaline kick in, a hard burst of energy. "What else do you want?"

"Don't worry. Already got it." She elevated the Magna slowly. "This is for Rocco Marin."

Jaleem gave her a helpless smile and tried to look confused. "I don't know what the hell you're saying. I'm just here for the pilot."

"Hey, then I'll owe someone an apology. But for right now, business is business."

Still smiling, Jaleem flicked his wrist.

Chapter 33

Flame blossomed in the the man's upraised hand. Like a holo from the Universal Catholic Bible, Rolen thought as he kicked his chair backward and dove for the floor. Christ imparting the Holy Spirit to the apostles. The concussion was his holy thunder.

Pulchek fired as she hit the wall, bullets ripping a path across the acoustic ceiling, causing a snowstorm of white foam to whirl through the air. Her eyes were wide; most of her throat was missing. Blood and flesh painted a ruddy abstract on the white paneling behind her head. Even while collapsing, she was trying to take the Akira man out, her mouth locked in a grimace of agony, fighting her own dying flesh to twist the Spencer toward him.

The man crashed into the table, flipping it as he lunged, his weight driving the wooden shield into the woman. Bones crunched. He snagged at her weapon with his good hand, but even in death her grip was like iron.

Whirling, Rolen clawed at the door. Jerking it open, he caromed off the bouncer standing uncertainly at the top of the stairs. The man swiped at Rolen with one arm, but his eyes were drawn to the blood-spattered room. Rolen ducked the blow and plunged down the steps into a scattering crowd of dancers. Screams wove a frantic counterpoint through the throbbing music.

He jumped the second flight of stairs. Behind him, he heard blows and swearing. The bartender was hunched behind the counter, frantically punching the emergency number on the comm unit.

The exit was standing open. As he darted into the corridor, Rolen glanced over his shoulder. The bouncer was on his knees on the dance floor, doubled over and clutching his groin.

The fixer was at the top of the stairs.

It was shift change, and traffic filled the corridor, fresh crews milling and surging along with knots of workers heading for home. Tired faces, angry and sullen, turned to watch his flight. His mind was racing, his brain laced with panic. He needed cover—a turn, a chute, a lift, anything to get him out of sight. His spine crawled, expecting the hard impact of a bullet in his back, the agony, then his life flowing out.

An angry, shouting mob blocked the intersection. Sirens wailed. Flashing strobes swept the passage. Teeth clenched, sucking breath down his burning throat, Rolen rounded the corner and ran headlong into a picket line.

Thirty or forty corpses were standing across the corridor, arms linked, swaying and singing. The mob of civilians congealed around them. Security was trying to keep them apart, but the citizens were raging, half of them staggering drunk. As he watched, two civs charged the line, fists swinging, driving one of the corpses to his knees.

Revolution.

It was starting—picket lines, work stoppages, and strikes. Farther down the passage he could hear more shouting, more chants. Red strobes gleamed. The chaos was spreading.

The lights blinked, flickered, then died. Somewhere, a corpse had punched an infocube into the informational cluster controlling the electrical system. The auxiliary lights kicked in, a yellow glow, dim and uncertain.

He imagined the madness on the surface: mines shut down; streets jammed with automated vehicles, their command modules scrambled; communications snarled in an indecipherable tangle. Looting would follow the power outages—and worse. If the turmoil was half as great on the docks, there was a chance of reaching the *Shadowbox*. But he had to hurry. There was no telling how long the opportunity would last.

Rolen stared back down the corridor, but the Akira man was lost in the confusion. Squeezing through a gap in the press, he headed for the lifts.

The elevators weren't operating, but someone had already broken the seal on the emergency exit and the door to the free-fall tube was standing open. He bailed through the opening and dropped, his body wedging through the plastic cilia, which slowed his rate of fall.

The scene was worse than he'd ever imagined, and better than he'd hoped. The docks were in an uproar, paralyzed, crazy. From the mouth of the tube, Rolen could see a wide arc of the staging area scattered with lift trucks and Security vans, stalled cranes, boxes, and pallets.

Hundreds of corpses choked the dock, a line four bodies deep spanning from ship bay to the interior bulkhead. ''Freedom! Freedom! Freedom!'' The chorus echoed in the depths, joined by other choruses from farther down the quay. There were civilians scattered in with the corpses, arms linked and voices joining in the chant. Liberals and radicals.

Yellow trucks and forklifts, fully loaded, waited in the corridor like predators. Stevedores and dockworkers had joined together in an army, carrying clubs of tubing, spanners, and lug wrenches. The two lines were a scant ten meters apart, separated by a dozen Security officers who looked nervous and worried.

The silver blister of a comm unit bulged along the wall to his left. Rolen steeled his nerves against agoraphobia and sprinted for the safety of the bubble.

Inside it was pleasantly confined, smelling of sweat and stale smoke. Rolen paused for a moment with his eyes shut and his hands pressed against opposite walls, drawing strength from the tight quarters. When he had calmed

enough to stop shaking, he called up the Port directory and
scanned the listing for the *Shadowbox*.

There were three possibilities. One: There *had* been a
bomb on board and it had blown her to hell. He'd already
decided that the bomb had been a ploy to get him off the
ship. Two: Zenyam had already written him off and shuttled
in a new pilot. If so, she wouldn't be listed at all and he'd
have to try for another ship. Three: The ship was undam-
aged and waiting for a pilot, either himself or another to be
brought in later.

SHADOWBOX - DOCK 31A. He almost cried as the name
scrolled up onto the display. Squinting through the smoked
glass of the booth, Rolen spotted a dock marker—Dock 23.
His luck was still holding. He was on the same side of the
port, ten minutes away, just around the bend.

Outside, the confrontation had turned ugly. The two
picket lines had merged. There was no sign of Security in
the melée. Heavy wrenches and iron bars chopped in vicious arcs as civilian hotheads slashed at the deaders. The
chants degraded into screams of pain. A barrage of dull
concussions pounded the docks. Clouds of gas boiled up
and covered the mob.

Fighting his fear, Rolen slid from the booth and headed
toward the bays, keeping one hand on the wall for support
and reassurance. The docks stretched ahead of him. Keep
moving, he thought fiercely, don't stop. But the fear was
strong in him, his chest tight, and his muscles vibrating like
a metal wire.

The youth was waiting for him beneath the dock marker,
a square sign identifying it as Dock 31A. At one time, the
boy had been a Maimer; his ears were notched in a series
of identifying cuts that proclaimed his allegiance to some
teen gang. The cartilage was serrated like the edge of a
steak knife, but his loyalty was to another group now,
stronger and more apparent. His skin was translucent. Light
played on his hairless scalp as he stepped out from the shadows of the conveyor frame.

"You're him."

Rolen spun and backed against the wall, watching him nervously.

"You're the pilot." The kid licked his lips. "I was your contact. Supposed to meet you on the docks. But you didn't show," he said, his voice breaking. "It was real crazy out there. Man, I couldn't wait forever. Figured if you got this far, you might need me. So I came ahead—after I waited." The boy held his hands up as if he were pleading. "Didn't desert or nothin'. Just tryin' to do my part."

Rolen stared at him. Just a kid trying to do a major job, so caught up in Vasquez's madness that he'd risked his life to find Rolen.

"Yeah," Rolen said, nodding slowly. "I had some problems. But looks like we made it."

Across the dock, the wall of the bay curved upward, the lift gantries clinging to the side like a child's construct. Home. He'd never seen anything so welcome.

"Could be we got a problem." The kid nodded toward the dock. "Vasquez didn't say anythin' about any civs. You expectin' someone?"

Rolen shook his head, puzzled.

"Can't see him from here, down behind the cable spools. Tall guy, dark hair, beard. Got a burner."

"Damn!" The fixer hadn't followed him—he hadn't needed to. He'd known right where the pilot was headed.

"Bad, huh?" The kid fingered one of his notched ears nervously.

"Very bad."

"Supposed to get you shipboard. So we do it this way." He jerked a thumb toward the *Shadowbox*. "Give me a count of a hundred. I'll go around and slow him up. You head for the ship. Never know what hit him."

Rolen shook his head. "The man's professional. Very dangerous."

"Hey, bro'." The kid laughed softly. "I'm already a friggin' corpse."

He moved away, staying near the wall, using the crates

and machinery as cover as he worked his way toward the side of the ship.

Rolen started counting slowly.

At one hundred, he pushed away from the wall, threading his way slowly through the stacked cargo and supplies and into the open expanse of the dock.

Suited, he thought to himself. Hard suit, pressure type. Moving out across the open, but safe in a protective shell of EVA gear. The fantasy was thin, the illusion strained by the sounds of the riot down the bay and the faint drift of tear gas in the cold air.

He focused his attention on the gantry—his goal. He ran the action down through his head like a prayer: reach the gantry . . . hit the lift and up . . . through the external airlock on the bay wall . . . cross the access tube which stretched from the bay wall to the ship, three centimeters of alloy and insulation separating the air inside from the vacuum beyond . . . one more airlock at the *Shadowbox*, and he'd be home free. Rolen could see it in his mind, see his fingers keying the access codes . . .

Akira's man waited until the pilot had almost reached the lift before stepping out from behind the cable drums. The Spencer was a wicked bulge, dark and angular, in his right hand.

"Waited a long time," he said casually. "Thought you might have rabbited, found a hole to hide. But not you— only one place for you. Right, pilot?"

Rolen tensed.

"Go on up. Slowly." The man grinned at Rolen's confusion. "Need a safe place to stay until the riot dies down. Plenty safe inside." He gestured with the weapon.

The Maimer dropped from the cargo conveyor.

Maybe he sensed the leap or maybe he saw Rolen's gaze twitch to follow the boy. Spinning, the fixer crouched and raised the pistol in a single move—pure ballet. The Magna roared. Momentum carried the kid into him, arms spread. The fixer rolled with the impact, grabbing a handful of jersey and levering the corpse over him with a hard kick.

Rolen scrambled for the lift, fingers stabbing at the controls. Electric motors howled. The box lurched. A bullet whined through the gantry above his head.

The fixer was on one knee, Spencer leveled. He had Rolen sighted and dead, but he didn't fire. He couldn't fire.

Logic slotted. The man needed him alive. The pilot was no good to him dead.

Dropping the gun, the fixer leaped onto the gantry frame, swinging up, almost pacing the slow rise of the lift. Rolen was punching the access code before the platform stopped at the ship's hatch. The man's arm snaked over a support behind him.

The hatch hissed, swinging open. Rolen shouldered it wide, staggering forward into the access tube. He tried to slam the hatch as the fixer rolled onto the lift, but the man wedged his shoulder into the narrowing gap, hands clawing at Rolen, clutching at his face, gouging for a hold. Rolen leaned hard into the door and heard something crack; he prayed it was the bastard's neck as he raced for the airlock.

Slapping the contact, he pivoted, keeping his hands up and trying to remember how to fight. The man came at him slowly, favoring his shoulder, one arm dangling. At the last instant, he pirouetted, driving a kick into Rolen's chest. Rolen tumbled through the half-open hatch, his head striking the floor and darkness edging his vision. Then the man was standing over him, reaching down for his collar and smiling grimly.

This was the man. The bastard who had set him up and used him as callously as his father had used his tools. The man's cold arrogance enraged Rolen, fueling him with blind hatred.

Rolen scissored his legs and, driving his knee up, hit something vital as the man fell. The fixer grunted in pain and surprise. Fingers knit, Rolen swung both fists into the damaged shoulder. The man rolled with the blow. Rolen kicked him in the sternum, and though he partially blocked the blow, the man fell into the tube.

Rolen scrambled toward the inner door on his knees,

hands instinctively seeking the access contact. The portal slid open and he squirmed into the ship.

The fixer staggered to his feet in the tube, his eyes wild, blood oozing from his lips as he coiled for another strike.

Rolen met his gaze, holding it just long enough let the bastard know that he was way too late.

"Just gotta be mad enough," he heard Carta saying.

The fixer lunged.

Palming the emergency disconnect, Rolen blew the tube away from the side of the ship.

For one heartbeat, he saw the man clinging to the external hatch, his face contorted with rage, air roaring past him. Then the inner door sealed and cut him from view. Dimly, Rolen heard sirens screaming from the Port as the bay hatch reacted to the dropping pressure and clanged shut to secure the docks.

Somehow he reached the bridge. The helm molded to him. He felt as if he were detached from his body, a rider in his own skull, some animal-part of him reacting instinctively. His fingers found the plugs and fitted them into his sockets. Information flooded into his brain.

Port was screaming for answers: the nature of his emergency, his identification, threatening fines and lawsuits, citations, penalties. Rolen ignored them.

The infocube was a glittering mass in his fingers, damp with his sweat, innocuous and subtle. He stared at it, looking for an answer. His mind was filled with crystalline fragments of data, visual images heightened by the adrenaline punching through his system.

The fixer pointing his Spencer . . .

Vasquez trying to smile . . .

Carta taking his hand in a darkened alley . . .

A pale Maimer taking a bullet in the chest for him . . .

It was all beyond his control, everything that had happened during the past few days, a nightmare of cause and effect that had sucked him along like litter in a hovercraft's wake. Every moment except this one. He was all alone now. No frigging codes to fall back on. His choice.

His hands were very still, two birds frozen in the air before him, elevating the crystal as a priest would raise a host. His mind was shuffling referents, seeking direction. Faces flickered through his skull. His mother. His father. Illana Vanos.

Something emerged; a face created as if by overlaying all their features; recognizable, different, insane. All laughing and speaking in unison.

"What the hell, boy. You're already a corpse," they said in a voice as derivative and distinct as the face.

His hands moved suddenly. The cube slotted into the drive with a distant click.

Outgoing message, he mentally ordered. *Line-feed and squirt*.

The ship computer interfaced with Port. The red telltale on the drive gleamed as the program downloaded and the tangler punched out on a burst of electrical impulses, a logical bullet fired deep into the brain of the Port comm system.

Chapter 34

The escort was a formality, a gesture by the Confederation to remind all of who was in control. The two troopers were female, but all signs of gender were hidden beneath spandex and body armor, black uniforms with gold epaulets and piping.

Three months of occupation had acclimated the civilian population to the sight of Confederation troops. Their passage through the Bacchus Council Administration Complex drew little more than passing glances from the people hurrying on their errands of commerce.

Despite occupation, business continued as usual on the civilian level. The Confederation had moved swiftly against the High Council and certain corporations, but strikes on such stratified levels created little more than ripples in the general populace.

The pilot was without baggage. His few personal belongings were already on board the liner, stowed in a cabin like those of the rest of the passengers. The ship was bound for Kosar at 0300. It was a two-jump trip to the Port where a jump-class freighter was waiting for his hand at the helm. The thought buoyed his step even against the suck of gravity.

They left him in the anteroom outside the office; a brief salute, and then they were remembered only by the fading click of heels in the corridor. For a minute, he stood in silence before the oaken door, studying the grain and the highlights in the wood, anxious to be leaving and yet somehow afraid. He finally summoned up the courage to knock.

"Come." The mechanically augmented command was growling and brusque.

Rolen pushed the door open, the knob cold in his hand.

Antonio Vasquez looked up from the viewer. His ravaged face was bright in the glow from the fiche projector, the plastic hemisphere gleaming in the light, his steel teeth sharp points in his smile. Even from a distance, Rolen could see the fatigue in his movements and the darkened circle beneath his good eye.

Freedom had not given Vasquez rest, and never would as long as there was work to be done, a cause to champion. He had simply redirected his efforts from leading a revolution to ramrodding the Corpsemen's interests in the Confederation hearings. There were rumors of twenty-hour days and endless poring over records and tapes. Rolen had not seen the man since his surrender to the Confederation forces.

Vasquez's successes were already legend. The Confederation representatives had accepted his suggestion that Confederation sentences be applied to the Corpsemen. It meant reasonable prison terms for crimes, and in many cases, time already served resulted in freedom. Other cases were being individually reviewed for adequacy. His own had received special attention.

"Ah, Iserye," Vasquez said, switching off the fiche projector. "So glad you could come."

Rolen smiled sheepishly. "You had but to ask."

"And try to pry a few free minutes from an already hectic schedule." He waved his good hand at the stack of folders on the desk and the other mountains of files and microfiche on chairs and on the sideboard. "Enough for a lifetime of labor. And everything needing to be done now." Silence stretched between them for a moment, comfortable and relaxed. "I wanted to thank you. You made a difference."

"No." Rolen shook his head. "You'd have won without me. You weren't at the Port. I was. Chaos. Your people did it. I was icing. Did my part as we agreed. Don't need thanks for that." He traced a pattern on the desktop with his fingernail, his skin translucent against the dark grain, still odd, still strange, but gaining recognition. "You, however. You went beyond, way beyond. Out on a limb for me. I can't ever repay you for that."

Vasquez gave a phlegmy grunt. "Don't blame me. You should have seen it, a hundred lawyers representing the Guild, Bacchus, Akira, even Zenyam, all scrambling to point out how badly you'd been used, every one of them disagreeing on exactly who did the using." He presented his self-deprecating half smile. "Lots of pointing fingers. All I did was clarify the stories—just made sure the Confederation had everything in proper perspective."

"Secured a pardon for me, plus compensatory damages from the Guild and the rest of them. You didn't have to do that."

"Part of the job." He pointed at the stacks of fiche. "Corpseman Representative. I'm doing the same for dozens of others."

Rolen stared at the man. Who had won? The Guild? Certainly not with the Confederation stepping in to seize temporary control, Confederation courts already moving against the monopoly, injunctions terminating all pilot contracts, and hundreds of corporations jockeying for position among the crumbling remnants. Akira had taken a terminal shot, fines and suits collecting around it like litter in a whirlwind. Rumors of bankruptcy swirled. Bacchus was under Confederation control, new leaders being hand-selected to protect Confederation interests.

Not the players, but the pieces. The pawns had won the game. Himself and the other corpses. An odd little quirk of fate that made him smile. Perhaps there was justice after all.

"So what will you do?" Vasquez asked, watching him quietly.

Rolen shrugged. "I've put a down payment on a freighter.

A little independent commerce. Take advantage of a changing situation.''

"Picked a home Port yet? Bacchus will need transport."

He shook his head slowly. "No offense. Too many bad memories." Rolen swallowed. "Maybe Thor's Belt. Maybe someplace new. I haven't decided."

Vasquez nodded, light glittering on the facets of his artificial eye. "Choices. That's the beauty of freedom."

She was waiting in the anteroom. A final bit of aid from Vasquez? He would never know for sure.

Carta stood slowly. She wore a jumpsuit of bright red, polished cotton fabric. Her face was childlike, beautiful, a smile on her lips at his surprise. "Hello," she said softly.

"Waiting for him?"

"You. Heard you had a ship. That you were leavin' this rock."

"Yeah."

Carta shrugged, a gentle roll of her shoulders. "What're your fees?"

"Don't know yet."

"Got insurance? Got a fuel supplier? Any contracts?"

He shook his head.

"Damn, you're green, pilot." She took his arm and turned him toward the door. "I'm probably gonna live to regret this, but I can't let you go by yourself. Be murder to send you out into that sea of corporate sharks . . ."

They walked out together into the bustle and hurry of Bacchus.

About the Author

A native Californian, Joel Henry Sherman was born in Pomona, a suburb of Los Angeles. At the age of twelve, he moved with his family to the mountain metropolis of Wofford Heights (pop. 426), trading the white shirts and navy slacks of St. Dorothy's Parish School for the bootcut denims of Kern Valley High. Reading was the preferred alternative to the marginal programming on the three local television stations. He learned the basics of writing from a ten-year-old correspondence course discovered in a box in the attic.

Joel has a BA in English from California State College, Bakersfield, and is presently employed by the state of California, operating under the dubious title of Worker's Compensation Insurance Specialist II. He and his wife, Carolyn, make their home in Bakersfield. His major hobbies include snow skiing and backpacking, and he has recently completed a 120-mile trip to the headwaters of the Kern River.

His short fiction has appeared in *Amazing SF* and *Aboriginal SF* as well as numerous small-press magazines. *Corpseman* is his first novel. His second is gestating in the womb of an Apple IIe.

MICHAEL McCOLLUM PRESENT'S

HARD CORE SCIENCE FICTION